A Portal for your Thoughts

Jeffrey Poole

Jeffrey Poole's Epic Fantasy Books
Bakkian Chronicles:
The Prophecy
Insurrection
Amulet of Aria
Disneyland Debacle (short story)
Winter Wonderland (short story)

Tales of Lentari
Lost City
Something Wyverian This Way Comes
A Portal for Your Thoughts
Thoughts for a Portal
Wizard in the Woods
Close Encounters of the Magical Kind
The Hunt for Red Oskorlisk (short story)
May the Fang be With You (Pirates trilogy #1)
The Hammer is Strong with This One (Pirates #2)
These are Not the Stones You're Looking For (Pirates #3)
Blast from the Past

Dragons of Andela
Harness the Fire
Strike the Spark
Clear the Water

Mysteries by J.M. Poole
The Corgi Case Files Series
18 delightful cozy mystery novels featuring corgi
sleuths, Sherlock and Watson

A PORTAL FOR YOUR THOUGHTS

Tales of Lentari, Book 3

JEFFREY POOLE

Secret Staircase Books

A Portal For Your Thoughts
Published by Secret Staircase Books, an imprint of
Columbine Publishing Group, LLC
PO Box 416, Angel Fire, NM 87710

Book layout and design by Secret Staircase Books
First Secret Staircase paperback edition: July, 2023

First Secret Staircase e-book edition: July, 2023
* * *
Publisher's Cataloging-in-Publication Data

Poole, Jeffrey
A Portal For Your Thoughts / by Jeffrey Poole.
p. cm.
ISBN 978-1649141385 (paperback)
ISBN 978-1649141392 (e-book)

1. Lentari (Fictitious location)—Fiction. 2. Epic fantasy fiction
3. Dragons and mythical creatures—Fiction. 4. Time travel—Fiction.
I. Title

Tales of Lentari : Book 3.
A Portal For Your Thoughts
Poole, Jeffrey, Bakkian Chronicles epic fantasy series.

BISAC : FICTION / Fantasy/Epic.

813/.54

For Giliane—

As ever, I count my lucky stars that I can always count on you to be by my side.

Love you always & forever!

Acknowledgments

As usual, my list of people to thank is long and extensive. Please bear with me.

First off, I need to thank my wife for continuing to be my inspiration. I strive to become a better writer because of you. I also would like to thank the beta readers who took the time out of their busy schedules to lend a hand proofreading a manuscript that clearly needed the attention—Susan Gross, Sandra Anderson, and Paula Webb. Next up would be anyone unlucky enough to have to listen to me prattle on and on about the books, possibly story arcs, battle scenes, and so on.

And finally, I'd like to thank you, the readers. Tales of Lentari exists solely because of you. If not for the continued interest in the series, then I'm sure I'd be wondering what I could possibly write about. Thank you for keeping Steve and Sarah with all kinds of new adventures!

Table of Contents

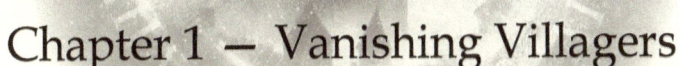

Chapter 1 – Vanishing Villagers

The setting sun laced the early summer sky with streaks of orange and painted the undersides of the few clouds a soft pink. A flock of bright yellow kytes circled lazily high overhead as they searched for a suitable place to perch for the evening. The writhing and pulsing mass of yellow feathers was a sharp contrast to the calm azure sky, causing many an onlooker below to lift their hands and point at the noisy, fluffy birds in wonder.

Directly below the flock of kytes sat the Lentarian capital of R'Tal. Nestled safely within its walls stood the majestic castle the king and queen of Lentari called home. It nestled up against Anakash forest on the north and sat fairly close to the great sea on the east. Inside the city walls, street after street of vendors eagerly peddled their wares to anyone that passed by, and residential houses ranged from simple thatched cottages to much more elaborate multi-level dwellings that only the city's elite could afford. Anyone strolling outside on this beautiful sunny day would typically encounter villagers selling baked goods, fresh meat, recently harvested vegetables, and bolts of fabric in vivid colors. If the prospective buyer wasn't looking for new clothes, or fabrics to make their own, and were able to pry themselves away from the tempting aroma of freshly baked food, then they'd encounter several rows of vendors selling all manner of tools, weapons, and services pertaining to each. Coins changed hands and goods changed possession.

The sounds of a galloping horse caught the attention of the gate master at the city's west gate. The guard frowned. From the sound of the hooves rapidly striking the cobbled pavement, it was clear that this rider wasn't out for a leisurely stroll. The guard's right hand rested easily on the hilt of his sword, while his left inched toward the tower's bell. In his three years of service in the castle's militia, it had only been necessary to ring that bell once.

Horse and rider came into view. The guard's eyes opened wide as he saw the rider. He barely had enough time to usher a few peasants out of the way before the horse thundered by him, on a direct line to the castle. The guard jumped back against the wall; the whinnying horse galloped by.

The gate master followed the rider's progression up the streets as numerous vendors voiced their alarm. Conversations halted and the streets became silent as the clatter of the horse's hooves echoed loudly on the paved road. After a few moments of silence, the general din of the day's activities returned.

Arriving at the castle's inner keep, the rider dismounted and tossed his reins to the closest guard. Catching sight of the rider's identity, the guard snapped to attention. He caught the reins with his left hand while simultaneously opening the door with his right.

"See to my horse," the tall soldier instructed. "I may have to depart as quickly as I arrived. He is to be ready at a moment's notice, is that understood?"

The guard bowed. "Aye, Captain."

Captain Pheron strode purposefully into the castle's

interior. He had to constantly remind himself not to break into a run as it was generally considered bad form to appear in front of the king and queen out of breath. The captain took several deep calming breaths as he neared the Great Hall. The king wasn't going to like what he had to tell him. He could only hope that his majesty was preoccupied with other things and he would have to impart his news to someone else. He doubted he'd be that lucky.

As luck would have it both the king and queen were present. Not only were their majesties holding court inside the large chamber, but the commander of the royal guards was also present. His superior officer's keen eyes had noticed Pheron first. The captain groaned silently. He watched the commander's eyes travel down his unwashed face to his dirty, disheveled clothes and then back up to his face. Or more specifically, his eyes. Pheron was certain his commanding officer had noticed the concern he was desperately trying to mask.

Rhenyon rose to his feet and dismissed the three lieutenants he had been speaking with. The commander glanced over at the king and queen and confirmed that neither had noticed the captain's arrival. Rhenyon gestured to an unoccupied corner of the Great Hall.

"I assume," Rhenyon began as he glanced again at the dirty countenance his subordinate presented, "that you have a good explanation for this."

Captain Pheron bowed. "My apologies, Commander. I was following the king's express orders. If I were to learn of any new developments with regard to the situation in Capily, then I should deliver the news personally."

Rhenyon straightened. "Something has happened in Capily?"

"It's more like something *else* has happened in Capily, Commander."

Rhenyon's full attention fell on Pheron. "Well? What is it?"

"Another person has gone missing. It happened just last night."

Commander Rhenyon cursed softly to himself. "His

Majesty will not like this."

Pheron nodded. "Aye. Those are my feelings exactly. But, now that you're here, perhaps you could tell him?"

Rhenyon considered for a few moments. "Aye, I suppose I could."

Relief washed over Pheron. "Thank you, Commander."

"However…"

Pheron had turned and taken a step back toward the keep when he froze.

"Didn't you just say that you were given strict orders to personally deliver any news to the king?"

Pheron swallowed nervously and nodded. "Aye."

"Then you should be the one to tell him. Wait here. I will see if he deems this important enough to halt these mundane proceedings."

Pheron watched as Rhenyon approached the king and tapped him softly on the shoulder. The king kept his eyes, and presumably his attention, on the people standing before him but did lean over to hear what Rhenyon had to say. Pheron held his breath. He already knew the king would want to hear about this latest development.

Sure enough, the king's head snapped up and instantly sought him out. Kri'Entu excused himself and said something to Rhenyon. The commander instantly looked at him and mouthed the word 'Antechamber.' Captain Pheron began automatically moving toward the king's private chamber tucked deep within the castle and far from prying ears. Once the three men had stepped inside the magically enchanted chamber where no jhorun—magic—could be used unless one had a very powerful ability, Kri'Entu faced the commander and the captain.

"What has happened?" Kri'Entu snapped. "Report."

Rhenyon instantly turned to Pheron. "Tell the king what you told me, Captain."

Pheron nodded. "Fifteen minutes ago I received word, via a village messenger kyte, that another disappearance has happened."

The king let out an exasperated sigh. "How long ago? Today?"

"Last night. A young girl never returned home and no amount of searching has turned up any clues."

Both the king and the commander scowled. Rhenyon ran a hand through his thick black hair.

"How young?"

"Perhaps twelve, maybe thirteen."

"Wizards be damned," the king muttered. "She was just a child. This has got to stop. This marks the second time this year a villager has gone missing." Kri'Entu looked up and met Rhenyon's eyes. "I instructed Capily's constable to inform us of anything unusual happening, no matter how irrelevant it appears."

"What would you have us do, Your Majesty?" Rhenyon inquired.

The king's response was quick and to the point. "We find our citizens and return them home. I do not care what it takes. This mystery ends now."

Kri'Entu walked over to his private desk and faced the wall directly behind it. He tapped one of the many stones on the wall's surface and waited for the false wall to slide out of the way. Once it did, a large pedestal, holding a statue of a griffin was revealed. Soft chimes began to play. The king approached the griffin and waited for it to raise its right front paw. As soon as it did, the king pressed the small, concealed button and pulled open the pedestal's door. He retrieved a small velvet case and turned to place it on his desk. Opening the case revealed a set of sparkling crystal keys of various colors. He selected a sky-blue key and handed it to Rhenyon, who nodded. The commander turned to Pheron and handed him the portal key.

"Captain, take one squadron to Capily and investigate. There has to be something we're missing."

Pheron was confused. "Were you not just there several months ago? What new leads do you think I would be able to find where you could not?"

"Unknown," the king answered. "We have faith in you, Captain. You will succeed. Why? Because you are going to be more methodical than we ever were. And aye, we were there nearly three months ago."

Rhenyon nodded. "We were investigating the disappearance of a woodsmith."

"Is there anything else I need to know?" the captain asked, as he mentally assembled the roster of men who would accompany him.

"There have been five disappearances," the king answered in a neutral tone. "However, I suspect this has been happening far longer than has been documented."

"Why are we just now hearing about this?" Pheron asked, perplexed. "Why didn't the constable report this long ago?"

"How would you be able to tell if a person went missing?" Rhenyon asked. "Unless there was someone actively looking for that person, and it is reported, then we'd never know."

"So what has changed?" Pheron wanted to know.

"The frequency of these disappearances have been increasing," Kri'Entu answered. "And that is unacceptable."

Captain Pheron lowered his voice to a whisper. "Could the renegade wizard everyone has been searching for be responsible?"

"It's plausible, but unlikely," Rhenyon told him. "That wizard has a history of conducting his or her activities in secret, so I very much doubt that he or she would do something so foolish as to draw attention to themselves. For now, we will assume this is something else besides the wizard."

Pheron nodded. "I understand, Your Majesty. Fear not. I will get to the bottom of this."

"See that you do, Captain," the king said as he turned to Rhenyon. "Now if you'll excuse me, I must return to the Board of Treasurers meeting. Nothing is as dull as listening to proposed changes to the taxes, I assure you."

The king departed, leaving captain and commander eyeing one another.

"Do you have an idea which men you will select?" the commander asked.

Pheron nodded. "I do."

"I will expect daily progress reports, Captain."

Pheron saluted. "You will have them, Commander."

* * *

"What would you like us to do first, here in Capily, Captain?"

Pheron fastened the crystal portal key to his dragon-tooth medallion and tucked it safely beneath his tunic. Adjusting his dark brown leather armor so that his chest was once more properly protected, he turned to his first lieutenant.

"We were tasked with solving this mystery, Graylan. I have no plans on disappointing the commander or the king."

"How long do you think this will take?" a young soldier asked.

Pheron made eye contact with the youngest member on the squad. A youth, barely eighteen years old, fidgeted under his gaze.

"We will be here as long as it takes, Gunnar. Do you have somewhere else to be?"

The young soldier shook his head and fell silent.

"Let's find the constable. We need to know more about what's been going on around here."

Captain Pheron stepped out into the brisk morning air and inhaled. He had always loved the smell of the sea. If he hadn't become a soldier, he was positive he would have ended up choosing an occupation out on the open water.

Pheron walked a few steps away from the large two-story building that housed the portal and spun around to verify the rest of his men had followed. When all twelve were standing in two rows of six men each, Pheron looked around the quiet seaside village.

"We need to find the constable. He was supposed to be in his office but clearly he's not. Spread out. Find him. Report back here every half hour until he's found. Move out."

All twelve men nodded and quickly fanned out, heading to opposite corners of the village. Surprisingly, it took less than fifteen minutes to find the missing constable. One of his men found the village official trying to drink away his sorrows at one of the village's three taverns. Ordering his men to take up positions all around the pub, Pheron approached the establishment's front doors and automatically ducked.

Being six and a half feet tall usually resulted in more blows to the head than he'd care to admit. As such, Pheron had learned long ago that it was simply easier to duck when entering a building for the first time. In this case, it was a good thing; he would have cracked his head against the door's six foot high frame.

Smells of roasted meat, burnt tobacco, and spilt ale assailed his nostrils; wooden tables worn smooth by countless years of use were haphazardly scattered about. There were only a few patrons in the tavern at this time of day and all, save one, left to find other things to do at the sight of Pheron and his impeccably dressed soldiers. The last patron hadn't even bothered to look up at the disturbance. The lone man kept his eyes glued to the heavily scarred table and the half full tankard of ale in his shaky hands.

"Are you Constable Fensham?" Pheron asked, standing stiffly at attention.

The constable didn't look up but he did nod. Barely. He was a burly man in his mid-forties. Standing just under six feet tall, the normally proud official was slumped over in his chair. The forlorn man finally looked up and met Pheron's eyes. The constable's own eyes were bloodshot. His face was unshaven. His clothes were heavily wrinkled and he reeked of alcohol. This was a man who hasn't slept in days, Pheron decided. He watched Fensham's eyes drop to the king's crest displayed on his right shoulder and then over to his left to note the gold bars signifying his rank as captain. Pheron motioned for his lieutenants to wait by the door and approached the constable's table alone. He pulled out one of the rickety chairs, spun it around, and straddled the chair as he sat down. Leaning forward to rest his chest on the back of the chair, he clasped his hands together and rested his elbows on his knees.

"It's a little early to be drinking," Pheron casually remarked. There was no sense in frightening the inebriated constable any more than he had to. "Would you care to explain why you're in here rather than conducting a search for this missing girl?"

"We won't find her," the constable softly said. "Once they disappear, they never come back."

"Why aren't you even trying?" Pheron snapped. "If this

was your daughter, wouldn't you want someone to at least make an effort to find her?"

"She *is* my daughter!"

Pheron hesitated. That explained the constable's presence in the tavern and the fact that he was inebriated. How should he handle this? Dole out a reprimand for his behavior? Pheron shook his head. The loss of the man's daughter had to be devastating. Perhaps he should show some compassion?

"Uh…"

Fensham's gaze fell back to the table and landed on his ale. He drained the mug and angrily tossed it back to the table, where it bounced several times on the hard wooden surface. Pheron caught it before it fell to the floor.

"We are here to help, constable," Pheron gently told him as he replaced the tankard on the table. "We need to get to the bottom of these disappearances. Do you want to see your daughter again? Snap out of this. Help us."

"What do you want to know?" Fensham asked in the tiniest of whispers.

"Everything," Pheron promptly answered. "Start from … I'm sorry, what is your daughter's name?"

"Lissa."

"Lissa. What was she doing? Where did you see her last?"

Fensham belched loudly. His face colored with embarrassment as he looked at Pheron.

"I am terribly sorry. I have been feeling sorry for myself. Everything I have is at your disposal."

Pheron turned to his two lieutenants and motioned them over. Once both soldiers were seated next to him, he turned back to the constable.

"These are two of my lieutenants, Graylan and Tyril. I need additional sets of ears to listen to this. Now. Start from the beginning. How many people have been reported missing?"

Fensham sighed and sat back in his chair. "Officially or unofficially?"

"Let's hear the official answer first."

Fensham sighed again. "My daughter is the fifth to disappear."

"And unofficially?" Graylan prompted.

"At least a dozen."

"Why did you wait so long to report it?"

"Many of our residents are fisherman," Fensham explained. "Boats go down all the time. It is not uncommon for the weather to turn precarious from time to time. When that happens there are always reports of missing ships. People presumed to be lost at sea oftentimes turn up several months later."

"But you think otherwise?" Tyril prompted.

Fensham nodded. "I do."

"Let's focus on those who we know vanished," Pheron suggested. "What can you tell us about them?"

"The first to be reported missing, where I knew it wasn't fishing related, was a young man by the name of Quinn. He was going to head the new school that Prince Mikal had just set up."

The captain and his two lieutenants had produced small notebooks and were taking notes.

"Appointed by the throne," Pheron nodded without looking up. "Very well. Please continue."

"He disappeared without a trace. He didn't leave any explanation or indication of where he was going. We found his cottage fully furnished. All his possessions were still there, as if he had just stepped out."

"How long ago was this?" Pheron asked. His two lieutenants paused with their quills hovering over their papers.

"Over two years ago."

"And the next?" Pheron asked. He dipped his quill in the ink bottle and waited for the next name.

"That would be Melvyn. He was known as the town drunk."

"How did you know he vanished?" Graylan asked, looking up from his notes. "How do you know he didn't wander off and, in his drunken stupor, bump noses with a dragon?"

"There are no dragons in these parts."

"You know what I mean."

"His father said he didn't come home one night. Melvyn may have been a drunk, and a fool, but he was a habitual drunk. He always made his rounds to the same businesses at the same time. Every day. When he didn't make it home his father became worried and began investigating. No traces were ever found."

For a few moments no one could hear anything but the three quills scratching away on three separate pieces of parchment. Pheron finally looked up.

"And the third?"

"Ruan."

"And who was he?"

"He was an avid hunter. Ruan was one of the most skilled hunters I had ever seen. When he disappeared, we just assumed he had been tracking something that got the better of him. I was prepared to leave it at that until a group of searchers found his camp site."

Pheron looked up again. He scowled at the constable and waited for him to continue. When Fensham never bothered to look up from his empty tankard, Pheron cleared his throat. "And?"

"All his supplies were there. Several bows, two quivers, a short sword, and a few daggers were all found at his camp. Since when does a hunter leave behind his weapons?"

Pheron frowned. "He wouldn't."

Fensham nodded. "Exactly."

"Who's next?"

"That would be the woodsmith, Ruskin."

"What was his story?"

"Only that he was very particular about which wood he used in his shop so he was constantly searching for the right species of tree."

"His disappearance brought the king here, did it not?"

Fensham nodded. "Aye. He chastised me, just as you did, for not reporting the disappearances earlier. I promised him that if I heard of any other peculiar occurrences then I would notify him immediately. I never dreamed my own daughter would be the next to vanish."

Pheron turned to Graylan. "Lieutenant, begin the search. You have the names of the previous victims. I will start working on the constable's daughter."

Tyril jerked his head up and raised an eyebrow at his superior officer. Pheron cleared his throat and tried again.

"That is, I will start searching for the girl. Have the men split into teams and begin investigating the four other cases. I want to know everything about them. What were their hobbies? What did they like to do for fun? Who were their friends? What was the nature of their jhorun? Where were they seen last? We need answers. Find them."

Both lieutenants nodded. They stood and excused themselves from the table. Fensham watched as the group of soldiers standing silently outside broke apart and appeared to go their separate ways.

Pheron turned back to the constable. "Tell me about your daughter. Her name is Lissa, correct?"

Fensham nodded. His eyes teared up. "My lovely Lissa. She was only thirteen. She—"

"Don't speak of her as though she's dead," Pheron scolded. "We will get her back."

"Lissa *is* thirteen," Fensham amended. "She was so bright. Is. She *is* so bright. She wants to be a healer." Fensham pulled a handkerchief from his back trouser pocket and blew his nose so hard that he was certain the king could have heard it back in the castle.

"Your daughter wants to be a healer?" Pheron nodded, impressed. "That is a very commendable occupation. The king can always use gifted healers."

"Lissa had a remarkable gift for finding natural remedies for everything from a common cough to the strongest of fevers."

"Is there anyone you can think of who would want to do her harm? Is it possible she may have been kidnapped?"

Fensham shook his head. "No. This is a small village, Lieutenant."

"Captain," Pheron corrected.

"My apologies, Captain. Everyone knew Lissa. She's an energetic girl who made friends easily and had a smile for everyone."

"What does she look like?" Pheron asked, as he picked up his quill.

"She has reddish blonde hair that sweeps down to her shoulders," Fensham began. "She has green eyes, stands about fourteen and a half hands high and weighs about seven stone."

Pheron was silent a moment as he mentally converted the archaic measurements into something he was more familiar with. He didn't know why the constable had used the old style of weights and measures, but figured it wasn't worth bringing up. After a few moments Pheron added a few more notes to his notebook. Fourteen and a half hands was the equivalent of about five feet tall while seven stone was just under a hundred pounds.

"Where was she last seen? Do you know?"

Fensham sadly shook his head. "She only told me she was going out to look for herbs. She never told me where."

"Will you take me to see her room?"

Fensham nodded. "Of course. Follow me."

The constable rose unsteadily to his feet and headed toward the door. Once outside Fensham turned to his left and headed south. After a ten minute walk in complete silence, Fensham pointed at a tiny, neatly kept cottage sitting on a small hill overlooking the water. A single gable stretched from one side of the house to the other. The cottage, Pheron noted, had been painted light blue while the trim around the windows and the doors was white. Rows of brightly colored flowers lined the walk up to the front door.

"You have a lovely home. Is your wife here now?"

Fensham shook his head. "My wife is dead. She died from complications during childbirth. Thank the wizards she delivered a healthy baby girl."

Pheron silently groaned. No wonder Fensham was in the tavern. His only daughter, the only family he had left, had vanished. He'd be distraught, too, if that had happened to him.

"I'm sorry. I didn't know about your wife."

"It was a long time ago, Captain. I have long since grieved for her."

"I will do everything in my power to return your daughter to you," Pheron vowed.

Opening the front door, Fensham turned and laid a friendly arm on Pheron's shoulder.

"I know you will, Captain. Lissa's room is just over there."

Pheron gently pushed open the door to the small room and looked inside. Several bundles of plants were hanging upside down near the window next to the small desk. The girl's bed had been lifted up and was resting against the wall, presumably to give the girl more work space.

To the right of the room's only window was a large map of Capily. Judging by its incorrect scale and distorted landmarks, Pheron deduced the girl had drawn it herself. Stepping up to the map he noticed that notes had been written all across it. Pheron nodded. The girl had been documenting where she had found specific herbs. Clever.

Pheron turned back to the desk. Bottles and jars of dried herbs were everywhere. The girl had enough herbs to make a full-fledged healer jealous. He would have to talk to the king about helping the girl with her education. Provided he was able to find her.

Pheron shook his head. He really shouldn't be thinking like that, either. He *would* get her back. He just had to find out where she had gone.

He turned to look at the desk again. Something caught his attention. As his eyes traveled over the surface of the desk, he noticed that all the herbs were labeled. Everything was in its place. All the bottles were full. All except one.

Pheron picked up the nearly empty bottle and rotated it so that he could see which herb was almost gone. It was goldenseal. While not knowing too much about herbs and their properties, he did know goldenseal was used as a contact disinfectant. It was a common ingredient used in many salves. Could Lissa have been looking for more?

The captain walked back over to the map and studied it. There. Northeast of the city, in a small section of the forest, was a tiny scribbled word: goldenseal.

"I noticed that, too," Fensham told him from the doorway. "That was the first place I checked. I didn't find anything."

"Noted. Nevertheless, it's a place to start."

Thanking the constable, and assuring him that he would

keep him apprised of any new developments, Pheron headed toward the closest inn to procure rooms for the next several nights. He didn't think this particular problem would be solved in one day so it was better to be prepared. He was anxious to see what his men had been able to find out about the other missing villagers.

* * *

Three hours later, the contingent from R'Tal reassembled in the same tavern where they had found the constable and were comparing notes. After three tables had been shoved together in the center of the room, Pheron pulled out his notebook and flipped through a few pages.

"Everyone, settle down. We need to find what these people had in common. We'll go through them one at a time, starting with Quinn, the schoolmaster. What did we find out?"

Lieutenant Graylan consulted his notes. "He didn't have any family here. The only relatives I could find were his parents, who lived in R'Tal. The house where he lived now has new occupants in it. I'm sorry to say, they didn't know him at all."

Pheron frowned. "Were you able to find anyone who did know him?"

Graylan nodded. "The cobbler. He remembers striking up several conversations with him whenever he mended Quinn's shoes."

"How often did his shoes need mending?" Pheron asked.

"Quite often. It seems he was fond of hiking. He was an outdoor enthusiast."

"Where did he hike?"

Graylan shook his head. "The cobbler didn't know. No one else I spoke with had any additional information."

Pheron consulted his list. "What about the town drunk?"

Lieutenant Tyril raised a hand.

"Melvyn's father tells me his son abused alcohol whenever and wherever he could. No amount of coercion could force him to surrender the bottle, so he was always in trouble."

"Did he frequent one tavern more than the other?"

Tyril shook his head. "Apparently, he was an equal opportunity drinker. Whenever one tavern threw him out, he'd just move on to the next."

"Friends?"

"None. There is something else I should point out, Captain."

"Go on, Lieutenant."

"Melvyn liked to roam about the city. I heard from numerous people that he had been found, passed out, in practically every street and behind every building."

"That doesn't really help us too much."

Tyril shrugged.

"What about Ruan, the hunter?"

Graylan flipped a page in his notebook and consulted his set of notes.

"He was an honest businessman who sold his game at a fair price. He was good friends with the owner of the Bustling Barmaid."

Pheron raised an eyebrow and suppressed a smirk. "The Bustling Barmaid?"

"It's a fairly new tavern," Graylan explained as he fought the urge to smile. "Ruan and the owner were quite close and frequently hunted together. The tavern owner couldn't remember anything other than Ruan telling him he was restless and wanted to go hunting that day. Ruan had invited him along, but the tavern owner declined because several of his serving girls had fallen ill. That was the last he ever heard from him."

"Fallen ill from what?" Pheron prompted.

His lieutenant looked at him blankly.

"Find out," Pheron ordered. "Any detail, no matter how seemingly unimportant, could be helpful."

Graylan nodded.

"And what of Ruskin, the woodsmith?"

Graylan answered. "His shop is located in the southern district. He turns quite a profit, I'm told. His wife showed me some of his work. It's truly amazing."

"Did he have any known enemies?"

Graylan shook his head. "On the contrary, he was an outstanding citizen. I checked with all the adjacent businesses and the owners had nothing but high praise for him."

"And finally, we have Lissa, the girl," Pheron added. "She was—*is*—an aspiring healer. She vanished while searching for herbs."

"How does that help us?" Tyril asked.

"I'm fairly certain she was searching for goldenseal. According to a map I found in the girl's room, there is an area northeast of the city that had the label 'goldenseal' next to it. I believe that was where she had found the herb before and was planning on searching again."

Tyril unrolled a map and spread it out on the table in front of them. He made a mark on the map.

"This is where you'll find the educator's house."

Graylan took the pen and made another mark. "Here is Melvyn's house."

Pheron took the pen and drew an X. "This is where the girl lives."

Several other marks were added to show the locations of homes and businesses. The final X marked the spot on the map where the hunter had set up his last camp. Pheron stared down at the map and groaned. The X's were scattered all across the village. There would be no help there.

"The educator liked to go hiking," Graylan recalled, as he tapped the mark designating Quinn's house. "The girl was presumably collecting herbs northeast of the village, here. Then there's the woodsmith and the hunter. All had reason and motivation to explore outside. Do you see this? The girl's goldenseal location and the hunter's camp are fairly close to one another. That must be significant."

"And then we have Melvyn, the drunk," Pheron reminded everyone. He tapped a mark on the southern edge of town. "His parent's house is nowhere near the northeast but we also know Melvyn was known to wander. Lieutenant Graylan is right. Ruan's camp and the girl's location for goldenseal are very close together."

"What does that mean?" Gunnar asked.

"My friends, it means we need to find ourselves some herbs."

* * *

An hour later, thirteen men fanned out and were carefully inspecting a nondescript section of the forest northeast of the city. Several of the men were down on their hands and knees as they carefully sifted through pine needles, acorns, and other forest detritus. Inch by inch they crept along, searching and hoping for some indication that any of the missing villagers had been there. So far their group was turning up just as much evidence as the king's investigators had several months ago, which was absolutely nothing.

His back sore and his knees aching, Pheron found a small shrub less than a foot high and was inspecting the plant's ovary. The leaves and stems resembled a raspberry bush, so he knew he had found a live specimen of the medicinal herb. The captain glanced up and watched several of his men poke and prod at various ferns and flowers.

"Just to make sure we're all looking for the same thing, does everyone know what goldenseal looks like? This shrub is what we're looking for. Or, more specifically, a shrub like this that looks as though it has been harvested."

One of the soldiers pointed at the shrub and looked up at Pheron. "We're looking for that? I thought we were looking for a tree."

"Goldenseal is a shrub no more than ten inches high. Men, come here and get a good look. Everyone know what it is now? Good. Spread out. Look again."

While the soldiers fanned out once more, Pheron turned to look back at the small seaside village nearly half a league to the south. He gazed silently at the distant rooftops of the village before slowly turning in place to look at the small shrub at his feet.

"What are you doing?" another soldier asked. It was Gunnar, the youngest member on his team.

"I'm trying to recreate what the girl would have seen had she come here straight from Capily. This cannot be the only plant. It shows no sign of harvesting. Either she didn't make it this far or there were other shrubs nearby that attracted her attention first. Look that way and I'll check over here. The roots of the goldenseal shrub are what's predominantly used, so look for signs of disturbance to the ground. She would have had to either pull them or dig them up. Either way we should see some signs."

Within moments Gunnar gave a shout. "Captain, over here!"

Pheron hurried to Gunnar's position on the ground and looked at where the soldier was pointing. Sure enough, a small shrub had been dug out of the hard ground and had been discarded, its roots missing.

"Excellent, Gunnar. Keep looking. Let's see if she found any more."

Twenty feet to the east they found another uprooted shrub, also with its roots missing. Thirty feet away, at the base of a rather large fern, they found a third uprooted plant, only this specimen still had its roots intact. Gunnar picked up the plant while Pheron knelt down to inspect the disturbed soil where the plant must have been growing. He could clearly see the marks Lissa's spade left in the soil as she worked to extricate the plant from its natural bed.

"She left these roots intact," Gunnar observed. He held the plant out to the captain. "Why?"

Pheron took the plant and straightened. He carefully looked around the quiet forest. "Isn't it obvious? Something distracted her and prevented her from harvesting this. The question is, what? What did she see?"

The hairs on the back of Pheron's neck suddenly stood up. His nostrils flared. His right arm instantly jerked up and he held it in place, signaling Gunnar to be quiet. The young soldier was more than happy to comply.

There was a faintly acrid odor in the air, much like what Shardwyn's workshop always smelled like after a failed experiment. Pheron squatted low—Gunnar instinctively dropped beside him—and scanned the surroundings. He couldn't see any smoke but he could still smell it.

"Do you smell that?" Pheron whispered.

Gunnar nodded. "It smells like a potion gone wrong."

"Exactly. Stay close by me. Whatever is causing that smell must be nearby. Don't let your guard down."

Gunnar nodded and rested a hand on the hilt of his

sword. Pheron pointed east, toward a huge fern with fronds that were easily three feet wide by five feet long.

"I think it's coming from that direction. Follow me."

"Aye, sir."

The two men carefully pushed aside the fern's enormous fronds and poked their heads into the small space directly behind it. More ferns stretched out in all directions. The small clearing was no larger than two square meters, but all traces of the actual ground were hidden from sight. Fronds from five different plants overlapped one another, but only in the one spot. Intent on seeing what the fronds were hiding, Gunnar pushed his way past the huge fern only to stumble.

Pheron caught Gunnar's wildly flailing left arm and gave him a violent yank backwards. Both men fell to the ground, away from the convergence of giant fronds. Gunnar rolled to his feet first and came up swearing.

"What the blasted hell is a stinking pit doing under all those leaves? Is this someone's idea of a joke? It isn't funny!"

Pheron rose to his feet. "A pit?"

"Aye. The ground disappeared. If you hadn't caught me then I would have fallen in. I probably would have broken a leg."

Pheron cautiously inched back toward the mass of huge ferns. "I want to see this pit."

"Be careful," Gunnar cautioned.

Together the two of them pushed by the closest fern and gently pulled the fronds away from the ground. This time it was Pheron's turn to swear.

"Wizards be damned! What the blazes is that?"

Hidden beneath the thick foliage, and floating several inches off the ground, was a disturbance of air. The swirling vortex beckoned invitingly.

Gunnar poked a finger at the vortex but Pheron caught his wrist before he could make contact.

"I wouldn't do that if I were you. You have no idea what that thing is."

Gunnar nodded. "You're right, Captain. Don't you want to find out?"

Pheron snapped a small twig off the nearest tree and held

it over the anomaly. He let go of it and the piece of wood blinked out of existence the moment it hit the swirling mists.

"I'll stand guard," Pheron told the soldier. "Find the others. Tell them they can call off the search. I think we found what we've been looking for."

Half an hour later all thirteen men were crowding around the vortex. Everyone wanted to not only get a good look, but to also toss in a rock, or a twig. As before, each item disappeared the moment it touched the swirling mists.

"So why didn't you vanish when you touched it?" Lieutenant Tyril asked. "It looks as though these sticks and stones we're throwing in disappear as soon as contact is made."

Gunnar was nonplussed. "So?"

"So why didn't you vanish? Find a large branch," Pheron ordered. "Let's see what happens when we only poke one end into the anomaly. Will the branch vanish? Will it be pulled down? I want to know."

Graylan chose two men from his group and retreated into the forest. They were back in less than five minutes with a seven foot long pole held between them.

Pheron smiled. "Excellent. Be ready. If there is a sudden pull downward, I want everyone to let go. Is that understood? I don't want anyone touching that thing."

The three soldiers nodded. Pheron indicated they should proceed. The tip of the pole was lowered and gently made contact with the disturbance.

Pheron watched the pole and the three men carefully. Nothing was happening. After a few moments the soldiers carefully inserted another foot of the pole into the anomaly and then carefully pulled the pole out. Pheron was expecting the pole to become a foot or two shorter but it wasn't.

"Try that again," the captain instructed. "Poke it down as far as you can safely go. I want to see if you can feel anything on the other side."

The pole was lowered once more into the vortex. As before, the tip of the pole vanished into the swirling mists. A few seconds later, however, the pole was ripped from the soldiers' hands and sucked into the anomaly.

Alarmed, Pheron ushered everyone away from the vortex. "Is everyone alright? What happened?"

Graylan was shaking his right hand back and forth. "What just happened was that I just got the biggest splinter of my life."

"Could you feel anything with the pole?" Pheron asked, as he pulled out his dagger and carefully dug out the sliver of wood that had lodged in his lieutenant's hand.

"No resistance," Graylan reported as he wrapped a strip of cloth around his injury. "It was as if someone grabbed the pole from the other side and yanked it in."

"On the other side? You're saying you think this is some type of a portal?"

"Captain, I don't know what that is."

"Captain?"

Everyone turned to look at Gunnar. His face was ashen. "Captain, if you hadn't been there to prevent me from falling in then I would be suffering the same fate as those other people. I— I—"

"Don't get all blubbery on me, soldier. Men, I think we can now explain what has happened to the missing villagers. I need a couple of volunteers."

Two men hesitantly raised their arms.

"Excellent. Eslac, Stamwick, relax. As tempting as it is, you two are not going in. Set up camp here. Stand guard. I don't want anyone coming anywhere close to this place, is that understood?

Both soldiers nodded and saluted. And breathed a sigh of relief.

"We have to inform the king and see what he wants to do. I'm sure he'll want to set something up so no other villagers will suffer the same fate."

"Do you think they died in there?" Tyril asked.

"We don't even know what *it* is," Pheron pointed out. "There's no sense in trying to guess what has happened until we have as much information as possible. We'll let the experts decide what to do."

* * *

"I honestly have no idea, Your Majesty."

"Shardwyn, you're a wizard. Surely you must have read something about this. Can't you tell us anything about it?"

Captain Pheron had notified the castle that a singularity had been discovered which explained the disappearance of the missing villagers. Kri'Entu hadn't wasted any time assembling a team and sending them to the kingdom's largest seaside village. Since there had been a lull in activity around the castle, the king himself accompanied the group west to see the strange phenomenon for himself and what could be done to neutralize it.

However, upon arriving at the scene of the anomaly, Kri'Entu had been informed by the captain that it was his opinion this wasn't a portal as it didn't conform to the same properties every other portal exhibited. There was no athe crystal to power it. There were no frames to contain it. It wasn't possible for a portal to exist without those elements, yet there it was, defying all known explanations.

"If I were to venture a guess," Shardwyn was saying, "I'd say this is nothing more than jhorun in its elemental form."

Kri'Entu frowned. "Jhorun does not exist in an elemental form. It's something we are all born with. We can temporarily increase our own jhorun through the use of the joriis but those spheres are rare. The few joriis that do exist are safe and sound. No, I do not think this is jhorun, and if it is, we have no way to confirm that."

Down on his knees, peering intently at the swirling disturbance just above ground level, Shardwyn shook his head.

"I mention it only as a possible explanation, Your Majesty," the wizard informed him.

"I have already sent for a second opinion," Kri'Entu said with the beginnings of a smile.

"Who could you possibly ask that would know as much as I would on the matter, Your Majesty?"

"Me," a strong gruff voice flatly said.

Shardwyn stiffened with surprise and slowly got to his feet. He looked down his nose and crossed his arms over his chest.

Standing in front of him, with a smug look on his face, was an elderly dwarf everyone was quite familiar with. His beard was streaked with gray and had been tightly braided together and tucked into an ornate black belt. The dwarf was outfitted entirely in black. Tunic, trousers and boots; all were of the same hue. Draped over his shoulders was a heavy gray robe adorned with all manner of pins, patches, and various other accoutrements. The dwarf's black eyes twinkled mischievously as they stared up at the tall wizard.

"You."

The dwarf nodded. "Aye. Me. It's a pleasure to see you, too, wizard."

"Master Maelnar. Don't you have better things to be doing? What would your Council think if they knew you … how did you get here so fast, anyway?"

Maelnar grinned and held up a glittering crystal key. It was such a bright yellow color that Shardwyn briefly wondered if the dwarf key maker had somehow managed to capture a piece of the sun's essence and imbue it within the crystal. The dwarf nodded at the king, who nodded in return.

"At Kri'Entu's request, and with the permission of the Council, a new portal was commissioned and linked to your castle straight from Bohragg. Now I can visit at a moment's notice. Isn't that grand?"

"It doesn't explain how you arrived *here* so quickly", Shardwyn pointed out. "We have Capily's portal key. What did you use?"

"I didn't use anything. I came over with you."

"You did? I didn't see you."

"I'm surprised. You're always looking down your nose so I figured you would have seen me. I was there, as clear as the wrinkles on your face."

Shardwyn's eyes momentarily flicked over to the king's, who had to turn away in order to keep from laughing out loud. The feud between the wizard and dwarf had been going on for years now and gave every indication that it would continue for years to come. Shardwyn shoved his hands into his pockets and came close to pouting.

"Well, you're here. You can at least make yourself useful.

What do you make of that?"

Maelnar followed the human wizard and looked where he pointed. The dwarf's eyebrows shot up. He slowly approached the anomaly and knelt down on the ground to get a closer look. With wide, wondering eyes Maelnar looked up at Shardwyn.

"There's something you don't see every day. What do you think that is, wizard?"

Shardwyn appeared ready to give a sarcastic answer when he caught sight of the king standing quietly nearby, watching the proceedings. The king frowned at him. Shardwyn closed his mouth and sighed. He forced a smile as he looked down at the dwarf.

"I say this knowing full well you'll ridicule me but I do so anyway. I think this is an example of jhorun in its purest form."

"Jhorun doesn't manifest itself physically," Maelnar pointed out.

"How would you know?" Shardwyn countered. "Dwarves don't typically have jhorun. We have more experience with it so maybe we know something you don't."

Surprisingly, Maelnar nodded. "I concede the point."

"What do you think it is?" Shardwyn asked as he squatted down to both inspect the anomaly closer and at Maelnar's eye level.

Maelnar stared intently at the swirling vortex. "I was told that it has the characteristics of a portal. Is that true?"

Graylan, standing nearby, raised a bandaged hand. "With the exception of having a long pole forcefully yanked out of our hands as we were conducting some tests, aye. It behaves like a portal."

"It just doesn't look like a portal," Shardwyn added, giving Graylan a friendly smile.

"It cannot be a portal," Maelnar concluded. "All portals require a power source. There is no frame or a place to conceal the athe crystal. If that's a portal then it's not one I'm familiar with."

"Can you detect a power source?" the king asked, as he appeared standing next to the two of them. "I would concur with Master Maelnar. If it's a portal, there should be a power source of some sort."

Maelnar pulled several small metal devices from pouches attached to his belt and began setting them up on the ground. He retrieved a small notebook from an inside pocket in his robes and mumbled quietly to himself as he made a few adjustments to the strange apparatuses on the ground. He flipped the page in his notebook and then pressed a button on the closest device.

Nothing happened.

Grunting softly, Maelnar returned the first device to his belt and concentrated on the second. He inserted a small metal key into the top of the flat rectangular device and twisted the key for several revolutions. Properly wound, the second device began whirring and emitting soft clicks. After ten seconds of listening to the whirring and clicking, Maelnar consulted his notebook a final time. He snapped it closed and pressed another button on the device, silencing it instantly.

"Nothing," Maelnar reported. He tapped the first device. "This one will detect energy signatures that many of the athe crystals produce. If there was an athe crystal, or something equivalent in the vicinity, then it would have made quite a ruckus. It didn't. Therefore, whatever that thing is uses a source of power I am unfamiliar with."

"And the second device?" the king prompted. "What does it do?"

"That is a geographical locator. I don't have to use it much so I beg your pardon for having to consult my notes. I had to make sure I was using it correctly. I was. Not only did this device not pick up the presence of a portal, it certainly was unable to determine where that portal, assuming it is one, would deposit the traveler."

The king sighed. He stared down at the anomaly with grim determination. There were missing Lentarians and more than likely this disturbance—this *thing*—was to blame. He had to know what was on the other end of … of … that portal.

"What about a teleporter?" Kri'Entu suggested. "Could someone with a teleporting jhorun be able to determine anything?"

In unison, both wizard and dwarf shrugged.

"It couldn't hurt to try," Maelnar answered.

Shardwyn nodded.

The king turned to look back at Pheron, who was standing off to the side as he gave orders to his men to properly secure the area for the foreseeable future.

"Captain, could you send for a teleporter?"

Pheron nodded. "At once, Your Majesty."

Less than an hour later Capily's only known teleporter, a slender man in his late twenties or early thirties, had joined the group and was staring intently at the anomaly. Dressed in khaki shorts and a green tunic, the nervous young man ran a shaky hand through his brown hair and whistled, then slid his hands into his pockets and grunted twice. He looked up at the king and realized he was being watched. He smiled sheepishly and returned his attention to the anomaly, stepping close to squat down for a more methodical inspection. A few seconds later he backed away a few feet, seeming undecided.

"I, uh, er… This is very peculiar, Your Majesty. I have never seen the like."

Kri'Entu smiled patiently. "I am sure. However, Mister Breet, I need to know if you can sense where this portal might lead. If it is a portal, that is. What can you tell us about it?"

Breet closed his eyes and went still. Kri'Entu glanced over at Maelnar and Shardwyn, who were standing nearby. Maelnar gave a quick shake of his head and smiled. Shardwyn was staring at a flock of kytes in a distant tree.

"It's perfectly acceptable to say you don't know," Kri'Entu told the quiescent teleporter. "I thank you for your time. You are excused and may return to your home."

Relief washed over the man's features. "Thank you, Your Majesty. I'm sorry I wasn't able to be of more help. Perhaps a stronger teleporter might be able to do better."

Kri'Entu's curiosity was piqued. "Who would you recommend, Mister Breet?"

"There's Tessler, in Donlari. Bertol is good. He lives in Avin."

The king smiled and nodded. "Thank you. That was incredibly helpful."

"If I may make a suggestion, Your Majesty?"

"Of course, Mister Breet. Go ahead."

"I would contact the strongest teleporter you can. Portals and teleporters perform the same task. As a result, most teleporters can get a sense of what's on the other side of a portal. The stronger the jhorun, the clearer the picture. I wish I could help but–I will be the first to admit this–my teleporting skills aren't the strongest. I will have to rest for days just to rebuild my own jhorun for my return trip home."

"Who is the strongest teleporter you can think of?" Kri'Entu asked.

"Lady Sarah." Shardwyn and Maelnar interrupted, in perfect unison.

Wizard and dwarf looked at each other and briefly smiled. Breet was nodding.

"They're right, Your Majesty," Breet agreed. "Her teleportation jhorun is unmatched and envied by all."

The king sighed. "I was referring to Lentarian teleporters. I know full well Lady Sarah is the strongest known teleporter. I was hoping there would be someone local we could ask instead."

"We're at a loss here," Shardwyn told him. "We need more information and so far we are coming up short. No offense, Master Maelnar."

The dwarf harrumphed.

Kri'Entu nodded and came to a rapid conclusion. "Very well. We will contact Lady Sarah."

Chapter 2 — Call Out the Cavalry!

"You don't want your arms to be too rigid. Loosen up a little. There you go. Now look through the peep sight and adjust your aim so that those fixed pins in the sight are straight ahead. Do you see them?"

"Yes. Which color am I supposed to be looking at? There are three of them."

"The pins denote distance to target, so it depends how far away you are from what you're shooting at. The bottom pin, the yellow one, would be the farthest setting. It's presently set to forty yards. The orange is set to thirty, and the green pin at the top is set to twenty yards. Since you're about twenty yards from the target I'd use the green pin on the top. Once you've got the green tip of that pin on what you're aiming at, then you release the arrow. It's that simple."

"Oh. I didn't know that. All the times I've watched you shoot one of these things I never knew how to properly aim it."

"Want to hear a secret? Up until about two months ago, neither did I."

Surprised, Sarah released the tension in her compound bow and turned to stare at her husband.

"But you've had your bow for over a year now!"

"I know. Let's just keep that between ourselves, okay?"

Sarah laughed and swatted her husband's arm. She tightened the wrist strap on her arrow puller and clipped the nock of her arrow back onto the bowstring. She attached her arrow puller to the D-loop and took a deep breath. As smoothly as she could, keeping the tip of her arrow pointed at the ground, she pulled back on the string in one fluid motion. Keeping her arms steady she felt the level of resistance drop as the cams on the upper and lower limbs reduced the pull to a fraction of the full draw weight. Sarah took aim at the square archery target Steve had set up on the huge lawn behind their house and gently touched the arrow puller's trigger.

There was a soft *swoosh* and the arrow was gone. A split second later it had sunk deep into one of the inner rings of the target's bullseye. With a triumphant smile, she turned to her husband and handed the bow to him.

"Yep. That's how it's done."

"What are you giving me this thing for? I have my own."

"I thought maybe you'd like to try mine, seeing how you're having so many difficulties with your own."

Steve's eyes narrowed. "Aren't we just full of it today?"

"I'm the one who is reliably hitting the target. How are you doing?"

Steve shook his head with exasperation. "You're not going to let me live that down any time soon, are you?"

Sarah smiled sweetly at him. "Well, ask yourself this. Have you gotten an arrow closer to the center of the target than I have?"

Steve pursed his lips and came close to pouting, not that he'd ever admit it. "No."

"Would you like me to give you some pointers?"

"I just gave them to *you*. You're not allowed to give me pointers. Besides, you're probably using your own jhorun to look good."

Ignoring the insult, Sarah pointed at the second compound bow that was leaning up against a nearby tree. "Your turn then. Let's see you do any better."

Steve handed Sarah's pink compound bow back to her and picked up his much more manly camouflage-colored Stringer bow. He inserted his left hand into the wrist strap so he wouldn't accidentally drop the expensive bow and clipped an arrow to the serving point. He hooked his own arrow puller to the bow's D-loop and drew the arrow back, simultaneously adjusting his posture so that the arrow and the ground were parallel with one another. He targeted the center of the large cube. His finger inched toward the release trigger.

Sarah sneezed.

Steve's arrow missed the target and sank deep into one of the bales of hay he had set up as a backstop. The arrow had practically disappeared into the backstop as only the tips of the feathers were still visible.

"No fair! You did that on purpose!"

Sarah sniffed loudly and rubbed her nose. "Shoot. My allergies are really bad right now. I should take something for that."

"Snot."

Sarah squinted at the target and frowned. She reached for a pair of binoculars on the small patio table next to them. She adjusted the focus and stared at the distant bales of hay.

"Your bow doesn't have to be set that high, does it? I mean, look at that arrow. Only the tip is left."

"It *is* set as low as it'll go," Steve pointed out.

"Oh."

Sarah nocked another arrow and targeted the bale. A moment later there were two arrows sticking out of the center of the target. Sarah took a seat in a nearby patio chair and laid her bow across her lap as if to say, 'I thought this would be difficult.'

Steve fired off four arrows, one right after the other, in rapid succession. Three hit the target and the fourth joined his first arrow in the backstop behind the archery cube.

"Perhaps if you aimed you might do a bit better," Sarah idly suggested.

Steve scowled and tried again. This time he took several

deep breaths and then held it, drew his arrow back, and twisted a little to the left so that the tip of the green targeting pin was touching the center of the bullseye. Standing completely motionless, and confident that his arm wasn't wavering, he hit the trigger.

The arrow streaked across the open countryside and embedded itself into the target. It was his best shot yet; unfortunately, the arrow was still at least three inches farther away from the center than Sarah's. He quickly glanced at his wife and caught her smug smile.

"Alright, alright, laugh it up. Congratulations. You're better at this than I am."

Sarah rejoined him and fitted another arrow to her bow's serving point. Taking aim, she released. Then another. And another. Every arrow was as close to the target's center as her first, if not closer.

Steve reached for another arrow but found his quiver empty. He watched Sarah fire the last of her arrows and then set her bow on her chair. She picked up the binoculars and again inspected the target. There were far more pink arrows than green ones sticking out of the three foot by three foot archery target. Sarah closed her eyes and concentrated. Fifteen pink arrows suddenly dropped into the soft grass at her feet.

"What about mine? Are you really going to make me walk all the way over there when you can teleport them just as easily as you did yours?"

Sarah gave him a devious smile. "Sure. I can do that. What's it worth to you?"

"What? What do you mean?"

"I said what's it worth to you? A ten minute back massage?"

Steve glanced irritably back at the target over fifty feet away and weighed the pros and cons of Sarah's offer. Laziness won.

"Fine. You'll get your back massage tonight."

His green fletched arrows appeared next to hers in the grass. Steve shook his head as he glanced back at the arrow-free target. He'd deny it under the most heinous of tortures but he did think Sarah's jhorun, her magical ability, was more useful than his own. He briefly thought back, years ago, upon their first visit to Lentari and how much their lives had changed since then.

Steve and his wife were the only two people on the face of the planet who could do magic. Thanks to their first visit to the magical kingdom of Lentari, he and Sarah had been gifted with jhorun and included in an ancient prophecy where they had become protectors of the young crown prince. Now, years later, Mikal no longer needed their protection so their babysitting days were over.

Steve sighed. Since retiring from the full-time nanny position, there hadn't been any situations that called for his jhorun. But that wasn't surprising. He could summon and control fire. It was a handy and very powerful jhorun to have in Lentari, but in Coeur d'Alene? It was only used when he wanted to light his barbecue. Or perhaps to safely light the fuse of one of the high-powered fireworks he was so fond of.

Was his jhorun useful?

Steve sighed again, which garnered him a speculative look from Sarah, and slid his arrows back into his quiver. Over the next half hour husband and wife continued to fire arrow after arrow at the target. Occasionally, Steve would move the target farther away, just to see if Sarah could hit it as easily.

She could. In fact, it seemed as though her aim improved as the distance increased. Steve silently vowed to practice more when Sarah wasn't around. "What's that face for?" Sarah asked, breaking more than thirty seconds of silence. "A penny for your thoughts?"

"Promise not to laugh?"

Sarah shook her head. "No promises. Out with it. What's the matter?"

"It's nothing. I was just thinking that if Rhenyon could see me now, he'd be laughing his butt off."

"Why?"

"Because your archery skills are far superior to mine."

"Oh, stop being so competitive. I'm a better shot, so what? As soon as you figure out the nuances of that bow then you'll be doing much better than me. Don't take this the wrong way, but if you actually practice more, you'll get better.

I don't see you shooting this thing that often."

"It's not fun shooting by myself," Steve informed her. He picked up her full quiver and held her bow while she gathered up the patio chairs. Sarah turned to smile at him.

"Why do you think I suggested we should buy me a bow, too?"

Steve felt his smile stretch from one ear to the other. "You wanted a bow so you can shoot with me? Awww, how sweet!"

"Don't get all mushy on me," Sarah warned. "You were just outshot by a girl. How do you sleep at night?"

Steve grinned. "Like a baby."

"A snoring baby," Sarah agreed. She hooked her arm through his as they walked back to the manor. "Are you going to take care of Annie's computer today?"

Steve groaned and sighed aloud. "Yeah, I need to do that. I've been putting it off."

"Any idea what's wrong with it?"

"It's the same problem that my mom's had. And your mom's. They've picked up extra software on their computers when they weren't paying attention and, as a result, their laptops have begun to slow down. I just gotta break up the party, so to speak."

"Well, put that stuff away and let's head over there. I'm looking forward to spending some time with the boys."

Half an hour later, after their archery equipment had been properly cared for and put away, Steve and Sarah were on the doorstep of one of the other three houses on their property besides the huge manor. Ever since they'd built a house for Annie and Tristan on their extensive property, Sarah had surreptitiously suggested that a third house might be in order.

"You never know if we'll have someone else move in here," Sarah had told him. "It could be your parents, or even mine. If that happens, wouldn't it be a good idea to be prepared?"

"By building another house?"

"Sure. We can afford it. And as long as we're doing that…"

Sarah trailed off and batted her eyes at her husband. Steve crossed his arms over his chest.

"What? What's the rest of that sentence?"

"We should build a lodge."

"Are you serious?"

"For gatherings and get togethers," Sarah explained.

"Are you suggesting the manor isn't big enough to entertain a lot of people?"

"I know it is," Sarah patiently explained to her exasperated husband. "But we live there. Do you really want that many people wandering around our house?"

Six months after Annie and Tristan's house had been finished, the final touches were put on the guest house and the enormous lodge. The massive lodge, at over four thousand square feet, sat several hundred feet away from the manor and was situated up against the base of the government-owned forest lands.

Sarah knocked again. She looked at her husband and shrugged. Steve walked over to the side of the garage and peered in one of the two windows.

"She's there," Steve helpfully told her. "Her car is parked in there."

"Stop peeping through the windows," Sarah scolded. "It's creepy. Get back over here before she sees you."

Sarah knocked again. This time they heard a piercing smash followed by a loud peal of childish laughter. The heavy front door briefly shuddered as someone on the other side unlocked the dead bolt, more than likely doing so as they were running by. Sarah suppressed a smile as one voice rose above the others.

"Christopher, get back here this instant!"

Sarah gently pushed the door open and stepped into a world of chaos that only a small child could create. Toy trucks, foot-destroying building blocks, half eaten plates of macaroni and cheese, and a handheld video game, complete with a jagged crack running across the length of the screen, met their eyes.

"I think I can safely say that a tornado must have touched down in here," Steve commented, shutting the door behind them.

"Yep," Sarah agreed, "and they call him Christopher."

Hearing his name, a tousle-headed boy of four appeared in the bathroom doorway. His cherubic face split into a grin as he ran toward Sarah as fast as his chubby little legs could manage.

"There's my little Christopher!"

Sarah hefted the boy onto her hip, being careful to avoid touching Christopher's shirt as it had a dollop of orange goo slowly running down the front of it. Annie appeared moments later. She caught sight of her son and smiled.

"There you are, you little stinker. I told you we need to get you cleaned up. Now hold still!"

Annie produced a wet washcloth and proceeded to clean the boy's face while he wiggled and squirmed in Sarah's grasp. With his face finally clean, Sarah set her nephew down on the ground and watched as he scampered off.

"Sorry about the mess," Annie began, but Sarah waved off her concerns.

"Don't worry about it. Clearly your hands are full at the moment."

"Where's Tristan?" Steve asked, while stepping over a large red firetruck that had been upended in front of the couch.

"He took Zachary for a walk. He knows how much Christopher hates his baths, so I think he opted for a quieter setting."

Steve knelt down as Christopher reappeared, holding a toy cement truck. "You don't like baths, huh? Well, trust me kid; you could use one right about now."

"He already had it," Annie pointed out.

Upon hearing the dreaded 'b' word, Christopher dropped the truck and ran, squealing, from the room.

Annie frowned. "Nice going, Uncle Steve. He was just starting to settle down when you had to go get him all riled up again."

"You think he was calming down? Really?"

Annie nodded. "Yeah, he was. Trust me."

"Alrighty then. I'll just go take a look at your computer, shall I?"

Steve ducked into the room Annie and Tristan used as an office and quickly shut the door behind him. He could hear Sarah and her sister laughing, presumably at him. That was okay. Quite often he found himself the butt of their jokes, but since he knew it was all in good fun, he never made an issue out of it. Most times.

He booted up the laptop and found a bunch of programs that had installed themselves—browsers, false security alarms, add-ons, and nearly a dozen demo games. He dumped them faster than a pizza would disappear at a kid's party, then pushed back from the desk and peeked out into the hallway.

"Umm, hello? Where'd everyone go?"

Movement caught his eye past the kitchen. It looked as though everyone was standing out on the patio. The sun had set moments before. He slid the patio door open and joined Sarah, who was standing by the railing and watching Christopher drive a kiddie-sized motorized truck around the backyard. The boy had a huge grin on his face as he plowed over smaller toy trucks, Frisbees, and anything else unfortunate enough to fall in his path.

A tall bald man wearing a simple gray tee shirt and a worn pair of blue jeans suddenly came through the front door pushing a three wheeled stroller with large rubber wheels. Tristan parked the stroller and gently pulled out a sleeping toddler, and ducked into a nearby room. A few moments later, he came into the kitchen, made eye contact with Steve, and joined the others on the patio. He smiled at Sarah as he took the bottle of water Annie offered to him. He joined Steve at the railing and together they watched Christopher grind more and more toys into the soft grass of their backyard. When his replica monster truck disappeared around the southwestern corner of the house, both men automatically followed.

"Christopher sure is a handful," Steve commented as a coiled hose became the young boy's latest vehicular conquest.

Tristan smiled. "He is, indeed. I would not have it any other way."

"You may be changing your tune once Zachary becomes old enough to give Christopher a run for his money."

"Perhaps." Tristan straightened and stared toward the

manor house.

"Are you expecting company?" Tristan asked, his voice flat.

Steve shook his head. "No. Why do you ask?"

"Several people are standing by your house and I did not hear any mechanized carriages arrive."

"Say what?"

Steve and Tristan peered over the stone perimeter fence where they could see the northern corner of the huge manor. Steve narrowed his eyes. Tristan was right. Two people were slowly starting to walk toward his detached garage and were staring at the surrounding countryside as though they were lost. He didn't recognize either of the two young men. Steve inclined his head toward the intruders.

"We need to take care of this."

Tristan nodded. "I want Annie and Christopher inside. Now."

"Come on. We need to warn them."

Steve ducked back behind the fence and ran toward the patio with Tristan hot on his heels. Sarah and Annie were sipping on tall frosty glasses of lemonade when the two of them burst onto the scene. Sarah, catching sight of her husband's alarmed expression, was on her feet first.

"What is it? What's going on?"

"Someone's at the manor. Several someones. We would have heard a car pull up. We didn't. However they got there, they didn't use any means we're familiar with. You three need to get inside, okay?"

Sarah nodded. The lemonade sat, forgotten, as Annie snatched up Christopher and ducked into the house. Steve waited for Sarah to follow her sister inside, then he and Tristan quietly snuck toward the manor.

"Did they come out of our house?" Steve whispered after both he and Tristan sprinted toward the huge exterior garage sitting next to the manor.

Tristan shook his head. "Unknown. I cannot see the front of the manor from the backyard."

"You didn't recognize any of them?"

"I do not know either of them."

"Do you think there's more than two?" Steve asked. He looked down at his hands; both had turned dark red.

"Unknown."

Both men cautiously inched around the corner of the garage and inspected the front of the manor. There, shuffling uncertainly about, were two men who appeared to be in their early twenties. Both were wearing matching dark gray shirts and pants, almost a uniform.

Steve was silent as he watched the two men move uncertainly about. He looked at Tristan and nodded.

"Looks like there's just two. Come on, we can take 'em!"

"What if more are nearby?"

"I doubt there are, but if so, I'm sure we can handle it."

Just then they heard a shout. One of the men walked around the back of the manor and paused at the corner. Looking furtively about, he focused his attention on the heavily forested government land behind the manor. The man shouted something in the direction of the forest. Then they heard an answering shout. There were at least three people present!

"Did you find anything?" the closest intruder shouted.

"Nothing here," an answering shout sounded. "Keep looking. They must be here somewhere! Search the structure again if you have to."

The intruder nodded and headed back toward the manor's front entrance. He called for his companion and the two of them walked up the steps to vanish inside.

His mind made up, Steve looked over at Tristan, who nodded.

"I will take these two," his introverted brother-in-law told him. "Do you think you can deal with whoever it is behind the house?"

Steve nodded. "Easily. Hell, I've taken on trolls before, so one or two—"

Tristan held a finger to his lips, cutting off Steve in mid-sentence. "Perhaps now is not the best time to boast about your adventures. Be quick and be silent."

Steve swallowed his annoyance and sprinted toward the back corner of the house. He looked toward the trees but couldn't see anyone moving about. He inched forward, pausing every ten seconds to see if he could hear anything.

Not a sound.

At the far northeastern corner of the mansion Steve eased his head around the corner and finally spotted the third man. Standing about a hundred feet in front of him, his back turned, this one was dressed in the same gray outfit as the others but with dark trim outlining his jacket. An officer? This had to be the leader of the small group.

Steve released his jhorun into his hands and felt both of them flame up. He stepped away from the house and cleared his throat.

"You, my friend, just made a big mistake coming here." In case he hadn't been heard, Steve blasted several jets of fire high up into the air. "You're personally going to see what it feels like to become 'well done' if you so much as flinch."

The third stranger jerked his hands upward.

"Hold your fire, Sir Steve," a familiar voice said.

"Turn around," Steve ordered.

The man complied. Steve's fires snuffed out. "Pheron! What the hell are you doing here? Showing up unexpected like that is a good way to get yourself toasted, pal."

"I am sorry, Sir Steve. I was under orders."

"You are? By who? Rhenyon?"

"No, not Commander Rhenyon. I am here by order of the king."

Steve whistled. "That can't be good. What's going on? What's the matter?"

"Is Lady Sarah nearby?"

"Yeah. Why? What do you want her for?"

"We need her help."

"You do? What could you … Wait. How many men came here with you?"

"Myself and two others. Why?"

"Because Tristan went after the other two."

Pheron looked alarmed and they raced toward the manor. They took the stairs two at a time as they bolted into the house. They burst into the mansion's foyer and slid to a stop. It was quiet. Way too quiet.

"Tristan?" Steve called out. "Are you okay? Speak to me, pal!"

"I am here."

"Where?"

"By the fireplace."

Steve and Pheron sprinted through the family room doors and came to an abrupt stop. Tristan had not only incapacitated the two strange men but had also hog tied them with black cord. Both men were lying on their stomachs with their hands tied behind their backs and then tied to their bound ankles. It looked very uncomfortable. Steve noticed the flatscreen television from the living room had been knocked from its perch on the wall. It and several electronic components were sitting haphazardly on the floor.

"I am sorry about your electrical devices," Tristan began apologetically. "I needed rope."

Steve waved off Tristan's concerns. "That's okay. I'll cry later. You did what had to be done. Besides, it gives me an excuse to do some upgrading. Anyway, it turns out they are harmless. They are Pheron's men."

Tristan nodded. "That must have been what they were trying to tell me before I gagged them."

Pheron knelt and before Steve could utter a word of protest, unsheathed a dagger and sliced through the cords immobilizing his men. Steve gave a quiet gasp of shock and managed to bite his lip before he let slip that Pheron had just destroyed two very expensive audio/video cables. If Sarah had been here, she'd be laughing her tail off.

Speaking of which…

"Let me go get Sarah. Tristan, hold down the fort. I'll be right back."

Five minutes later Steve returned and escorted Sarah through the front door. Pheron instantly bowed and smiled. A quick frown at his two subordinates caused them to mimic their captain.

"Lady Sarah. It is a pleasure to see you again."

Sarah beamed her smile up at the tall captain. "It's nice to see you, too, Pheron. You surprised us. I don't think anyone has ever come through the portal unannounced. Is everything okay?"

Pheron shook his head. "Not really. Several villagers have vanished."

"That's what the king told us the last time we were there," Steve recalled. "That was what, a little over three months ago?"

Pheron nodded.

"Aye. Since that time another person has gone missing."

Sarah took her husband's hand. "How can I help, Pheron?"

"We found something in Capily that we'd like your input on, Lady Sarah."

"O-kay. You found something. Can you tell me what?"

Pheron shook his head no. "I wish we could. We were hoping you'd be able to help identify it."

Intrigued, Sarah looked at Steve.

"Alright, I'm curious. You?"

Steve smiled and turned to Pheron. "Go back to Lentari. Tell the king we're on our way and that we'll be at the Constable's office in Capily in about an hour."

"Can you not meet us at the anomaly?"

Sarah clapped her hands together.

"Ooooo! An anomaly? This is sounding better and better! And no, I can't."

"Her reference point is the constable's office," Steve explained to Pheron. "She's been there before so she can take us directly there."

Pheron nodded. "I will report back to the king. We will expect the two of you there in an hour's time."

Pheron and his two men walked back up the stairs toward the master bedroom and the portal contained on its entry doors. In a few moments they heard the chiming from the portal as it was activated. Ten seconds later all was silent upstairs. Steve and Sarah both nodded. Perhaps an outing to Lentari was just what they needed to brighten up an otherwise uneventful day.

* * *

"It has to have something to do with a portal," Sarah was

saying as they exited the constable's office in Capily. Fifteen minutes had passed, and that was only because they had changed into their Lentarian outfits. "Why else would they want my help?"

"Are you the only teleporter?" Steve asked.

"No. There are others. I don't know why they haven't asked them."

"Maybe they have and they weren't able to do anything," Steve suggested.

"Perhaps. Look, there's Pheron."

Pheron waved them over and together they turned to the north and headed off, following one of the village's main roads in and out of town. In the fifteen minutes it took to reach the anomaly, as Pheron had called it, the friendly captain shared what he had learned thus far. Sadly, it wasn't much. That it was some type of portal seemed to be the only certainty. The problem was no one knew where the portal went. If several of the villagers had fallen through this mysterious portal, then the only way they'd be able to mount a rescue mission was if they knew what was on the other side.

"Watch your head, milady," Pheron cautioned as they crested a rise and began their descent into a shallow depression.

The captain held a few low branches out of the way while Steve and Sarah pushed by. Both of them came to an abrupt halt as they saw the flurry of activity before them. Tents had been erected everywhere they would fit. Marching guards patrolled by every thirty seconds. A large maroon tent had been erected just off to the side facing south. In the direct center of all the commotion was a small group of people that were huddled around recently pruned ferns. Several makeshift tables had been set up nearby where a gaunt man dressed completely in black was busy adjusting various devices that had been set up in several rows. The thin gray haired man looked up and smiled at the two of them. Shardwyn's familiar face sparkled with wonder. The castle wizard was clearly enjoying every minute of his involvement with whatever this anomaly was.

"Sir Steve! Lady Sarah! So good of you to join us!"

A small figure that had been standing so still he could have been mistaken as a part of the surrounding environment looked up and bowed. The top of the dwarf's head may have only come up to Shardwyn's chest but he still managed to project an aura of confidence and intelligence. The dwarf pushed by the wizard and smiled at both of them. Shardwyn crossed his arms over his chest and scowled.

"Lady Sarah! Sir Steve! Welcome!"

Sarah gave the dwarf a hug. "Maelnar! It's nice to see you!"

Steve grasped forearms with the dwarf and grinned. "Looking good, pal. How've you been?"

"Quite well, quite well. I don't recall enjoying a mystery as much as this since Nar was discovered."

"What did you guys find out here?" Steve asked, genuinely bewildered. "I have to admit you've definitely piqued our curiosity."

Shardwyn appeared and swept Maelnar out of the way. He took Sarah's arm and started to guide her toward the anomaly.

"You'll be most interested in this, Lady Sarah. What we have here is—"

Shardwyn tripped over Maelnar's outstretched foot and tumbled to the ground. Without missing a step Maelnar took his place and hooked his arm through Sarah's.

"What we have here," Maelnar continued, as he smiled victoriously at Shardwyn's sprawled form, "is what we have decided must be a natural portal."

"I don't think I've ever heard about a natural portal," Sarah commented.

Steve grasped Shardwyn's outstretched hand and pulled the wizard to his feet.

"Neither have we, if you must know," Maelnar added with a wink. "But, we know about it now."

"And you don't know where it goes?" Sarah asked.

Together she and Maelnar approached a ten-foot by ten-foot burlap tent that had been constructed over the portal. Maelnar gently pulled the flap out of the way and let Sarah get her first look at the anomaly. Steve appeared at Sarah's side and together they gazed at the swirling vortex.

"If that's a portal," Steve began, "then what's powering it? I thought it needed some type of special crystal."

"An athe crystal," Maelnar confirmed. "And you're right. It does. However, this one doesn't."

"What would you like me to do?" Sarah asked as she looked down at Maelnar. "How can I help?"

"We're told," a new voice chimed in, "that teleporters can get a sense of where a portal will lead if they concentrate in close proximity. We would like you to do just that."

Everyone turned to see the king exit his giant maroon tent and approach the group. Steve bowed while Sarah curtsied.

"We didn't think you'd still be here," Steve jovially told the king.

"As Master Maelnar has indicated, this is an intriguing mystery; one that must be solved. I will devote as much time as needed to guarantee our villagers are returned safely."

"Trying to avoid some boring meetings at the castle, huh?" Steve said under his breath, but loudly enough for the king to hear. Sarah elbowed him in the ribs. Kri'Entu smiled.

"Whatever could you be referring to, Sir Steve?"

Steve gave the king a knowing smile and returned his attention to the small vortex. Sarah squatted about three feet from the portal and closed her eyes. Maelnar knelt on her left. He, however, had his eyes wide open and fixed on Sarah. Steve nodded as he understood what the dwarf was doing. Maelnar was there to make sure Sarah didn't become the next victim to fall through the portal.

"Can you see anything, lass?" Maelnar asked.

Sarah was frowning. "It's worse than trying to picture someone in Lentari when we are in our world. Every time I start to get a picture something happens and I lose my concentration."

"Like what?" Steve asked, curious.

"Like you breathing," Sarah instantly answered. "Or Pheron coughing or Shardwyn fidgeting from foot to foot, which causes his robes to make a rustling sound. Every time I hear something like that, I lose the picture."

"You're saying you need absolute quiet, is that so?"

Kri'Entu nodded. He looked at the many people bustling about. "That can be arranged. Attention! I need everyone to vacate the area. That means everyone! Fall back to the edge of this clearing. You need to be at least a thousand feet away. Captain Pheron, secure the tents, the packs, the equipment, and anything else you can think of. No noises. Is that understood?"

"Be careful," Maelnar warned Sarah. "We will give you your required privacy but do remember that there will not be anyone here to prevent you from falling into the anomaly."

Sarah nodded. "Got it."

Five minutes later, watching from as far away as they could while still keeping the anomaly in sight, Steve saw Sarah lower herself to sit cross-legged on the ground. She went perfectly still.

"How long should we give her?" Shardwyn whispered to Steve.

"She will be given as much time as she needs," the king promptly told him.

Sarah remained on the ground for another ten minutes before she finally rose to her feet and signaled it was okay to come back. Maelnar and Shardwyn both noticed at the same time. Wizard and dwarf eyed each other. Both wanted to inform the king first, but Kri'Entu was standing off to the side and talking with Pheron. Maelnar was much smaller than a human and therefore easily able to maneuver around the men that were milling about. Shardwyn tried to thread his way through the crowd of people but found he spent more time excusing himself than making progress toward the king. Maelnar ducked under Pheron's arm and tugged a corner of the king's robes to get his attention.

The king looked up and then over at Sarah's distant form. He smiled gratefully at the dwarf and ordered everyone back to the clearing. Shardwyn could only glower from a distance.

Arriving at Sarah's side first, Steve looked into her eyes to see for himself that she was okay. His wife's unconcerned look puzzled him. He wanted to press her for more information but decided to wait until everyone had arrived.

"What did you see?" Kri'Entu asked as soon as everyone

had returned to the small clearing. "Could you see our people?"

"I didn't see any people," Sarah began, which elicited a frown from the king, "but I did see several pictures. I couldn't keep them in focus for very long."

Steve leaned forward. "Pictures? Plural?"

Sarah nodded. "That's right. I actually saw at least a dozen different visions. I'm convinced that if I were to sit there long enough, I'd keep seeing new ones every thirty seconds or so."

Steve shoved his hands in his pockets. It was his telltale sign he was thinking about something that was bothering him.

"Were you seeing the same scenes more than once?" he asked.

Sarah shook her head. "It was the weirdest thing. The pictures took so long to focus that I was only able to look at them for a few seconds before the scene would shift and I'd have to start all over again. That's why I waited so long."

"That is very peculiar, lass," Maelnar commented. He stroked his beard. "Have you ever encountered a vision like that before?"

"The closest experience was when we were all fighting Celestia, and her sister, Caladonia, and the vision showed me the approaching monsters. This, however, didn't feel like that. It didn't feel like anyone was in control of what I was looking at this time."

"It sounds like someone changing the channels on the television," Steve said quietly, more to himself than to anyone. Sarah, with her keen Vulcan hearing, as Steve called it, easily heard him.

"Yes! Like that. Exactly like that!"

"What can you remember about your vision, Lady Sarah?" the king asked. Kri'Entu turned to make eye contact with one of the scribes he had brought along and pointed at a nearby table with a stack of blank parchment and several quills and ink bottles. The young scribe hastily took a seat and looked expectantly up at Sarah. His quill was poised and ready to go.

Sarah took a seat at the table, which prompted everyone else to do the same. Sarah closed her eyes and went through the images she could remember.

"Let's see. The very first picture I saw was of trees and water. I could see tree-covered hills and a large lake."

Sounds of a scratching quill were heard as the scribe took notes.

"The second picture showed an oblong clearing with a small river running through the center, like a tributary of a larger river. I remember thinking this vision was one of the prettiest. Pine trees surrounded the clearing. Moss, or a light-colored grass, covered the ground."

"Excellent, Lady Sarah," Kri'Entu praised. "Do continue."

"The next picture was of a rock formation and waterfall. Some parts of the forest were visible, but this vision's main theme was rocks. There were smooth, rounded river rocks everywhere, as though the area had been underwater but wasn't anymore. The pool formed by the waterfall wasn't that big, either. The water flowed off to the left. I couldn't tell which direction it was."

The scribe called for a pause while he hastily uncorked a fresh bottle of ink and resumed his work.

"The image that stands out next was another image of the forest. There were trees everywhere I looked, including off into the distance. Speaking of which, it looked like the area was surrounded by a slight hazy fog. I remember thinking that the one thing lacking from each of these pictures was civilization. No houses, no roads, no signs of people nearby. This one was no exception. The forest was pristine; picturesque. It looked untouched."

The king nodded thoughtfully. Steve raised a hand. "I have a question."

Kri'Entu gently pushed Steve's arm down. "Let Lady Sarah finish her narrative and then we will ask some questions. It is important for her to recall everything she can before any details fade from her memory."

Steve nodded. "Right. Sorry."

"I'm trying to think of any other images that stood out. Oh. The mountains. Okay, this next picture showed snow-capped peaks in the distance. The mountains were just rock, as far as I could tell. Gray and brown with only the tips of the peaks dusted with snow. Sitting before the mountains was an enormous field of broken rocks. They were jagged and looked as though they were out of place, like someone had dumped them there. Several dead trees were nearby. They were twisted and gnarled."

Shardwyn opened his mouth to ask a question but Maelnar stomped on his foot to silence him. The wizard muffled a curse but did refrain from saying anything.

"The last vision I can recall is of a shallow river running along the base of several hills. I remember thinking that I was looking at a road because the river ran fairly straight before curving off to the right. A moment later I knew I wasn't looking at a road. White cumulus clouds were visible up in the sky and more mountains could be seen to the right."

Sarah opened her eyes, looked around the table, and smiled. "Alright, I will now field any questions you may have."

Steve snorted and hesitantly raised his arm. "Yes, my dear. You have a question. Go ahead."

"Did any of the trees look familiar? I mean, you know a lot about trees and plant life. Could you recognize anything?"

"Not from the perspective I had when I had those visions. I was too far away. I'm sorry."

Steve frowned. "You don't have anything to be sorry about."

"I concur," Kri'Entu agreed.

Maelnar cleared his throat. Shardwyn instantly crossed his arms over his chest.

"I wonder if Lady Sarah was seeing the same forest but from different angles?"

"There's no way to verify that," Kri'Entu informed him. "But it's a very good point."

"There's something about that scene with the shallow river I thought was a road."

Everyone turned back to Sarah.

"What of it?" the king gently inquired. "Was there something odd about that last vision?"

"Steve will tell you that I'm no camper and I don't really like spending too much time outdoors. However, that picture of the river reminded me of the very few camping trips I took when I was a child."

"What about it?" Steve inquired. "What makes you say that?"

"It was just the whole scene. I thought it would be a perfect place to camp for a few nights provided they had an RV hookup nearby."

Steve chuckled. His wife was a confirmed city girl, no doubt about it.

"Not once," Sarah continued, "have I looked at any river here in Lentari and thought that."

Steve leaned forward and rested his elbows on the table. "Interesting. Are you saying your visions weren't in Lentari?"

"The pictures were all outdoors and showed trees and mountains. From a distance they could be anywhere. However, not once have I ever seen dancing lights in the sky, either."

"Dancing lights? Like the aurora borealis?"

Sarah nodded. "It is similar, yes. However, the pictures I've seen of the aurora borealis aren't nearly as bright and colorful as what I saw in several of those visions. Wherever that was, it wasn't Lentari."

Kri'Entu frowned. "Then it is confirmed. The anomaly is a portal, and from the sounds of it, it's a portal to another world. Our missing villagers no doubt happened upon this very spot and fell through. It also means they have become stranded. This pleases me not. We *must* render aid. I want ideas, no matter how preposterous they may sound."

An entire table full of people sat with their hands clasped in front of them as they helplessly looked at each other.

"We have no idea where that thing leads," Pheron said, breaking the silence. "Our only option is to send a teleporter through that portal and hope they can make it back."

"Teleporting across worlds has only been accomplished by one person," Maelnar reminded them. "And that person is sitting at this very table. Lady Sarah, what do you think?"

"I'd like to think that I could return safely," Sarah slowly began, "but I can think of one problem no one has addressed."

"And what would that be?" Kri'Entu asked. He, along with everyone else at the table, had given Sarah his complete attention and was waiting, transfixed, at what she was about to say.

"What if my visions weren't of the same forest? What if my visions jumped among random areas? What if one person fell through the portal and was dropped in location A? Then person two comes along a few months later, falls in, and is sent to location B. How would we even know?"

More silence ensued.

"You're saying it's too dangerous to risk a trip through?" Kri'Entu slowly asked.

"I'm not comfortable with her going through there," Steve told the king. "Even you have to see that, Your Majesty."

The king nodded. "I do, Sir Steve. As much as I want our villagers returned, there would appear to be no method available to assure the safety of a rescue team. It pains me to say this but I must order this location off limits. A stone structure will be built around the anomaly and permanently sealed. No other villagers will lose their lives, is that understood?"

Those sitting near the king at the table solemnly nodded their heads. The king rose to his feet.

"This meeting is adjourned. Captain, you will oversee the building of whatever structure is necessary to keep our people safe."

Pheron nodded. "Aye, Your Majesty."

"I want this area evacuated. Right now. Shardwyn, collect your equipment. Master Maelnar, would you give Shardwyn a hand in dismantling his devices?"

Maelnar nodded. "Of course."

Kri'Entu turned to face Sarah and was startled to see her openly crying. "Lady Sarah, are you alright?"

"I'm sorry, Your Majesty. I want to help those people so badly. I feel like we have sealed their fate. Maybe if I were to at least try I might be able to save someone. I can try, can't I?"

Kri'Entu shook his head at the same time Steve scowled.

"Your suggestion is commendable, Lady Sarah," the king told her, "but impossible. Your safety cannot be guaranteed. If the victims of the anomaly have suffered some horrible fate, then you'd be sharing that fate. I am the one who must live with this decision, not you. I will bear that grief."

Steve put his arm around Sarah's shoulders and guided her away from the throng of people that were rapidly taking apart tents, tables, and other gear. They slowly walked over to the anomaly and stared at the gently swirling mists within the small vortex.

"I sure would like to know where that goes," Steve murmured.

Sarah was still upset. "Think of all those poor people who have disappeared. And the girl! What will her parents think? Oh, honey, I feel so bad."

Steve wrapped his arms around her in a hug and held her while she quietly sobbed against his shoulder. He watched as the giant maroon tent was pulled off its frame and rapidly packed. Poles were pulled apart and packed away. Maelnar was hastily plucking various devices off the wizard's allocated work table and handing them over when Steve saw the dwarf hesitate. Maelnar held the most recent device he had picked up, one that was spherical in shape, up to his ear. He heard the dwarf say that it was making noise. Maelnar examined the pewter colored device by gently turning it over in his hands.

"What is this, wizard? It's giving off a soft hum and it's vibrating."

Shardwyn looked up from where he was hastily shoving his instruments into a large trunk.

"That is a mobile levitator. I used it earlier when I was conducting experiments with the anomaly."

"Ah. You used this to lift large objects?"

The wizard nodded. "That's right. I wanted to see if an object of increased mass made a difference when going through that portal. It didn't. It's making noise, you say? I must have left the silly thing on. Go ahead and press that red button right there."

Maelnar did so. Instead of going quiet, as expected, the round machine became louder and started shaking even harder.

"That did not shut it off, wizard. What's it doing?"

Shardwyn rushed over.

"All you had to do was turn it off. Here, give me that."

"If you tell me the correct button to hit then I will," Maelnar angrily shot back.

The wizard reached for the device but before he could get both hands on it, Maelnar yanked it away. They both heard a loud click and suddenly Shardwyn was floating several feet off the ground.

"Very funny, dwarf. Now put me down."

"I didn't do it on purpose," Maelnar snapped back. He punched a few more buttons on the device.

Shardwyn let out a terrified shout as he found himself hurtling away from the surprised dwarf as though shot out a cannon. The wizard collided with Steve. Sarah flew from her husband's embrace, stumbling forward. She shrieked in terror as she tripped over an exposed root and fell head first into the vortex.

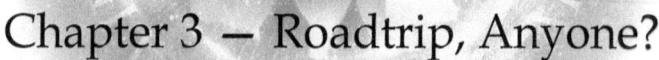

Chapter 3 — Roadtrip, Anyone?

"NO!" Steve stared in horror at the anomaly's swirling mists. He spun toward the king, his face ashen. They both turned on the wizard and dwarf. "You two and your stupid feud!"

Maelnar instantly dropped to one knee. "This is my fault. I alone share responsibility for this catastrophe."

Shardwyn shook his head and pulled the dwarf to his feet. "I cannot allow that, friend Maelnar. I should have —"

"I don't give a crap about pointing blame!" Steve shouted. His hands, which had turned dark red, flamed up. The fire climbed up his arms and spread across his chest. Ignoring the rapidly expanding flames that were quickly engulfing his body, Steve ran a shaky hand through his hair. "What are we going to do? The way I see it, we only have about twenty seconds to decide."

Kri'Entu looked up. "Twenty seconds? I do not see ... Sir Steve, please lower your flames lest you force us to vacate the area."

Steve glanced down at his chest and noticed most of his torso was engulfed in fire. "Right. Sorry."

"Thank you. You said we have only a short amount of time. Please explain."

"Sarah said that her mental picture shifted every thirty or so seconds," Steve reminded the king. "If that's true, whatever we're going to do must be done in that time or else we run the risk of the portal moving to a completely different location. If that happens, we'll never find her! I have no choice. I'm going after her."

The king looked angrily back at Shardwyn and Maelnar before beckoning to a nearby soldier. "Your water bag and provisions. Now! Hurry!"

The guard instantly handed over his provisions to the king, who shoved them into Steve's hands.

"You're right. There is no time to lose. You must hurry! You're going to need a weapon. Here, take my dagger."

Maelnar unbuckled his small hand axe and handed it to Steve.

"May it bring you as much luck as it has always brought me. I am deeply sorry, Sir Steve."

"The guard has a bow he can take," Shardwyn informed them, visibly shaken.

"There's no time!" the king snapped as he slid his personal dagger, sheath and all, into one of Steve's jacket pockets. Kri'Entu took Maelnar's axe and held it up, handle first, and waited for Steve to take it, only it was declined.

Water bottle and bag of provisions were slung over Steve's shoulder as he nervously stared at the anomaly. He smiled fleetingly at the king before turning to face a very somber wizard and dwarf. In the blink of an eye both hands turned red and were threatening to ignite once more.

"If I make it back, you two are going to officially bury the hatchet, is that clear?"

Dwarf and wizard both nodded.

"When," Kri'Entu corrected with a meek smile. "*When* you make it back, not *if.*"

Steve swallowed hard and looked once more at the anomaly. "Right. Wish me luck."

With the image of Sarah ingrained firmly in his head, Steve gritted his teeth, took a deep breath, and jumped feet first into the anomaly.

"Good luck, Sir Steve," Kri'Entu whispered as he stared at the empty space where the fire thrower had just been standing.

* * *

He was floating and falling at the same time, if that was possible. The dizzying sensation nauseated him and reminded him, unpleasantly, of the most extreme roller coaster he had ever been on. Steve ordered his lunch to stay put and kept his eyes screwed tightly shut. Even though his eyes were closed he could see bright lights flashing unmercifully on the other side of his eyelids.

A headache erupted, pounding away at the base of his skull. *Wham wham wham!* Steve couldn't tell if his eyes were open or closed as all of a sudden he was seeing stars. From the headache? From the nauseousness? Was he still falling? Could he even tell which way was up?

His headache hammered mercilessly away at him. He screwed his eyes shut and waited for the pain to pass. It didn't. He couldn't think straight. Why was this happening to him? Could he remember what he was supposed to be doing?

Sarah. He had to find Sarah!

His awareness latched on to that single thought and held it as though it was the most precious thing in the world. Sarah. His wife. She was his whole world. Somehow he'd find her. He didn't care what it took, he *would* find a way to bring her back.

Sometime later he woke, face down, on the ground. Every muscle in his body ached as though he had put it through the most intensive workout he could have imagined.

He could feel pine needles. Taking a deep breath, he sat up and unkinked his arms to try and restore circulation. After suffering through several minutes of prickly sensations running up and down his arm, Steve took stock of his surroundings.

The first thing he saw was pine needles. They were everywhere. He was still in a forest, no doubt about it. But, after patting down his pockets, he realized he no longer had Maelnar's axe, nor the king's dagger. They must have tumbled loose during his transit here, wherever that was.

Steve quickly glanced around. No sign of Sarah.

"Sarah!"

The forest was utterly still, with the exception of the evergreens gently swaying in the breeze. Steve sniffed the air. Pine, pine, and more pine. The overpowering scent from the fragrant evergreens was the only thing he could smell.

Steve rose to his feet and dusted off his clothes, noticing a handful of pine needles had decided to stick to his knees. Even a pine cone had managed to find its way into his pocket. How had that happened? He must have been thrashing about when he landed.

Curious, Steve turned to look back at the place he had woken up. No, there wasn't any evidence he had been there at all save a slight disturbance in the blanket of pine needles covering the forest floor. Wherever here was, he certainly hadn't walked here.

So, this was where the portal had deposited him. Great. Once again, he was stranded in the middle of some forest. The problem was, which forest? What kingdom? For that matter, what world? And, most importantly, was it the same world that the portal had dropped Sarah?

Steve plucked one of the errant pine needles off his pants and studied it. It had a single point, unlike the multiple points Lentarian pine trees were known for. He sniffed it and nodded sagely. Yep, he hadn't a clue as to what he was looking at other than he was holding a simple pine needle.

Steve dropped the needle and noticed several nearby shrubs. He wandered over to study the tall stems protruding from the base of the shrub. Each stem was covered with bright yellow flowers which resembled elongated tubular bells.

Nearby was a large bushy plant covered with multi-petaled flowers. A closer inspection of the plant revealed there was only one flower head per stem and that the flower didn't have any scent that he could detect. Was the flower Lentarian?

Why was he studying flowers, anyway? He had to find Sarah!

He stared around the quiet forest, looking for hope. There were no paths, no signs of habitation, and no indication of which way to go. He spent the next hour methodically scouring the surrounding area looking for some signs of Sarah's presence and frantically shouting her name, but was unable to find so much as a single footprint other than his own.

With a heavy heart Steve realized it could only mean one thing: Sarah had never been here.

"I really should have thought this one through," Steve muttered, quietly turning in place.

Hopefully he'd be able to get a sense of which way to go just by facing in that direction. It always seemed to work for Sarah. After stopping every three seconds to see if he could detect anything, Steve came to a stop. Nothing. *Nothing* stood out. Once more he was lost and this time he was by himself.

"Get a grip," Steve berated himself. "Sarah's out there. Somewhere. I *have* to find her."

He looked up at the evening sun and turned so that it was on his left side. He held up his hands and ordered his jhorun to ignite. In moments his hands were lit. He gave them a quick flick to extinguish them and headed off.

"This has got to be Lentari," Steve thought to himself as he pushed his way through several shrubs. "My jhorun works fine."

Your jhorun works fine in your world, too, a little voice said in his mind.

Steve nodded. "True. I concede the point."

And the pine needles had only one point. Lentarian pine needles have two, sometimes three points.

Steve shrugged. "Noted."

You don't know enough about flowers to determine which type they are, let alone where they typically grow.

"What's your point?"

And you're arguing with yourself.

"Shut up and leave me alone."

How then do you plan on finding Sarah when she could be in a different world?

"You're not helping," Steve grumbled to himself.

Do you want help or not?

"You're *me*," Steve thought to himself crossly. "I know what you know, remember?"

And yet you still haven't noticed it.

"Noticed what?"

Must I tell you or would you like to guess?

"Wow, I must have really hit my head hard when I landed here. I can't believe I'm having this conversation. No, dude, I don't want to guess. Just tell me."

Didn't you smell the water?

Steve froze in mid-step.

"Water? Where?"

And could you smell any brine? No? What does that tell you?

Steve was silent as he thought back. Had he smelled any water? He didn't think he had but … Wait. Wait! One of those directions he had faced did remind him briefly of rain yet there weren't any rain clouds in the sky.

Very good!

"Don't get snarky with me. I have no qualms about kicking my own ass."

Yeah, right. Don't flatter yourself. You couldn't get your leg up that high.

Steve's eyebrows shot straight up. Had some part of his own brain just insulted him?

"You do know that when you insult me, you're actually insulting yourself, too, right?"

You need to keep moving. Wake up and get going.

"Excuse me? Wake up? I'm not dreaming. I'm not even asleep."

Yes, you are. You were feeling light-headed, so you sat down on the ground and rested your back against a tree. Naturally, you were out like a light.

"Oh. I don't remember that."

Wake up. Follow the water, young grasshopper. Hurry!

Steve groaned and shook his head. He must have been really tired.

"And how do you propose I do that? That's assuming that I even believe you."

The scene shifted and suddenly he was driving his truck. A motorcyclist zipped by him and cut him off. Steve gasped with alarm and reacted instantly by slamming on the brakes.

Steve's whole body gave a violent, spasmodic jerk, effectively knocking him off the fallen log he had been sitting on. Once more Steve found himself rising painfully from the ground and dusting himself off. He looked down at the fallen log and grimaced. He hadn't even remembered sitting down to rest. How sad was that?

Steve stretched his back and looked around. It was time to get moving. Clearly Sarah wasn't anywhere nearby. Logically, if she had been dropped in an area similar to this then she would start searching for some signs of civilization, too. He could only do the same.

A more detailed investigation revealed the existence of a shallow river. He decided to follow it north. The slow moving water was flowing south, so something had to be feeding the river. Whether it was runoff from the nearby mountains, or being fed by a lake, he didn't care. It was a direction to go and he stuck with it.

Noticing that the sun was setting much faster than he cared for, he picked up his pace. It was one thing to go camping outdoors; he was very fond of spending time under the stars. However, when there wasn't an RV or trailer to return to, or a hotel room to check in to, it was another matter entirely. He did not want to be stuck out here overnight, alone. He could only hope that he'd find a town before it got too dark. Another glance at the sun told him he had one, maybe two hours of light left before it'd become too dark to see. Either he'd have to find a place to hole up for the night or he was going to have to pray his luck would hold out and he'd be able to find someone who could help.

As he walked, his thoughts drifted to that which worried him the most: what if Sarah had been dropped in another world? What if he had become stranded here? She, on the one hand, would more than likely be able to get herself home. Her teleporting skills were unparalleled. His jhorun, on the other hand, had nothing to do with teleporting, so if he couldn't find her then he was going to be up a proverbial creek without any means of propulsion.

Steve angrily shook his head. He had to stay positive. He had to believe that he and Sarah were on the same world. He just had to find her.

His thoughts turned dark again. What if she had been dropped on the other side of the planet? What if she had landed in a nest of monsters? What if she was in danger right now? What if she'd already returned to Lentari and he'd made this trip for nothing?

Steve groaned. In his rush to help Sarah he hadn't even considered the possibility that his wife could have made it back on her own. What if she had already returned and was preparing to go out after him and THEN got herself dropped onto a different world? A headache formed. There were just too many variables to consider. He needed more information and the only way was to keep moving forward.

A small hard object suddenly dropped onto his head as he passed under the branches of a large tree. Rubbing the stinging welt on his head, he glanced up at the overhead branch to see a tiny pair of beady black eyes regarding him. Steve caught a glimpse of grayish-brown fur with spots of red and a striped tail; it was a squirrel. The furry creature was motionless as it studied him.

Steve glanced down at the ground to see what had hit him. It was an acorn. Typical. He retrieved the nut from the ground and stretched up to gently place the acorn back on the branch the squirrel was perched on. He held it in place while the squirrel hesitantly inched forward. It grabbed the nut and darted away, running down the trunk, across the ground, and disappearing into a dark hole nestled in the roots of a nearby tree.

"That's gratitude for you," Steve muttered as he absentmindedly rubbed his welt a final time. "I dare you to come out here and—"

An ear-splitting crack shattered the peaceful tranquility of the forest. Squirrels scampered back to their nests. Flocks of birds took to the sky. Within moments a deathly silence had fallen over the forest. Steve nervously looked about. It had sounded like gunfire!

A second blast ripped through the air, followed shortly thereafter by a third and then a fourth. Intent on discovering what was making the noise, Steve took off northwest. Using skills one could only acquire by watching way too many action movies, Steve darted from rock to bush to tree in an attempt to mask his approach. He drew up short. He could hear voices! That could only be good, right?

Steve crept to the base of a massive pine tree and quietly peered around the trunk. Six men were there, two of which were astride horses that were nervously chomping their bridles. He was about ready to hail the strangers when their attire caught his eye and he hesitated. Steve blinked a few times as he stared at the strangers' clothes.

All six men were wearing blue button-down coats that had four pleats running each side from the shoulders all the way down past their waists and partially covering their light blue trousers. A single white stripe ran from hip to presumably ankle, but he was unable to tell as the cuffs of the pants were tucked into black calf-high boots. Adorning the blue coats were five gold buttons, all polished to a mirror-like shine. Wide brim slouch campaign hats, worn by all of them, completed the picture. The two men on horseback also wore dark blue double-breasted overcoats with five pairs of buttons running down the front.

Steve stared in shock at the scene before him. Had he stumbled onto a reenactment of some sort? Why did it look like those men just came from the battlefields of the Civil War? Something didn't add up here.

One man cuffed another on the back of his neck, causing his hat to go flying off his head.

"You still use that thing? Get with the times. No one uses black powder rifles any more. It's messy, loud, and quite frankly, it's embarrassing."

Once the fallen hat was retrieved, and sitting back on the man's head, he turned to glare at his companion.

"I prefer 'em. It's the traditional way to hunt. The only way, if you ask me."

"Well, I ain't. It's a good thing you hit it 'cause you damn near spooked everything else away."

One of the men on horseback guided his mount up to the two men, cleared his throat, and dismounted.

"Just tie the deer over my horse so we can get out of here. We're overdue and I don't want to be late. You follow?"

The rest of the men snapped to attention. The man who had lost his hat saluted.

"Yessir!"

The men finally parted and Steve saw that they had indeed killed a deer. Did people typically hunt in a getup like that? Something about this whole situation didn't sit well with him. Something was wrong. He was missing something here.

Once the deer had been tied across the back of the horse, the men silently left, walking off in the direction that he was originally planning on heading. Following from a discreet distance, Steve watched the men marching in front of the horses in a tight two by two formation, while the owner of the horse carrying the deer—an officer?—guided his mount by the reins. The other mounted rider was motionless and sat stiff as a board on his horse's saddle.

Chatter was kept to a minimum. Only the occasional command by the mounted rider could be heard as the men marched in silence. After an hour of walking, they crested the hill they had been traveling up and began angling east. Anxious to not lose sight of his escorts, Steve hurried to the top of the hill and paused to catch his breath. There they were, still marching in step, even if they had to navigate around obstacles in their path like the cluster of trees that were rapidly approaching.

The rider barked out an order and the company instantly executed a flawless left turn, marched about ten steps, turned to the right, marched another ten steps and then made another right turn, and then finally a sharp left turn to put them back on the same course as they had been on before. Steve nodded with admiration. He had been a member of band class in school and had marched in several parades. None of their turns had looked as sharp and clean as those. Someone clearly took pride in making his men look as professional as possible.

"Sherman's not that far away," the rider suddenly announced. "I will go on ahead. I expect you there in no less than fifteen minutes. Is that understood, Lieutenant?"

Steve surreptitiously moved closer so he could better hear the conversation.

The man guiding his horse nodded. "Yes sir!"

"Good. See to it that you're not late."

Once the rider had galloped off, the men let out a collective gasp of relief. The men all relaxed their postures and allowed themselves to fall out of step together. One of the men rose up on the tips of his toes to peek over the nearby shrubs to verify that the rider was indeed gone.

"Who in their right minds insists that we march together on the way back from a hunt? It's preposterous!"

Another man chuckled.

"Not only that, but a successful hunt. Winter'll be here in the next month. Game is not as plentiful. Lieutenant Hall should have been pleased."

The man guiding the horse spoke up. "He was pleased. You don't know him as well as I."

"He has a funny way of showing it," another man grumbled.

The group broke ranks and started walking together as a group of friends would do: laughing, chatting, and slapping each other on the back. Gone was the military precision marching. Gone was the feeling of unease. Steve smiled. Clearly the men didn't think too highly of their commanding officer.

Commanding officer. That meant that these were, in fact, real soldiers. What were they doing wearing those uniforms? Had he really been dropped in some type of alternate reality? They were talking in English so they had to be somewhere on Earth.

No, Steve thought as he shook his head; speaking English didn't mean this was Earth. When he and Sarah had first arrived on Lentari they were startled to learn that the people there spoke English, too, although it had been referred to as simply speaking 'human' at the time, as crazy as that had sounded. No, there were no guarantees he was on Earth.

Actually, there was no way he *could* be back home as no one from his world wore getups like that. However, they did look like authentic American military uniforms. Perhaps he should start leaning toward the alternate reality theory?

Exactly fifteen minutes later Steve rounded a bend and came to an abrupt halt. The soldiers had disappeared from view but he had heard a slew of new voices. Had they arrived at their camp? Steve ducked into the nearby trees and cautiously peeked around the corner. Sure enough he could see the group of soldiers with the dead deer chatting with more soldiers under a large white canvas tent. Many more of the same tents were lined up neatly side by side along the left of the road. Visible in the distance was a large two-story structure with numerous windows and columns. Smaller wooden buildings lay to the right. Out in front, guarded by four men, was a large white sign that stretched from one side of the road to the other. Written across the sign in big black letters was 'Fort Sherman'.

Fort Sherman? Where was that? What was a fort that looked like it belonged on a movie set doing out here in the middle of nowhere?

Steve only had time for a quick look when he shifted his weight to his left leg and took a step back. The twig he landed on snapped loudly and drew the attention of several guards. Steve cursed silently and slipped deeper into the forest. Three guards followed.

Steve hurried through the forest, intent on getting as far away as possible from the strange fort. Where was he, anyway? Why did the soldiers all dress in period clothing? Either he'd have to subscribe to the alternate reality theory or else he would have to believe that he'd stumbled upon a group of die-hard history buffs.

Steve exited the forest nearly a half mile away as the sun was setting. He had seen several lights in the distance and automatically headed in that direction. The farther he walked from the soldiers, the more lights appeared in front of him. A town? He hoped so.

A light breeze began blowing. With it came the unmistakable scent of water. Was it the same as he had smelled before? Steve didn't know and at this point, he didn't care. He had to find a place to stay for the night because he was clearly going to be here a while. If he was stuck here in this land then how was he going to survive? He wasn't a hunter and he could barely fish. There had to be something here that he could do to be useful.

Steve angrily shook his head. He refused to think any further on the subject. Life without Sarah wasn't an option. Whatever predicament he had found himself in would have to be solved. He had to find his wife. Failure was not an option.

A row of buildings came into view. The first thing Steve noticed was the set of railroad tracks running down the middle of the street. It reminded him of Main Street, Disneyland, and he briefly wondered why someone would put buildings so close to the track. It never occurred to him that the city had trolleys. Curious, he knelt down and knocked on the rails a few times with his knuckles. The metal chimed softly in response. He glanced up at the row of buildings on either side of the tracks. They were, Steve noted with dismay, in less than pristine condition and reminded him of a deserted town, although there was nothing abandoned about this place.

People were milling about on the street. Horses were tied to hitching posts in front of saloons. Somewhere in the distance Steve could hear someone playing an energetic little ditty on a piano.

As he slowly walked down the street, taking care to not walk on the rails or tread on piles of horse manure, Steve noticed that no one was even bothering to look in his direction. He briefly considered igniting a hand to see how people would react but a quick check of several of the seedy looking men leaning up against a couple of nearby buildings confirmed the presence of weapons. In fact, just about every male he passed, save for the band of small boys playing a game of tag in the street, seemed to have a gun on his hip. A few of the nicer dressed gentlemen tipped their top hats in his direction as he passed by. Steve turned to stare back at two men who had just passed him. Top hats? Another man approached.

"Umm, how's it goin'?" Steve offered, as he passed the man who was wearing a maroon corduroy jacket. The stranger had tipped his black bowler hat at him, which prompted Steve to offer a greeting.

The man turned to regard him. After a moment of silence, he held out his right hand. "You look lost, mate. I am Cecil Cook. May I be of assistance?"

Steve hesitantly shook the friendly man's hand. "Steve Miller. Can you tell me where I am?"

"Gadzooks, my dear fellow. You don't know where you are?"

"Of course I do," Steve hastily corrected. "I mean, I got turned around. I was looking for a place to stay. Can you point me in the right direction?"

"There are three hotels in town, friend. As far as I am aware, none have any vacancies, what with the mining boom that has hit our fair city. No doubt that's why you are here?"

Steve wisely nodded. "Right. That's me. I'm going to be panning for gold."

Cecil scoffed loudly. "There's no gold in these parts. Now silver, on the other hand, that's what we're here to find."

"Right. That's what I meant."

"Of course you did. So you'll need a place to stay."

"Ummm, yeah. Can you recommend a place?"

Cecil turned and pointed farther down the road. "Continue on Burke here for another quarter mile. You'll find a number of houses on your right. The last I heard the home owners there are willing to rent their rooms at a fair price. I assume you have money."

"Ummm…"

Cecil sighed. "You really didn't think this through, did you?"

"You have no idea," Steve muttered under his breath.

"Here's what we'll do." Cecil turned and pointed off to the south. "Forget what I just said. Continue past those houses until you reach the next street. Turn right. Continue on for another ten minutes or so and you will find another row of houses. One will be painted blue. Find that house and check in with my wife, AnnaBelle. She'll see to it you have a place to sleep."

Steve was amazed. Yet again here was someone he didn't know who was offering to let him stay in their house and all within a span of a few minutes. Perhaps he was in Lentari after all! The people from his world certainly didn't act that way.

"Why are you doing this for me?" Steve asked, genuinely bewildered. "You don't even know me."

Cecil clapped him on his right shoulder and turned to go on his way. "Because, my good man; your face reminds me of a trusted friend. Go now before it is too dark to see."

"I will." Steve thrust out his hand. "You have my thanks."

Cecil shook it. "Think nothing of it. Now, if you'll excuse me, I do believe there's a poker table that needs an extra player."

Steve watched as Cecil pushed his way through the swinging doors of the closest building. He shook his head. If he didn't know any better, he'd say that he had somehow landed in the Old West.

Following Cecil's instructions led him to a row of identical box-like houses. Some had been painted different colors, but most were a shade of off-white. He approached the only blue house he could see and introduced himself to AnnaBelle, the lady of the house. Happy and lively, the lady was more than willing to open her home to honor her husband's wishes.

After giving Steve a tour of the small house, AnnaBelle walked with him back to her humble kitchen and leaned up against the sink with a hand pump next to it.

"So, where are you from? What country?"

Taken aback, Steve blinked a few times and gazed at the woman who was slightly younger than he was. He noticed callouses on her hands the moment he shook her hand. This was a woman, Steve decided, who knew what it meant to work. A quick glance around the simple kitchen revealed everything was clean; everything was stowed in its proper place.

"I'm from the same country as you are," Steve assured her.

"You are? Are you sure? I have never seen clothes like

that before."

Steve glanced down at his dark green tunic and khaki trousers. "What's wrong with it?"

"No one wears things like that around here," AnnaBelle patiently explained. "Much can be gleaned by observing what a person wears."

Steve smiled. "What do my clothes tell you about me?"

AnnaBelle pushed herself away from the sink and smiled. She slowly walked up to Steve and studied him. She quietly murmured to herself as she walked around him. After a few minutes had passed, she put her hands on her hips and faced him.

"I have it."

Steve crossed his arms over his chest. "Okay, let's hear it."

"You're a professor."

Steve's eyebrows shot up. "I'm a what? A professor? Nope, sorry. Not even close."

"Hmmm." The lady of the house did another pass around Steve. "A banker, like my Cecil?"

"Nope."

"Jeweler?"

"No."

"Ah! I have it now. You're a preacher."

"Say what? No, I'm not."

"Very well. Tell me what you do."

Steve hesitated. What should he tell her? He was willing to bet all the silver that was apparently buried in them thar hills that she wouldn't know what a computer tech was. "Er, would you believe a miner?"

AnnaBelle crossed her arms over her chest. "No."

"What? Why not?"

"You don't have any callouses on your hands. Mining is hard work. Even a blind man could tell you don't work the earth."

Steve looked down at his hands. "I have callouses."

AnnaBelle held out a hand. "Let me see."

Steve reluctantly held out his right hand. AnnaBelle took his hand and pulled it up close to her.

"Pah. I have callouses on the soles of my feet that are

thicker than these. A miner you are not."

"Fine. You win. I'm not a miner."

AnnaBelle stared at him as she waited for an answer.

"You've never heard of my profession, trust me. The only thing I'll say is that I'm here to look for my wife."

"Your wife? Is she missing?"

"Yes. She, uh, disappeared earlier today and I came here looking for her."

"I know everyone in town. I have heard of no one else arriving by coach or train today."

"Damn," Steve swore softly. "Are you sure? This would have been a few hours ago."

"The 5:15 from Wallace only had supplies, no passengers. The 3:30 coach from Harriston carried three passengers but they all were gentlemen."

"Then the honest answer is I don't know what I'm going to—"

AnnaBelle let out a shriek of dismay. Her eyes had alighted on a small bottle of tiny white pills sitting obtrusively on the counter.

"Is everything alright?" Steve asked, alarmed. Had he done something to upset her? AnnaBelle and Cecil seemed to be nice people. The last thing he wanted right now was to cause either of them duress.

AnnaBelle snatched up the tiny glass bottle and held it out for Steve to see. "Cecil's medicine! He has a heart condition and I don't want him to be unprepared in case he has a flare up."

Steve held out a hand. "I know which casino he went in. I can give it to him."

AnnaBelle looked up at him with uncomprehending eyes. "What's a casino?"

"Oh, um, it's another name for a saloon."

The bottle was thrust into his hand.

"Please get this to him as quickly as possible. I will feel much better once he has it."

Steve nodded and pocketed the pills. "Got it. I'll take care of it."

"Thank you, Steve. Your generosity just paid for your

first night here."

Steve nodded appreciatively and exited the small house. It was very dark outside. What little light there was came from the curtained windows of the houses lining the street. Steve looked up. The full moon had just risen over the mountains in the northeast and was beginning its trek across the sky, giving Steve enough light to find his way back into town, which was bustling with activity.

Two people left an establishment on his right, each carrying a bottle of liquor with one hand and had the other wrapped around their companion so they wouldn't tip over. Each was singing at the top of their lungs. Too bad it wasn't the same song, Steve mused. He scowled. Each was wearing a gun belt.

"Right. Moving on."

Retracing his steps, Steve found the bustling saloon and pushed his way into its interior. Both doors swung back into place with a noisy clacking sound. A small part of him was afraid that the entire place would go deathly quiet and everyone would turn to stare at him.

Not one person bothered to look up. An upright piano stood against the far corner closest to the roaring fireplace, and the farthest end of the long wooden counter served as a bar. Small wooden tables were everywhere. Four, five, and sometimes six people were crowded around the tables laughing, drinking, smoking, and having a good time. Three serving girls moved with grace and ease through the jostling patrons as they served drinks and food. More than once he saw a female derriere get pinched as a way of thanks. And, as expected, the patron got a slap in the face in return, much to the delight of his companions.

Catching sight of Cecil sitting uncomfortably close to five other people around a tiny wooden table, Steve reached into his pocket and withdrew the bottle. He tapped Cecil on the shoulder and waited for him to turn around.

"You never, *ever* interrupt a man when he's playing poker, friend," one grizzled man dangerously said without even bothering to look up.

Cecil waved his hand. "It's okay. I know him. Steve, it's

good to see you again. Did you find the house?"

"I did, yes. I'm repaying part of that debt. Here. Your wife said you forgot to take these."

Steve held out the tiny bottle of white pills. Several men who were sitting around the table snickered loudly. Cedric forced a smile.

"Ah. My nitroglycerin pills. I had hoped I made it out of the house before she noticed."

"Don't screw around with your heart, pal," Steve warned him.

Cecil smiled. "Easy for you to say, friend. You don't have to take the accursed things. They taste horrible."

Steve gave a friendly smile to the rest of the players; it wasn't returned. "Sorry to interrupt you guys. I'll, uh, let you get back to your game now."

He turned around and bumped into one of the serving girls, threatening to tip over her large tray of filled mugs. Steve caught the tray before any of the drinks could tumble to the ground.

"I'm really sorry. I didn't mean to —"

Steve trailed off. He was looking into Sarah's surprised eyes.

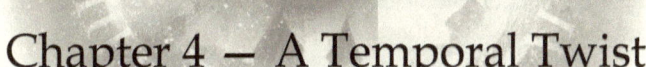

Chapter 4 — A Temporal Twist

Steve stared in shock. Wearing a frilly purple off-the-shoulder gown, with her hair pulled up high and styled so that it fell evenly across her head, and sporting a dark purple ribbon tied around her neck, was Sarah. Noticing that she was also several inches higher than he was used to, Steve looked down to see shiny black leather shoes with two inch heels. She was even wearing fish net tights!

Sarah continued to stare at him as though she was looking at a ghost.

"What are you doing in that outfit?" Steve asked with a bewildered look on his face. He noticed that her tray was starting to tremble. "Here, let's put that down. How did you—"

He was cut off as Sarah threw herself into his arms and started sobbing uncontrollably.

"Hey, hey, it's okay. I'm okay. Ummm, are you okay?"

"Where have you been?" Sarah managed to get out between sobs. "I thought I would never see you again!"

Before Steve could respond, two men who were each the size of small locomotives, packing revolvers on each hip and wearing twin ammo belts crisscrossing their chests, appeared out of the shadows and stared menacingly at him. Steve paled.

"Alrighty then, we need to get you out of here. This party is about to turn ugly."

Sarah turned to see what he was scowling at. Hastily wiping her eyes, she waved at the two men and then returned her attention to Steve, who was staring in shock at the two brutes who, having been dismissed, were shuffling back to the bar.

"How did you do that? They looked like they could spit nails."

Sarah took several deep breaths and focused her hazel eyes back onto his blue ones. Her eyes began to water once more. She gripped him by the shoulders and gave him a fierce shake.

"Where have you been? What took you so long?"

Finding himself on the unwelcome side of an interrogation, Steve began back pedaling.

"Hey, I ended up following some soldiers here. They were a little slow, okay? You know me. My sense of direction isn't the greatest. Cut me a little slack, huh?"

"Cut you a little slack? I've been worried sick for so long now that I'm sure I gave myself an ulcer."

"I got here just as quick as I could," Steve said in an attempt to defend himself. "Besides, how did you get that outfit? And what are you doing serving drinks in a saloon? What am I missing here?"

A small elderly woman wearing a dress similar to Sarah's, in shades of brown, approached the two of them and laid a friendly hand on Sarah's shoulder. A dark brown Victorian hat that had several fluffy white feathers sticking out at odd angles was perched askew on the newcomer's head. To Steve it looked as though she had walked into a bird's nest and, without realizing it, was now wearing it as a hat.

"Sarah, dear, is everything okay?"

Sarah patted the matronly lady's hand. "Everything is fine, Mrs. Jones."

Steve cleared his throat. Sarah smiled.

"Mrs. Jones, this is my husband, Steve. Steve, this is Mrs. Rosamund Jones, wife of Gerald Jones. They own this tavern, the Silver Spike Saloon."

Rosamund Jones, who would've topped five feet if she was wearing three-inch heels, smiled with relief.

"Ah! Your prince has come at last! I am so happy for you, dear. We should get you two off the floor. Follow me."

The tiny woman spun on her heel and led them toward the long, curved bar. Steve briefly wondered how Rosamund Jones managed to see over the counter, but held his tongue as the answer was revealed when they saw what was behind the bar: boxes. Small wooden boxes were strategically placed three feet apart so that the diminutive tavern owner could see her customers from behind the counter.

Rosamund swept her foot across the wooden floor to push a threadbare gray rug out of the way. Even though it didn't look as though it revealed anything, Rosamund stepped on one floorboard in particular and then grasped the end that had risen slightly off the ground. Reaching inside the dark opening in the floor she yanked her hand back out just as a hidden trapdoor swung noiselessly downward. A steep staircase was revealed.

"Down there. Be quick about it."

Steve leaned over the dark opening and frowned. "Why in the world would I want to go down there? What exactly are we hiding from?"

"What you want to talk about must be done privately," Rosamund told them in a hushed tone. She looked at Steve and her eyes softened. "She isn't from around here. I know that. You clearly know that. Other people know it, too. Questions have been asked; questions for which I don't have answers."

Sarah stared at the small woman with an indignant expression on her face. "*What* questions?"

Rosamund pointed into the darkness. She handed Steve a lit oil lamp and took one for herself. After the three of them had descended the ten or so steps into the darkness, Rosamund adjusted the flaming wicks of both oil lamps. The room brightened considerably. Steve looked around. It was no more than ten feet square, with several chairs and a tiny table against one wall and an old couch and even smaller table against the opposite wall. Rosamund set the lamp down on one of the two wood tables, walked over to the wall closest to the stairs, and flicked a switch. A single bulb illuminated. Rosamund then climbed up onto the couch. She motioned for Steve to swing the trapdoor shut. As soon as he did so, she folded her hands primly in her lap and looked at both husband and wife expectantly. Steve and Sarah settled hesitantly into the two easy chairs. Fanning away the clouds of dust that had risen up, Sarah caught Rosamund's eyes and held them firmly in place. Mrs. Jones sighed.

"I didn't tell you because I didn't want to alarm you, dear."

"What is going on?" Steve demanded. "How do the two of you know each other?"

Sarah laid a hand on her husband while simultaneously frowning at Rosamund.

"Mrs. Jones took me in when I couldn't find you. She knew I needed help and didn't have anywhere to go. I've been helping out around here as a way to say thanks while I waited for you to show up."

Steve stared at Mrs. Jones for a few moments before looking over at his wife.

"Why would she need to take you in? We've been separated for less than a day. That's no reason to panic."

Sarah gave him an incredulous look.

"Steve, I've been waiting for you here for over six months!"

"What?" Steve sputtered. "Six months? That's not possible!"

"How long did you wait before you followed me through?" Sarah asked. "I thought for certain that you would follow me straight in."

"I *did* follow you straight in," Steve clarified with a frown. "I went through about twenty, maybe twenty-five seconds after you did."

That drew Sarah up short.

"So you weren't kidding when you said you literally saw

me earlier today?"

"What kind of question is that?" Steve retorted. "You know I did."

"But for me it was months ago."

"That explains the outfit," Steve murmured.

"Where are you two from?" Rosamund asked. "I know you're not from around these parts."

"Actually, we are," Sarah contradicted.

"We are?" Steve asked. "You're saying this is Idaho? Whereabouts in the state did we get dropped?"

"Well, this territory is known as Idaho," Rosamund clarified. "We haven't become a state yet."

"Territory?" Steve repeated as he turned to Sarah. "Territory? Did she just say—"

"This is Coeur d'Alene," Sarah confirmed. "It's just not the Coeur d'Alene we're familiar with."

Steve grimaced. "What's the date?"

Sarah took a deep breath.

"This may come as a shock, honey, so just—"

"Sarah, what is the date?"

"It's still September."

"Of course, it is. Why wouldn't it be? Can you be a little more specific? What's the year?"

"1884."

Steve's eyes shot open. He alternated his gaze between Sarah and Rosamund.

"1884? This is 1884? How the hell did that happen?"

Sarah quickly glanced at Mrs. Jones and then back at her husband. Rosamund smiled and made herself comfortable on the sofa.

"Don't mind me, dear. Do go on."

Sarah patted the elderly woman's hand. "I'm not sure how much you can handle, Mrs. Jones. If we were to explain where we're from it might freak you out."

"Freak? Are you calling me a freak?"

"Heavens, no, Mrs. Jones. Umm, what I meant to say was that I don't want to alarm you."

"Oh. I have given birth to ten children, dear. I made the journey all the way from New York in a covered wagon.

There isn't anything you can say that would surprise me."

"Just tell me one thing, Mrs. Jones," Sarah began. "What questions were you talking about before? Have the people been asking about me?"

"They know you're not from around here," Rosamund told her. "A pretty young thing like you showing up in this town without a husband is an invitation for trouble. Almost immediately, I had to start fending off matrimonial advances from just about every male around here. If they see you now, with Steve here, they're likely to try and do him harm."

Steve scowled. "I'd like to see them try."

"These aren't arrows we're talking about," Sarah reminded him as she frowned at her husband, "but bullets. You cannot incinerate bullets."

"Incinerate arrows?" Rosamund said, with a laugh. "One day I hope to hear all about who you two really are."

"Mrs. Jones, you've been so kind to me. Let me repay the favor by not having you hear what's about to be said. It would cause you undue stress and you don't deserve that. Besides, I need you to cover for me upstairs, okay?"

The feathers on Rosamund's hat bobbed up and down as she nodded.

"Very well, dear. If you need me, I will be upstairs."

"Thank you, Mrs. Jones," Steve told her. "I am indebted to you for taking care of Sarah for me. I owe you one."

"I'll be sure to collect, dear," Mrs. Jones assured him with a wink.

After she disappeared up the steep stairs, and the trapdoor was firmly back in place, Steve turned to his wife once more.

"Okay, spill. How is it we've gone back in time? And is it safe to say that you can't teleport through time?"

"If I could," Sarah told him, "then I would have joined you long ago. I tried. Trust me, I tried. I cannot picture anywhere I want to go. The only thing I can figure is that it's because those places just don't exist yet."

"Yes they do," Steve argued. "Our home is a place and it damn well exists."

"Yes, it does," Sarah patiently explained, "but not *here*. My visions show me where I'm teleporting, right? Since the manor as we know it doesn't exist yet, then I cannot picture it."

"Oh. That sucks."

Sarah was incredulous. "Is that all you can say? That sucks? We are stuck here, do you realize that? We do not have a way to return home!"

"What about that portal? Can't we just use that to get back?"

Sarah clamped her mouth shut and gave herself a few moments to compose her thoughts.

"There are several things wrong with that. First, the portal keeps jumping around. If we could somehow catch that portal, or figure out where it'll be next, then we might have a chance. As it is, there is no predicting where it'll be next, or *when*. Speaking of when, that brings me to my next point. If we were to somehow get to a point where we could use the portal, how do we know we would even be dropped back off at the correct time?"

Steve cursed silently to himself as the ramifications of their predicament began to settle in.

"The portal took us back in time over a hundred years," Sarah continued. "Who's to say that it wouldn't throw us several hundred years into the future? No, that portal needs to be considered off limits."

"You've given this some thought, haven't you?" Steve asked.

"I've lain awake for nights thinking about how to get home," Sarah confessed.

"What have you come up with?"

Sarah sighed and slid her hand down her face. She looked at him and didn't say anything.

"You don't have any idea how to return home, do you?"

"I've only come up with one solution."

Steve sat up straight and leaned forward. "Yes?"

"I use my own jhorun and figure out what is blocking me."

"I assume you've been trying?"

"Every waking moment," Sarah admitted.

"Have you made any progress?"

Sarah's gaze fell to the floor and stayed there. Steve felt the blood drain from his face. Sarah didn't have a clue how to get home and that was after six months of trying. Steve reached out a hand and laid it on his wife's.

"We've been through worse. We'll figure this out." Steve sat back in his chair and gave a little cough as some of the dust flying through the air tickled his throat. "Fort Sherman. I should have known when I saw that sign."

"You saw that big white sign and you still didn't know where you were? Honey, we drive past that sign every time we go to the Cook Book Nook. How is it you didn't remember seeing it before?"

Steve let out an exasperated breath. "I ended up following what I now know was a bunch of Civil War era soldiers on their way back from a hunting trip. There were no roads, no houses, and no signs of anything that I recognized. When they finally did make it to the fort, the only thing I was focusing on was not being discovered."

"Were you?" Sarah asked.

"They heard me but didn't find me. I disappeared into the trees and found my way here. Thankfully I bumped into Cecil and he offered me a place to stay. I guess I can let him know I won't need the room after all."

Sarah shook her head no.

"Don't you remember what Rosamund just told us? If people see us together then they're going to know you are with me. The last thing we need right now is some jealous nitwit with a gun causing problems."

Steve suddenly stared at Sarah for a few moments.

"What?" Sarah slugged him on the shoulder. "Why are you staring at me like that?"

"Can you still teleport?"

Sarah nodded. "Of course. I just can't teleport anywhere that I'm familiar with. It's like I have to recreate all my safe zones. Consequently, I have several around town now. What about you? Does your jhorun still work?"

Steve ignited a hand and held it up. Relieved, Sarah nodded. Then they both clearly heard a gasp of shock. Husband and wife whirled around on the couch and stared straight up at the closed trap door. Someone had been watching! Sarah closed her eyes and went still. Several seconds later Mrs. Rosamund Jones appeared in front of them.

Rosamund straightened and looked around the tiny room in undisguised shock. She looked at Steve and then down at his lit hand and gasped again. Steve sighed and flicked his hand out.

"Mrs. Jones," Sarah began as she rose to her feet, "please don't panic."

"All I have to do is scream," the elderly proprietor nervously told her. "There are dozens of people in the saloon right now."

Steve shook his head. "I doubt it. You'd be serving them right now. In order to hear and see what you did, you'd have to be lying flat on your stomach on the floor. You're short, yes, but people would still see you."

"There's no one upstairs?" Sarah gently asked.

"The last customer walked out a few moments before his hand started burning," Rosamund reluctantly admitted.

"Stop looking so scared," Steve scolded. "We're not going to hurt you. In fact, you're free to go if you want. If you'd like to stay, we'll tell you what we can and hope you'll be willing to help us out."

Surprised, Sarah glanced his way and nodded her head in agreement. They both stared at the small woman before them and waited. After a few moments Rosamund was back on the couch.

"Nothing exciting ever happens here anymore," Rosamund admitted with a smile. "I would like to know how he can make his hand burn and how I was taken from up there to down here when I don't remember coming down the stairs."

"That's because you weren't," Sarah told her. "I teleported you down here."

Mrs. Jones stared at her uncomprehendingly.

"It means she can instantly move things from point A to point B," Steve added helpfully. "That goes for people, too."

"She instantly moved me from upstairs to here?"

Sarah disappeared from her chair and appeared next to

Rosamund on the couch. The poor lady let out a yelp of surprise.

"It takes some getting used to," Sarah admitted. "Trust me when I say that I am harmless. I'm not here to hurt anyone. Neither is Steve. We're just trying to figure out how to get home."

Getting over much of her fright, Rosamund looked over at Steve and pointed at his hand.

"Can you make your hand burn again?"

Steve ignited his right hand and held it up.

"Incredible. How can you do that?"

"It'd be too hard to explain," Steve informed her. "I'm not here to hurt anyone, either."

Rosamund shifted her position on the couch until she was facing Steve. "You said before that you were familiar with Idaho, but were surprised when I referred to it as 'territory.' You had also mentioned the state of Idaho. Then you were shocked to hear the date. What date did you think it was?"

Steve looked at Sarah for help and guidance. The only thing she could do was give him a look which said *your call.*

"Let's just say that we're not from your time, either. We really need to leave it at that."

Rosamund clapped her hands together excitedly. "You're from another time? How extraordinary! How can I help?"

Amazed, both husband and wife stared at their tiny benefactor.

"You are a lot more understanding than I originally gave you credit for," Steve admitted with a smile. "We appreciate that. The best thing you could do for us now is to keep the rest of the people from asking too many questions."

"How long will you be in town?" Rosamund inquired. "For several more months?"

"I sure as hell hope not," Steve muttered under his breath. He looked over at Sarah. "We're going to make it home. I promise you. There has to be a reason why that portal exists on Lentari."

"Lentari?" Rosamund repeated. "Is that where you're from?"

"We're from Idaho," Sarah reminded her with a smile.

She turned back to Steve. "Do you think those poor people fell through the portal for a reason, too?"

Steve looked up, surprised. "The missing villagers. I had forgotten about them. Have you heard anything about them?"

Sarah slowly shook her head no.

"Assuming those people came here, there's no way we can guarantee that they came to the same time as we did."

Rosamund wrung her hands together. "You're now looking for more missing people? And they came here the same way you did?"

Steve nodded. "Yes. The problem is, they could have been dropped here at another time. They could have been here longer than Sarah now. Hmm. What if they have been dropped into the future? Say, instead of 1884 then maybe 1885?"

Sarah shrugged. "Who knows? We were dropped in the past, and in two different points in time, so it's possible, I suppose."

Steve turned to Rosamund and began smiling. Mrs. Jones noticed and returned his smile.

"Is there something I can do for you, dear?"

"You know what? Actually, there is. How long have you lived here in town, Mrs. Jones?"

"Oh, let's see. Gerry and I moved here back in the spring of '47, so that would be almost forty years ago."

"So you know most people in town, is that right?" Steve guessed.

"Dear, I know *everyone* in town."

Sarah suddenly smiled. She met Steve's eyes and nodded.

"Well, I'm hoping you can help me out then, Mrs. Jones. We're looking for more of our people and it's hard to say when they would have shown up. Do you think you could discreetly make some inquiries and perhaps see if you can locate any of them?"

The brown bird's nest that was supposed to be a hat nodded so violently that several feathers were dislodged and fluttered to the ground.

"Why, I would be delighted! If those people are here, I am certain I could uncover their present whereabouts. You leave it to me, dear."

Sarah was nodding. "Thank you so much, Mrs. Jones. That's a big help."

Rosamund got to her feet. "I believe I will start making some inquiries. If there are people out there that need our help, then by God, I will find them."

"I'll give you the descriptions we were given," Sarah announced, as she rose to her feet and searched for something to write on. She found a stack of dusty parchment on a table near the stairs. A cup of pencils was nearby. "I don't know if you can find out what happened to them, but if you can, that'd be great."

"Don't draw attention to yourself," Steve cautioned. "Be discreet."

Rosamund waved a dismissive hand. "Honey, I perfected the fine art of acting discreet long before you were born. You have nothing to worry about."

She climbed back up the stairs, opened the trapdoor, exited the room, and securely closed it after her.

"That was a nice move," Sarah admitted as she took her husband's hand. "Giving her something to do will keep her from worrying about everything she heard and saw. Think she'll find any of them?"

"I don't know," Steve admitted, "but I figure it couldn't hurt to try."

"There's something else you need to see," Sarah told him as they both rose to their feet.

"Oh? What's that?"

"The manor."

"Our manor? I had assumed it hadn't been built yet."

"So did I. Steve, it's being built. Right now."

"Okay. What's your point?"

Sarah smacked him on his arm. "Didn't you tell me that your ancestor built that house? Something like your great-great-grandfather, or maybe your great-great-great-grandfather?"

Steve thought a moment. "Yeah, that's right. Luther. Luther Miller built the house. He's my grandfather's grandfather. He's here? You've met him?"

Sarah shook her head no.

"He's something of a recluse. He rarely comes to town, and from what I hear, when he is in town, he's here only long enough to pick up whatever supplies he needs and then it's back to the manor."

"Wow. That's weird."

"I think we need to talk to him."

"What? Why?"

"Don't you get it? I think that's how Luther got here. Honey, he must have used that portal! That's probably why it was created. I think it was how our world was originally linked to Lentari!"

About to ask another question, Steve's mouth snapped shut. "How in the world did you come up with that?"

"When you're stuck in the Old West for months on end, with no internet, there's not much else to do but ponder. I took the time to think things through. Do you know who Luther's parents are? Didn't you tell me that Luther was the first Miller to take up residence here in Coeur d'Alene?"

"That doesn't mean he used the portal," Steve pointed out. "It just means he's the first Lentarian to visit our world."

"He used that portal!" Sarah insisted. "How else would he have gotten here?"

"I had assumed by whatever wizard is living in R'Tal at this point in time."

"Wouldn't you like to know?" Sarah asked. "Wouldn't you like to know if he knows how to use the portal and see if there's a way to get back?"

Steve finally acquiesced. He wasn't too sure how he felt about meeting an ancestor of his, and was hoping to avoid it, but since Sarah deemed it important, then so be it.

"Fine. We'll go see this relative of mine. Should we tell him who we are?"

"I don't want to," Sarah admitted, "but we might have to in order to win his cooperation."

Steve and Sarah trooped back up the stairs and were startled to see the saloon completely dark. Rosamund was just finishing tipping several chairs upside down on a nearby table.

"Maybe we should call it a night," Steve quipped as

he looked around at the eerily quiet bar. "What time is it, anyway?"

"Closing time," Rosamund announced, as though it should be perfectly obvious. "Business has been slow, ever since the White Elephant opened earlier this year. I've been in there. It's nothing spectacular, believe me. It's just a tent. A tent! Our establishment is much cleaner and we serve better liquor."

"We know you do, Mrs. Jones," Sarah assured her. She looked at her husband and winked. "Remind me to tell you about the Elephant, okay?"

Intrigued, Steve nodded. He looked around the quiet saloon. "So is there room for me at wherever you're staying?"

Rosamund automatically shook her head no.

"Appearances must be kept, dear. It would be best if you find another place to stay while you're in town."

"What? We're married! Do you think there will be some hanky panky going on?"

Sarah blushed bright red and looked straight down. To her credit, Mrs. Jones chuckled softly.

"What I mean is that your wife has had a lot of admirers asking about her."

Steve's left eyebrow rose up as he swiveled his head to look at his wife. "How many are we talking about?"

"A lot," Rosamund confirmed. "If you start parading about town on her arm then you're going to find yourself the recipient of a lot of unwelcome attention."

"It's okay," Sarah assured the friendly barkeep. "He has a place to stay for the night. He's staying with Cecil and AnnaBelle Cook."

"Ah. Excellent choice. Very well, you'll be off now. We open at sunrise so you can see Sarah then."

Steve was ushered to the door much like an unwanted guest. He was barely able to kiss his wife goodnight before a heavy wooden panel was pulled across the front entrance of the saloon and bolted in place.

* * *

The following morning, after they had eaten a light meal at the Silver Spike, Steve followed Sarah out into the bright morning sunshine. The sun was just appearing over the eastern horizon, streaking the dark blue sky with reds and oranges. Steve stretched his back and groaned aloud.

"How'd you sleep?" Sarah asked, casting a sideways glance at him.

"Not too well. I might as well have been sleeping on a bag of bricks. That bed in Cecil's house is not very comfortable."

"You have a number of years to go before our adjustable beds will be invented, you know."

Steve grumbled something, but Sarah ignored it.

"So can we at least teleport there?" Steve asked with a hopeful tone. "I'm so done with walking it's not even funny."

"Yeah, I can, but let's get away from town first so no one sees what we're about to do. Funny story about my teleporting."

Steve grunted.

"I said, there's a funny story about my teleporting. Would you like to hear it?"

Steve's bloodshot eyes rose from the ground and found hers. "Sure. Would love to. What about it?"

"It took me some time to figure out how to do it."

"What, teleporting? That doesn't make any sense. You've been teleporting for years now."

"If I do line-of-sight teleporting it's a breeze. If I'm trying to teleport someplace, I've been in our time but trying to teleport to the present-time equivalent of it, it becomes very difficult."

Steve's curiosity was piqued. "Why?"

"None of my safe zones work. I usually just bring up a mental picture of where I want to go and voila, I'm there. In this time, namely the nineteenth century, I have to think generic. I remember what those images look like, what scents I remember smelling, if I felt a breeze, etc. It helps me remember. Are you with me so far?"

Steve nodded.

"Now, the problem is that none of those places as I remember them exist anymore. I have to concentrate on the location and forget about the little things that help me remember the locale. Trust me, it's a lot harder to do than you realize."

Steve still didn't say anything. Sarah continued.

"So, once I was able to think about just the location and not about any other specifics, then, and only then, would I be able to teleport."

"How long did it take you to figure that all out?" Steve wanted to know.

"About a month," Sarah recalled. "Once I knew what I had to do, it was another two weeks or so before I could figure out how to do it. It's still hard for me to do. My teleporting is not as instantaneous as it used to be. Then again, that's only to locations that we've been to in different times. If it's a brand-new location, then it's a piece of cake."

Once they were certain they weren't being followed, Sarah took his arm and pulled him into the nearby trees.

"Ready?"

"Where are we going?"

"My safe zone is now what used to be, I mean, what will be French Gulf Street."

"So we're going to our street, is that it?"

"Yes. Here we go."

The surrounding forest winked out and just as quickly was replaced by another scene, this one with trees visible in the distance all around them. Steve slowly looked around. The other three houses that were at the end of the cul-de-sac back in their time were nowhere to be seen. Clearly, they hadn't been built yet. Steve looked down. The street wasn't paved, either. Although now that he thought about it, none of the streets in town were paved. A dusty gray gravel road overrun with weeds was the only indication they were in the right spot. That and the brightly polished brass plaque set into a newly mortared set of brick walls framing a solid iron gate.

Steve walked up to the name placard and knocked his knuckles against the metal surface. "Wow. This thing looks brand spanking new. This is seriously weird."

Sarah turned to him. "Why? Is it because we're about to

see our future house over a hundred years before we'll ever live there? What could be weird about that?"

Just like the name placard, brick wall, and iron gates, the chain and the lock were practically new and very formidable looking. However, the chain was lying, discarded, on the ground and the lock was right beside it. Steve nervously looked at his wife.

"Either someone forgot to lock the gate, or maybe they have company at the moment?"

Sarah frowned as she looked down at the discarded chain and lock.

"That's probably the same lock and chain from our time. I don't think I've ever seen them off the gate before."

"Should I put it back on for them?"

Sarah shook her head.

"No. We have to think about the consequences while we're here. That chain is on the ground for a reason. If we pick that up and put it on the gate then we could change something that could affect us back home."

"How could a simple chain affect us?" Steve wanted to know.

"Let's say they were supposed to meet some important person here. At first glance, the gate would appear locked and they might turn away. What if it was to meet with the land owners next door so that he, namely Luther, could purchase more land? We could mess up that meeting and when we get back we could discover half our land no longer belongs to us."

That sobered Steve. About to retrieve the chain from the ground he instantly straightened and held out his arm.

"Chain stays on the ground. Got it."

"Just remember where we are," Sarah told him as she slipped her arm through his. "We cannot interfere, no matter what happens."

Steve nodded. "Right. How does us meeting my ancestor not qualify as a paradox waiting to happen? Don't you remember *Back to the Future*? Marty McFly messed up how his parents met and ended up almost not existing."

Sarah laughed. "Well, aside from that. We just have to be careful."

Steve gently pushed the gates open. Both heavy iron gates quietly swung inward on well-greased hinges. Together they turned to walk down the weed-free gravel road. Sarah whistled. Everything was pristine. Everything was perfect. The trees were trimmed away from the gravel road and there were no low-lying branches that needed to be cut back. The future fruit orchard hadn't been planted yet, but there were a number of other trees that were all being meticulously cared for.

A gentle breeze blew in from the south, carrying with it scents of wet leaves, moss, fresh grass, and blooming flowers. By Steve's estimation they had a few hundred more feet to go before they'd round the bend and see their house. Well, the house that belonged to Luther at the moment. Steve shook his head. Trying to keep everything sorted out in his head was starting to give him a headache.

"So, what do you know about Luther?" Steve asked, Sarah as they continued to stroll along the well-manicured grounds. "You say he's a recluse?"

"Rosamund has talked about him several times," Sarah recalled. "She can't imagine anyone living the way Luther does, all holed up on his property like that. She did say that he has one of the biggest plots of land in town, though."

"Is he married?"

"Obviously, or else you wouldn't be here."

Steve fixed Sarah with a stare.

"I mean, is he married at the moment?"

"Yes. I've actually seen his wife more than I've seen him. She comes to town more than he does. Not much, mind you, but enough to sell or trade her gowns."

"Excuse me?"

"Oh, sorry. Cora is a seamstress and a very gifted one at that. She made the purple dress I was wearing last night and this blue one I have on now."

Steve looked at the snug blue Victorian style dress Sarah was wearing. The skirt was embroidered with dark blue thread and looked as though it was as flimsy as lace. The patterns were exquisite. Obviously, this Cora person knew her way around a sewing machine. Sarah's dress even had an old-fashioned bustle in the back. The dress was long sleeved, had a button-up collar that stretched up Sarah's neck to just below her chin, and the hem extended all the way down so that it was less than an inch off the ground.

"Is that thing comfortable to wear?" Steve asked yet again. "How do you move around? Granted, it looks great on you."

Sarah looked at him and smiled.

"Not that there's anything that *wouldn't* look good on you," Steve hastily added.

Sarah leaned in and brushed her lips against his right cheek. "And that's why I love you so much."

"So she made the dress for you? That must have taken her ages."

"Two days. It only took her two days to make it. Can you believe it? I was shocked. Mrs. Jones was rendered speechless. I don't know how Cora does it. Oh! I forgot to tell you that she's made dresses for many of the girls in the other two dozen saloons scattered about town."

"Two dozen? Really? How many saloons does one town need?"

"Not that many, that's for sure. Coeur d'Alene is a dangerous place right now. Everything centers around mining and the search for silver. If someone thinks you're hoarding silver or your mine has struck it rich then you'll most certainly be hit by claim jumpers."

"I'm surprised Luther lets his wife go to town unescorted," Steve commented, more to himself than to anyone.

"I had thought that, too. I figure he must have his reasons."

"So what does Luther do? How does he make his money?"

Sarah shrugged. "I have no idea. I haven't talked to him. No one has. If you were to ask me, I'd say he's sitting in his house paranoid with fear." Sarah suddenly turned to Steve and grabbed his arm excitedly. "I forgot to tell you and you forgot to remind me! Last night. Remember when I said you had to ask me about the Elephant?"

Steve nodded.

"You're never going to believe who owns it!"

"Okay, who owns it?"

"Wyatt Earp!"

"*The* Wyatt Earp? Really? He's here right now?"

Sarah rocked back and forth on the balls of her feet. "Yes! And I even talked to him! He tipped his hat at me and said 'good morning.' I returned the greeting and then Rosamund told me who it was. I was flabbergasted!"

"Where did you see him?"

"At the Silver Spike. I think he was checking out the competition."

"So you met Wyatt Earp! That's so cool!"

Husband and wife finally rounded the bend in the road and they came within sight of their future house. Steve nodded. Sarah was right. It wasn't quite complete. The southern-most section of the house still had several exposed walls and the roof hadn't quite been extended over that area yet. Also, Sarah's beloved garden had yet to be planted, as there was nothing but a large field of overrun weeds and grass.

Steve nudged Sarah's shoulder and pointed at the garage. "Check it out. Looks a lot different than what we're used to."

The large four stall RV garage that they were familiar with was instead a large, mostly completed structure with four open bays. A carriage with two bench seats was parked in the far-left stall and a single-seat buckboard wagon was in the one next to it. Several bales of hay were in the third, while nothing was in the yet-to-be-completed fourth stall.

Sarah let out a small gasp and quickly pulled him to a stop.

"What? What's the matter?"

Sarah pointed at two men who had just come out of front door. Both were seedy looking types that sported several days of growth on their faces, and since they were downwind from the two characters, they could tell that both were in dire need of a bath. Two horses, one an Appaloosa mare and the other a buckskin stallion, were saddled and tied to a hitching post nearby. Both men instantly spotted the newcomers and changed course to intercept them.

Steve gritted his teeth. "Let me handle this."

"Remember," Sarah whispered in his ear, "you cannot

hurt them. Scare them, sure, but don't hurt them."

"Got it. I'll be the epitome of restraint."

"Lookee what we got here, Pete!" one of the men sneered. He was tall, thin as a rail, and had a single holster on his left hip. "This day keeps gettin' better an' better!"

Pete, a short rotund man who was wider than he was tall, scratched his belly and spat a stream of brown juice from the huge wad of tobacco in his lower lip. He grinned lecherously at Sarah and displayed his brown, rotting teeth to her. All ten of them.

"I got me first dibs on her," Pete told his companion. His hands started for the buckle on his pants. "You take care of that feller there. Since the lady of the house is off limits, we should at least have some fun with this looker here. Come on over here, princess. I'm gonna make you a queen!"

"If I heat those things," Steve nonchalantly told Sarah as he indicated the guns, "then I could run the risk of setting them off. Someone might get hurt."

Sarah cupped her hands together and then opened them. A dozen shiny brass bullets fell to the ground. Sarah smiled at him.

"You were saying?"

Steve interlaced his fingers and cracked his knuckles.

"Let the good times roll. Now, let's see what we have here. You, Beanpole, on your knees. Mr. RolyPoly, you too."

In a flash both of their assailants had their guns in their hands.

"You just signed yer death certificate," Pete sneered. He pulled the trigger.

The click of an empty chamber was music to Steve's ears. His gaze dropped to Pete's gun. Within moments Pete dropped his revolver and was howling in pain. Beanpole, as Steve had referred to him, drew a bead on Steve and tried his luck, too. Everyone heard a second loud click. Moments later Beanpole's gun was lying on the ground next to Pete's. Both were glowing red.

"Here's what's gonna happen, guys," Steve jovially told them. "You're going to drop anything you're carrying that's metal. You're also going to drop those ammo belts."

Sarah tapped him on the shoulder and she pointed at the two horses.

"I see rifles over there," Sarah softly murmured.

"Good one. Okay, after all that happens, you are going to go to your horses and drop those rifles, along with any other weapons you may have in hiding."

"Why the hell should we do that?" Beanpole asked as he glared at Steve.

"Because you're wearing a belt full of bullets. Know what happens when a bullet is heated? Want to see?"

Pete hastily stripped off his ammo belts and pulled a six-inch hunting knife from his hip. Beanpole followed suit a few moments later. Once their weapons were all laying discarded on the ground, the two thugs hesitantly turned to Steve.

Deciding a little incentive was in order, Steve blasted out two jets of fire and whipped them through the air like unattended fire hoses. Both goons screamed like small children and dove to the ground. Steve continued his pyrotechnical demonstration for a few seconds longer before pulling his jhorun back into his hands and snuffing them out.

"Stand up."

Both men leapt off the ground as though they had been lying on a hot plate that had just been switched on.

"You wanted to kill me to have your way with my wife. I'd be well within my right to finish you two off right here, right now. As it is, you're not worth my time, so you two had better pray that we don't ever meet again. Is that understood?"

Both goons quickly nodded.

"Good. Get out of here. Now."

Both men turned toward the distant gate and began running.

"Hey geniuses!" Steve called out in his loudest voice. "You can take your horses."

Pete and Beanpole reversed directions and ran to their mounts. Within moments they were gone. Steve looked down at the discarded weapons.

"What do we do with all of that?"

The weapons vanished.

"I've got it covered," Sarah told him. "I put them in the

hidden snug back at the Silver Spike. No one ever goes there so they'll be safe."

"We were just down there," Steve reminded her.

"Did you see how much dust there was? We were probably the first people in years to use that room. Trust me, they'll be fine."

The front door of the manor opened and a young woman in her mid twenties slowly came down the steps. She was slender, had blond curly hair, and was wearing a twin to Sarah's dress, only this one was maroon. She nervously eyed the two of them before offering them a tiny smile.

"Thank you for what you've done," the woman said in a soft, childlike voice.

The voice didn't match the person, Steve thought with a smile.

"Are you Cora?" he asked, already knowing the answer.

The woman nodded. "I am. You look very familiar. Have we met before?"

Steve shook his head. "I guarantee that we haven't. You might have met my wife, though. This is Sarah."

The two pale green eyes that were peeking out from beneath her mop of blond curls widened with recognition.

"I do know you. You're employed at the Silver Spike Saloon, aren't you?"

Sarah nodded. "I am. I love your gowns. You do exquisite work."

Cora gave them a meek smile. "Thank you. I would invite you in for refreshments, but now is not a good time."

Without any warning, Cora broke down in sobs and began weeping uncontrollably. Sarah rushed forward to encompass her in a hug.

"There, there; everything will be alright."

Cora shook her head. She looked up at Sarah with tears streaming down her face. "No, it won't be."

"Those men are gone," Steve assured her. "They won't be back. What were they doing here, anyway?"

"You don't understand. They came with the others. They've taken him!"

Steve and Sarah risked a glance at each other.

"Who?" Steve asked, once it became clear that Cora wasn't offering any more information.

"My husband. They've taken Luther!"

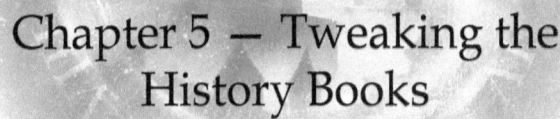

Chapter 5 — Tweaking the History Books

"Who in their right mind would do that?" Steve demanded, angrily addressing Cora, as though she alone were responsible for Luther's disappearance. "What could he have possibly done to deserve that?"

Cora, already distraught at losing her husband, doubled over in agony and would have collapsed to the ground if Sarah had not been there.

"Nice going, Ace," Sarah murmured, elbowing her way past him. "Why don't you give her a paper cut and pour some lemon juice on it? She's already hurting. There's no need to make it worse."

"I didn't mean that the way it sounded. What I meant was…"

Cora wailed in misery. Sarah gave her a friendly, but stern, shake to get her attention. "Hush now. We're here to help. Who took Luther?"

"Who else?" Cora managed to get out between sobs. "Sheriff Bixby. He's got the people thinking Luther found a rich silver mine and now he wants it."

"Has he?" Steve asked. "From what I hear he doesn't really sound like he'd make a good miner."

"He's not a miner!" Cora insisted. "I tried to tell them that but they wouldn't listen. We have too much land. Our house is too big. My gowns are too ornate. He thinks we must have a plentiful supply of silver and gold."

"What'll he do when he discovers Luther doesn't have a mine?" Sarah wanted to know.

Cora let out another wail. "Then he is as good as dead! Oh, my poor Luther! Whatever will we do?"

There was a distant clang, followed moments later by the ringing of a bell. Someone was waiting at the gate.

Steve shook his head and hooked a thumb backward. "Wouldn't the gate still be open if those two men just rode out? And a bell? I didn't see any bell."

Cora groaned. "It's Cecil and AnnaBelle. I had forgotten this is the day we play cards together. What am I going to tell them?"

"Cecil and his wife are the least of your worries," Sarah assured her.

"Who is this Sheriff Bixby person?" Steve demanded. "And where can I find him?"

"Cool your jets, Sparky," Sarah scolded. "You need to not only remember where you are but *when* you are, too."

Cora stifled her sobs just long enough to gaze speculatively at the two of them.

"What's that supposed to mean?" Steve asked, as he crossed his arms over his chest. "What does that have to do with anything?"

"The people here are armed," Sarah clarified. "In fact, I think just about everyone is packing. Your, umm, hands won't stop bullets."

Cora frowned. "Packing? Why would the folk be packing? No one is moving anywhere."

"Packing heat," Steve helpfully added. "Carrying guns."

Cora nodded. "Everyone carries guns. It's our right to

bear arms."

"And this sheriff? What's his story?"

Sarah escorted Cora inside the incomplete manor and guided her toward a pair of Victorian arm chairs covered with dark blue upholstery, taking the neighboring chair for herself. Steve decided he'd be more comfortable pacing.

"That'd be Sheriff Marcus Bixby," Sarah answered with a frown. "From what I've been told he moved here years ago, from New Jersey, I think. He has an incredible knack for wresting control of lucrative mines away from the townsfolk. Legally. I don't know how he knows which mines are in financial trouble, or how he knows which people are about to be foreclosed on, but he does. He's a cattle wrangler, gambler, and saloon owner. He's about as corrupt as a person can get. Everyone around here is afraid of him, and as a result, no one would ever cross him."

"Where's it written that every town has to have someone like that?" Steve exclaimed with a sigh, rubbing his temples. "This is just what we don't need right now."

"Everyone in town has become accustomed to simply looking in the other direction whenever he's around."

"That's no way to live," Steve grumbled. "Man alive, this sucks."

"I didn't plan on this happening," Sarah stated matter-of-factly.

"Have you met him before?" Steve asked.

Sarah shook her head. "Not really. I've seen him from a distance several times, and have even waited on him once, but I have never talked to him."

"What was he like?"

"Cold," Cora's quavering, high-pitched voice spoke. "Heartless."

Steve turned to Sarah. "And your take on him?"

"Smart," Sarah instantly responded. "Ruthless and cruel. He's used to getting what he wants, and if you happen to have what he wants then it's too bad for you."

"I don't like this guy," Steve decided. "At all."

Sarah sighed and shook her head. She leveled a gaze at Steve. "We're going to have to break him out."

"You're breaking someone out? Of jail?"

Everyone turned at the sound of the incredulous voice that had spoken up behind them. They had been so engrossed in their conversation that they had failed to hear Cecil or his wife approach in their wagon. The two were standing just outside the front door and both wore surprised expressions. Cecil recovered first.

"Er, knock knock? We're sorry to barge in like this. In our defense, the door was open. Well, with that unpleasant bit of business out of the way I'll say hello, friends!" Cecil stepped inside and took off his black bowler hat. He pulled AnnaBelle across the door's threshold and then smiled at the three of them. "I must be hearing things. I thought I heard someone say that they were going to break a person out of jail. Tell me I misheard that."

AnnaBelle cleared her throat and physically pushed Cecil out of the way.

"I'm sorry; you'll have to forgive Cecil for his impetuousness. I tried to tell him that..." AnnaBelle trailed off as she took notice of the three stern faces before her. She clasped Cecil's hand tightly in her own. "What's happened? Where's Luther?"

A single tear trickled down Cora's face. She was unable to look her friend in the eye. AnnaBelle sighed and looked over at Sarah.

"Hello. I do not think we have been formally introduced. I am AnnaBelle Cook. Cecil is my husband."

"Sarah Miller," Sarah automatically answered as she extended a hand. "I'm Steve's wife."

Shock registered on AnnaBelle's face as she slowly turned to her new tenant. "Steve, you found your wife already? Good for you! I am impressed." AnnaBelle squinted as she studied Sarah's face. "Do I know you? Have we met before?"

"I've seen you in the Silver Spike a few times," Sarah admitted. "However, we have never met until today."

Cecil glanced worriedly over at Cora. "What happened to Luther? Has someone taken him? Was it the sheriff?"

Cora nodded again. She evidently thought she couldn't keep her voice from breaking. Cecil muttered a curse under his breath. He looked over at Steve and forced a smile.

"That imbecilic moron still thinks Luther and Cora are sitting on one of the richest veins of silver in this county. No amount of explaining will convince him otherwise."

"What's going to happen to Luther?" Cora asked in a very timid voice.

"Knowing the sheriff as well as I do, he'll probably keep Luther incarcerated until he gets what he wants."

Steve scowled. "And when he doesn't? He wants a silver mine. Luther doesn't have one to give. This isn't going to end well for him."

Sarah took both of Steve's hands and held them tightly. "We need to do something."

"I'm not sure how much we *can* do."

Sarah fixed him with a stare. "I am certain we can lend a hand here."

Steve returned Sarah's frank stare and nervously cleared his throat. "Sorry, let me rephrase that. I'm not sure how much we should get involved."

Sarah hesitated a few moments as she considered their predicament. She suddenly smiled and looked over at Cora's tear-streaked face. With a triumphant grin, she looked back at her husband. "Oh, I think we *need* to get involved."

Steve was taken aback. "What? Why? Have you forgotten our previous conversation?"

"What's going on?" Cecil asked suspiciously. "What do you two have planned?"

"We'll have to explain later, Cecil," Sarah told him. "I'm sorry. A bigger issue has just presented itself."

Steve folded his arms across his chest. "Nuh uh. You need to explain yourself. I'm under the impression if we get involved, we could end up changing a few things back home and I really don't want to mess with that."

"I'm sorry. I'll explain. First, let me ask a few questions." She looked at each member of their small group. "Are we all in agreement what's going to happen to Luther if we don't get him out of jail?"

Everyone nodded, including Steve.

"Good. Now. Cora, the next question is for you. Do you

have any children?"

Cora slowly shook her head. Sarah turned back to Steve and smiled, as if to say *what more do you need?* To Steve's credit, comprehension slammed into him hard and fast. His eyebrows shot up as he stared at Cora.

"What? Why do you stare at me so?"

"You don't have any kids?"

"No. I just said that I don't."

Steve met his wife's eyes. "There's some incentive for you. Hoo, boy. Count me in."

Confused, Cecil looked first at Sarah, then Steve, and finally back at Sarah. "What just happened? What does having kids have to do with Luther?"

Steve gave Cecil a cryptic smile. "Let's just say that I am, er, highly motivated to keep Luther safe."

Cecil nodded. "Good. That goes for me, too. Whatever it is you're planning, count me in."

"You might want to rethink that, buddy," Steve told him, slapping a hand on Cecil's shoulder. "Luther's in jail. I'm going to bust him out."

"Excellent. As I said before, count me in."

"What exactly do you think you're going to be able to do?" Steve asked. "I appreciate the help, but you probably ought to sit this one out."

"And what, pray tell, do you think *you're* going to do?" Cecil countered. "You just get into town and you think you're going to be able to pull off a successful jailbreak? You don't know this town, you don't know where to hide, and you certainly don't have the resources to pull this off. Not without help."

"He'll have help," Sarah informed him. "Me."

"You?" Cecil scoffed. "No offense, ma'am, but you're not in any position to render aid. Not dressed like that."

Sarah glanced down at herself and had to suppress a giggle. She'd have to concede the point to Cecil. At the moment, wearing her full-length Victorian gown, she certainly didn't present the appearance of someone capable of assisting in a jailbreak. Then again, little did Cecil know that she alone could get Luther out of jail without anyone knowing she had been there.

"Luther is a friend of mine," Cecil announced, using as firm a tone as he could command. "I want to help and you will need it. Therefore, I'm going with you."

"Fine. You can come with me. I could use a guide." Steve looked over at Sarah and frowned. "However, I need *you* to stay put."

As expected, Sarah was on her feet and spitting mad in just a few seconds. She stalked over to her husband and put both hands on her hips, daring him to refuse her.

"Are you kidding me? No one is capable of pulling off this jailbreak better than I am! You can't possibly think it's too dangerous for me. Not after everything we've been through!"

Steve smiled and held up both hands in a show of surrender. "Trust me, I know. You are more than capable of handling yourself. However, I need you here."

"Why?"

"To look after my, uh, well, I need you to look after Cora. Can you do that for me?"

"What do you think will happen here?" Sarah asked, confused. "I can be of more use to you by your side."

"And I want you by my side; however, you know how these things go. We drove off two of the sheriff's men. I need you here in case he tries to retaliate."

Sarah slowly nodded. "Alright, I'll give you that one. What's your plan? How are you going to bust him out?"

Steve shrugged and gave her a sheepish smile. "Haven't a clue. I'm making this up as I go."

* * *

It was a few minutes after sunset and the temperature was steadily dropping. The streets slowly emptied of people as the townsfolk moved inside for the remainder of the night. The small residential houses went dark and quiet early on, but the saloons were the exact opposite. All two dozen or so saloons in the greater Coeur d'Alene area were a hive of activity, as saloon girls strutted in front of their respective establishments and beckoned to passersby. Beer and whiskey flowed freely while numerous card dealers went to work.

One street in particular, with only a handful of large buildings scattered along the road, had only one structure that showed any signs of life. It was a two-story Romanesque style building composed of local brick and stone masonry. Bright light streamed out of long narrow windows along the northern half of the edifice.

"What can you tell me about that place?" Steve whispered, as he and Cecil knelt by a copse of trees just south of the building's formal entrance. "I don't know what I was expecting to see but that certainly wasn't it."

"I assume you've seen a great many jails?" Cecil countered.

"Of course, I have," Steve retorted. "And in the movies, they never made 'em look like that."

"Movies?" Cecil repeated. "What's that?"

"It's way too hard to explain. Forget about that for now. Have you been inside that building before?"

Cecil nodded. "Only one time."

"Tell me as much as you can remember."

"Once you step inside the front entrance, you'll find two flanking offices and a double height cage room. There are five jail cells on the mezzanine, along with a small jailer's office."

Steve groaned. "The cells are on the top floor? I would never have called that one."

"What's your plan?" Cecil asked.

"I can only think of one way. Break him out from the inside."

"Meaning you'll allow yourself to be captured?" Cecil asked incredulously. "Help me understand something, friend. What makes you think you can successfully break out of a jail cell in a two-story building without alerting the entire town? Did you hit your head on something?"

Steve smiled, and patted Cecil patronizingly on his back. "There are some things that are better left unsaid."

"This is madness!" Cecil sputtered. "You don't even know he's in there!"

That drew Steve up short. "Are you saying he might not be? Where else could he be?"

"The sheriff has his own private compound up in the

mountains. No one who goes up there ever comes back alive."

"Not true," Steve countered with a smile. "Obviously the sheriff goes up there. Clearly, he makes it back in one piece."

"You know what I mean," Cecil scolded. "If the sheriff hasn't taken Luther up there yet, then he most certainly will soon."

"All the more reason to get him out of jail," Steve told him. "Now listen up. Once we're out of there we'll need to beat a hasty retreat. See if you can find some transportation and meet us behind the Silver Spike, okay?"

"If you make it that far," Cecil muttered, as he slipped away into the night.

Steve turned to look back at Coeur d'Alene's town jail and shook his head. He really shouldn't be doing this, as he had no idea what would happen once he made it inside and came face-to-face with one of his ancestors. These people had guns. Guns shoot bullets and no matter how hard he tried, he would not be able to melt the bullets before they made it to their targets. Arrows, sure, but bullets? That was a different story.

How could he not do anything? How could he not help out? Cora had no children yet, which meant unless he helped Luther successfully break out of jail then the chances were he'd cease to exist.

Steve swallowed nervously and slowly stood up. There was no time like the present; even though the present was the past and he fervently wished he and Sarah were back in *their* present. Steve chuckled to himself. Had he spoken that last statement out loud in front of Sarah, she would have laughed in his face.

As he approached the jail's front entry, a deputy, who must have been watching from one of the windows, slowly sauntered down the stairs. He was hastily buckling his gun belt around his waist when Steve stopped in front of him.

"This is no place for you to be, stranger," the deputy warned him, as he finished buckling his belt. His right hand rested on the hilt of his Colt revolver. "State your business."

"I'm here to see someone," Steve began, but was cut off by the deputy's short bark of laughter.

"You're here to see someone? At this hour? What kind of fool do you take me for? Visiting hours are from ten to two. Come back then."

Steve crossed his arms over his chest and thought about what he could do to get himself arrested. Several possibilities sprang to mind. He could punch the deputy. That was sure to get him an overnight pass to the jail. Maybe he could insult the sheriff? Perhaps a not-so-subtle reference to the sheriff's parental lineage would do the trick?

"If you don't move off, I'll personally grant your wish, only it won't be in a way you'll like, I guarantee it."

Steve smiled. Well now! This was going to be easier than he thought. "You know what? I think you're mistreating your prisoners. I demand to see the inside of one of your jail cells. Now!"

The deputy's eyes widened with disbelief. Clearly no one ever waltzed right up to the jail and demanded to be let inside. The deputy shrugged. He pulled his gun and trained it on Steve. "You want it, you got it, pal. You're under arrest."

Steve decided to play along. "For what? Wanting to make sure you're not mistreating your prisoners?"

"Oh, you'll see for yourself how well we treat our prisoners," the deputy sneered. "You're gonna have yourself a ringside seat. Get inside. Now."

Steve reluctantly raised his hands and allowed himself to be led up the steps into the jailhouse. The deputy snickered loudly behind him as the front door slammed closed behind them. Steve paused as soon as his eyes adjusted and he saw the two-story holding cell. Three men were inside, lying on cots. None of them elected to look up.

"You're putting me in there?" Steve asked. He squinted at the man closest to him. Was it Luther? He looked at the other two. Unfortunately, all three had their backs to him so he couldn't tell if one of them was his relative.

Steve automatically began walking toward the large cage but the deputy grabbed his collar and yanked him to a stop.

"Where do you think you're going? You wanted to see a cell, right? Well, your wish has been granted. Start walking. Head for them stairs right over there."

Steve looked down the hall and saw a flight of steps leading to the second floor. While he grudgingly headed toward the steps, he mentally hoped that Luther wasn't one of the men in the large holding cell. It was out in the open! How was he supposed to discreetly melt the bars when everyone in the whole damn building had a front row seat?

The deputy gave him another shove as he made it to the top step. Steve stumbled forward. He would have taken a nasty crack to the head had he not caught himself on the bars of the cell directly in front of him. There was no one in the cell.

Steve turned to give the deputy a scowl. "Would you take it easy? I almost took a header right into those bars."

The deputy stared at him for a few seconds. "You almost took a what?"

Steve shook his head. "Forget it."

The deputy smiled and unlocked the cell farthest on the right, the same one Steve had almost collided with.

"Consider it forgotten, friend."

Chuckling loudly, the deputy pushed Steve into the cell and locked the door behind him. The deputy whistled merrily as he clomped back down the stairs and disappeared from sight. Steve looked at the cell adjacent to his. Two men, dressed in dirty long-sleeved blue shirts and equally dirty brown trousers looked back at him. Steve gave them a smile.

"Whatcha in for, buddy?"

Both men stared silently at him.

"What were you two arrested for?" Steve translated. He spoke in slow, careful tones he was sure the other two men would be able to understand.

Neither man in the adjacent cell said a word.

"Right. You two are certainly a talkative bunch. I don't suppose either of you are named Luther?"

One man looked at the other. Both slowly shook their heads no.

"Figures," Steve mumbled under his breath. He moved around his tiny seven foot by nine foot cell to see if he could tell who was in the other cells. He already knew the adjacent cell had two men in it. Past that he could see two loudly snoring men in the third. The fourth cell appeared empty and there was a single man in the last one. He, too, appeared to be asleep on a cot.

"Excuse me," Steve whispered, in the loudest voice he dared to use, "but could any of you fine gents tell me if there's a Luther present?"

The two men in the third cell awoke and sat up on their cots. Steve repeated the question for them. The two men looked blearily in his direction before collapsing heavily back onto their cots. Within moments twin resonating snores echoed loudly through the space.

Steve rose up on his tiptoes to see to the end of the row. The lone occupant was still stretched out on his cot.

"Excuse me down there," Steve repeated, this time a little louder, "but could you tell me if your name is Luther?"

"Keep it down, pal," one of the men in the next cell over hissed at him. "You don't want to attract attention in here. Trust me."

"How many deputies are here right now?" Steve softly asked the tenants of cell two. "Is it just the one guy?"

The man who had spoken to him earlier nodded. "Come sun up two more idiots will arrive to relieve the one already down there."

Steve nodded. "Just the one guy. That'll do."

"What is it you think you're gonna do, friend?"

"I'm getting out of here," Steve promptly told him as he turned to face the thick iron bars before him.

The second man finally spoke. "Not unless you got a stick of dynamite hidden up your arse you're not."

Steve approached the two men watching him from the adjacent cell and squatted down until he was eye level with them.

"If I get you out of here, will you keep your mouths shut and do as I say?"

Both men swung their legs over their cots and stood up. Together they approached Steve and squatted down low.

"If you can get us out of here, friend, then feel free to do so. Just tell us what you want us to do."

"It means you'll need to lay low and not get caught again," Steve warned them. "You're going to have to ignore what you're about to see and don't ask any questions. Can you do that?"

"We all can do that," one of the occupants from the third cell told him in a hushed tone.

Steve glanced at the wall of bars separating the cells and then back at the door. The bars were equally thick so it really didn't matter where he started. "Again, ignore what you're about to see and above all, keep quiet. Got it?"

Four men fervently nodded their heads.

"Someone keep an eye on the guy in the last cell," Steve said over his shoulder as he ignited both hands. "If he starts to stir, make sure you tell him to keep quiet, okay?"

The men gasped with alarm when they saw Steve's hands go up in flames. One of the men pointed at Steve's hand and opened his mouth to say something. Steve snapped his fingers a few times to get his attention. "Nuh uh. Don't say anything. Remember our arrangement. I'll get you out but you have to ignore what you see. Agreed?"

Wordlessly the four men all nodded. With his hands still blazing, Steve leaned forward and wrapped them around the locking mechanism on his cell's door. In moments the iron was glowing red. Steve pumped more jhorun into his hands and ordered the iron to heat as hot as it could. Out of the corner of his eye he could see the two men in the second cell backing as far away from him as they could. He couldn't blame them. The ambient temperature in his cell must have jumped at least thirty degrees.

Steve experimentally squeezed the metal in his hands. It moved! The metal was becoming malleable! He shoved the metal into a ball, like he was wadding up a large piece of paper. The metal groaned just a bit as it was stretched thin in several places. Steve gave the molten metal a violent twist to the left and then to the right.

Suddenly he was holding a handful of hot metal and was looking at a basketball-sized hole in the cell door. It had worked! There wasn't a lock to keep his door closed! Still holding the heated metal in his hands, he nudged the door with his right knee. The hinges creaked noisily as they swung outward.

Cursing silently Steve hooked his foot through the iron bars to keep the noisy door from opening any further. He withdrew his jhorun and waited for the wadded-up lock to become nothing more than a misshapen piece of metal. He gently placed the iron lump onto the floor under the cot and turned toward the second cell. Both occupants were gaping at him.

"Who are you, friend? How did you do that?"

Steve held up a finger and shook his head. "We agreed there'd be no questions. Now, step away from the door. This is going to get warm for you guys."

Using the same technique, Steve melted the cell lock and pulled it free from the door. Holding a lit finger to his lips, Steve approached the third cell and repeated the process. He gently opened each of their doors and beckoned the occupants to follow him. There were a few minor creaks but nothing to arouse suspicion.

His followers gathered around him as he stared into the fifth and final cell. The person inside was still on his cot and wasn't moving. Was he alive? Steve watched the man's chest for a few moments and was starting to convince himself that the poor fellow was dead when he saw the chest rise into the air. He was breathing. Good.

"Leave him," one of the men told him. "He hasn't been in there that long."

Steve turned to the man who had spoken and scowled. "Exactly how long has he been in there?"

"Since earlier today. Right about noon, I reckon."

"Why didn't you say so before?"

"You didn't ask. Only wanted a name. We don't know his name."

Steve slowly counted to ten. The man was right. He should have asked if anyone had recently been brought in. Oh, well.

Steve melted the lock from the last cell and stepped inside. He placed the former piece of cell door onto the ground and gently shook the sleeping man's shoulder. The man groaned and finally rose to a sitting position. He rubbed his eyes and groaned again.

Steve gave the man's shoulder another nudge. "You need to keep it down. We're getting out of here."

The man finally looked up. Steve's mouth dropped open. He was looking at a spitting image of himself. The face was unshaved and the hair was longer than he had ever worn it, but there was no doubt about it: this man was related to him. It had to be Luther.

"Would your name be Luther? Luther Miller?"

The man warily eyed him. "I am. Who are you? What do you—"

Luther trailed off as he noticed his cell was open. He slowly inspected the other cells and saw that all the doors were open. "How did you get in here? What happened to the cells?"

Steve helped Luther to his feet. "I'll explain later. Right now, we need to get out of here."

"How do you propose to do that?" Luther asked. He pointed toward the stairs leading to the ground floor. "We may have gotten out of the cells but that doesn't mean we're free. We'll still need to sneak by Gabriel."

"Well, let's see what we can do." Steve motioned for the men to gather round. "Who knows this area best? Which wall doesn't have any other buildings behind it?"

One of the occupants of the third cell raised a hand. "This building faces into town. Directly behind us is Maple." The man headed back toward Steve's cell and motioned him over. He pointed at the one wall not made of iron bars. "On the other side of this is forest. Nothing but trees for miles around."

Steve nodded. "Then this is our exit point."

"How do you plan on getting through that?" the man asked. He knocked on the wall a few times. "The wall's gotta be made of brick and stone and is at least a foot thick."

"You just watched me melt iron bars and you're questioning me about bricks? Really?"

The man held up his hands in defeat. Steve pointed back at the other cells. "We're going to need a rope or something. See if you can use the material from the cots and make us a rope."

The man nodded. He and the others quickly went to work stripping the fabric from the wooden frames. Steve turned back to the wall and ran his hands along its surface. This wasn't going to be easy.

Steve sank to the floor and contemplated his options. Several times before he had created a tiny pinprick of intense fire and heat and had used that to cut through leather and wood. Could he use that to burn through the stone? There was only one way to find out.

"Someone keep an eye out for Gabriel. There's a good chance he'll be able to smell what I'm about to do."

One man, a prisoner from the second cell, positioned himself next to the doorway leading to the stairs and gave him a thumbs up. Steve nodded. He turned to the wall and closed his eyes.

Breathing slowly, he focused all his jhorun onto one tiny point. He needed his Dot of Fire to be hot enough to burn through solid stone and since he was certain ol' Triggerfinger downstairs was sure to smell burning bricks, he had to do it as quickly as possible. He opened his eyes. A tiny orange dot had appeared directly in front of him on the wall's surface. A single tendril of smoke also appeared.

Here we go, Steve thought.

He channeled all of his jhorun into the tiny dot and then proceeded to draw a two-foot circle down near the floor. Uncertain if the dot had adequate time to burn its way through the stone, Steve decided to run it over the same line again. He moved the dot a few feet to the left, holding it there while it smoldered in place. He put both hands on the circle and pushed.

Nothing. The rock was clearly thicker than he had thought.

Determined, Steve ordered the tiny point of light back over to the circle, tracing a few more times. Steve spent the next ten minutes, finally making progress. It now looked as though someone had used a tiny chisel to cut a circle into the wall. He again ordered his jhorun to move the dot to the side and then pushed against the wall.

There was a loud grating noise as a chunk of wall, in a

slightly squashed circular shape, moved forward a few inches.

"I think we have it," Steve told the others. "Is the rope ready?"

One of the men held up a twenty-foot section of braided burlap.

"It ain't pretty, but it'll do. We're ready."

"Remember, you need to lay low for the foreseeable future," Steve reminded the motley group.

"That sumbitch ain't ever gonna find me again," one man vowed. "Locked me up for no reason. Was just trying to work my mine."

"You didn't tell him where to find it, didja?" another asked.

"Hell no. That's my mine. He can get his own."

Steve turned around and held a finger to his lips. "Guys, not now. Worry about that later. Tie that rope off. As soon as I push this out it's going to make a loud ruckus. Everyone ready?"

The makeshift rope was tied to the closest bar.

"We're ready here, friend. Do your thing."

Steve gave the cut rock a violent push and grimaced as a loud grating sound erupted. The rock slid forward another few inches.

"What's going on up there?" a voice hollered from below. "What are you doing? So help me if I have to come up there…"

Steve shoved the rock and winced as it fell, crashing noisily below. He lowered the rope through the hole. Steve pushed Luther through first.

"Get going! Hurry!"

Luther scurried down the rope. Fortunately, it was only a dozen or so feet to the ground. Steve leapt next and turned to look up at the rapidly descending prisoners. Just as soon as each person's feet touched ground, they were off like a shot. Within moments every man, except Steve and Luther, had disappeared into the forest.

Gabriel poked his head through the wall, shouting with alarm. "Hey! You! Halt in the name of the Law!"

The deputy grabbed a handful of the homemade rope

and leveraged himself through the hole. He was in the process of drawing his gun when Steve sliced the rope in two. Gabriel fell the remaining five feet and lay motionless on the ground. Steve pulled the deputy up into a sitting position and patted his shoulder reassuringly. "Relax, you'll be fine. You've just had the wind knocked out of you."

Gabriel tried to swing his gun around so that he could point it at Steve, who caught the man's hand and easily disarmed him. He looked at the Colt revolver and shook his head. Steve's thumb and index finger glowed red as he pinched the gun's barrel closed. A quick check revealed this was the only gun Gabriel had on his person.

Steve handed the disabled gun back to the deputy. "Think carefully about what you just saw," Steve told the man, who had begun trembling. "Who do you think melted those bars up there? Who cut through the wall? That was me. Don't ever draw a gun on me again. Ever. Are we clear?"

Gabriel vehemently nodded his head.

"Good. I'll be on my way then. For the record, those cells were terrible. They're way too small."

It was too much for the deputy. He passed out.

Steve took Luther's arm and ducked into the woods.

"Who are you?" Luther asked him yet again. "Do I know you?"

"Nope."

"How did you cut through that wall?"

"I'll explain later. Right now, we need to get to the Silver Spike."

"I don't want to go to a saloon. I hate saloons."

"Noted. However, Cecil should be waiting for us with some horses, I hope."

"You dragged Cecil into this?"

Steve glanced irritably at his great-great-grandfather. "Don't look at me like that. He wanted to come. He insisted he help break you out."

"You went there for me?"

Steve nodded. "Yep."

"Why?"

"I'll —"

"Explain later." Luther sighed. "Yes, you've told me that before."

Ten minutes later, they arrived at the Silver Spike. Steve guided Luther to the back of the building. There, as he hoped, was Cecil. He was astride one horse and held the reins of two others.

Steve hurried up to him and stepped into the left stirrup. He swung his right leg over the horse and took the reins that Cecil tossed to him. He looked back and saw that Luther was already seated on the third horse, ready to go.

"Cecil, we need to move. Go!"

"Where to?"

"Where else? The manor. Go!"

"You know about my manor?" Luther called from the back as the three horses galloped off. "How?"

Just then Cecil twisted in his saddle to look behind him. "It's too dark to see where I'm going! We're going to kill ourselves if we try to gallop through the woods at night!"

Two fireballs sprang into existence; one on the left side of the riders and the other on the right. Cecil gasped with astonishment.

"They'll pace you," Steve told his shocked friend. "Now you can see. Get going!"

Luther spurred his mount so that he was galloping side by side with Steve. "Wizards be damned! You're Lentarian! You're using jhorun!"

Steve turned to Luther and smiled. "It's a bit more complicated than that. I'm using jhorun but I'm not Lentarian. Well, mostly not Lentarian."

"What does that mean?" Luther asked, perplexed.

"It's a long story. The short version of that is I've been to Lentari before. Many times. I love it there."

Cecil reined in his mount so that the three of them were galloping side by side. "You're from Lentari, too? I thought Luther had made all those stories up!"

Luther leaned back and spoke to Cecil behind Steve's back. "You didn't believe? Not even a little?"

Cecil shook his head. "I wanted to believe, Luther, I really did. Look at it from my point of view. Would you have believed me had I come up with a story like that?"

Luther looked back at Steve. "You have no idea how glad I am to see you. Fortuitous timing indeed! I had almost given up hope!"

Baffled, Steve looked at his ancestor. "Given up hope about what? What's the matter?"

"If those stories are true," Cecil was saying, more to himself since no one was paying attention to him, "then that means magic is real! You can do magic! That's incredible, my friend. You'll have to give me a demonstration!"

Luther shook his head. "I told you before, Cecil, that I cannot do that. My jhorun no longer works here."

Steve stared straight at Luther. "You mean your jhorun worked here before and it doesn't now?"

It was Luther's turn to smile. "It's complicated, my friend."

"Let's see if I can uncomplicate it. On Lentari your jhorun worked fine. When you came here you knew there was a chance your jhorun wouldn't work so you took measures to make sure it worked at least long enough to complete the portal. My guess is they gave you a jorii or two, but have since used it up. How am I doing?"

Luther stared at him in utter shock. "How do you know this?"

The three horses continued to gallop through the woods as Cecil guided them toward the manor.

"No one knew the nature of my mission. I told no one. The king told no one. Even the wizard wasn't told, although I suspect he knew."

"Trust me, Luther, you wouldn't believe me even if I told you."

"Try me."

Just then they came to the familiar iron gates and led their horses through, one at a time. Once Luther was through, he dismounted, closed the gates, and locked them from the inside. Five minutes later, they brought their horses to a stop by the four-stall carriage house that would one day become Steve's garage.

The front door banged open. Cora, AnnaBelle, and Sarah

came bounding down the steps. Cora threw herself into Luther's arms and sobbed hysterically. AnnaBelle embraced Cecil and whispered words of encouragement to him. Steve held out his arms for a hug. Sarah approached and gave him a high-five.

"Good job, honey!"

Steve remained motionless with his arms up and still open. Both eyebrows lifted as he gazed at his wife. Sarah burst out laughing and threw herself into his arms, giving him a passionate kiss.

"Oh, just kidding. Nicely done!"

Luther led the horses into stalls and pulled a gate closed. He ushered them all inside the manor. Finally, Luther got his first good look at his rescuer.

Standing side-by-side, the resemblance was uncanny. They were the same height and weight. Same color hair. Same nose. While Cecil and Cora eyed them curiously, Steve watched Luther. He watched his ancestor's eyes widen. Comprehension dawned. Steve nodded at him, knowingly, and Luther's mouth dropped open.

"Who ... who are you?" Cecil suspiciously asked him.

Steve cleared his throat. "Steve. Steve Miller."

Cora gasped. She leaned forward for a better look. Cecil and AnnaBelle quickly glanced at each other.

"I am their great-great-grandson."

"Impossible," Cecil told him. "They have no children."

Steve smiled and looked over at Cora. "Yet."

Cora's hand fluttered to her heart. She stepped over to the closest chair and sank down on it.

"What—what are you doing here?" Cecil sputtered.

"Honestly? I came here because my wife fell through the same damn portal that brought Luther here."

Luther looked over at Sarah. "The interdimensional portal? I was told it should have closed by now."

"Interdimensional portal? Is that what you call it? Trust me, sport, it's still there. At least a dozen people, that we know of, have disappeared through it. We didn't know where it went and were prepared to seal it off when Sarah accidentally fell through. I went in after her. The problem is, it clearly messes with time. I went through thirty seconds after she did but Sarah ended up getting here six months before me."

"I've been here for three years," Luther told him. "You were most fortunate. The amount of time between arrivals were in months and not years."

"We seriously need to seal that thing off," Steve told his wife. "It's way too dangerous."

Sarah nodded. "I couldn't agree more."

Cora turned to look at Luther. She took his right hand and brought it to her lips. "I'm so sorry."

Puzzled, Luther looked at his wife. "What are you sorry for, love?"

"I'm sorry for doubting you."

Luther stared at his wife in shock.

"You, too? You didn't believe me, either? I tried to tell you both that I wasn't from this world."

Cora hung her head and her cheeks reddened.

"Be that as it may," Steve interjected, "we have a bigger problem. We need to find a way home. You do know how to use the portal, don't you?"

Luther slowly shook his head no.

"You said it was an interdimensional portal!" Steve argued. "That has to mean it can move between worlds! You used it to get here so there's got to be a way to use it to get back, right?"

Again, Luther slowly shook his head.

"How do you know? Have you tried?"

"I was there when Zevern created it," Luther explained. "The king had found some book about a prophecy and became obsessed by it. He said that a link to another world must be created so he tasked Zevern with finding a way to do it."

"There's got to be a way to figure out where it'll be next."

"I'm afraid not," Luther sadly told him. "I tried tracking it for over a year. The most reasonable explanation I could come up with is that the portal is only one way."

Sarah began crying. AnnaBelle and Cora rushed to her side. Steve swore under his breath.

"Who in their right freakin' mind would create an unstable

portal?" Steve demanded. "Is Zevern that inept?"

Luther nodded and lowered his voice as if he was somehow afraid the wizard might be able to hear him. "You'd be surprised. He's not that good. Zevern is very absentminded; some might say batty."

"Is that a trait common with all castle wizards? The wizard from our time is just like that."

Luther gave a hollow laugh.

"Our wizard was partly responsible for bringing us here," Steve continued. "He and a dwarf have an ongoing dispute. They were in the middle of one of their arguments when Sarah was accidentally knocked into that portal."

Sarah suddenly stopped sobbing and looked hopefully over at Luther. "Wait a minute. Weren't you supposed to have built a portal? We can go to Lentari. This Zevern fellow should be able to help us. If he created an interdimensional whatsit to bring you here, then he should be able to create another one that will take us home."

Cora looked worriedly at her husband. Luther was staring at the floor.

Sarah was confused. "What? What'd I say? What's the matter?"

"The portal is complete," Luther confirmed, using a very sullen voice, "but is unable to be activated."

Steve was curious. "Okay, I'll bite. Why? What's the problem?"

"The athe crystal is broken," Luther admitted. "It has shattered. There is no way to activate my portal. I have no way to return home to get another; therefore, I have failed in my mission. Zevern probably could help you, my friends, but without a way to get to Lentari I'm afraid we are all stuck here. Forever."

Steve and Sarah both began to smile. Cecil noticed first and became defensive. "Why are you two smiling? Their discomfort pleases you?"

Luther looked up and saw Steve's smile.

"Perhaps we should finish our introductions," Steve suggested.

Disinterested, Luther shrugged.

"My name is Steve Miller," Steve began. "I am from Coeur d'Alene, Idaho. I am married to this lovely lady, Sarah Miller. I am a fire thrower, as if you couldn't tell. Sarah, perhaps you'd like to tell them about your jhorun?"

Sarah smiled. "I'm a teleporter."

Luther's head jerked up and his eyes landed on hers. "A teleporter?"

"One that's strong enough to make the jump between worlds. I can get us to Lentari!"

Chapter 6 — Pesky Powerless Portal

Allow me to see if I understand you correctly," Luther said slowly as he collected his thoughts. "You both have jhorun, yet you're not Lentarian. You are both able to use your jhorun here, whereas I cannot. You also say that you, Steve, are a descendant of mine and live here in this manor, yet that won't be for over a hundred years? Have I missed anything?"

"You missed the part about needing us in order to complete your mission," Steve reminded him. "Specifically, Sarah. Her jhorun is strong enough to span our two worlds."

"How?" Luther demanded. "No teleporter is strong enough to jump between worlds. Better yet, explain how your jhoruns work here when mine doesn't? No. Wait. If what you say is true, explain to me how you even have a jhorun in the first place when you're not Lentarian?"

Steve returned his ancestor's frank stare. "*You* are

Lentarian, which makes me Lentarian."

"Part Lentarian," Luther corrected. "By at least five generations. That would suggest you should have a jhorun but it wouldn't be very strong."

Steve shrugged. "Our jhorun had a little help."

"From who?" Luther wanted to know.

Steve cleared his throat. "A sorceress by the name of Caladonia."

"Why would a sorceress be willing to help you?" Luther wondered aloud.

"Do you remember what you told us about the king?" Sarah suddenly asked.

"Aye. Kri'Calin had found a book about some prophecy and wanted to create a link to another world. What of it?"

"She's the one who made the prediction," Sarah answered. "Trust me, it's a long story. Look, I don't blame you for having a lot of questions. If I were in your shoes I'd want answers, too." Sarah was silent for a few moments as she thought of how to best explain their situation. "You said earlier that you were there when that interdimensional portal was created, right?"

Luther nodded. A look of puzzlement was written across his features.

Sarah took her husband's hand and smiled at Luther. "Let's just say that it worked."

"What worked? The portal? Obviously."

"No, the prophecy," Sarah corrected. "You've heard of the Nohrin?"

Luther nodded. "It was in the prophecy. The Nohrin are the off-world protectors responsible for protecting the future prince."

Steve spread his arms wide as if to say, *here we are!*

"You two? You're the protectors?"

Steve ignited his left hand and blasted a jet of fire at his right hand, which absorbed it upon impact. Both hands then snuffed out.

"Why else would our jhorun work here? It had to be strong enough to protect the prince regardless of where we were."

"Prince? What prince?"

"The young prince from our time," Sarah told him, deliberately omitting Mikal's name.

Luther shook his head in wonder. "If only the king were here now. He'd be ecstatic! My friends, he talked incessantly about you. Where were you from? What was your world like? When would you arrive? He wanted to know everything."

"I'm sorry to say he won't learn anything. At least, not in his lifetime," Steve said.

Luther sat down on the closest chair and gazed up at his descendant. "Simply incredible."

"What is?" AnnaBelle prompted.

"That the old fool was right about something."

"Who?" Steve asked. "Your king or Zevern, the wizard?"

Luther smiled. "Yes."

Steve smiled back. "Trust me, we were just as surprised to learn about our involvement in that prophecy as you were. It took a while before I was willing to believe. Anyway, what did the king say about us?"

"There wasn't a lot of information about the Nohrin," Luther admitted. "There was no clarification about who the Nohrin were, let alone what world they lived on. Besides, how were we supposed to contact another world? How were we supposed to search for the Nohrin if we didn't know what they looked like? Were they human? The king decided the only thing he could do to facilitate their arrival was figure out how our world could link to another. On and on, over and over, it's all he talked about. Quite frankly, I was sick to death of hearing about it."

"So your job, your *mission*, was to come here and set up a way for these Nohrin people to find their way to your world?" Cecil hesitantly asked.

Luther nodded sheepishly. "Aye, and because of my clumsiness, I failed. I allowed a sunbeam to fall upon the athe crystal."

"That's the crystal that powers the portal," Steve explained to Cecil and his wife. "It's very delicate. If the crystal is exposed to the sun, then it'll break apart."

"More like shatter," Luther agreed solemnly.

"How did you break the crystal?" Sarah asked. "Did you accidentally take it outside?"

Luther anxiously looked at Cora before he dropped his eyes back to the ground. Steve chuckled. "Out with it, grandpa. What did you do?"

"Don't call me grandpa."

"Sorry. Out with it, great-great-grandpa. Better?"

"Egads, no."

Sarah giggled.

"It doesn't really matter how it was broken," Steve decided as he raised an eyebrow at his ancestor. Both Luther and Cora blushed and then looked at each other when asked about that crystal. Clearly, they knew more than they were letting on. Was it possible that his great-great-grandparents had been horsing around with the crystal? Whatever the reason, this wasn't the time to pursue it. He'd have to inquire later. "The fact is, it's broken. There's no fixing it. You need another one. Therefore, we need to get to Lentari. Sarah and I can do it."

Luther shuffled uneasily from foot to foot.

"What's the matter?" Steve asked, annoyed. Luther's hesitation and his lack of excitement angered him. Why would Luther have a problem with going back to Lentari to get another crystal? Would that not complete his mission? Shouldn't he be happy? Grateful?

Sensing Steve's unspoken questions, Luther sighed. "If I go back to Lentari and tell them I mishandled the athe crystal and need another, what will they think? I don't want it known that my folly caused this predicament."

Steve shrugged. "The only reason you're here in Idaho is to link this world with Lentari, right? If you, or someone else, doesn't make it back to Lentari to get another then we–Sarah and I--will never make it to Lentari in the first place and all this will be for naught. Suck it up. Everyone needs help from time to time."

Sarah raised a hand. "I have a question. Let's assume you get the portal working upstairs. How is that supposed to help us get home? That portal is not designed to move us through time."

"No, but it will get you to Lentari," Luther pointed out.

"So what? I can get there without the portal."

"I understand, Miss Sarah," Luther patiently explained. "However, the portal must be fixed to assure your future will not be altered, but in order for you to *have* a future you must see if Zevern can create another interdimensional portal to return you home. To your own time."

"And if he can't?" Steve prompted.

Sarah's eyes teared up again. Luther gave them all a furtive smile. "Ask the king for another jorii. I will see if I can do anything from my end here."

Steve turned to Luther and raised an eyebrow. "What's that supposed to mean? What would you be able to do with it?"

"What's your jhorun?" Sarah asked. "Did you already tell us and I missed it?"

Luther smiled and shook his head. "You didn't miss it as I haven't revealed it. I am a gatekeeper."

"You're a gatekeeper?" Steve chuckled. "Are you sure you're not the key master?"

Sarah, standing directly on Steve's left, punched him on his arm. True to her deadly aim, Steve's arm tingled like crazy for a few moments. Steve gave his stinging arm a quick rub.

"Hit the funny bone on that one. Ouch. That smarts."

"You watch way too many movies, dear," Sarah informed him. "He's not going to have a clue what that means."

"Fine. Guilty as charged."

Their four companions stared uncertainly at them.

"It's a joke," Steve told them. "It's from ... forget it. Luther, what does a gatekeeper do?"

"I can take an unlinked portal and direct it to where it's supposed to go, without the aid of any instruments or machines. My jhorun is quite rare. Only a handful of gatekeepers have been known to exist. In fact, most of them were from my family."

Sarah nodded, comprehending. "That's why you're here. You can build this portal and link it back to Lentari."

Luther nodded affirmatively. "Correct. That's why I was perfect for this mission. They just had to get me here. I alone could link the portal back."

Cecil spoke up. "Does that mean you can take this portal you're building and —"

"Already *built*," Luther corrected.

"Very well, built. So you can take this portal that you've built, wave your hands at it, and it'll send them home?"

"I've never tried to modify a portal to move someone through time," Luther confessed. "That doesn't mean I can't try."

"Do you really think you can do it?" Sarah hopefully asked.

Luther shrugged and held up his hands. "I cannot make any promises, my friends. But I would definitely give it my best attempt, since I have a vested interest in getting you two home."

Steve whooped aloud, grabbed Sarah, and started twirling her around in a circle. "Now *that* is what I'm talking about! Yes! We have a plan. What do you need me to do? How can I help?"

Cecil cleared his throat. "Pardon me, but I have a question."

Caught up in Steve's contagious good mood, Luther slapped his friend on the shoulder and nodded. "Yes, Cecil. What's on your mind?"

Cecil turned to Steve and Sarah, still spinning around, and pointed at the two of them.

"If what they say is true, if what everyone says is true, should they get involved? Wouldn't they be jeopardizing their own existence if something went wrong?"

Steve stopped their spinning and turned to regard Cecil. "Way to rain on my parade, buddy."

Cecil gave a curt bow as a form of apology. He addressed Steve. "What I mean is, how can you be certain that what you're doing will not somehow be changing something back in your time? I mean forward in your time. I mean ... I don't know what I mean. Hopefully you do. Are you not afraid?"

"You're damn right I'm afraid," Steve answered. "We'd be fools not to be. Back in my time this would be called a damned-if-you-do-and-damned-if-you-don't situation. Do I want to mess with anything that could hurt Sarah or myself?

Absolutely not. But, if we don't get involved, our lack of action will undoubtedly cause a paradox."

Cecil blinked his eyes a few times. "A what?"

"A paradox. It's something that is made up of two opposite things, which seems impossible, but is actually true or possible. The easiest way to explain myself is to give you an example. Let's say I killed Luther right now. Thankfully, I won't, nor will I ever do that. But what would happen if I did? Think about that for a moment, Cecil. Tell me. What do you think would happen to me?"

Cecil considered. "If Luther died right now, he would obviously be unable to give any children to Cora, and therefore … you would be in trouble, friend Steve. I understand now."

"We are the only ones on this world who can help Luther complete his mission," Steve continued. "What he needs is simple. His portal needs a power source. The power crystal he needs is in Lentari. Ordinarily, he'd use his portal to get there; however, without the athe crystal to power the portal, it's pretty much useless. So, unless we step in to help, the portal will never work. And if that happens?"

Steve trailed off as he waited for Cecil to come to the same conclusion.

"If the portal remains powerless, then you'll never get to Lentari," Cecil slowly answered. He turned to look at Luther and his wife. "You're going to need their help."

Luther smiled and nodded. "I came to the same conclusion as you, my friend. Only I got there about fifteen minutes ago."

Cecil chuckled. "This is all very new to me. My experience with magic has been limited to stage shows and card tricks."

Steve held out a hand, as though he was greeting Cecil for the first time. When their hands were clasped together, Steve released his jhorun into his hand and held on as Cecil automatically flinched and tried to yank his hand out of Steve's flaming grip.

"Trust me," Steve told him. "You won't be harmed."

Cecil and AnnaBelle watched, amazed, as Steve's flames spread to Cecil's hand and flickered merrily over their clasped hands.

"Does it hurt?" AnnaBelle asked, staring as his two clenched hands. She frowned at Steve. "You'd better not harm him."

"Then tell him to stop trying to pull his hand free," Steve told her. "I can only prevent him from being burned provided he's in physical contact with me."

AnnaBelle turned back to Cecil and cuffed him on the back of his head.

"You heard him. Stop trying to pull your hand away. You'll get burned!"

With great reluctance, Cecil ceased his struggles.

"Feels like something is tickling your hand, doesn't it?" Steve commented as he rotated their hands this way and that to inspect for possible damage. Just as he expected, their hands were blemish free.

Steve finally extinguished his flames and released his grasp on Cecil's hand. Cecil yanked it away and held it up before his eyes for a close inspection. Satisfied he was unharmed, he silently regarded Steve for a few moments.

"Simply incredible. If I had that ability, my friend, I would use that power at every opportunity."

Steve sighed. "Ordinarily, I'd agree. However, I think I should keep the fires to a minimum. What would the people of Lentari think if all of a sudden a fire thrower appeared in their midst?"

Sarah took his hand. "Don't you remember what the king and queen said to us when we first met them?"

Steve thought a moment. "I think so. What part are you referring to?"

"Do you remember what the queen said when she found out you were a fire thrower?"

Steve slowly nodded. "Yeah, I do. She said there hadn't been another fire thrower for over a hundred years. So?"

"Honey, don't you see? I think she was talking about you!"

"You have no way of knowing that. She could have been talking about someone else."

"If that was true she would have said something about multiple fire throwers. No, she only mentioned one. Do you realize what this means?"

"No."

"It means," Sarah continued, "that you were meant to go to Lentari. Once there, you must have used your jhorun for some reason. Someone obviously noticed. Whatever that reason may be, it was noteworthy since it made it into their history books."

"You're saying we're supposed to do this."

"Not we," Sarah corrected. "*You.*"

"You're not going? How am I supposed to get where I need to go without you?"

Sarah shrugged. "The old-fashioned way, I guess."

"You mean I'd have to walk? That sucks! Are you sure you don't want to come with me?"

"I want to, but someone has to stay here."

"Why?" Steve demanded.

"Sheriff What's-his-name. We can't risk Luther or Cora. Someone has to protect them."

Steve looked over at his great-great-grandparents before fixing his wife with a stare. "Protection is my department, not yours."

Sarah nodded. "I'm aware; however, your jhorun is way more noticeable than mine."

"Meaning?"

"If it comes to it, and someone has to use their jhorun here, it'd better be me 'cause you'll freak people out."

"And you won't?"

"I can play the innocent damsel in distress pretty well. They'll never know I'm responsible for anything. We've both read up on Coeur d'Alene's history. We've been to the museum. Have you ever seen or read anything about a serial arsonist in the area?"

"I'm no serial arsonist, thank you very much."

"That's how the people would see you," Sarah told him.

"She's right," AnnaBelle added. "There's no one around here even remotely like you, Steve. If it becomes known you can control fire, then the townsfolk will turn on you."

Cecil scoffed loudly. "If that happens, I'll give you three guesses who'll be out at the front of the pack screaming for your head. However, you'll only need one."

Steve scowled. "The sheriff."

"Miss Sarah is right," Luther agreed. "If someone has to use their jhorun around here, it'd be best if it was an ability that wasn't easily noticeable."

"I really don't like separating like this," Sarah admitted as she took her husband's arm. "So many things could go wrong."

Steve patted her hand reassuringly. "Not as many as what could go wrong if we don't do this. Hey, I just thought of something. Have you tried going to Lentari since you made it here?"

Sarah shook her head no. "As soon as I saw what the year was, and realized the portal dropped me at a different time, I decided not to risk it. Besides, I wanted to make sure I was here when you came looking."

Steve smiled tenderly at his wife. "Based on everything we've seen, I'm very thankful I made it. Now, speaking of trips, how am I supposed to get back from Lentari? Without you, or a portal, I'm screwed."

"Don't be so melodramatic. We'll meet at a pre-arranged location at a specific time."

"What happens if I get into trouble? What if you do? What then? We're taking a hell of a chance separating like this."

Sarah nodded. "I know. It's risky; I don't like it either, but what choice have we? We can't leave them unprotected. I just don't like the idea that you'll be by yourself."

"He won't be," a new voice chimed in. "I'm going with him."

Everyone turned to look at Cecil, who was nervously clutching his bowler hat in his hands.

"I appreciate the support, pal," Steve began as he approached Luther's friend, "but we're talking about some rough territory here. This isn't going to be any picnic you're familiar with."

"I am not afraid," Cecil stoically declared. "I have a firearm."

"Which you've never used," AnnaBelle pointed out.

"And have never loaded," Luther added.

"Steve should not have to suffer that abominable land by himself."

"Abominable?" Luther repeated as he frowned. "Have a care how you speak about my homeland. It is a wonderful place to live."

"He's right," Steve added. "I've been to Lentari many times."

Cecil visibly relaxed and offered a smile.

"Don't you remember how scared we were the first time we saw those two griffins in person?" Sarah asked with a mischievous twinkle in her eye.

"What are griffins?" Cecil wanted to know.

Steve gave Cecil's shoulder a reassuring pat. "Mythological creatures with the body of a lion and the head, wings, and forelegs of an eagle. They are a wonder to behold, that's for sure."

"Mythological monsters?" AnnaBelle repeated. Horrified, she looked at Cora. "Is this true?"

"Luther has told me about them before. Apparently, they are noble creatures. Luther is fascinated with them. I personally wouldn't want to come face to face with one."

"You're not helping," Cecil accused.

Steve grinned. "It could be worse."

Cecil moaned. "I sincerely doubt it."

"You could run into a dragon."

"A dragon? As in fire breathing, heavily scaled, and you need to be a knight in shining armor in order to survive?"

Steve shook his head. "That's where the fairy tales got it wrong. I don't care how much armor you've got on. There's no way a single human, armed with only a sword, would ever be able to successfully take on a dragon. Not only could the dragon simply melt the armor right off you, but they wouldn't have to. They're so big that they could simply step on you and squish you flat."

Cecil's face had turned ashen white.

Sarah gave Steve a disapproving look before smiling at Cecil.

"Don't worry. The chances of running into a dragon there are slim to none. They stick to the northern mountains and will rarely venture south."

The color had yet to return to Cecil's face. "That's not very reassuring."

Steve clapped his hands together and vigorously rubbed them together. "So! Sounds like a blast, doesn't it? When are we going? Now?"

"The sooner you go, the sooner you can come back," Sarah agreed.

"Where are you going to drop us?" Steve asked as he started going through his pockets in search for anything he didn't want to risk losing in Lentari. As it turned out, the Lentarian trousers he was wearing didn't have any pockets, nor did his tunic. A quick pat down revealed only one extra item.

Sarah, observing her husband fumble with something behind his back, approached Steve from behind and gingerly prodded his back. Feeling the small club sitting in its holder she quizzically turned to her husband and raised an eyebrow.

"What is that? Is it the Nohrstaf? What prompted you to bring that?"

Steve shrugged. "I can't say. I don't use it that much and thought it might come in handy."

"What is a norestaff?" Luther asked.

Steve reached behind his back and slid a hand under his shirt. He tugged the small club free. He held the unremarkable weapon out to Luther and waited for him to take it.

"This is a special weapon that I was given by Sh … by the wizard from our time. It is capable of assuming the form of most weapons, but only when the situation calls for it. The problem is, my definition of pertinent and its definition of pertinent are clearly not the same."

"It's temperamental," Sarah translated, causing Cora and AnnaBelle to giggle with laughter.

"I'll go retrieve my firearm so that we may leave straight away," Cecil told the group.

Steve hooked his arm through Cecil's as he was passing by. "Don't bother, Cecil. Most creatures that call Lentari home would not be stopped by a single bullet. The only thing you'll end up doing is severely annoying whatever it is you're shooting at."

"You're suggesting I don't bring my firearm?"

"Remember the description of the dragon? We weren't kidding. Those dragons are huge. A simple gun is not going to do anything against them. I would be nothing more than a bug to them. The best thing is avoid them."

"But you can generate fire out of your hands! Could you not hold off a dragon?"

Steve shook his head no. "I wouldn't stand a chance. A dragon's flames get much hotter, so my jhorun is no help there."

Cecil swallowed nervously at the same time Steve grinned. "Sure you don't want to stay here?"

Cecil shook his head. "I told you I'd accompany you. I will not back down now."

"You may want to reconsider when you realize where you have to go," Sarah informed him.

If possible, Cecil paled even further. "What do you mean?"

Curiosity piqued, Steve also turned to Sarah.

"What do you mean? There are no dragons in R'Tal."

"You're not going to R'Tal, are you?"

Steve blinked with surprise. "If we're not going to R'Tal, then where are we going?"

"Who do you think has the athe crystal you need?" Sarah asked, adopting a tone she would have used to address a group of school children.

Comprehension dawned. Steve's eyes widened. Cecil saw Steve's expression and fidgeted uneasily from foot to foot.

Sarah nodded. "That's right. The dwarves. We have to get you to the dwarves. I can't take you all the way down there. They don't know you. Yet. So it'll have to be the valley."

"That's gonna be a problem," Steve muttered darkly.

"Why?" Cecil demanded. "Why is that a problem? A valley sounds nice."

"Not when it's in the heart of dragon territory," Steve informed him. "Way up in the Bohanis."

"Bohanis?"

"The northern mountains."

"But … but … Isn't that where you said we shouldn't go?"

Luther whistled. "Most of the dragons live around Lake Raehón, up north. You're talking about the valley that lies just to the south of the lake, right?"

Steve nodded. "Yes. In our time it'd be no problem at all 'cause we're friends with the dragons."

Luther's mouth gaped open. "You are?"

"Yes. We're even good friends with the Dragon Lord, if you can believe that. The problem is, that's in our time. At present, no dragon knows us nor will they think twice about attacking. Humans and dragons aren't typically a good mix, especially when they aren't allies. Yet."

All color drained out of Cecil's face. "And this is where we have to go?"

Steve nodded again. "No one ever said this was going to be easy." He gave Cecil a speculative look. "Last chance to back out."

Cecil gave a quick shake of his head. "No, I am still going."

Resigned to visiting the Lentari of the past, with a complete Lentarian newbie in tow, Steve turned to Sarah.

"Alright, hon, there's no time like the present. No pun intended. Let's get going."

AnnaBelle tearfully embraced her husband and whispered something in his ear. Cecil nodded. He took off his overcoat and handed it, along with his bowler hat, to AnnaBelle.

"Keep them safe for me. We'll be back as soon as we can."

* * *

"There are so many things that can go wrong with a stunt like this," Steve murmured softly to Sarah as he held her tightly. "What if something delays us and we can't make it back here within two days? What if…" He trailed off as sounds of someone retching could be heard from the other side of a clump of bushes.

Husband and wife turned to the large group of bright

green leafy plants. Cecil was down on his knees, hunched over close to the ground, and politely offering the shrubs some fertilizer. Steve crossed his arms over his chest, while Sarah clasped her hands together in front of her. She cleared her throat.

"Cecil? Are you okay?"

The retching paused. "Give me a minute, will you?"

"Take your time, pal," Steve called out. "I guess I should have warned you that Sarah's teleportation jumps can cause quite a jolt to the system. Trust me, it'll pass."

Wiping a sleeve across his mouth as he stood up, Cecil gave them a weak smile. "I have never experienced anything of the like before, and I would rest easy knowing I never have to experience it again."

Steve looked around. They were standing in a clearing where a section of the forest met the mountains. A veritable wall of rocks was directly south, signifying the base of a nearby mountain. Falling from the heights above was a steady waterfall, which landed in a pond at the base of the rock cliffs. Excess water flowed east as a small river.

"It's very picturesque," Cecil commented.

"This is a known watering hole," Steve told him. "This is where we saw our first griffin. Scared the hell out of us."

"Is the castle nearby?" Cecil wondered, as he noticed all the nearby trees.

Steve and Sarah both cocked their heads at him as though they had just heard a high-pitched sound

"Do you see any castles around here?" Steve asked incredulously.

Cecil's cheeks reddened. "Well, no, but… Why are we here then?"

Steve turned back to Sarah. "Good question. Why are we here?"

"This is the easiest safe zone to visualize," Sarah explained. "What I'm used to in my time doesn't exist here."

"You couldn't picture anything else?"

"Not a single thing," Sarah confessed. "I won't bore you with details, so trust me when I say it's more complicated than that. The waterfall still looks the same to me. I think that's why it worked."

Understanding, Steve nodded. "So that explains why you couldn't picture the villages. They've probably changed in appearance, too."

"Right. I decided to try a more generic location. The first place I thought of was here, at this waterfall. Surprise, surprise, it worked."

"And now that we're in Lentari? Are you able to move us around or do we need to hoof it?"

Sarah went quiet and closed her eyes. She nodded.

"Whatever was blocking me from our world is no longer at work here. Maybe my jhorun needed some time to acclimate? I don't know. Yes, I can take us to just outside one of the gates. Perhaps the landscape there hasn't changed much? Who knows. Will that do?"

"Perfect."

"Are you sure you don't want me to take you north? I realize you have recently changed your mind but I still do think that you should be talking to the dwarves first and not the king."

"Professional courtesy. This is his kingdom. Do you really think we can show up at the dwarves' home and ask for the one type of crystal that can power a portal? I guarantee you they will notify the king. It would be best to inform the king first."

"Okay, it's your call. Here we go."

Cecil moaned aloud. "Oh, lord, no. Not another—"

His protest was cut off as Sarah teleported the three of them over a hundred leagues northeast. Once the dizziness passed, and Cecil had finished groaning on the ground, Steve straightened and saw that they had been deposited just outside the west gate of Lentari's capital city. The turrets and towers of the castle, home to the king and queen, stood on a gentle sloping hill, visible above the rest of the city. Steve nudged Cecil and pointed.

"That's where we're headed. The king and queen should be there."

"What if they ask us what our business here is?" Cecil wanted to know.

"It'll be no problem," Steve assured his friend. He turned to look back at Sarah, who was nervously clasping her hands together.

"If you're not back at the waterfall, our backup will be right here at the gate," Sarah told him. "Be at one of those two spots in two days' time." She hugged him tightly. "Be safe, okay? I don't want anything happening to you. To either of you two, for that matter. Agreed?"

Steve smiled. "Agreed. Do you have any idea what you're going to do if the sheriff tries to retaliate?"

"I've been thinking about it. The answer would be yes. I do have an idea."

"Care to share the details with me?"

"Let's just say that I think I have a way to ensure no one, especially the sheriff, will ever bother Luther and Cora again."

"Oh? Now I am really curious. What's your idea?"

Sarah smiled and blew him a kiss.

"I'll tell you all about it when you get back."

"You tease. Fine. Just promise me you'll stay safe, okay?"

"I will."

They embraced a final time. Sarah stepped back and smiled at the two of them. "I'll be back here in two days," Sarah told them. "Let's say by sunset?"

Steve automatically looked at his left wrist. He hadn't worn a watch for years but apparently the habit was hard to break.

"We'll be back at the waterfall in two days," Steve vowed. "Or here, at the edge of the West Gate by sunset."

Sarah blew him a kiss. "Miss me!"

Steve nodded. "Always."

Sarah vanished. Steve and Cecil looked at each other.

"What now?" Cecil wanted to know.

Steve pointed at the distant castle. "We go that way. The sooner we check in with the king, the sooner he'll give us his blessing to get another athe crystal."

"And if he doesn't?"

"We'll cross that bridge when we come to it."

Steve strode confidently over the drawbridge, gesturing for Cecil to follow.

"Let me do the talking," Steve called back to him as Cecil hurried to catch up. Steve nudged Cecil's shoulder with his own and nodded toward the two guards leaning languidly against the stone wall of the castle's keep. Both men were more involved with their own argument than in keeping an eye on the foot traffic crossing the drawbridge.

Steve kept watching as they crossed into the city, surprised that the soldiers weren't at least asking them the nature of their business. As the two of them slowly made their way across the wooden drawbridge and passed under the heavy iron portcullis, a family of six noisily pushed by them and made their way into the city. The father was unsuccessfully trying to stop two of the older boys from squabbling, while the mother held a crying toddler on her hip, all the while dragging a petulant looking four-year-old behind her.

A merchant pushing a cart full of purple fruit passed them next. The two-wheeled cart, with wide wooden wheels, clattered noisily past as the villager disappeared into the milling throngs of people.

The guards, Steve noted, hadn't even bothered to look up.

"You made this sound like it'd be difficult to get inside the castle," Cecil whispered.

"It usually is. If we were back in my time, we'd never have made it across without someone asking us who we were or what we were doing. Well, that's not exactly true. Most everyone knows me there so we still wouldn't have been bothered. But you, on the other hand, would have been stopped."

Steve led Cecil down the busy streets, steering him away from dozens of eager vendors looking to make a sale. He had to pull Cecil away from a cart that was piled high with linens of all styles and colors.

"Oh, AnnaBelle would love some of these," Cecil remarked more to himself than anyone. "Imagine the clothes she could make if only she had—"

Steve appeared at his side and pulled him gently, but firmly, away. Cecil looked longingly back at the colorful fabrics.

"We should make a point of coming back here so I can select a few fabrics for AnnaBelle."

Steve eyed his friend with a stern expression. "Really? With all that is going on right now, including leaving your wife and mine unprotected, you want to go clothes shopping? Dude, we need to work on your priorities."

"I thought you said Sarah can take care of herself," Cecil complained, as he cast one last furtive look behind him. The vendor was still standing in the middle of the street, waving several examples of his wares back and forth.

"She can, yes, but do you think that makes me feel better? We need to get this damn crystal and get home as soon as possible."

"How difficult do you think this will be?" Cecil asked yet again.

"As I told you before, it all depends on the dwarves. We may get lucky and the king will tell us he has a spare crystal here in the castle that he'd be willing to let us have."

"Or we could be thrown in the dungeon," Cecil whispered, remembering Steve's uplifting suggestion on possible outcomes after they met the king.

Steve grinned and shook his head. "Trust me, we have nothing to worry about. Let me do the talking."

Thirty minutes later the two of them were standing in front of the castle drawbridge and eyeing the four fully armed guards who were standing stiffly at attention. All four of the soldiers had spotted the two foreigners and were warily eyeing them back. Their armor had been polished to a mirror shine, causing spots to dance before his eyes whenever Steve looked their way.

"Come on, follow my lead."

Steve strode confidently across the wooden planks of the open drawbridge. They hadn't quite made it halfway across when the first guard stepped into their path.

"Halt. State your business."

"Hey there," Steve said jovially. "We're on our way to see if we can get an audience with the king."

"Peasants are not allowed to address the king until next week. Return then."

Steve held his ground. "I have an important matter I need to discuss with him. Trust me, he'll want to hear what I have to say."

Two more guards flanked the first. The soldier addressing him dropped his right hand down to let it rest on the hilt of his sword. "Be gone. You will not be pestering his majesty with trivial matters today."

Cecil shrugged and started to turn around. Steve caught his arm and held him in place. "Look, pal," Steve said, growing angry, "we have come a very long way to see your king."

"A very long way," Cecil repeated in a rather high-pitched voice.

Steve shot him a concerned look and pressed on. "Can you at least take a message to him? You'll see that I'm not making this up."

The final guard, one that was easily half a foot taller than Steve and full of muscles, joined his companions.

"Be off, peasant," the soldier rumbled. "You heard him. This isn't the day his majesty hears from the villagers. Return next week. Off you go now."

Steve crossed his arms over his chest and returned the huge guard's patronizing stare.

"Off you go? Do I look like I'm five years old? You know what? We're wasting time." Steve walked over to the side of the drawbridge and looked down at the murky moat water. "Is Bredo in there yet?"

"What was that?" the burly guard asked, confused.

"What was that?" Cecil echoed. "Did you ask if there was a burrito in the moat?"

"Bredo is the name of the moat monster from my time," Steve answered, in a low voice. He turned to look back at the four guards standing abreast before him. "Are there any monsters in there?"

The big guard shook his head no. "It's not a bad idea," he admitted. "It would be a great deterrent to keep pipsqueaks like you away from the castle."

"How deep is it?"

The first guard scoffed loudly. "Wouldn't you like to know?"

Cecil again tried to run. Steve sidestepped to his left and blocked his retreat.

"Okay, guys, I'm sorry to do this to you. Just remember that we asked nicely first."

Thinking they were about to be ambushed, all four guards drew their swords. And then dropped them. Cursing and madly shaking their hands through the air as though they had just grabbed the handle of a hot frying pan, the men stared at their fallen swords in shock. The hilts were *glowing*!

"How the ruddy hell did you do that?" the first soldier demanded. He reached for a crossbow hanging from a nearby rack of weapons.

Steve instantly clenched his fists and sent out an order to his jhorun. Before the soldier had taken more than a few steps toward the weapon rack, all four men shouted with alarm and started the most ridiculous strip tease Steve had ever seen.

"Get it off me!" one man screamed, as he frantically pawed at his armor. "It's burning me up!"

Since strapping a person into a suit of armor can be time consuming, and obviously the process to remove oneself from said armor can be just as time consuming, two of the guards elected to dive headfirst into the green algae infested water encircling the castle. The guard who could give a certain barbarian from Cimmeria a run for his money managed to pull off his gauntlets and one greave by brute force alone, but ended up splashing into the moat as well.

A few seconds later, the final guard gave up trying to get his armor off and joined his companions in the moat. There was a chorus of "Aaaahs" as the dirty water cooled the hot metal. Thankfully the moat wasn't that deep as each man had sunk into the mud of the moat's floor and was now up to his chest in the filthy water. Four sets of eyes glared angrily at him.

Steve shrugged. "I tried to warn you. For what it's worth, I am sorry."

Steve pulled Cecil across the drawbridge and vanished into the castle interior.

"What are you going to do when those men make it out of the water?" Cecil wanted to know.

"By that time, we should have found the king," Steve told him as they came to a junction in the hall. "Okay, to the left is the Great Hall. That's where the king should be. Stay close to me. If a pyrotechnical demonstration is necessary, the last thing I want to have to worry about is you."

"If a *what* is necessary?"

Steve mentally rolled his eyes. "If I have to play with fire," he translated.

Cecil nodded. "Got it. If the fire comes out, stick close to you."

Steve pushed the double doors open and stepped into the Great Hall. Right away he noticed the layout of the royal reception room was different than he remembered. In his time, the two golden thrones were against the eastern wall, with tables and chairs arranged in the center of the room, much like a conference room.

In this time, however, the thrones were nothing more than ornately carved wooden chairs, and they were along the northern wall of the large chamber. Something else was different. With a start, Steve realized what it was. The light. The room was dim. There were few windows for such a large area, and those were nothing more than narrow slots that ran horizontally for a few feet. Steve imagined they were a throwback to the days when the castle had to be defended on a daily basis. It'd be perfect for archers or soldiers with crossbows.

Steve turned his attention back to the darkened room and took a few steps in. The king was there, and he was looking bored out of his skull as some castle noble was regaling him with a tale of woe about something or other. Physically, the king looked to be younger than Steve. However, as was usually the case when a single person carried the responsibility of so much on their shoulders, the king had a thick mop of premature gray hair atop his head.

"Halt!" a voice shouted. "Intruders! Stay where you are!"

Steve and Cecil whirled to see four soldiers running toward them, trailing water and green sludge out of the chinks of their armor.

They might as well have smacked the side of a bee hive,

Steve thought angrily. The Great Hall exploded with activity. Steady streams of soldiers poured out of nearby doors. A wall of men sprang into existence all around the thrones, as the safety of the king must have been drilled into each and every soldier present. Those who weren't guarding the king drew their swords and advanced angrily on the two of them.

Steve glanced over at the king but was unable to see him anymore as there were too many people between them. Hoping that the king could somehow see him, or someone was describing what was happening, Steve raised a hand up into the air and gave a smile in the king's general direction.

"Pardon me, Your Majesty," he called out in his loudest voice. "Please, I need to talk to you. Hang on a sec."

He didn't know how he knew it but Steve was sure the king's eyebrows had just shot up in surprise.

Steve turned to the dozens of soldiers flanking them on all sides. He smiled. All were wearing armor. Steve cracked his knuckles and elbowed Cecil in the ribs.

"Here we go. Watch this."

The shouts and the dancing began. Soldiers began hopping around on one foot, then the other, as various implements began heating up. The dancing became frantic. Pieces of armor were flung off and tossed across the room. Swords, daggers, axes, and an assortment of other weaponry fell unceremoniously to the floor as they were abandoned by their owners.

"Enough of this."

Thinking the king had addressed him, Steve turned to face the thrones but his attention was drawn to a single guard walking toward him. Slightly shorter than he was, the guard had shoulder length jet black hair with streaks of gray visible on the sides of his head. From the way he was holding himself, Steve figured he had to be an officer. In deference to his status, he instructed his jhorun to leave this soldier alone. Besides, he was decked out in leather armor, not plate.

"What spell have you put on my men?" the guard demanded.

Steve crossed his arms over his chest. "There's no spell. Who are you?"

"Sauer, Captain of the Royal Guards. You want to speak to the king?" Sauer swept his arm around to indicate his men. "Convince me of your peaceful intentions. Cease this frivolous nonsense."

"How do you know I'm peaceful?" Steve wanted to know.

"If you had wanted to harm the king then you would have. Who are you? What do you want?"

Steve instructed his jhorun to stop heating the guards' armor.

"I don't know how much I can tell you," Steve confessed. "Can you get me a piece of paper and a pen? If you'd be so kind as to deliver a message for me, I believe I can put your mind at ease."

"Do I look like a messenger to you?" Captain Sauer demanded.

"Tell you what. If the king doesn't want to talk to me then, fine, we'll leave."

Captain Sauer motioned to a nearby court page and told the young man what he wanted. Once the paper and pen had been retrieved, the captain pushed the items into Steve's hands.

"This had better be good, peasant," the captain growled.

Steve took the paper and began to write. "First of all, I'm no peasant."

Unconvinced, Sauer remained motionless. "I haven't seen you before. You're no noble."

Steve wrote one sentence on the paper and then folded it in half. He handed it to the captain. Sauer looked at the folded parchment and unfolded it to see for himself what was so important. The captain quickly looked up. Without saying another word, he headed straight toward the knot of soldiers guarding the king. Thanks to the gap that had formed as Sauer pushed his way through, Steve was able to see the captain and the king. Steve watched as Sauer handed the king the paper.

The king pulled a pair of spectacles from one of his pockets and perched them on his nose. He peered at the paper and gasped so loudly that even Steve and Cecil heard him. The king's eyes shot over to Steve's and stayed there, as though the king were trying to bore holes into him. The king finally shifted his gaze to Sauer's and mouthed a word. Sauer nodded. He returned to Steve's side and gestured toward an open door to their right.

"Let's go. He wants to see you in—"

"The Antechamber," Steve cut in. "I know. I saw him."

"You know about the Antechamber, too?"

"Yep."

"How?"

"I'll be telling you shortly."

Once they were inside the room especially created to repel all but the strongest of jhorun, and the guards and servants were ushered out, the king turned to him. He held the paper up questioningly.

"Explain this."

Cecil looked at the paper and finally saw what Steve had written on the paper:

Luther needs help or his mission will fail.

Steve gave a subtle nod of his head in the king's direction. "Kri'Calin, I presume?"

"How do you know me?" the king demanded. "I have never set eyes upon you before."

Steve took a breath. "My name is Steve. This is Cecil. We're from the world you sent Luther to. His original athe crystal broke and he needs another."

The king gasped aloud at the same time captain Sauer's mouth dropped open. Kri'Calin suddenly frowned.

"Wait a moment. That's impossible. According to you, Luther needs another athe crystal. That means his portal is powerless. How do you expect us to believe you are who you say you are? How did you get here if you didn't use Luther's portal?"

Steve nervously cleared his throat. "You picked up on that amazingly fast. I, er, hmmm. This is harder than I thought."

"Out with it," Sauer barked. "We've been more than accommodating with you. How did you get here?"

"My wife brought us. She's a teleporter and is strong

enough to make the journey from our home to here, without a portal."

"Impossible," Kri'Calin breathed.

"Is it? Refresh my memory. What did your prophecy say?"

"The prophecy? What does that have to do with…" The king trailed off as he stared at Steve. His eyes widened even further. "Wizards be damned. I think I know who you are."

In response, Steve held up both hands and blasted a jet of fire from his left hand and absorbed it with his right. Sauer leapt backward with a cry of alarm. Cecil, on the other hand, leapt forward to encompass him in a bone-crushing bear hug from behind. Thrown off balance, Steve stumbled forward and toppled to the ground.

The absurdity of the situation struck and Steve burst out laughing. "Man, this is wrong on so many levels. Cecil, get off me."

"You said that if the flames came out then I should get close."

"I did say that, didn't I? Okay, clearly that was a poor choice of words."

Sauer pulled Cecil to his feet but was hesitant about offering an arm up to Steve.

"My flames are out," Steve grumbled as he rolled to his feet.

Kri'Calin made it to his side first. He looked as excited as a school boy that had been told there wouldn't be classes today.

"By the Wizards, you are one of the Nohrin!"

Chapter 7 — Persona Non Grata

I am sorry I ever doubted you, Your Majesty," Sauer was saying. Again. "Not only did I think that Luther's mission was a long shot, I never dreamt he'd be successful so soon."

"So soon?" Steve interrupted as he frowned. "He's been gone for several years! If you consider that to be a short mission then I'd hate to see what is classified as 'long'."

Captain Sauer and the king both shook their heads.

"You are mistaken," Sauer told him. "He left almost two fortnights ago."

It was Steve's turn to shake his head. "You might want to check your facts. He's been in Idaho now for over three years."

"The facts are," Sauer angrily shot back, "that Luther was here last month, finalizing plans for his journey. That's when we traded with the dwarves for that blasted crystal."

"Last month?" Steve repeated, frowning. He turned to Cecil. "How is that possible?"

"I would imagine it has something to do with you standing

beside me right now," Cecil quietly answered.

Steve looked up. "Where's this Zevern character? I have a few choice words for him."

"What does our wizard have to do with this?" Kri'Calin demanded, instantly growing defensive. "We are fortunate to have a man of his talents at our disposal."

"His talents are what have gotten this whole situation so mucked up in the first place," Steve countered.

"Mucked? I'm not familiar with that word."

"Zevern created a portal that dropped Luther off in my world," Steve explained. "Since he's a gatekeeper, he'll be able to modify the portal he built so that it will link up with your portal here, in R'Tal. That was the plan, right?"

Monarch and soldier nodded.

"Well, the portal Zevern created jumped Luther not only to my world but backwards in time. I kid you not, he's been there a while now. He had pretty much given up hope of ever completing his mission until Sarah and I showed up."

"Who's Sarah?" Kri'Calin interrupted.

"My wife."

"What do you mean 'showed up'?" Sauer asked.

Steve took a breath. "That same portal, which Luther said should have dissipated not long after its first use, remained active. It was still active in my time. Villagers have been stumbling through it for years. My wife fell in and I went in after her."

"Zevern assured me that the portal would collapse in only a matter of minutes," Kri'Calin insisted. "How long has it lasted? What time are you from?"

Steve bit his lip and tried to look serious for a few moments. He glanced over at Cecil before taking a deep breath. "If I tell you that, you two have to promise me that it stays here in this room. No one else can know where I'm from. And that goes for Cecil, too. Is that understood?"

The king frowned. "I am unaccustomed to being given orders by mere peasants."

"I am no peasant," Steve informed him. "Don't you get it? Neither of us are. We're not even Lentarian!"

Kri'Calin sighed and rubbed his temples. He took his seat

behind his desk and took off his crown. He stared at the two of them. "When is your time? Tell me. Please."

"About a hundred twenty years from now."

The king's eyebrows jumped straight up. Steve was certain that if the king had still been wearing his crown, his eyebrows would have knocked it completely off his head.

"One hundred twenty years! But that means…"

"That you will not live to see the prophecy fulfilled," Steve finished for him. "Your Majesty, consider this a second chance. If we weren't here, you'd always wonder if Caladonia's prophecy would come true. Trust me, it has. I'm living proof."

The king was silent as he digested this.

"Can we count on your help, Your Majesty? Do you see the problem we have? If we don't get an athe crystal back to Luther, his portal will never be completed. If it's never completed, I'll never get around to using it back in my time."

Captain Sauer gave an exaggerated shake of his head and scoffed loudly. "What you say cannot possibly be true. Your Majesty, he's jesting. He must. What he suggests simply isn't possible."

"Tell him about the Nohrin, Your Majesty," Steve suggested. "I'll be more than happy to give him a full demo of my jhorun."

Sauer turned quizzically to the king. "I've heard you say that word a few times now, Your Majesty. Nohrin. Can you tell me what it is?"

"According to the prophecy, the Nohrin are the bodyguards of the future prince," Kri'Calin answered. "It was prophesied that the Nohrin will be non-Lentarians yet will have powerful wizard-class jhorun. One will have power over an elemental and the other will be just as powerful, but more cunning."

Steve ignited three chasers and juggled them in the air. "Got any other fire throwers around here?" Steve asked as he caught the flaming spheres and tossed them back into the air.

"Can you juggle four?" Kri'Calin suddenly asked.

The fireballs all poofed out.

"Why isn't three good enough?" Steve grumped. "No one ever says 'hey, that's pretty good!' It's always 'can you juggle more?' I'd like to see you juggle three."

The king gave him a good-natured smile. "You sound just like our jester."

Cecil clapped a hand over his mouth to prevent himself from snorting with laughter.

"And your wife?" the king continued. "What is her jhorun, if I may ask?"

"I already told you. She's a teleporter. She's the one who brought us here."

"Simply incredible. I cannot even begin to imagine how powerful her jhorun must be if she can teleport across worlds."

Steve nodded. "Yes. She's amazing, that's for sure. Look, are we done proving ourselves? Can we get down to business now? What about that athe crystal? The sooner we get it the sooner I can meet…"

Steve trailed off as he realized the last thing he wanted to do was reveal he needed to meet Sarah at their prearranged spot. He was pretty sure he could trust the king but the captain, true to his name, was a sourpuss who rubbed him the wrong way.

"That's not going to be easy," Kri'Calin began. He caught sight of Sauer's darkened expression and frowned. "Enhance your calm, Captain. They are no threat. In fact, they are helping one of your soldiers complete his mission."

Captain Sauer's suspicious expression slowly melted into a look devoid of any emotion. Steve didn't know which face he liked better.

"Now," the king continued, turning his attention to the items on his desk. He selected a sheet of parchment and uncorked a bottle of ink. "I will notify the Kla Guur and the Kla Chanus. One of them should have an extra crystal or should be able to mine one for us. I'm not sure what they'll want in exchange for it, so assure them that I will honor whatever they demand."

Steve groaned. "We have to wait until we can contact the dwarves? How long is that gonna take? I don't think we have the time for them to mine another crystal."

"Do you have somewhere else to be?" Sauer asked in a

clipped monotone.

"As a matter of fact, we do," Cecil announced before Steve could shush him.

The king leveled a stern gaze at the two of them. "If you want our help, you must be honest with us."

The two Idaho residents eyed each other. Steve cleared his throat. "Fine. I'll tell you the truth, but I ask again for your assurance that nothing leaves this room. That includes Mr. Sourpuss here."

"My name is Sauer."

The king's lips quivered. "You have it."

"We have two days," Steve told the king. "Only two days to get the crystal and get back to our rendezvous point so that my wife can take us back to our world."

"Two days?" the king repeated incredulously. "It will take nearly a week just to make it up to Lake Raehón and back, not accounting for the time it will take to locate the dwarves and ask them to open negotiations to trade for another suitable crystal."

"The success of your mission is speed," Sauer told them. At least it sounded as though his attitude was improving somewhat. "You need more time. Could you not arrange to delay your departure?"

"How?" Steve demanded, at the exact time the king asked the same question.

"How, exactly?" Kri'Calin asked.

Sauer shrugged. "I'm trying to tell you that a journey to the valley, even on our fastest horse, wouldn't make it in time."

"You should have given yourself at least a week, if not a fortnight," Kri'Calin thoughtfully observed.

"I didn't want to leave my wife unprotected for that long," Steve informed them.

Captain Sauer cleared his throat. "She is a teleporter, correct? Could she not get herself to safety?"

"Yeah, she can. However, she can't leave the area."

"Why?" Sauer wanted to know.

"She's looking after Luther and his wife."

Both king and captain were rendered speechless. Steve nodded.

"That's right. Luther found a wife. I would imagine that since he thought he wouldn't be able to complete his quest, he'd be forced to live the remainder of his life there in my world. It must have been lonely for him. I can assure you he met a wonderful lady."

The king stared at Steve for a few moments longer before he leaned back in his chair. "I sense there's something else you're not telling us."

Steve nodded again. "There is. You did catch the part about me coming from over a hundred years in the future?"

The king nodded.

"Well, there's a reason my wife and I found that portal and went through it. We inherited that house from my relatives."

"Your relatives," Captain Sauer repeated. His eyes widened with comprehension. "You're his kin, aren't you?"

"I am, yes."

Both of the Lentarians were silent as they studied Steve's appearance.

"Aye, I can see the resemblance," the king muttered. "He has the same eyes and nose."

"And mannerisms," Sauer added.

Steve frowned. "Is that a good thing or a bad thing?"

Ignoring him, the king turned to his captain. "We need to get these two north as quickly as possible. I will authorize your use of the castle portal to Verdayn. From there, it will be several hours' walk to the southern edge of the valley. That's the best we can do, I'm afraid."

"It beats walking several days straight," Steve gratefully told the king. "We'll take it. And thanks. For everything. Oh, I forgot to mention something."

"Oh? What's that?"

Steve turned to captain Sauer. "Would you apologize to your guards for me? I really don't like causing anyone pain. I'm sorry I heated up their armor."

Sauer dismissed Steve's apology with a wave of his hand. "Think nothing of it."

"And those guards? By the west gate?"

"What of them?"

"Tell them to ask a few more questions before letting

people through the gate."

"What manner of questions did they ask when you came across?"

"They didn't."

The captain's face darkened. "I'll take care of it."

The king rose from his place behind his desk. "Good luck, Nohrin. I am honored to have met you. Captain, escort our guests to the portal room and see to it they make it safely to Verdayn."

The captain bowed.

* * *

Several hours later, Steve and Cecil found themselves sitting wearily on an overturned log, looking north. Steve removed the stopper on his bota bag and took a long draught. He nudged Cecil and passed him it to him. Steve pointed north, through the trees, at the open valley floor not twenty feet away.

"Do you see those large boulders that are several miles away?"

Cecil rose to his feet and cautiously approached the edge of the forest. He stopped short of exiting the safety of the trees and held a hand over his eyes. "Yes."

"One of those is the door leading down to the dwarves. We just have to make it out that far."

Cecil brushed by him and strode confidently out into the bright sunlight. "Then there's no time to lose. Let us be off."

Steve grabbed Cecil by the arm and gave him a violent yank back inside the quiet forest.

"Okay, just because you don't see any dragons doesn't mean there aren't any nearby. The last time I made this trip we were guided by an actual dragon and even he warned us that hostile dragons were nearby."

"So how are we going to make it?"

Steve sighed. "Ordinarily I'd say we should just run for it. However, the dragons fly quicker than we can run. By a long shot. They spit fire hotter than I can absorb, and they are so large and powerful that they can hammer us into the ground like railroad spikes."

Cecil gave a hollow laugh. "Might you have any good news to impart?"

"Not really."

"Can you run, Steve?"

"With a dragon on my tail, I'm pretty sure I could run across water."

"Then do try to keep up."

"Excuse me?"

Cecil broke free of Steve's grip and ran out across the valley floor.

"Cecil! Get back here! Cecil!"

Resigned to a lung-bursting sprint across the valley floor, Steve tore off after his companion. Twelve minutes later, gasping, wheezing, and clutching a painful stitch in his side, Steve smiled to himself. The large boulders were close. They had finally caught a break and Cecil had been right. There were no dragons nearby. What luck!

Movement out of his peripheral vision had him veering slightly off course to see around Cecil's running body. One of the piles of boulders had started shimmering and changing shape. Whether Cecil had detected movement and had unwisely decided to run toward it, Steve didn't know, but what he did know was that Cecil was in for a reality check that was clearly wyverian in nature.

A long sinewy tail seemed to materialize out of thin air and placed itself directly in Cecil's path. Cecil, already winded and gasping for breath, collided with the tail and was knocked backward by nearly a dozen feet. Low growls sounded as the heavily scaled black tail continued to extend. More shimmers appeared and the bulk of the dragon's massive body materialized. The dragon growled again as it thumped its stinging tail against the ground.

The majestic jet-black dragon lifted its enormous head off the ground and surveyed the area. Twin silver orbs peered intently at the surrounding countryside, as it was evidently searching for whatever had crashed into it. Thankfully, the grass was waist high and with Cecil stretched out on the ground, the dragon wouldn't be able to see him. Yet.

Steve dove head first into the grass the moment it was obvious Cecil had clashed with a dragon. He only had a few seconds before the dragon was bound to notice Cecil's prone form in the grass. There, not twenty feet away, was the boulder that concealed the entrance to the dwarven realm below. Somehow, he had to get the dragon away long enough for him to grab Cecil and get underground.

Cecil sat up and groaned. Loudly. "Ohhhh…"

Steve rolled his eyes and cursed to himself.

"I have got *such* a headache. What happened? It felt like I just smashed into a tree."

Steve sighed. He risked a glance at the dragon, who was now staring straight at Cecil. If he didn't know any better, he'd say the dragon had just licked his chops. There wasn't anything else he could do. The dragon knew they were there.

Steve stood up. The dragon's eyes jetted over to his.

"Ummm, greetings. Would you believe we mean you no harm? We didn't see you there. Sorry. We'll just go about our business now."

"You dare touch me, human?" the dragon's gravelly voice bellowed. "For centuries I have avoided your ilk, never once having the misfortune of touching your kind. Now thanks to your blundering arrogance, all my efforts are for naught!"

Irked, Steve glared at the massive wyverian towering over him. "One of my ilk? What are we, some type of disease?"

"One that is easily eradicated," the dragon agreed.

Both nostrils snapped closed. The huge reptile began taking deep gulps of air. Its jaws opened and from deep within the scaly body they could feel the rumble of internal combustion as the dragon's furnace was stoked. It was gearing up to spit fire and there wasn't a damn thing Steve could do about it. Cecil, realizing what was about to happen, stared up at the dragon with huge saucer-like eyes.

"Oh, this can't be good."

The black dragon's jaws opened even wider and it belched forth a huge jet of flames. Steve was barely able to get his hands up in front of him before Cecil slammed into him from behind. Already in a defensive stance, Steve managed to stay on his feet. However, a human standing out in the open made for an easy target.

Steve instantly made a fist with his left hand and grasped it with his right hand, effectively turning his arms into a rudimentary plow. He knew that he'd never be able to absorb the ferocity of the dragon's flames so he didn't bother trying. He crouched low and braced for impact.

The blast of fire hit Steve's arms and was instantly bifurcated. Half of the dragon's fiery breath blasted harmlessly away into the air while the other half shot downward and hit a point on the ground nearly twenty feet away. The grass blackened and crumpled, leaving a huge scorched mark on the earth. Steve could feel the sheer power and intensity of the dragon's breath as his arms began trembling under the massive assault. His fingers and knuckles were glowing red, which he was quite certain had nothing to do with his own jhorun. The dragon's flames were so hot that even his clothes, which were typically immune to his own fire, blackened and became singed. He tried to move a few degrees to his right to shift his weight onto his other leg, but his right shoulder grazed the jet of fire. His skin felt as though he had brushed up against a red-hot oven. Steve let out a curse that would have curdled his wife's blood.

The dragon's relentless barrage of flames finally lessened and came to a stop. Steve hesitantly turned to glance over his shoulder at Cecil. "Still alive back there?"

Cecil had wrapped both his arms around Steve's chest and had him in a white-knuckled death grip. "Is it safe?"

Steve looked up at the dragon who was now gulping more air for round two.

"Nope. Heads up! He's ready to go again!"

Cecil muttered something under his breath and buried his face in the back of Steve's shirt. Once more the dragon spat fire at them, clearly perplexed that they weren't succumbing to its flames. They heard the dragon growl louder; the flames grew hotter and more fierce.

"We can't keep this up much longer!" Cecil hollered from Steve's back.

Steve risked a glance at the nearby boulders. They were less than twenty feet away. If memory served, the way they got into the hidden door last time was by blasting fire at the door until the boulder opened up. He might get the dragon to open the door for him. If he could angle his right arm and aim half of the dragon's deadly breath at the door ... Steve smiled

The fire lessened and came to a stop. Steve lowered his aching arms, warily eyed the dragon, and inched toward the closest boulder. Once more the dragon gulped air. Both nostrils closed and it took a step toward them.

"What are you doing?" Cecil hissed with alarm as they both stumbled over a small rock on the ground. "Are you trying to kill us? Stop moving!"

The third blast of fire hit them with unerring accuracy. Steve made his move. Half of the blast slammed into the dwarven door.

Nothing happened.

Startled, Steve kept the jet aimed at the large rounded boulder for a few more seconds. Maybe it needed time. Nothing.

"Whatever you're doing, do it faster!" Cecil cried from behind him.

Steve risked a glance at the other boulders. Could he have forgotten which one was the door? Cursing silently, he repositioned his arm to target the next closest boulder. This one, too, began glowing red from the constant blast of fire.

Desperate, and fighting fatigue, Steve targeted a third boulder. The same red glow. And then ... the boulder smoothly swung upwards, as if on hydraulics. Finally!

"Get ready to run!" Steve called back to Cecil. "Look behind you. See that staircase going down? Get ready!"

The flames ceased. The black dragon saw that its prey was about to escape and roared angrily. It lunged forward, intent on snapping up both of the impudent humans. Steve cried out and threw himself backward, pushing Cecil. Both of them tripped over the slight lip at the base of the rock door and tumbled down into the inky blackness. Moments later the faux boulder slammed down, plunging them into instant darkness. From outside they heard the dragon pounding on the giant stone.

Steve painfully got to his feet and ignited his hands for light. The incessant pounding increased. Dust and bits of pulverized stone filtered down, getting into their eyes and noses. Cecil sneezed.

"Come on," Steve ordered, as he headed down the stairs. "I don't think the dragon closed the door for us. I'm hoping there was some type of failsafe built in. Whatever the case, that's one pissed off dragon. I don't want to be around if he manages to get that door open."

"He won't, human," a voice came out of the darkness. "There *is* no failsafe on the door, although I will admit it's a good idea. *I* closed it."

"Who's there?" Steve increased the flames in his hands.

"Get your arses down the stairs. Hurry! I've set the tunnel to collapse!"

"Why are you —"

A small, bulky figure dressed in a dark outfit brushed by them, running down the stairs two at a time. "Move, human!"

Not about to wait for further explanation, Cecil brushed by him and bolted down the stairs. Steve dashed after. The walls and floor had begun to tremble, getting stronger.

"Move! Move! Move!" the voice urged from farther down the stairs. "We are too close. Too close! Run!"

Sprinting down the stairs for nearly four minutes at breakneck speed, Steve was sure he would tumble end over end. They finally drew to a stop. They had emerged into a familiar cavern. Well, familiar to him, anyway.

Cecil whistled. "Look at the size of this cave! It's enormous!"

Steve hunched over and tried to catch his breath. His wheezes came out in large gasps and had Cecil staring uncertainly at him.

"Don't worry about me," Steve wheezed. "I'll be fine. Just give me a moment."

A small figure dressed in black leather armor, brandishing a single-bladed black battleax, pushed past Cecil to glare angrily at Steve.

"Who the ruddy hell do you think you are, human? We just lost a perfectly serviceable tunnel because of you. Do you have any idea how long it takes to dig a proper tunnel to the surface? Hmm? Do you?"

Steve stopped sucking in massive gulps of air and finally looked up at the angry dwarf. "Don't give me that. I know perfectly well how fast a dwarf tunnel can be dug."

The dwarf's eyes narrowed.

"Who are you? What are you doing here?"

"We need —"

"Isn't that just the way with you humans?" the dwarf interrupted. "You humans. You need something and you automatically think the rest of us exist only to service those needs. Well, forget it."

"There's a cordial fellow," Cecil whispered softly.

The dwarf's angry black eyes swung over to Cecil. "Don't even get me started with you, human. What moronic imbecile runs all pell-mell toward a sleeping dragon?"

Steve grunted as he turned to look at Cecil. "He's got a point."

"And you!" the dwarf continued. "You deliberately provoked a conscious dragon! Are all humans as daft as you two?"

"Now wait just a minute," Steve exclaimed. "First of all, the dragon was camouflaged, so there's no way we knew he was there. Second of all, we survived a direct frontal assault. By a dragon, no less. Three times! Let's see you do that, pipsqueak."

"How *did* you do that?" the dwarf inquired. "I didn't know humans were fireproof."

Cecil glanced down at Steve's flaming hands. "Ordinarily I would agree with you; we're not. However, that being said, Steve here would have to be the exception."

Together they looked around the vast subterranean cavern. Great stone stalactites and stalagmites were everywhere, not that they could see much. Steve noted that some of the bioluminescent moss that was prevalent in many dwarf tunnels was growing on a select few of the stalactites. However, no amount of glowing fungus would be able to properly illuminate the enormous cavern.

"Is this place as big as it feels?" Cecil asked in awe. His

question echoed back at him from all directions.

Steve nodded. "Yep. Trust me, it's huge."

Skeptical, the dwarf crossed his arms over his chest. "You're insinuating that you've been here before? Prove it."

Steve confidently strode toward two darkened tunnels visible toward the south. He made it about ten feet when he suddenly stopped and looked back at the dwarf. "Who are you, anyway? What's your name?"

The dwarf automatically bowed low. "Brugar, at your service. No, wait. No, I'm not. You are responsible for the destruction of one of our six main entrances. You are no friend to us, human."

"What? I didn't destroy it. The dragon did!"

Brugar stood motionless, dividing his angry glare equally between the two of them. "You were lucky in finding our southern door. However, you'll never find the gate. Give up now and you can save yourself a lot of embarrassment."

Steve's smug smile returned. "Tell you what, Brugar. If I point out where your precious gate is, will you at least escort us down?"

Brugar adopted his own smug expression. "Very well. Find the gate on your first try and I'll escort you down. Trust me, you won't find it."

Steve pointed at the right-hand tunnel. "It's over there. That tunnel is only about a hundred feet long. Your gate is at the end."

Brugar's defiant expression vanished instantly. "How could you —?"

"Lead the way, my good dwarf."

"How much farther do these stairs go on?" Cecil wondered aloud. "We've been doing nothing but descending for half an hour now."

Their reluctant guide hadn't said a word after twisting two stone protuberances on the unfinished tunnel's end-- something Steve would have sworn wasn't there in their time-- and opened the dwarves' precious gate. Steve had tried his best not to gloat too much, but admittedly, he was horrible at keeping secrets.

"Aren't you curious about how I knew where the gate was?" Steve asked their guide after another five minutes of silence had passed.

"I didn't want to know when you asked ten minutes ago and I still don't," the dwarf grumped.

"I've been here before, Brugar. That's how."

"Hmmph. Lucky guess."

Steve pressed on. "Then how do I know we're going to Borahgg? How do I know the city's western edge backs up against a huge black lake? How do I know that the Council meets in a huge domed structure sitting northeast of the city center?"

Brugar had paused in mid-step and turned to look behind him. "Impossible. I don't know how you know those things, but what I can tell you is that no human has ever stepped foot inside the city."

Steve went to jam his hands into his pockets, but had forgotten his Lentarian trousers didn't have any. He switched, rubbing his hands together, and hoped no one noticed.

"I just hope you guys have a spare athe crystal lying around."

Brugar cast him a speculative look, but elected not to say anything.

Less than an hour later, the small group emerged into Borahgg's main cavern. This space easily made the first great cavern feel like a dragon cave. The domed ceiling rose hundreds of feet into the air, with a circumference at least ten times that of the gate cavern above.

He nudged Cecil on the shoulder. "Pretty impressive, huh? Look. You can't even see the other side."

Cecil whistled softly. "I had no idea this was down here. From the surface one would suspect nothing but solid rock. Simply incredible."

Brugar scoffed. "That's the way we prefer it, human."

Steve leaned forward and gave the dwarf a grin. "Trust me, pal, it works. No one knew this city existed until fairly recently. In fact, it won't be until—"

Cecil stomped on Steve's foot.

"Ow! What did you do that for?"

"Perhaps a full explanation would not be in your best interests, my friend."

Steve paled and nodded his head. "Right."

Brugar stared at him a few moments before he pulled off his axe and dropped the handle onto a glowing circular plate outside the mouth of the tunnel. A loud crack reverberated throughout the cavern. Dwarves came streaming out of buildings. Guards rushed to grab their arms. Within moments Steve and Cecil were surrounded.

"Humans! How the blazes did you find us?"

Steve turned to look at the speaker, an older dwarf soldier who was wearing a light tan set of leather armor. The dwarf glared at their guide. "Explain yourself, Brugar. It doesn't appear you have been taken prisoner. I don't see the humans holding any weapons. How did they coerce you to bring them here?"

Brugar frowned at Steve and jabbed a finger in his direction. "He knew the way. He knew where the entrance was, which tunnel held the gate, and even the name of our city."

The dwarves erupted into heated arguments as each thought their neighbor had something to do with the appearance of the humans. Brugar put two fingers in his mouth and let out a loud, shrill whistle.

"My brothers! Still your mouths! The news worsens, I'm afraid. These two humans also caused the demise of the southern entrance. The tunnel had to be collapsed."

More indignant shouts and conversations.

"What happened?" the dwarf in the tan armor inquired. "How did two humans manage to destroy one of our tunnels?"

"I had to destroy it," Brugar clarified, drawing an instantaneous hush from the crowd. "It was for all our sake. They provoked a dragon and it was attempting to gain entry. I had no choice."

"What the ruddy hell did you accost a dragon for?" the first dwarf exclaimed angrily. "I know you humans aren't that sharp, but I never dreamt your level of intelligence was so low that you'd have to dig in order to find it."

Steve turned to Cecil. "He's implying that I'm stupid, isn't he?"

Sensing the growing hostility amongst the many dwarves, Cecil had to clear his throat a few times before he could speak. "Er, I believe so."

Steve crossed his arms over his chest. "Where's the Council? I want to talk to someone in charge."

"The Council isn't in session today," Tan Armor informed him. "And even if they were, they wouldn't want to talk with the likes of you."

Steve took a couple of deep breaths. Sarah had said that oftentimes he came across as being too brash and ill tempered, especially with strangers. He couldn't expect the dwarves to do him a favor if he ended up angering everyone, so it was time to change his tactic. He smiled.

"That has to be the creepiest smile I have ever seen," Cecil whispered to him. "You're forcing a smile. Don't. In fact, let me."

Cecil turned to the dwarf spokesman and gave them a short bow. "Good afternoon, my friends. What my large companion is trying to do, albeit not too successfully if you ask me, is…"

Several dwarfs snickered.

"…to ask for a favor," Cecil finished.

The chattering of the dwarves tapered off and it became eerily quiet.

"I realize you don't know us," Cecil continued, "and we have no right asking this of you, but I was hoping, er, *we* were hoping you would grant us this favor so we can return home."

"Who are you?" the lead dwarf asked, completely ignoring Steve and not bothering to look his way.

"I am Cecil. This is Steve. What is your name, friend?"

"I am Selwyn, Head of Security. And I am not your friend."

Unconcerned by Selwyn's brusque manner, Cecil gave the dwarf the friendliest smile he could muster. "Understood. I don't blame you. Before today I have never seen a dwarf before, so if one strolled into my home, I'd be taken aback, too."

Selwyn's scowl lessened. A little. "A favor for a favor, eh? What do you—"

Sensing movement behind him, Selwyn turned to look at the many faces that were still staring at them. He crossed his arms over his chest. "Show's over. There's nothing to see. Back to work, all of you."

The crowd dissipated.

"Come with me, humans, and we'll talk. Brugar, assemble a team to scout for a location for a new tunnel."

Brugar nodded and wandered off. Once they were alone, Selwyn turned to the intruders and raised an eyebrow. "Well? What type of favor do you want?"

"I don't know much about these things," Cecil confessed, "but I am led to believe that they are difficult to come by. We need a crystal."

Selwyn stopped so abruptly that Cecil walked right into him. "A crystal? Let me guess. You humans want another athe crystal, am I right?"

Steve nodded. "Yes. Due to technical difficulties beyond our control, the first crystal was destroyed. We need another."

"You're working for the human king who wants to put a portal on another world, is that it?"

"As a matter of fact," Cecil began, but this time Steve stomped on his foot.

"Yes, that's it," Steve told him. "Can you get us another? The king was afraid you would have to mine another, and apparently that takes a while. We need to get this crystal as soon as possible. If it takes longer than two days, then we're in serious trouble."

"Two days, eh? You don't ask for much, do you?"

"Can it be done?" Cecil asked the dwarf. "Do we ask the impossible?"

"Impossible, no," Selwyn admitted. "The Council mined an additional half dozen crystals when the human king asked for one. So there are others, aye."

"How do we get our hands on one?" Steve wanted to know. Hearing that the crystal was within their reach lightened his mood considerably. "What would we have to do?"

Selwyn shook his head. "The only way to get you approved

for one of those crystals is to get every single member of the Council to agree. It took the human king several months of endless pestering and convincing before the entire nine members of the Council were swayed."

Steve groaned aloud. "Several months? We don't have that kind of time."

Cecil held up a hand. "You did say it was possible, right? There has to be another way. What is it?"

Steve swallowed several choice expletives he had been ready to fire off and nodded appreciatively at Cecil. He had completely forgotten about that part.

Selwyn nodded. "Aye, I said there was a way. However, I think it would be easier and quicker to convince the Council to give you another."

Steve's hackles rose. This wasn't going to be good. "What? What is the other way?"

"Steal it."

"Excuse me?"

"You heard me. Steal it. The only way you're going to get your hands on an athe crystal is if it is stolen."

Steve eyed Cecil before he looked back down at the dwarf. "Let me get this straight. You're *recommending* we steal an athe crystal? You. A dwarf. Recommending to us, two humans, to *steal* property from the dwarves."

"I didn't say that."

Steve frowned. "Yes, you did. You want us to steal it."

Selwyn sighed. "Human, you'd have an easier time trying to steal a diamond from a dragon. There is no way a mere human is capable of stealing a gem from us dwarves."

"Then why did you…"

"I would have to do it."

"Come again?"

"Are all humans as deaf as you?"

Steve cleared his throat. "Let's see if I have this right. You. Steal from your own kin. Why would you do that?"

Selwyn crossed his arms over his chest. "I wouldn't."

"Okay, I'm confused here. You just said…"

Cecil laid a hand on Steve's arm. "I believe I know what he's doing. The agreement was a favor for a favor. He is saying that he'd be willing to do it, but he wants a favor from us."

Selwyn nodded. "Aye. I really don't want to have to face the Council and explain why I would steal one of our own crystals, so no, I don't want to. However, that being said, there *is* something that I want even more."

"What's that?" Steve wanted to know.

"Grant my ailing daughter her fondest wish."

Taken aback, Steve knelt down to stare at the dwarf at his own level. "Of all the things I thought you were gonna say, that was nowhere on the list. You know what? I'll agree to that without even hearing the request. What's wrong with your daughter?"

Selwyn's eyes filled. He angrily blinked a few times in rapid succession.

"Her heart. It doesn't beat as well as it should. Our healers have told me that there's nothing they can do for her."

Both Steve and Cecil quickly wiped their eyes when they thought the other wasn't looking.

"What can we do?" Steve softly asked.

Selwyn pulled the tip of his braided beard out of his belt and began twisting it into knots, a telltale sign that he was nervous. "You find a way to grant her wish and I'll see to it you get your crystal, in whatever time frame you need."

Still kneeling, Steve nodded. Cecil placed his hand on Steve's right shoulder in agreement. "You got it. What does she want?"

"To ride a dragon."

Chapter 8 — An Eerie Encounter

What are we to do if he comes back?" Cora asked as she sat beside her husband on a plush navy-blue camel-back sofa in the manor's living room.

"Believe me, he *will* be back," Luther told his wife, as he laid a reassuring hand over hers. "Sarah is right. He's been thwarted. He will be angry. Not only will the sheriff undoubtedly return but this time he'll bring whatever forces he deems necessary to ensure his success."

"But what are we to do?" AnnaBelle asked, voicing her own concern. "Do you not think it prudent that we simply hide in the forest until he goes away?"

Sitting directly across from two of her husband's ancestors, and one new friend, Sarah leaned forward in her armchair and shook her head. "What if he doesn't go away? You'd just be prolonging the inevitable. He must be dealt with."

Luther nodded. "I agree."

Cora turned to her husband and frowned. "What would

you have me do? I am no fighter. I've never handled a gun. You cannot possibly think I can defend myself."

"Nor can I," AnnaBelle agreed.

Before Luther could respond, Sarah cleared her throat. "It is my belief that not only can we defend ourselves against that lunatic but in such a way that no one ever bothers you or this house again."

Cora let her hands fall dramatically to her lap. "How? They have guns. We don't own a single firearm!"

"Cecil has a pistol, but neither of us has ever used it," AnnaBelle added. "I wouldn't be of any help there, I'm afraid."

"If we were only standing on Lentarian soil then the advantage would be ours," Luther muttered.

"Your jhorun allows you to modify portals," Sarah pointed out. "What exactly would you have been able to do?"

"I'm a king's soldier. My fellows would have been by my side at the slightest sign of trouble. That's what soldiers do for each other, Sarah."

"Well, you're not in Lentari and your soldier buddies aren't here to help. What you have is me."

Luther snorted. "You? No offense, Ms. Sarah, but what can you possibly do?"

In answer to his question, Sarah smiled and rose to her feet. "I have a plan. Come on, we have work to do."

An hour later Cora deposited another armful of her best linen down onto the growing pile of fabric in the living room while AnnaBelle scouted the house, looking for more.

"There are none in here," AnnaBelle called out from somewhere within the depths of the house.

"Try the cupboards in the guest rooms," Cora answered back. She turned to look at the mound of sheets and towels and frowned at them. "You cannot possibly think this will work, Sarah."

"Oh, it'll work. Trust me."

"How can you be so certain?"

Sarah sank down to the floor and began sorting the linens by size. Pieces that were deemed too small were handed back to Cora. All others were tossed haphazardly onto the blue couch. Cora took the delicate silk handkerchief Sarah was holding out to her and dropped it onto the discard pile. She stooped to retrieve one of her luxurious white towels, a gift from the mayor's wife, from the growing 'acceptable' pile next to Sarah.

"How is this supposed to frighten anyone?"

Sarah finished inspecting the large ivory colored tablecloth and decided it wasn't white enough. She draped it over the discard pile. She looked up at Cora and paused. She held out a hand and waited for the towel to be passed over to her. Then she took one of the smaller unacceptable cloth napkins she had recently discarded and wadded it up. Next, she wrapped the wadded-up cloth in the sheet, making sure to use as little as possible to cover the crumpled cloth. She then tied a short black ribbon around the lumpy shape so that the sheet wouldn't fall off. Sarah triumphantly held her makeshift 'ghost' up to Cora for her approval.

"That? You think that will frighten away the sheriff's men?"

"Nobody likes ghosts. Even you. As soon as I suggested turning this place into a haunted house you and AnnaBelle almost fainted. Even Luther's face turned a little bit ashen. We obviously can't make it haunted but we sure as heck are going to make it *look* as though it is."

The makeshift ghost Cora was holding suddenly sailed high up into the air. Sarah let the ghost hang in midair for a few moments before directing her jhorun to move it around the room in an impromptu demonstration. The towel flapped in the breeze as it soared around the ceiling of the living room.

Sarah glanced up at Cora. Luther's wife wore a bemused expression on her face as she watched the homemade ghost fly around her living room. She knew what Cora was thinking. During daylight hours they didn't have much chance of scaring anyone. But, once the sun had set, maybe, just maybe, their plan might work.

"Perhaps if we drew some faces on them, they might be more believable," Sarah suggested.

Cora frowned. "I will do no such thing. That towel was a

welcoming gift from the mayor's wife."

The large towel cruised silently through the air as Sarah made the ghost fly circles around the crystal chandelier in the center of the room. AnnaBelle walked in, took one look at the object sailing overhead, and let out a shriek that could have shattered glass. The stack of folded sheets and blankets she was holding flew into the air as she flailed her arms and ran from the room.

Sarah laughed, her concentration evaporating in the blink of an eye. The ghost promptly nosedived straight to the ground. Moments later Luther sprinted through the front door. He was holding a large net and a wooden bucket with a square piece of fishing net draped over the top.

"What has happened?" Luther wheezed as he fought to regain his breath. "What—"

Sarah let out a shriek, followed almost immediately by Cora. Both women backed away, pointing shaky fingers at Luther. The wooden bucket was positively crawling with bugs—grasshoppers, crickets, beetles. A large red-banded dragonfly buzzed angrily in the net in his other hand.

"Get those things out of here!" Sarah shouted as she turned to sprint after AnnaBelle. "Are you mad? You don't bring bugs inside a house!"

"But I heard…"

Cora appeared by Sarah's side and she, too, was ready to leave.

"We're fine," Sarah assured Luther. "We spooked AnnaBelle. That's all. Get those things out of here! Hurry!"

Luther sulked a bit but reluctantly returned to his job of collecting as many bugs as possible. Only when the buzzing bucket was out of her sight (and earshot) did Sarah visibly relax. She wandered over to the closest window and watched Luther pull the dragonfly out of the net and drop it into the wooden pail. Brandishing the net as though he was holding a two-handed broadsword, Luther spotted another insect and hurried off after it.

Sarah smiled. It had been an interesting couple of hours. She could only hope that people from the nineteenth century were just as gullible as the people from her time.

"I've shown you what else my jhorun can do," Sarah began, as she faced her audience. "This mansion is going to be, I'm sorry to say, overrun with ghosts. Yes, they're nothing more than towels and sheets floating through the air, but to an outside observer? It can be nerve-wracking."

AnnaBelle nodded. "I'll attest to that."

"Continuing on, I know practically everyone dislikes bugs. What happens when one lands on you? If you're like me, you freak out. Now, imagine getting a whole bunch of them dumped on you. You wouldn't like that, would you?"

As one, all three listeners vehemently shook their heads.

"In order to make this believable, we have to make sure everyone believes this house is haunted. I'm not going to be able to do that by myself. I've got a few other ideas to make happen. Now, listen closely."

For the next thirty minutes, Sarah relayed her instructions. When everyone knew what they had to do, working together, they prepped the manor for the arrival of their inevitable *guests.*

While she worked, Sarah's thoughts traveled back to Luther and his bucket of bugs. She shuddered. He had brought the infernal bucket of bugs inside! Chivalry or not you never, ever, EVER brought insects into a person's home.

She shook her head and turned back to the piles of fabric. After cutting holes in several sheets, much to Cora's chagrin, and drawing contorted facial expressions on some of their larger ghosts, they were ready. Sarah, with Luther's help, tied ropes to various items and, after giving them an experimental yank, nodded with satisfaction as the object seemingly levitated. Sarah made sure each of them knew where to find the ends, and when they should be used. Once done, Sarah tasked Cora with seeing what might pass as blood. Who wouldn't be upset by seeing blood drip down a wall?

"Will these do?" Cora asked nearly thirty minutes later. She held up several jars of a thick dark red liquid. "It's raspberry syrup I made last summer."

"It's close enough. Take them to the top of the stairs and conceal them. Take the lids off, too. Chances are, if we have to use them, we're going to be in a rush."

Cora nodded.

Luther returned an hour later and announced his buckets were so full he couldn't contain any more.

"Perfect. Let's hide one of the buckets in that large forked pine tree where the driveway bends to the right. What about the other? Can you think of somewhere we could hide it so that we'd get maximum results?"

Luther thought a moment. He slowly nodded. "I know where I can put it. The hitching post. There's a large herb bush growing next to it. Cora calls it basil. I can conceal the bucket behind it."

"That'll be perfect. Which side of the house is it on?"

"It faces the southern side of the manor."

"Wonderful. We'd best get going. It'll be dark soon. You and Cora know what to do."

An hour later, as the sun set and the darkness crept closer and closer, Sarah was beginning to think that all of their hard work had been for naught. The sheriff was a no-show. No cowboys on horseback, no mobs of people holding lit torches, nothing.

Sarah sighed. Maybe she, like her husband, had watched too many movies. But wasn't that how it worked? The villain, if thwarted, wanted vengeance and returned with a small army. At night. Always at night.

She briefly rose to her knees from her seated position and repositioned the blanket she had been sitting on. Crouching behind the manor's chimney up on the roof, anxiously awaiting the arrival of people with guns, terrified her. What if someone got hurt? Worse, what if someone was killed? What would happen to Steve if something happened to Luther or Cora? Sarah shuddered.

A grim resolve appeared on her face.

She wasn't going to let that happen. She had to protect them. She *would* protect them no matter the cost. Her plan *had* to work. Someone had to experience the terrifying show and relay what they had seen to others. She needed the townsfolk so afraid of the manor that they wouldn't ever speak of it, let alone want to visit it.

She sighed. The only thing she could do now was … she

heard a cough. She held her breath. Was someone nearby? Did they know she was hiding up on the roof? Then she heard soft whispers. Cora was hiding in an upstairs closet within reach of half a dozen of the ropes. Luther was outside, presumably hiding until his turn came.

She heard another cough. A single lit torch became visible as someone on horseback rode around the bend in the road. More torches were lit from the one the rider was holding and were passed around. Sarah squinted. She could make out at least a dozen men gathered around the lone rider. Was that the sheriff? Sarah smiled. She hoped so. That power hungry lunatic was going to have a ringside seat to tonight's performance.

Sarah teleported herself back into the manor near the closet Cora was hiding in. She softly knocked on the door and peeked inside.

"They're here," she whispered. She motioned for Cora to follow her to the window. "Do you think that's the sheriff? The one on horseback? I can't tell from here. It's too dark out."

Cora joined her by the window. She nodded. "Yes. I recognize his hat. I personally think his wide-brimmed ten-gallon hat is the most ridiculous thing I've ever seen. He must believe it makes him more intimidating. I heard that someone actually ridiculed his hat and he shot and killed him, in cold blood. I've never met a more ruthless man than he, Sarah. He frightens me."

"Me, too," Sarah admitted. "Let's return the favor, shall we?"

The beginnings of a smile appeared on Cora's face. She nodded.

Sarah closed her eyes and brought up a mental picture of the tree that Luther had pointed out earlier. Several dead branches had been propped up against the tree's trunk. Sarah focused on one and ordered her jhorun to push it forward, but only in the middle. The other sections of the branch were to stay put.

The branch snapped in half. In the darkened and quiet countryside, the crack sounded like a thunderclap.

Guns were unholstered and rifles were cocked. Nearly two dozen weapons were trained in the direction the noise had come from. The rider pointed at two of the men and then back toward the direction of the tree. He then pointed at the ground.

"Go check it out."

Two men nodded, dismounted, and disappeared into the trees. The others also dismounted, but they were far from quiet. Leather creaked, horses whinnied, several of the men shuffled about on the ground.

The voice was deep, gruff, and meant business. This was a person, Sarah mused, who was used to getting his own way. What was it with small towns like this? Why was there always a bad apple in every bunch?

Sarah nodded. So far, so good. She focused her attention on the men's torches and ordered her jhorun to push a gust of air directly at them. She smiled as several of the torches poofed out.

Several men were now fidgeting as they stared expectantly at the quiet trees. She was pretty sure she knew what they were thinking: why had their torches gone out? Was there someone out there? Were they being watched?

The men holding the extinguished torches hastily relit them.

Getting bolder and more accustomed to manipulating air currents with her jhorun, she created a brisk breeze and directed it toward the ground. Leaves, twigs, and a few plants rose into the air.

"Tell me yur doin' that," she heard one man whisper to the other.

"How? I've been over here the whole damn time!"

"Keep your voices down!" the sheriff snapped at them. "If you let them know we're here I'll personally skin you alive, is that clear?"

Heads nodded.

"YESSIR!"

"I said keep it down."

"Yessir!" several men whispered back.

The two men sent to explore the surrounding trees returned.

"Well?"

"There ain't nuthin' there, boss," the first man reported.

"Fine. It's got to be my imagination then. Spread out. I want everyone in position when I give the signal."

"Why are we burnin' the place down, boss? It makes no sense."

The sheriff's face remained in the shadows, but Sarah knew the man wasn't smiling. Sure enough, the sheriff's horse was nudged forward until it had intercepted the man foolish enough to question him.

"If I want your opinion I'll give it to you, you got that?"

Wide eyed with fear, the man nodded.

"I ain't payin' you to think. When I tell you to do somethin', I expect you to do it."

Properly cowed, the man took off his torn and filthy hat and stared at the ground. "Yessir, boss."

"Good."

With her jhorun tingling like mad, Sarah focused on her mental picture of the same tree and snapped two more branches in half, one right after the other.

"What was that, boss?" one man asked.

"Who's out there?" another blurted out.

The sheriff spun his horse around and was looking off into the trees as though he had spotted something.

"Somebody's gotta be out there. You two, go … no, not you two. Step back. You and you. Get up there to … no, I told you two to stay put. You two couldn't find your ass if I handed you a map. I'm talking to you two. Head out there and check for … look. You two on the right, I want you to … your other right, idiot. I swear to whatever gods exist, if someone moves besides you two, then I'll personally shoot a toe clean off your foot. Is that clear? Now, you two move and everyone else stays put."

No one moved. Sarah grinned. The sheriff was becoming flustered.

"Well? Git!"

Before anyone could take a step, two torches leapt out of their owners' hands and floated through the air. They serenely passed each other and slowly presented themselves to their new owners. The torches flickered merrily, untouched.

The first man to lose his torch stared, aghast, at the floating torch before him. His companion nudged him on the shoulder. "Go on, take it."

"You take it. There ain't no one holdin' the blessed thing up!"

"Well, whoever's got it wants you to take it," the friend urged.

"That's what I'm afraid of. Ain't no way in hell I'm touchin' that thing."

As if on cue, the torch wiggled and lunged closer to its new owner. The man let out a bellow and backpedaled as fast as he could. He collided with the person behind him and was angrily pushed away.

Doubled over with silent laughter, Sarah extinguished the torch and let it drop to the ground. She did the same for the second torch as that man hadn't reclaimed it.

"What the hell was that?" the sheriff inquired. He had been facing the other direction and hadn't witnessed the torch exchange. "What's goin' on over there?"

"What's goin' on is I'm clearin' out!" the owner of the second torch informed him. "There somethin' not right about this place."

The sheriff glanced down and saw the two torches lying on the ground. "You dropped a torch. Big deal."

"It *floated*, boss! Torches ain't s'posed to float!"

"Yeah, right. Just pick it up and be done with it."

"Hell no."

From her vantage point outside, Sarah heard a gun's hammer pulled back in the universally recognized sign that something bad was about to happen. The nervous chatter of the men fell silent.

"Pick it up, Earl. Now."

Unable to resist, Sarah made the torch twitch just as poor Earl finally mustered the courage to grab the handle. He dropped the torch as though he had accidentally grabbed the tail of a rattlesnake. He bellowed loudly and ran into the woods. The rest of the men turned to look up at the sheriff, who was staring at the torch with a puzzled frown on his face.

"Boss? What do we—"

"We stick to the plan. The loss of one man changes nothing. Luther needs to be taught a lesson. No one crosses me. Let tonight be an example."

Before the sheriff could re-holster his prized Colt Peacemaker, the cylinder snapped out and ejected all six bullets.

"Umm, boss?"

"What?"

"You dropped your bullets."

"Really? Thanks for the bulletin, Merrith. You're a real barrel of laughs."

Sarah smiled as she watched the men become more nervous by the minute. Blowing leaves and snapping twigs were enough to make a person jumpy, sure, but Luther was right. Nothing unsettled a person's nerves faster than seeing something move around on its own accord.

The hats were the next to go. One after the other, the hats were shoved down over the wearer's eyes or blasted upward as though caught in a strong vertical breeze. Sarah focused her attention on the sheriff. Using her jhorun, she lifted the hat from his head and gently placed it on the head of someone who hadn't located his own hat yet.

The sheriff scowled, as though losing his hat in such a supernatural manner was a huge inconvenience. The man who ended up with the sheriff's hat had actually squealed like a pig. He snatched it off his head and returned it to its owner. The sheriff accepted his hat without a word. He scanned the trees, a little nervously. Sarah smiled. It was time for the second act.

The trees to the west creaked ominously, but the air was still. The quiet, nervous chatter amongst the men abruptly ceased. A small white object suddenly lifted straight up and careened toward the house. It disappeared into an open window on the second floor. Moments later they heard a loud crash as Cora, who was waiting for the ghost to come sailing through the window, dropped several plates on cue.

Multiple fingers pointed toward the manor. "Did you see that? Did you? What the hell was it?"

"Looked like a ghost t' me!"

"There's no such things as ghosts," one voice squeaked out.

"There ain't? Didn't you just see the same thing we did? This place has ghosts. One just flew into the house! I heard the crash! I'll betcha they done took care of whoever's in there. One thing's for certain. I ain't goin' in there!"

"You'll go in there or I'll put a bullet between your eyes!" the sheriff snarled at them. His right hand rested on the handle of his gun.

Another ghost rose up. Then another. And another. Suddenly the air was filled with white objects. After floating silently in the air for a few moments they all raced toward the manor and disappeared through the same window.

More crashes ensued. From the sounds of it, Cora had just smashed every single dish she owned.

"Now don't you feel stupid?" the one man asked the other. "You say there ain't ghosts but we both just saw the same damn thing. Listen to them in there! This place must be riddled with spooks!"

Sarah held her breath and hoped Luther was ready. She had just guided the last of the makeshift spirits into the window Cora had opened for this purpose. It was time for Luther to utilize one of his buckets. She strained her eyes to spot him concealed in the large pine tree next to the dirt driveway. She couldn't. It was too dark. Fortunately, at least half of the men were standing under the tree's canopy.

Almost immediately after the last crash sounded Sarah heard bloodcurdling screams, loud and high pitched. Five men dropped their torches—which she extinguished—and began doing the fastest striptease she had ever seen before in her life. She had to turn away once it became clear that the men intended to shed every scrap of their clothing. Even the sheriff had taken his hat off and was waving it as a swarm of crickets, butterflies, beetles and a myriad of other flying insects swarmed him.

"They done got in muh private parts!" one man hollered as he yanked his thermal underwear down to his ankles. "Someone get 'em off me!"

Four hairy nude men turned tail and sprinted back down the gravel driveway and disappeared into the darkness. Not once did they look back to see what the sheriff thought about the matter. The fifth man, with his pants still around his ankles, tried futilely to extricate his legs from his trousers while wearing his boots. He practically hopped after his companions, desperate not to be left behind.

The three remaining men turned to look up at the sheriff. "I don't like this boss. We need t' get outta here!"

The sheriff was silent as he stared at the ground. The writhing, pulsing mass of insects grew smaller as the once incarcerated bugs scrambled for freedom. The sheriff turned to look back at the manor and then around at the forest. He seemed to come to a decision. "Fine. We'll burn the place down at a later date, when I can find some men who aren't cowards. For now, get in there and fetch me the woman."

Sarah sat up straight. They wanted Cora? The men began grumbling amongst themselves. This was not what they had wanted to hear; no one wanted to go inside. One soul, braver than the others, was foolish enough to vocalize his objections.

"You mean we ain't leavin'? Can't you find a woman in town, boss?"

Sarah winced as she heard the loud crack of a fist striking a man's face.

"I don't need no whore, you imbecile. I need Luther's wife. If we have to cut our losses tonight then we need to get some leverage against him. I want the location of his gold mine."

"Gold? There ain't no gold in these here parts, boss! Only silver."

Sarah quietly agreed. Coeur d'Alene was known for their rich veins of silver, not gold.

"He pays for his supplies in gold coin," the sheriff flatly answered. "I know. Old man Hutton keeps me informed."

Up on the roof, Sarah groaned. Luther was paying for his supplies in gold coin? He must have been using grifs, gold Lentarian coins that he brought with him. No wonder he had attracted the sheriff's attention!

"You three. Bring me that woman. If you don't come

outta that house with her, then don't come back at all."

The three men swallowed nervously. They walked toward the porch steps and hesitated. One man turned to look behind him. "You sure you don't want to come with us, boss?"

The sheriff had drawn his gun and was pointing it straight at them.

"You got five seconds to get inside before I start firing. Now get going!"

The three men reached the bottom of the porch stairs together. As one they looked up at the small flight of six steps and swallowed noisily. Calmly, carefully, they drew their guns and ascended the stairs. Each stair creaked ominously.

As soon as the front door's doorknob was within reach Sarah used her jhorun to open the door, which creaked as it opened. She couldn't have planned that any better. An outside observer would say that it looked as though the house was beckoning the brave, or foolish, to enter.

"Oh, hell no," one of the men defiantly said.

"Duncan, you're oldest. You first."

"What are we, ten years old?" Duncan hissed back. His knees were shaking so badly it was a wonder he stayed upright. "Do I look that stupid? Besides, you're older than I am, Brent."

"Am not. Get going! The sheriff has a gun trained on our backs. I ain't goin' out like this."

The third man, a tall fellow sporting a bright orange beard, boldly covered the distance to the front door in a few paces and strode through.

"Bob, what the hell are you doing? Get back here!"

Cora had been watching through one of the smaller side windows. She was waiting for him. She gave a hard yank on one of the closest ropes. One of the spooks, hidden within a large vase, leapt upward and zoomed up the stairs. Less than two seconds later it had vanished.

Bob stood trembling in the foyer of the darkened house.

Sarah teleported herself from her hiding place on the roof to the third story, just outside of the master bedroom. She ducked behind an armchair and peered over the balcony where she could see the entire foyer, from the front door to the base of the stairs.

She watched the three men inch their way inside the dark house. Sarah decided some additional light was needed.

She closed her eyes and pictured the lit candle and its holder in the kitchen. True to her word, Cora had left the candle on the counter in case she needed it. Well, she did. She ordered her jhorun to move it from the kitchen to the foyer.

The candle levitated a few inches off the floor and deftly navigated its way through the house. Sarah was careful to keep a mental picture in her mind the entire time lest she lose her concentration and drop the candle. Setting the house on fire was not part of the plan.

The three men gasped as the lit candlestick floated into the room and settled on a small table near the base of the stairs.

"Tell me that ain't blood!" Brent whined.

Duncan swallowed nervously at the sight of a dark red liquid slowly oozing down the wall.

"Sure looks like it."

"There's blood on the walls," Brent whined, in a louder voice this time. "The walls are bleedin'! Do you know what that means?"

Sarah sniffed the air. She hoped no one else would identify the sweet fragrance. Despite the circumstances, Sarah smiled as she briefly imagined what Steve would say if he were by her side. He'd look her straight in the eye and tell her he was in the mood for a raspberry filled doughnut.

She had to give the three intruders credit—they remained side by side and inched farther into the house. In moments they detoured to the left and disappeared from her sight.

Sarah scowled. She teleported one story down and quietly leaned out over the second story balcony railing. She teleported herself down to the ground floor and peeked into the dining room.

"They must be hiding!" the sheriff shouted from outside. "Luther never leaves the house. His wife has gotta be with him. Find them!"

"Betcha them spooks got 'em," Bob whispered, looking anxious.

"I'm tellin' ya there's no one here!" Duncan whispered.

Sarah smiled. She knew what she had to do.

The doors to the china cabinet sprang open, causing the three men to yelp. The dishes flew out of the cabinet and soared about the room before neatly stacking themselves back into the cabinet. It only took about ten seconds.

Sarah glanced at the men. They were rooted in place, rigid with fear. Enjoying herself, she ordered her jhorun to reorganize the books on bookcases. Within moments, books were flying through the air and passing through more, returning to the shelves, albeit in a different order. The neatly executed maneuver was more organized than a marching band executing a flawless performance out on the field.

The men stared, wide-eyed at each other. As one, they opened their mouths, took a deep breath, and screamed.

The men bolted from the room, their worst nightmare chasing them into the foyer. Sarah ducked out of the way behind a suit of armor as she giggled to herself. This was actually quite fun!

Wait. The armor. The Lentarian crest proudly displayed on the cuirass. This wasn't anywhere in her house in her time, either. She pushed the thought aside as the men came rushing by her hiding place.

Deciding that an additional act certainly couldn't hurt, she directed her jhorun to the heavy metal suit.

The visor clinked loudly as it dropped into place. Bob, intent on reaching the outside door as soon as possible, risked a backward glance and gasped with horror as the suit of armor stepped down from its pedestal and raised its two arms up in a proper 'undead' fashion. It slowly ambled toward them.

"Sweet Jesus, Mary, and Joseph!" Duncan shrieked out as he spotted what had captured Bob's attention.

The third man, Brent, also watching the animated suit of armor clank rapidly toward them, sprinted toward the manor's open front door but forgot that only one of the double doors was open.

WHAM!

He slammed headfirst into the heavy wooden door. Dust flew off the top of the frame, and Brent slammed into his two companions, who hadn't been watching where they were going, either.

Sarah slapped a hand over her mouth to keep from laughing out loud. The armor mimicked her.

Duncan made it to his feet first. He and Bob both saw that Brent wasn't moving. He got a not-so-gentle kick on the butt.

"Get up, idiot! We're clearin' out!"

Bob glanced backward and saw the armor doubled over in laughter. "That rat bastard is laughing at us!"

Duncan didn't care. "Let 'im laugh. I'm outta here!"

"What about Brent? He ain't movin'!"

Duncan slung his companion's inert form over his shoulder and rushed outside, completely ignoring the sheriff's frustrated shouts. He and Bob, with their friend over his shoulder, disappeared into the woods.

Sarah teleported herself back to her hiding place on the roof. She peeked over the edge and saw the sheriff sitting astride his horse. When his shouts and threats brought no one back, he turned to the manor and sat, motionless, holding the last remaining torch.

Sarah summoned her tiring jhorun for a final task: gently push down on every board on the porch below. Sounds of the creaking wood grew progressively louder. She risked a glance at the sheriff. He was doing his best to keep the skittish horse under control.

She pushed a final blast of air at the sheriff's torch and extinguished it. The horse spun and took off in a flurry of curses from his rider.

Sarah watched him leave from one of the manor's darkened windows. If she didn't know any better, then she'd say the sheriff hadn't been that scared at all. If anything, he had looked pensive.

She frowned. That couldn't be good.

Chapter 9 – Royal Pain in the Athe

Steve stared at the dwarf in utter silence. Had he heard him right? Selwyn's daughter wanted a dragon ride? How in the world would he grant that request? He alone had permission to ride a dragon, and a very specific one at that. Pryllan. Thanks to an agreement he had with the new Dragon Lord, Steve had earned the right to ride other dragons, but only with their consent.

He sighed. He fervently wished Pryllan was here now. The Pryllan from his own time, that is. He knew that his large wyverian friend would be willing to give a small dwarf child a ride, especially if Pryllan knew it would probably be the last exciting thing the child was ever able to do. Unfortunately, if anyone tried to hop on Pryllan's back now, in the current time, they'd more than likely end up eaten.

"Are you sure there isn't anything else she wants?" Steve hesitantly asked. "Maybe we could get a dragon to carry her around in its talons. Do you think that would suffice?"

Selwyn fixed him with a blank stare, saying nothing.

"You're aware that riding a dragon is forbidden?"

"I'm well aware of Rinbok Intherer's decree," Selwyn snapped. "Do you not think I pleaded my case with the Dragon Lord himself? I am one of only a handful who have ever met the dragon king and lived to tell the tale."

Steve was instantly contrite. "I'm sorry. I don't mean to be insensitive; it's just that your daughter's request isn't an easy one."

"Don't I know it," Selwyn grumbled. He fixed Steve with a stare. "That's why I'm willing to steal you a crystal. Anything that will make Aislinn smile one last time will be worth any price."

Cecil put a friendly hand on Steve's shoulder. "We have to help her. We *must* find a way to grant her wish."

Steve looked back at his friend. "I know that, Cecil. You know that. However, as you've personally witnessed, dragons aren't overly fond of humans. It's mutual distrust. They do not allow riders."

Steve eyed the dwarf and refrained from saying that in his time, he happened to be a dragon rider. There simply wasn't any way to convey that thought without revealing too much. "You need to trust me on this, Cecil. There's no way they'll allow a dwarf rider on their back." He sank down on one knee to look Selwyn in the eye. "Is there no other way?"

The dwarf adamantly shook his head. "It's the only thing she wants. I am unable to grant this wish and it tears me apart. No father should have to experience this hell. Your arrival just might be the blessing I need. If you really want that athe crystal, then you'd best hope your powers of persuasion are significantly better than mine."

Cecil tapped him on the arm. "Didn't I hear you say you were friends with the dragons?"

"I am," Steve automatically answered as he nodded his head, "but in my own time." Realizing his mistake, Steve cursed silently to himself. He smacked Cecil on the arm. "Dude, you weren't supposed to ask me that."

"What? Why not?"

"Think about that, man."

Cecil nodded sagely. "Oh, right. Sorry."

"What did you mean?" Selwyn asked, confused. "How can this not be your own time?"

Steve cringed. He quickly shot a dark glance at Cecil. "It's a long story," he assured the dwarf, "and I just don't have the time to tell it. Selwyn, could you give us a minute? I need to have a little chat with my companion in private."

"Very well." The dwarf turned and pointed at a paved road leading down into the heart of the city. "I'll be over there. Don't keep me waiting too long."

As soon as they were alone, Cecil grabbed Steve's arm and pulled him around until they were face to face. "We have to grant that wish."

"That's the problem, Cecil, we can't. Only a dragon can."

"You said before that you were friends with the dragons. Contact them. Plead our case. Perhaps they'll be willing to help."

Steve began ticking off points on his fingers. "First, the dragons here don't know me. I can't go walking right up to a dragon, tap it on the nose, and ask to speak to Rinbok Intherer. Yes, I could do that in my own time, but not here. They don't know me and they certainly don't trust me.

"Second, even if I could agree to convince the dragon that I know to allow me to ride her, there's no way she'd agree to allow a stranger on her back. The human wyverian alliance won't be created for over a hundred years. Third, the dragon-dwarf alliance is almost as new as the alliance with us humans. It hasn't happened yet. This request is practically impossible."

"How long do dragons live?" Cecil wondered. "Are any of the dragons you're friends with alive right now? Couldn't we ask them?"

"I've ridden several dragons," Steve admitted, "but I only have permission to ride Pryllan. She's an emerald green dragon who just so happens to be mated to the Dragon Lord himself, Kahvel. However, in this time, the present Dragon Lord, Rinbok Intherer, will be the sourpuss that I remember him to be, and I guarantee you he won't allow this to happen."

"Couldn't we prevail upon his sense of morality to do

what needs to be done?"

One of Steve's eyebrows jumped up. "His sense of morality? Trust me, his Royal Grumpiness doesn't have one."

"Then you must try this Pryllan character. She sounds like she would be our best bet for success."

"In my own time, I might be able to…"

"I do not care about your own time, Steve," Cecil snapped at him. "We must focus on the here and now. There's a sick child who wants to ride a dragon. Let's make it happen, shall we?"

"You have no idea what you're getting yourself into," Steve muttered.

"Then let's find out. Excuse me, Mr. Selwyn? Can you come back here for a moment?"

Steve watched Selwyn approach. As soon as the dwarf was standing before the two of them, he nervously pulled the tip of his beard from his thick corded belt and began twisting it around a finger.

"Well?"

"We accept," Cecil informed him.

Selwyn's eyes darted over to Steve's and remained there, waiting for acknowledgment. Steve slowly nodded.

"Fine. We agree. We'll get your daughter up on a dragon. Question: how do we contact you? Once we get a dragon lined up you'll need to get your daughter to the surface."

"You worry about the dragon and I'll worry about my daughter. As for contacting me, there'll be no need. I'll be watching you. Do we have an accord?"

Steve nodded. Selwyn extended his right arm. Steve reciprocated and they grasped forearms. "We have an accord."

Cecil laid his hand on their two clasped arms. "We will find a way, Mr. Selwyn. For Aislinn's sake."

Selwyn cursed and instantly released Steve's arm to brush at his rapidly filling eyes. A few seconds of silence passed before the dwarf was able to compose himself. For the first time, he smiled.

"Excellent. You'd best be going. You have work to do."

Steve raised a hand. "Is there another way out? The way down for us is no longer the way back up."

Selwyn paused a few moments before nodding his head. "You'll need a guide. I know just the person."

* * *

Hours later, Steve and Cecil finally stopped inside one of the many caverns they had passed through and sat down on the closest rock formation that could loosely be considered a seat. Steve cleared his throat. Loudly.

"Why have you stopped?" their guide inquired. Steve found it difficult to guess the dwarf's age, as his bushy beard and moustache obscured all but his eyes and nose. There were no traces of gray anywhere in the dwarf's beard or in his hair, nor were there any wrinkles on his face. "We must keep moving. We won't make it Topside at this rate."

"At this rate, we'll be in here forever," Steve crossed his legs at the ankles and tried not to scowl. "Admit it, Jonquil. You have no idea where we're going, do you?"

The dwarf's eyes opened a little wider. Steve could swear he saw a bead of perspiration trickling down Jonquil's nose. The dwarf gave a nervous cough.

"I'm not sure I follow, human."

"I sure as hell don't want to follow you," Steve grumpily returned. "We're walking in circles."

Cecil sat up straight. "What? Are you sure?"

Steve pointed a flaming hand at one of the stalagmites nearby.

"See that? There's a black scorch mark on it. I put that there the last time we came through here. I thought this cavern looked familiar once before so I deliberately marked it to see if it turned up again. That means this is the third time we've walked through this blasted cave."

Cecil stared at the black mark for a few seconds before turning to confront their guide. "Is he right? Do you not know how to get us out of here?"

"I may have made a wrong turn somewhere," the dwarf admitted.

"Well, let's just retrace our steps until you see something familiar," Cecil suggested.

"I, er, tried that," Jonquil reluctantly answered.

"You're saying we're lost? Underground, with a dwarf?"

"Please don't tell my father," Jonquil pleaded.

"Why did Selwyn tell us he knew just the right person then?" Steve demanded. "Jonquil, we don't have a lot of time. Has your father told you what we have to do?"

"Aye, he told me. You're trying to help my sister."

"That's right. We can't afford to walk around in circles like we have been doing for the past hour or so."

"I will find the way out, I promise," Jonquil vowed. He turned left, waited a few moments, turned right, and finally pointed uncertainly toward the direction they had already gone. Twice. "I'm certain it's that way."

Steve wasn't convinced. "Nuh-uh. Let's try this."

He launched a huge fireball into the air. He allowed the raging ball of fire to burn itself out, but not before he saw tendrils of residual smoke reaching out toward the tunnel ahead.

"There's an air current flowing in that direction. Alright Jonquil, you have me convinced. Let's go."

Thirty minutes later, they emerged into an almost spherical cavern devoid of any stalactites or stalagmites. The cavern's dome, Steve noted, had what looked like elongated narrow dragon scales covering every bit of the curved ceiling. He hadn't ever seen a cavern with a roof as unique.

Suddenly, the ground gave a shake, as though it was trying to relieve an itch, before it settled down and moved no more. All three froze, mid-step. Steve tapped Jonquil on the shoulder. "Do you get many earthquakes around here?"

"I do not believe that was a terra tremor," Jonquil told him, with a frown. "Terra tremors are much more powerful, and they cause unfortified rock to flex and crack. That didn't happen in here."

"So, what exactly was that?" Steve wanted to know. "What would shake this cave like that?"

Jonquil was silent. Something about this abnormally spherical cavern was bugging Steve. He nudged Cecil on the arm. "Come on, let's go. I don't like this place."

"Look at Jonquil!" Cecil hissed at him.

Alarmed, Steve looked over at Jonquil, who still hadn't moved. He was staring, wide-eyed, at the cavern's ceiling.

"Jonquil, let's clear out. I want to get away from this place."

The dwarf didn't budge. In fact, he hadn't even blinked.

"Jonquil? What's going on? Don't freak out on me. We need to get going, okay?"

Cecil gasped with alarm. Steve reflexively pumped more jhorun into his hands and his flames grew hotter and brighter. Cecil pointed a trembling finger up at the ceiling and automatically inched closer to Steve.

"What are you doing? Why are you—"

Cecil gently but firmly turned Steve's head until he, too, was looking up.

"What are we looking at? I don't ... wait. What's that? Is that ... oh, *hell* no!"

The overlapping scales covering the entire surface of the cavern's ceiling were gently swaying back and forth. They heard quiet groans that grew louder.

"Jonquil! What is it? What are those things?"

The dwarf reached behind his back to pull his single-bladed black battleax free of its holder.

"Tsak! We call them rock biters! There was a rumor that they had a new nest but no one could ever find it."

Steve groaned. "Oh, lucky us. Whoopee. We found a nest of bugs."

"They aren't bugs," Jonquil clarified. "They're tsak. This isn't good."

"Their 'sack'?" Steve repeated, certain he had misheard Jonquil's description. "As in find one and throw them in it or that's the location they need to be kicked?"

Jonquil stared at him. "What?"

"What about their sack?"

"No, they are tsak. They're vertebrates that have adapted to living in deep subterranean caves over thousands of years."

Steve looked at the curved dome over their heads. Each scale had inched away from its neighbor, as if the roof was being stretched in all directions. Each scale then split right down the middle, forming thin, translucent wings that began flapping in place. In seconds, they created a downdraft.

Steve snorted and waved a hand in front of his face. Whatever these creatures were, they certainly didn't smell very good. A strong whiff of body odor forced him and Cecil to cover their noses. Steve studied the sea of flapping wings and shook his head in amazement. There were so many!

"What can you tell us about these things?" Steve asked the dwarf. "Why do you call them 'rock biters'? Do they bite the rocks? Are they dangerous?"

"They *eat* the rock," the dwarf clarified, still not taking his eyes off the undulating ceiling.

"They eat the rock? Of course, they do. Why wouldn't they? So let me venture a guess. These things are as dangerous as they look?"

"Aye."

"Venomous?"

"Aye."

"Think it's time to leave yet?"

"Undoubtedly."

"Are we screwed?"

"Are we what?"

"Sorry. Let me try that again. Is all hope lost?"

"Only if we are discovered."

"What? What does that mean? They're all moving when they weren't a few minutes ago. Clearly, they know we're here."

"The terra tremor must have awoken them. Start moving toward the exit over there. We may get out of here with our lives after all."

A scraping noise, like two heavy rocks being ground together, sounded from behind them. As one, the two humans and the lone dwarf turned to look at a conical mound of rock. A rock biter emerged from the tip of the cone and was facing their way, affording Steve and Cecil with their first clear look of a tsak.

Steve shook his head in disgust. It was an ugly thing, like a cross between an earthworm and a bat. Its narrow black body was being propped up by its two wings, which it was using as arms. It had a flat, squished face with a tiny slit for a nose, no eyes that he could see, and an unnaturally large mouth with jaws full of razor-sharp teeth. It leered at them from its vantage point on top of the rock formation.

"How's their eyesight?" Steve asked as he absentmindedly began searching his clothing for additional power crystals. He sighed. No mimets. He had forgotten he didn't have Mythrin with him, nor its scabbard with the extra mimet pouches sewn in.

"Nonexistent," Jonquil told him. "Do you see how small and narrow the face is? It's our belief that there simply wasn't any room for eyes."

"You're telling me it's blind?"

Jonquil shrugged. "We believe so. Notice the head moving erratically from the left to the right? It's picking up scent particles from the air. It's trying to find us."

"Did it come from within those rocks? Are the rocks hollow?"

The dwarf nodded. "Aye. That's their nest. Their young are kept below ground, where there are fewer predators."

Steve started inching away from the nest. Cecil followed, and Steve grabbed Jonquil's arm.

"I don't care what they are, we are leaving," Steve told the dwarf. "Get ready to run!"

The tsak turned to face the three of them and headed straight toward them.

Steve's right hand blazed bright as he readied his jhorun. Just before it could take a bite of fresh human, or dwarf, he blasted the creature with a bolt of fire.

"Killing bugs is one thing," Steve announced with a frown, "but these are mammals. I don't like this."

Several more tsaks emerged from within the nest. Both of the thin black creatures calmly climbed down to the cavern's rocky floor and headed toward them. Steve blasted them both.

The rock biters on the ceiling ceased their flapping. Startled by the absence of the foul- smelling draft from above, Steve and the others looked up. One by one, almost in military precision, the tsak dropped down from the ceiling and began buzzing around the cavern. At the rate they were dropping, they'd have no more than fifteen seconds before there'd be so many tsaks in the air that they'd be unable to see.

A dozen of the creatures passed over his head. An instant later he stumbled forward, as if someone had shoved him from behind. A large shield was strapped to his back. His shape-changing weapon, the nohrstaf, had switched from club to shield moments before a tsak had collided with it.

"Head for the closest exit!" Steve shouted to the others as he blasted out a wall of fire and held it in place. Jonquil took Cecil's arm and pulled him across the cavern. Once they had made it to safety Steve pumped extra jhorun into his pyrotechnical barrier to keep it nice and hot in the hopes it would act as a deterrent for the swarming rock biters. He felt several more thumps as apparently the tsak kept ramming his back and coming into contact with the nohrstaf-shield.

Unfortunately, the wall of flames wasn't successful in making the advancing monsters stop. In fact, they didn't even slow down as they approached the blistering hot wall of flames. Nearly three dozen of the ugly creatures flew right through the fire wall and were instantly reduced to ash. Another dozen or so then tried to attack from above. They would have been successful had Steve not increased the size of the flaming barrier and arced it to cover their heads.

Steve risked a glance behind him. Jonquil had just joined Cecil on the far side of the cavern. He looked up. Several tsaks on the ceiling started gnawing at the stony surface they were clinging to, gouging out large chunks of stone in the process. Falling stones, the size of softballs, began raining down from above. Steve let out a shout of alarm as several fist sized chunks of rock fell harmlessly through the wall of flames and narrowly avoided striking him on the head.

"Why are they trying to drop rocks on us?" Cecil asked from his position by Jonquil.

"They're rock biters," Jonquil answered matter-of-factly, as if that alone could answer the question. "That's what they do. It's their defense mechanism. Why do you think we try to drive them out?"

Steve cursed as he ran for the exit. These weren't gravel-sized pieces of rock falling from above where, if struck, it'd leave a welt. No, these were chunks of rock large enough to be fatal if one managed to find its mark.

"We are going to have to work on our communication skills," Steve told the dwarf as soon as he made it to the safety of a tunnel. He hooked an arm through Cecil's and grabbed Jonquil by his shoulder. "Just get us the hell out of here, okay? No more surprises."

"At least they weren't guur," Jonquil mumbled.

"Not funny," Steve told him.

"What's a guur?" Cecil asked.

Steve cast him a worried look. "You don't want to know."

Rounding a turn in the tunnel, they literally ran into a bit of good luck. Two dwarves in black leather armor and helmets came around the same bend, and unfortunately, weren't quick enough to jump out of Steve's path. The three of them went down in a jumble of arms and legs. They heard the telltale crack of glass as the dwarves' lantern made contact with the ground. Their candles went out and Steve had been so surprised by the encounter that he had let his flaming hands extinguish.

Darkness quickly enveloped them, rushing in at them from all sides. No one moved. Steve had fallen on one dwarf and he could tell the poor fellow was trying to get to his feet.

"What in the name of Usol just happened?" a gruff voice barked out. "Who are you? What are you doing here?"

"Someone's got their hand on my arse," another voice said. "If you don't move it, I'll make you genuinely sorry you didn't."

They heard a loud clang as one metal object struck another.

"Trevl, that's me, you imbecile. You're sitting on my hand. If you fart on me, I will personally cut off your beard and feed it to you."

They heard a grunt. "You wish."

"Who's there?" Trevl's voice asked. "Identify yourself."

"I will just as soon as I can stand up," Steve told the two dwarves. "I'd like to light my hands but I won't do that until I know you're out of the way."

"You want to light *what*?"

"We need some light. I can provide it once I know you're not standing right next to me."

They heard some scuffling as everyone cautiously regained their feet.

"My lantern's broke."

"Forget about your cursed lantern, Bhradain. There are intruders here!"

"Jonquil," Steve called out, "any time you want to jump in here, please do so, okay?"

"Jonquil? Son of Selwyn?"

"Aye," Jonquil's soft voice answered.

"What the blazes are you doing here?"

Two torches sprang to life as Steve reignited his hands. The two dwarves turned to give him an appraising look.

"Who are you, human?" Trevl asked.

"I am Steve and this is Cecil. From the sounds of it, you already know Jonquil."

"We know his father," Bhradain corrected. "Selwyn is head of enforcement in Borahgg. Everyone knows this. You, young Jonquil, I haven't met before."

Trevl took off his helmet and held it out to Steve. "Would you mind?"

Steve held out his right hand and waited for the dwarf to relight his helmet candle. Bhradain followed suit moments later. With their helmets providing light once more, the two dwarves looked at the small party.

"What are two humans and a Kla Guur doing in these parts?"

"These parts?" Steve repeated, frowning. He looked up and down the length of the desolate tunnel. As far as he could tell it was just as unremarkable as the other dozen or so tunnels they had seen today. "What parts are these, anyway?"

"You're in Kla Chanus territory," Trevl proudly told him.

Steve and Cecil turned back to Jonquil. The two Kla Chanus turned to stare at Jonquil, too.

"He got us lost," Cecil helpfully supplied, "but not before we found a nest of something called rock biters."

Trevl and Bhradain both visibly straightened. "You found the nest? We've been looking for it for days! We need to neutralize it before the nest becomes too big. Where did you find it?"

Steve smiled and held up a lit hand.

"Let's do a trade. You tell us how to get up to the surface and we'll tell you everything you need to know about that nest."

Trevl and Bhradain grinned and bowed. Steve and Jonquil returned the bow. Cecil, not wanting to appear like an outsider, hastily offered them a small bow, too.

Once the information had been exchanged, and they had successfully located the correct branch of tunnel, which revealed a steep ascending staircase, Steve finally smiled. It had taken much longer than anticipated but at least they were back on course.

He still didn't have a clue how he was going to convince a dragon to let a dwarf child ride on its back. Could he ask Pryllan? Would that mess something up in his future if he met Pryllan now and asked a favor?

He scowled. No, that wouldn't work. Pryllan didn't know him now. Neither did Kahvel. Why would they? They had absolutely no inclination to interact with a human in this time. Why would they start now? What could he offer them in order to agree to Selwyn's request?

Less than an hour later they had reached the top of the staircase. Steve's calves were burning. He was wheezing, short of breath, and was sure his heartbeat could be heard by his companions. A quick look at Cecil confirmed that he was in no better shape. Only Jonquil appeared unaffected by the long climb up the stairs.

Oh, how he missed Sarah.

Jonquil approached a heavy iron bar that was embedded through parts of the door. He made a few adjustments and then pushed forward. Sunlight flooded through the cracks and blinded all three of them. Blinking profusely, they stumbled out into a partial clearing in the middle of a forest.

"Where are we?" Steve asked. He had no idea which way the dragon valley was, let alone which way was north.

Jonquil pointed. "The lake is west, through there, about half a league away." The dwarf kept his finger pointed to the left. "We should go toward the valley. You will have a better chance of finding a dragon there."

"Have you any ideas how we should proceed?" Cecil asked.

"I've been thinking about it," Steve admitted. "The only thing I can come up with is to approach Pryllan. I'm just worried about her reaction since we haven't officially met yet. That won't happen for quite a while."

"Afraid you'll end up changing your timeline?" Cecil quietly asked. Jonquil had cocked his head and was listening intently, even though he tried to hide it.

"Wouldn't you be? I'm treading on thin ice here. The slightest screwup now could have major ramifications for Sarah and me. I have to be careful."

"Is Pryllan the only chance we have?"

Steve nodded. "That's what I'm afraid of. I think she is."

"Then that's your answer. If you don't ask her, we will most certainly fail."

They emerged from the thick of the forest onto the eastern edge of the Lake Raehon valley. They could see the lake's eastern shore to the west, while the wide-open grassland of the valley stretched off to the south. Jonquil made a move to brush past him and take the lead when Steve pulled him back inside the forest.

"Just a moment there, pal," Steve warned. "We need a game plan before we go out there. The last time didn't end well for us."

"What do you want to do?" the young dwarf inquired.

"I'm going to try contacting the dragon that I know. If things don't go well, then we can at least get back to that door fairly quickly. You know how to get back through that door we came out of, right? I don't need you fumbling with that huge stump when there could be an irate dragon on our tail."

Jonquil nodded.

"Good." Steve took a breath. "Here goes."

Pryllan? Are you there? Can you hear me?

Silence.

Pryllan? Are you there?

No additional voices sounded in his head.

Pryllan, I realize you don't know me, but believe it or not, you and I are going to become good friends in the future.

"Anything?" Cecil asked, after ten minutes of silence had passed.

"Nothing," Steve glumly told him. "I haven't heard so much as a peep from her. There's nothing else we can do except to keep trying."

An hour later they were back at the stump door, the Kla Chanus dwarf entrance. Cecil was sitting on the ground while Jonquil had climbed up onto the door and was sitting on the stump, swinging his legs like a schoolboy. Steve had paced back and forth in front of the stump so many times that he had created a path through the thick grass. Cecil cleared his throat.

"Could we go look for her? Does she live nearby?"

Steve looked down at him. "Her nest is miles from here," he told him. "It would take us weeks to find the nest and to walk there. We don't have that kind of time."

How do you know this, human?

Steve's head jerked up and he froze in place. Sensing something amiss, Jonquil jumped down from the stump and pulled out his axe.

"What is it?" the dwarf asked. "What has happened?"

Steve held up a finger. "Just a moment. I think Kahvel just contacted me."

You know my name? How do you know wyverian communication?

I have been to your nest, have communicated telepathically with you.

I know no humans, and I certainly would never disclose the location of my nest.

Yeah, this is where it gets confusing. We won't meet for quite some time.

Kahvel's voice was silent as the gold dragon no doubt tried to process that cryptic piece of information.

We are acquaintances, but we have not yet met? This makes no sense, unless ...

That's right, Kahvel. I'm not from this time.

You are a traveler from another time?

An unwilling one, yes.

I find your claim difficult to believe.

I don't blame you, not in the slightest.

How do you know Pryllan? I know that you have been trying to contact her. I have been blocking your attempts.

I was wondering why she wasn't answering. I figured she'd at least demand to know who I am.

Hence this conversation. How do you know Pryllan, may I ask?

Through you. She saved my life when I first met her.

You are referring to the future?

Yes.

I sense no malice or deception in your thoughts.

Nor will you ever. Pryllan is one of my closest friends.

My mate? Close friends with a human?

I can't explain it. I don't know why she chose me, only that I am incredibly fortunate that she did.

Why contact her now?

I'm in a mess here, Kahvel. There are certain things I need to do in order to get back to my own time.

Elucidate.

For starters, I came through what I'm told is an interdimensional portal. It took me back in time more than a hundred years. The only chance I have to get back is to acquire an athe crystal, used to power portals, from the dwarves so that the portal in my world can be activated.

Why aren't you down below? That's where you'll find the dwarves.

I know that. I just came from there. There's something they want before they'll give me what I want. Trust me, it's a royal pain in the butt.

What is it they require?

That is what I need to talk to Pryllan about. Only she can help me.

Why should I help you? Why should I trust my mate with a human?

Because I'm the one human the two of you trust more than anyone else in the kingdom.

So you say.

You actually did, Kahvel. You told me that quite recently.

You may be telling the truth. However, I do not wish to become involved. Leave us out of your scheme.

I have no other wyverian friends to appeal to. If you don't help us, then Sarah and I will never make it home.

Sarah is your mate?

Yes.

There were several seconds of silence before he heard Kahvel's voice again.

Would Rinbok Intherer approve of what you're trying to do?

Steve sighed. *No. Definitely not.*

You speak the truth.

I told you once, years from now, that I wouldn't ever lie to you. To you, Pryllan, or Pra...

Steve trailed off as he realized he almost revealed the existence of their future offspring. Had Kahvel caught his slip?

To learn too much about one's own future can be detrimental.

Uh, thanks. I think.

Will you guarantee Pryllan will not be put in danger?

Absolutely. I would never hurt her.

You are a strange human.

My wife tells me that all the time.

Steve felt Kahvel snort, whether from irritation or amusement, he couldn't tell.

Very well. You may contact Pryllan. Be advised, human. I will know if you cause her duress.

I understand.

Kahvel's voice fell silent. Was he gone?

Steve took a deep breath.

"Are they going to do it?" Cecil interrupted, breaking his concentration.

Surprised, Steve released the breath he hadn't realized he was holding. "I'm not there yet. I just managed to convince Pryllan's mate that our intentions are pure and we mean her no harm. He has been blocking me from contacting her and has now told me that he will step aside, so to speak, and let me talk to her."

"Good luck," Jonquil told him. "I hope you can convince her. For Aislinn's sake."

"Me, too," Steve agreed. He took another breath.

Pryllan, are you there?

Several seconds passed before he tried again.

Pryllan? I need to talk to you.

Who are you?

Gone was the friendly banter. He reminded himself that this dragon was a stranger and he had to be careful. Kahvel was surely tuned in to Pryllan's emotions and would cut him off if he alarmed her too much.

Tread carefully, Steve reminded himself.

Tread carefully? Is this a prank? Are you Kahvel's friend?

Pryllan, I know this is going to sound strange, but you don't know me. Yet. My name is Steve. You and I are going to become friends. Good friends. I'm not a dragon but a human. I trust you with my life, which you have saved quite a few times I might add. I have even had the privilege and honor of saving yours once or twice.

I find that hard to believe.

That's what Kahvel said.

You spoke with Kahvel?

Yes. He didn't tell you he talked to me? It's okay if he didn't. He was trying to protect you, which is what I would have done with my own wife.

You actually spoke with my mate, identified yourself as a human, and he agreed to let you speak with me?

Surprised?

Very. You say the two of us become friends?

Yes.

When?

Are you open to believing the impossible?

Tell me more.

Good. Here's the thing. I'm from the future. I... wow, that makes me sound like a complete dork. Let's try that again. I'm from another time. I accidentally came back in time and all I'm trying to do is find a way home.

What do you need to return to your home?

An athe crystal.

The dwarves will give me an extra athe crystal if I do them a favor. I have less than two days to get this crystal to a pre-arranged location so that I can return home.

What favor do they require?

Steve mentally prepared himself and took a breath. *One of them wants to ride on the back of a dragon.*

He felt Pryllan's shock ripple through him as though he was experiencing the emotion himself.

You can't be serious.

I am.

If you and I are as close as you say, then you would know dragons don't carry riders.

Oh, I'm aware.

He felt Pryllan give an exasperated snort. **I've allowed you to ride on my back, haven't I?**

Steve smiled. *Yes, you have.*

How have we managed to keep this a secret from the Dragon Lord?

We haven't.

He knows? Wasn't he angry?

Yes.

And I continue to allow you to ride on my back?

Yes

So you're asking me to allow a dwarf on my back, is that it?

I'm asking you to allow a dying dwarf child to ride on your back. It's the one wish she has that her father cannot grant.

She's dying?

Yes. There's a problem with her heart.

You want to put an ailing dwarf child on my back?

Yes. Will you allow it?

They know. I don't know how they know, but they clearly do. Have they told you, too?

A long pause ensued before Pryllan's voice came back to him.

An ailing child, if placed on the back of a dragon, will be completely healed and become whole, as if the ailment had never occurred.

Really? Why didn't I know that?

I never told you?

No, you didn't. You make it sound like this is a bad thing. Why?

It's complicated.

Uncomplicate it for me. Healing a sick child cannot possibly be bad.

I see that I need to explain. When a wyverian willingly takes a terminally ill person on their back, and the rider is inevitably healed, then a shachar will be placed upon them.

A what?

A shachar. A life debt. The rider becomes indebted to the dragon. Forever.

Oh, snap.

Chapter 10 — A Dragon's Dilemma

Steve stared at Cecil and Jonquil in shock. A life debt? Did that make little Aislinn Pryllan's slave? That didn't sit well with him at all.

"What is it?" Jonquil hopped down from his seat on the stump. "What's happened?"

"Hold on," Steve quietly told him. "Now we have another problem."

"What problem?" Cecil asked.

Steve held up a finger, signaling him to wait a moment.

It means, Pryllan's voice cut in, **that until the shachar has been repaid the child would have to accompany me. I don't think Kahvel would approve of this.**

Tell me about this shachar thing. Is it a spell? How is it created?

All wyverians have the ability to heal, Pryllan began. **We —**

Hold up, Steve interrupted. *That makes no sense. I've seen you dragons in peril before. I've seen dragons close to death that were unable to heal themselves.*

We can heal others, Pryllan clarified, **but not ourselves.**

Figures. You can heal other people but not yourselves. How annoying is that?

Very, Pryllan agreed.

So let's say I have a small cut on my finger. If I was to hop on your back, and my finger was healed, then would I have a life debt with you? If that's the case then I must have at least a dozen of these shachars with you.

Unlikely. A shachar is created only if the ailment is terminal. May I continue?

Sorry. Go ahead.

Several seconds of silence ensued.

Pryllan? Are you still there?

Aye. You are my rider? I have saved your life?

I know where you're going with this. I was joking before. No, there isn't one between us.

How have I saved your life?

Oh, you know, swooping in to save the day, that kind of thing.

You were never physically injured?

Right.

I understand.

Can a shachar be broken?

Broken? No. It must be repaid.

Something tells me you don't want this shachar, do you?

Correct.

What if the child returns to their home and you return to yours? Couldn't you just pretend it never happened?

Someone suffering the effects of a shachar is unable to be at peace until the life debt has been absolved.

What? Are you saying the kid's going to be in pain?

That is not what I said. Let me give you an example. You say you have a mate.

Right. Her name is Sarah.

If Sarah were taken against her will do you think you would be at peace knowing she was out there waiting for you to rescue her?

Oh. I think I'm beginning to understand.

The child might not survive being burdened with a shachar.

Then here's what we need to do. Find out what it'll take to break one of these shachars.

I've already told you what will absolve one.

In that case find out if there's anything else that can do it, too. We need to know everything there is about them if we're going to break it.

We won't be able to break it.

Where there's a will, there's a way. Think positive. We'll find a way to make everyone happy.

How can you be so certain?

You need to trust me, Pryllan.

How odd. I feel as though I do.

Good. If we can break this shachar, will you consent to being ridden by a dwarf?

Aye.

Thank you, my friend.

I must be crazy.

Why? Because you've agreed to give a ride to a dwarf child while telepathically communicating with a human who you've learned will be your rider in the future?

That about sums it up.

You're taking a lot on faith. I appreciate that.

What do we do now?

I think now would be the time for us to contact the child's father and see if he was aware of any of this, and if he isn't, then he needs to be told about it.

If you do, then the dwarves will learn of the existence of the shachar.

Not if we swear him to secrecy.

Will he agree?

We're going to save his daughter's life. Yes, he will. He'd better.

If the child's father agrees to the shachar, how soon will you need my services?

Almost immediately. I'm under a serious time crunch. I have to be back at a certain place at a certain time so that Cecil and I can return home.

Acknowledged.

Pryllan, let me ask you something. How often does this type of situation come up?

By that do you mean how many shachars have been created? Not many.

How long ago was the last?

Several hundred years.

Is this a closely guarded wyverian secret? I've known you for years now and not once has this ever come up.

It is a closely guarded secret. I'm sure you can understand the importance of keeping this conversation secret.

I do. Humans already want to give dragon riding a try. If it becomes known that hopping on the back of a dragon would cure any sickness or ailment, then humans everywhere would be searching for you dragons. Can't you just see it now? Humans all across the kingdom would be throwing themselves on the backs of the dragons, just to heal a wound or cure a disease.

Precisely. I trust you will not mention this to anyone else?

Mum's the word.

I am not familiar with —

Sorry. It means that I'll keep your secret safe. I'm pretty sure Selwyn, that's the girl's father, will want to do this. The alternative is death for his daughter. Once we get them Topside, how soon before you can make it here?

Unknown. Where are you?

Umm, east of the lake?

Can you be more specific?

I wish I could. Can't you just look through my eyes like you usually do?

Once more Steve felt Pryllan's shock course through his veins.

We have shared senses?

Er, yeah, many times. Is that bad?

You have given me much to consider, my friend Steve. Very well. I will access your senses now.

Go ahead. You have my permission.

Steve turned to face the west. He walked the short distance through the trees until he arrived at the valley's edge. He looked out across the open valley and then slowly turned to look left and then right.

I have seen enough, Pryllan told him. **I can locate you now. Contact me again when you are ready.**

I will. Thanks again!

You are welcome.

Pryllan's presence faded from his mind. He turned to look back at his two friends, who had followed him.

"Good news?" Cecil inquired, hopefully.

"Yes. She's agreed."

Jonquil smiled. "I don't know how you convinced them but I do know my father will be pleased. He just wants to see my sister smile again."

"We need to get in touch with Selwyn as soon as possible," Steve informed the dwarf. His face had become stern. "There are pros and cons to this dragon ride."

"I'm not sure I follow," Jonquil admitted.

Steve strode purposely back to the stump and waited for Jonquil to open the door. "I'll explain everything once we see your father."

* * *

"I had no idea. I swear!"

"You see now why we had to find someplace quiet to talk? Pryllan is agreeing to do you a huge favor, Selwyn. I hope you remember that."

"I will be forever indebted to the dragons for this."

"You do understand the consequences of this lifetime debt? If we can't find a way to break it, or absolve it, or whatever, then little Aislinn's going to suffer."

"How do we break it?" Selwyn anxiously asked as he twisted the tip of his beard around one of his thumbs.

"I don't know. I asked Pryllan to discreetly check. Logically, the only thing I can think of is if Aislinn were to somehow save Pryllan's life."

"How would my daughter be able to save a dragon's life?" Selwyn demanded.

"Lower your voice!" Steve hissed back at him. They were standing in a narrow alley near the outskirts of Borahgg. He cast a quick glance down the darkened corridor to make sure no one was listening. "I'm just telling you that you need to be prepared. If Pryllan does find something, and you don't like the answer, you need to prepare yourself. For Aislinn's sake. Got it?"

"I will pay whatever price she asks," Selwyn vowed. "If what you say is true, and my little Aislinn lives to see another year, I will do whatever must be done."

"You do understand that Pryllan doesn't want this shachar any more than you do?"

"Aye. When is the dragon expecting my daughter?"

"Her name is Pryllan, and she's expecting to see your daughter as soon as I tell her we're all ready. As much as I'd like to do this tonight it's probably dark up there by now. We'll wait for first light. I think we should let Aislinn enjoy this. She's earned it."

Selwynn nodded, pleased. "She has, aye. Very well, we'll retire for the evening and … do you and your accomplice have lodging for tonight?"

Steve shook his head. "No, we don't."

"If you don't mind sharing a room, the two of you may stay with me and my family."

Steve and Cecil both assured him those arrangements were fine.

The following morning Steve awoke to the smell of roasting meat. His mouth began to water. He looked over at Cecil, who was snoring just as loudly as Steve probably had, and nudged him in the ribs.

"Rise and shine, sleepyhead. It's time to get going."

Cecil groaned and slowly sat up on the bed. About to protest, his nostrils flared as he picked up scents coming from the kitchen.

"Good heavens. That smells like pot roast!"

"Rest assured it's better than any pot roast you've ever had. No one can roast meat and potatoes better than a dwarf. If there were dwarf women back in my world then I'm sure they'd all have their own cooking shows with legions of fans."

"Is that a good thing?"

"Yes. Without a doubt. Want a piece of advice? Don't ask where the meat comes from."

Cecil paused in his attempt to lace his boots. "I'm sorry? What was that?"

"Take it from someone who's very finicky that the food is good here. Don't ask too many questions about the meat. See any cows around here? Things work differently here. Hmm, that reminds me. There's something else you ought to be aware of."

"What's that?"

"Dwarf women have beards, too."

"Er, excuse me?"

"Their beards are just as full and pronounced as the men."

"Are you serious?"

"Very. You didn't see Torya last night when Selwyn brought us inside. I'm telling you now so you don't freak out when you see her today."

"Does that mean Selwyn's daughter has a beard, too?"

Steve scoffed. "No. Too young."

"Oh. I'll, ah, try not to react any differently to her than I would to him."

"Good plan."

After breakfast, Cecil belched loudly and covered his mouth with embarrassment. "I am so terribly sorry. Please forgive me."

Steve grinned and slapped a friendly hand on Cecil's back. "Nonsense. Every cook loves to be complimented. Isn't that right, Torya?"

Selwyn's wife, a stout middle-aged dwarf wearing a dark blue smock with a steel gray apron tied around her waist, turned to bow appreciatively at them. Her beard, while not quite as full or long as Selwyn's, had been braided and tucked into her apron to get it out of her way while cooking.

"I'm just not used to having beer for breakfast," Cecil whispered conspiratorially. He grinned. "I might have to bring it up to AnnaBelle."

"At least you drank it," Steve returned. "I've tried dwarf ale before and I don't care for it. Then again, I don't really care for any type of beer."

"Then what did you drink?"

"The green pitcher has water in it. Quite honestly, it's the best tasting water I've ever had. Talk about pure mountain spring water."

"I would have preferred the water over the ale," Cecil quietly moaned.

"Well, now you know."

Cecil belched again as they rose to their feet. Torya, busy tending the fire in the hearth which still had half the roast spitted across it, paused to look back at them.

"Is it time, then?"

Selwyn nodded. "Aye. I will go fetch Aislinn."

"I will help you prepare her," Torya informed him. She handed the poker to Steve as she walked by him. "Can you be certain the fire doesn't burn the meat? I'm going to make a lovely stew with it later today."

"I personally guarantee those flames won't get any higher," Steve assured her. He cast a speculative eye at the fire as it crept toward the haunch of meat. Seconds later the flames shied away from the spitted roast and settled down.

Selwyn appeared in the doorway leading to the back of the house. He was cradling a large bundle of blankets in his arms. Torya appeared and started fussing with the blankets.

"You'll need to rest every thirty minutes," she told her husband. "Aislinn mustn't over exert herself. She really shouldn't be out of bed."

"We've been over this," Selwyn told her curtly. "She'll be fine. She's going to have the time of her life."

"Perhaps I should accompany you to—"

"That would arouse suspicion," Selwyn told her as he shook his head. "If all of us are seen leaving this house at the same time, people are going to wonder what's going on. Our neighbors know Aislinn is unwell. No, we must be discreet."

"Then give her to me."

Surprised, Selwyn and Torya turned to Cecil, who was holding out his arms.

"Give her to me," Cecil repeated. "If Selwyn goes outside, people will think he's holding his daughter. They're never going to believe that a complete stranger would be holding her. It will arouse less suspicion this way."

Selwyn hesitated.

"It would only be until we're away from here," Steve softly added. "Then you could take her back."

Selwyn nodded. "Very well. Cecil, is it? Do be careful. Try not to move the blankets. She cannot maintain her body heat the way we can."

Steve approached the blankets. "She's cold? May I?"

"May you what?" Torya wanted to know.

Steve leaned over Selwyn's shoulder and peered into the depths of the blankets. He saw an elfin face looking back at him with wide, alert eyes. The tiny, thin girl was shivering but she smiled at him. Steve returned the smile.

"Aislinn, would you like to be warmer?"

The girl gave a perceptible nod.

"Remove most of those blankets," Steve told Aislinn's parents.

"But she'll freeze!" Torya protested. She looked to her husband for support. Selwyn had a curious look on his face as he studied the tall human.

"Let's get some of these blankets off of her."

Torya frowned, but complied. Once all but two of the blankets had been removed, Steve laid a hand on the girl's shoulder and ordered his jhorun to warm the blankets and to maintain the heat. Selwyn grunted with surprise; it suddenly felt as if the blankets had been warming by the fire for hours.

Steve leaned over to see how Aislinn was faring. The girl was all smiles and, most importantly, not shivering.

"Better?"

He heard the faintest of whispers. "Aye. Thank you."

Selwyn gingerly handed his daughter to Cecil, who smiled down at the tiny girl. He held her to his chest and nodded his readiness. Selwyn picked up his battle axe and flipped it neatly around his back to hook it in its holder. He slid several daggers into place, slung his water bag across his chest, and then turned to see if everyone else was ready. They were.

Once they had made it away from the city's center and were approaching Borahgg's outskirts, Selwyn finally asked

Cecil to return his daughter to him. Only when they were all climbing the stairs leading Topside did Selwyn start to speak.

"You're going to love this," Selwyn was telling his daughter. "No dwarf has ever ridden on the back of a dragon. You will be the first, little princess."

"What is the dragon's name?" Aislinn asked. "I must know what to call her."

"Her name is Pryllan," Steve answered as he turned to look down at the small girl in Selwyn's arms.

"Doesn't that hurt?" Aislinn's soft voice asked.

"Does what hurt?" Steve asked as he glanced back down at the tiny underling.

"Your hands. They're burning. Does it hurt?"

"Nope. I could make it look as though my hair was on fire and it wouldn't hurt me. I can control fire."

"Can you walk through fire?"

Steve grinned. "Yes."

"Can you hold a burning log and not be hurt?"

"Yes."

"Can you spit fire?"

"Like a dragon? No."

"Can you stick your hand in a burning fire and —"

"Aislinn," Selwyn groaned. "You don't need to pester him with all these questions."

"It's okay," Steve assured the dwarf as he looked down at the girl. He winked at her. Aislinn smiled and winked back.

Once they were standing Topside, Steve called for Pryllan. When she failed to acknowledge his call, he started to worry. Had she changed her mind? Had Kahvel decreed that she couldn't carry the dwarf child?

Pryllan? Can you hear me?

"What's going on?" Cecil wanted to know.

"I'm calling her and she isn't responding. I don't know what's happened to her."

"Perhaps she's already here?" a female voice suggested.

Steve smiled as he turned to survey the area. He knew that voice. It was Pryllan! What was she disguised as this time?

Nearby, a large grass covered hill began shimmering, as though it was throwing off massive heat waves. Steve shook his head. It still amazed him to see how flawlessly a dragon could camouflage itself. The grassy hill, Steve noted, had blended seamlessly with the surrounding landscape.

The hill shimmered a few more times before the illusion dropped. Pryllan had been curled up in an almost fetal position. No doubt she had been napping while she was waiting. She stretched her forelegs while extending her wings to give them a good stretch. She gave her head a final shake before she eyed the four of them.

Cecil whistled with admiration. Pryllan was a vibrant emerald green color. Every one of her scales practically glowed in the bright sunshine. Two spiraled horns protruded from her skull and were trained on them as the dragon studied their small group. Steve grinned as he looked at Cecil's shocked face. He knew full well what it felt like to see a live dragon for the first time. The sight had taken his breath away. He shot a quick glance at Selwyn. The dwarf was no different.

Pryllan was only marginally smaller than the last time he had seen her, back in his own time. However, that didn't make her any less formidable. She was, as all Lentarian dragons, huge in comparison to a human. Her talons were easily two feet long, and he could sit comfortably on her palm. When on all fours, Pryllan stood nearly twenty feet high, and if she were to rear up on her hind legs and stretch out her neck, she could easily triple that height. Each wing, when extended, was at least twenty-five feet long, making her more than sixty feet wide from wingtip to wingtip. Steve knew there were many dragons much larger than she was, but he also knew there were dragons much smaller, such as the two-headed zweigelans.

Pryllan brought her long graceful neck down to the ground so she could see the group up close. She moved to each person and gave them a cursory sniff. Her eyes remained on Selwyn longer than the others as she gently nudged the bundle he was holding with the tip of her nose.

Aislinn extended a thin arm out of her blankets and held it away from her father. Pryllan flicked her tongue, barely grazing the child's skin. The dwarf girl squealed with delight when she had felt the dragon's hot tongue briefly make contact with her own skin.

"Welcome, young one," Pryllan began, as she raised her neck back to a comfortable level. "I understand you wish to go for a ride?"

The bundle gently shook as Aislinn nodded her head as strongly as she could. Pryllan's gaze shifted to Selwyn. The dwarf gently laid his daughter down on the grass and turned to face the dragon. He reverently dropped to one knee.

"I know not why you agreed to this, dragon," Selwyn began.

"Her name is Pryllan," Steve reminded him.

"My apologies. Pryllan, I don't know why you agreed to this but I hereby swear, in front of you and these witnesses, that I will do whatever I can to repay your kindness. I am forever indebted to you for making this happen."

Noticing that the bright sunlight was shining directly into Aislinn's face, Pryllan extended her wings and provided shade.

"Are you fully aware of what's going to happen once you place your daughter on my back?"

"If you're asking me if I was aware of this life debt then no, I wasn't. This is Aislinn's wish, not mine."

"And now that you are?"

"I have spoken with my wife about this. Until you have a child and see her in pain you can never imagine what it's like to sit idly by, like an underling, and be able to do nothing. Now there's a chance. I don't like the idea of Aislinn having debt hanging over her, but I also will say that I have faith in my new friends here. We will find a way to absolve this debt, isn't that right Steve? Cecil?"

Steve cringed at the same time Cecil gulped noisily. They eyed each other and both approached the dragon.

"I promised you before, Pryllan, that we will do whatever it takes to absolve this shachar thingamajig. I meant it."

Pryllan looked down at the girl wrapped in the blankets before returning her attention to Selwyn.

"What does your daughter have to say about this? Is this something that she wants?"

Steve turned to look down at the frail girl who was now struggling to sit upright. With her father's help she shrugged off the blankets and looked up, adoringly, at Pryllan.

"Father explained it. I would gladly agree to this. I love all dragons."

Well? Steve mentally asked Pryllan. *Satisfied?*

I do hope you know what you're doing. I was unable to find a way to break a shachar without repaying the debt. There haven't been enough recorded shachars. There was no mention of any being broken, let alone absolved.

And you're certain one is about to be created?

Look at the child. She is weak, frail. Her condition will not allow her to survive another season.

Then let's do this.

Very well.

How soon before Aislinn will be cured?

Unknown. I have never done this before. Will you put her on my back?

Sure.

Steve walked over to the little dwarf girl. He knelt down and smiled at her. "Ready to make a dream come true?"

Aislinn enthusiastically nodded. Steve blinked a few times. Did it look as though Selwyn's daughter was getting her strength back? He seemed to recall that she had struggled to smile when he had first met her. Now she couldn't stop smiling as she gazed adoringly up at Pryllan. She was sitting upright, unattended, and didn't appear to be in any pain. Steve smiled. The dwarf girl's smile was contagious.

"Selwyn, would you help her up onto Pryllan's back?"

Aislinn's father started to move the blankets off of his daughter when he gripped one tightly and looked up at Steve.

"The blankets are still warm. How is that possible?"

Steve snapped his fingers. "Right. I forgot about that. I'll let them cool off now."

Within seconds the blankets' warmth receded. Selwyn shook his head. "Incredible."

He gently picked his daughter up and turned to face Pryllan. Selwyn paused. He looked up at the dragon's imposing figure and looked over at Steve.

"I, er, uh … I don't think I can climb up there while

holding my daughter."

"Would you like me to place her up there?"

"Please."

Steve approached Selwyn and held out his arms. "Aislinn, would you allow me to carry you?"

The dwarf girl shyly nodded. Selwyn passed her to him and then stepped back. Steve straightened. The little girl was so light in his arms. He stepped up onto Pryllan's tail and carefully picked his way along her back until he was at the large flat scale at the junction of her two wings near the base of her neck that had served as his seat in the past. Future. Whatever.

Steve paused. He placed Aislinn down onto the scale and immediately noticed that her legs were swinging freely. She couldn't touch Pryllan's back. Steve eyed the mass of scales on either side of where Aislinn was sitting and frowned. There was no way this tiny girl would have the strength to hold on while Pryllan was in flight. Someone was going to have to go with her. He felt Pryllan's concern.

What's the matter?

He explained his concern.

Someone will have to accompany her. Perhaps her father?

I don't know about the dwarves in this time, Steve began dryly, *but all of them from my time, other than their kids, suffer from acrophobia. They're afraid of heights. I'm pretty sure Selwyn is going to be the same.*

At least give him the benefit of the doubt.

Alright, I will. Have you ever seen a dwarf's face turn green? Watch this.

"Hey Selwyn, we're going to need you to come up here."

The dwarf's eyes widened in shock. "Whatever for?"

"Aislinn is too small to ride alone. She's going to fall off if there isn't someone here to hold on to her. That should be you. So come on up here so we can get you situated."

Selwyn's face drained of color. "I, er, ride a dragon? Up in the sky?" His voice cracked and came out as a high-pitched squeak when he said 'sky'. He cleared his throat and tried again. "I, uh, don't think I'd be the best person for that.

Ummm…" He slapped a hand over his mouth and spoke no more.

You're right. It looks as though he's about to be sick.

Told you.

Then you must ride with her.

Me? It ought to be her father.

I really don't want him to soil my scales, which we know will happen if we press the issue.

Steve chuckled. *Very well. I'll ride behind her.*

Perhaps you should ask the father's opinion?

Right.

"Selwyn, would you like me to accompany her? I can keep her safe."

The dwarf merely gave a quick nod of his head. Steve turned to look down at Aislinn, who looked up at him with her big brown eyes.

"Would you mind some company for this ride? I guarantee you won't be cold."

Again, the girl gave him a shy nod. He gently lowered himself into position behind her and gently wrapped an arm around the girl. She was growing cold, so he increased his jhorun to help keep her warm for the duration of their flight. Steve leaned to his left and gave Pryllan's back a friendly pat.

"Ready when you are."

"Did you just pat me like you would a horse?"

Steve smiled sheepishly. "Sorry."

"Where will you be taking them?" Selwyn managed to ask.

Steve twisted to his right to look down at the ground. Aislinn spotted her father and turned to wave at him.

"Feeling alright there, buddy?" Steve asked. The dwarf still looked incredibly pale.

"I'll live. There's a reason a dwarf's legs are so short. We're meant to be close to the ground."

"I think Aislinn would disagree with you."

"Where are you planning on taking them?" Selwyn asked again, addressing the dragon.

Pryllan's enormous head swung around until it was oriented on the lone dwarf standing in the grass.

"Wherever the wind takes us."

With that, her muscles bunched together and launched her straight up, over a hundred feet. Pryllan snapped her wings open and began pumping them, gaining altitude frighteningly fast. A few seconds later the dragon and her riders had disappeared into the clouds.

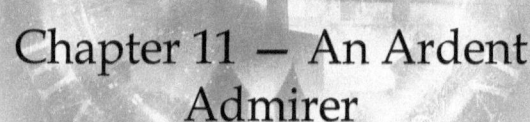

Chapter 11 – An Ardent
Admirer

Is the town much different in the future? Are there just as many people living in your time as there are now? What can you tell me about places to shop? I'd love to see what goods and services people have to offer. It's my favorite pastime."

Sarah smiled. She had persuaded Cora to make a trip into town so that they could see for themselves how well their ruse had worked. Ever since Cora had learned she'd be going into town with another female she hadn't stopped talking. Sarah only wanted to know if the people were talking about the events of last night. Had the sheriff and his men been properly frightened? What part scared them most? Was it her ghosts? Would they avoid the manor in the future? She had to know!

Sarah had offered to teleport the two of them into town, but Cora had something else in mind. She then surprised Sarah by bridling one of their three horses and guiding the mare over to her and Luther's buckboard. With Sarah's help, they pulled out the oval padded collar and gently placed it around the horse's neck. Using skills she'd acquired after living in the old west for the past six months, Sarah helped Cora harness the horse to the wagon. Tying the animal to the hitching post, rather than climbing up into the wagon to set the brake, Cora then retreated inside the manor and changed into her finest attire.

Sarah took that opportunity to teleport back to the room she was staying in at the Silver Spike to get herself cleaned up and to don her finest dress. If Cora was going to dress in her best gown, then at least she could follow suit. It was a sunny day outside so Sarah selected a dark navy blue dinner dress from her closet. It consisted of a long thin jacket with dark blue embroidery and a matching skirt with ruffles, complete with a bustle. She also selected her favorite pair of black patent leather shoes that sported thick two-inch heels. Properly outfitted for their excursion Sarah teleported herself back to the manor's foyer, just in time to hear Cora coming down the stairs.

The moment Cora saw Sarah she clapped her hands with delight. "I remember making that gown! It was one of my favorites. I am so glad to see that you ended up with it."

"It's one of my favorites, too," Sarah told her. "I'm still trying to figure out how I can take them all with me when I go back home."

Cora was wearing a cinnamon-colored dress that buttoned all the way up to her throat. It had gold accents decorating the front, with ten gold buttons running from chest to navel. The skirt had gold pleats mixed in with the cinnamon and gold embroidery along the edges.

Sarah eyed the dress with undisguised jealousy. "I love the color! You are so talented!"

Cora flushed with praise. "Thank you. Styles seem to change so fast that it's nice to incorporate new techniques here and there." Cora ran her hand along one of the golden edges of her skirt. "See the way this embroidery makes it look as though the skirt is flaring open? It really isn't but is deliberately designed to look as though it does."

"Very nice," Sarah said appreciatively. "I'll bet Luther loves that one."

"It's one of his favorites."

Taking care not to rumple her dress, Cora climbed onto the wagon's seat and waited for Sarah to untie the reins from the hitching post.

"I'm used to going into town by myself," Cora told Sarah as she tightly gripped the reins in her hands. She nudged the horse forward once Sarah had joined her on the rickety seat. "Too many people will make Luther scowl. If my husband scowls then he becomes irritable and I have no desire to be anywhere around him when that happens. I find it easier to make these journeys by myself."

Sarah was staring at her in shock. Cora guided the mare down the driveway and glanced over at her.

"What? What's the matter?"

"You just described my husband!"

"Your husband scowls, too? Don't you just want to smack it right off his face?"

Sarah burst out laughing. "Who says I haven't?"

Cora giggled at the thought. "I thought it was only Luther and I who had *that* particular problem."

"Have you forgotten that Luther and Steve are related?"

"A very good point, Sarah." Cora urged the horse into a trot. "What do you hope to find in town?"

"I want to see what people's reactions are when we come strolling into town. If they avoid us then we'll know our ruse was a success."

The wagon bounced and rattled down the gravel road. Sarah had to grip the wooden plank seat tightly so she wouldn't be bucked off. Since her arrival six months ago, she'd had the misfortune of riding in several of them.

"How do you get used to all the bumps?" Sarah managed to get out between clenched teeth. "This is far and away the most uncomfortable way to travel. I wish you had let me teleport us there. We'd already be there by now. You do realize that, don't you?"

Nearly half an acre of pines trees passed by before Cora turned to look at Sarah. "Of course, but then you'd miss all this scenery. Isn't this lovely?"

"Yes, it's great, but…"

"But?" Cora prompted. "What's the matter?"

"This seat is uncomfortable. There's no padding, or cushions, or anything else to make the journey pleasant."

"Do you not have wagons in the future?" Cora asked, curious. "How do you get around town?"

"I teleport," Sarah told her, matter-of-factly.

"And for those who don't?"

"We have cars."

"Cars?"

"It's something that hasn't been invented yet. I don't want to mess anything up and tell you something that you shouldn't know. Yet. So, I'll just ask you to trust me. You'll love them."

Approaching town, Cora guided the wagon past the city jail, which had several wagons and at least half a dozen horses tied up in front. Sarah groaned inwardly. Apparently, Steve had made a bit of a mess when he had broken Luther out. They watched several men carry new cell doors into the jail as three men carried out two of the damaged doors.

Cora's eyes widened as she glanced over at the damaged bars. "Steve cut through the cells? That's impressive. Most impressive, indeed."

"Hey, I could have been in and out of there without damaging anything," Sarah told her. "I still say I could have handled that jailbreak better."

"I am thankful you stayed behind," Cora told her as she guided her horse to an open patch of green grass that served as a sort of parking lot. She set the brake and carefully climbed down. She waited for Sarah to join her before she hooked her arm through Sarah's and guided them toward the closest row of shops. "I am envious. I would love to have a magical ability."

"Steve wishes he had my jhorun all the time, too," Sarah told her. They stepped up onto a wooden boardwalk spanning the entire length of the shops lining the street. "I personally think he's just being polite and wouldn't trade his fire throwing abilities for anything."

Sarah looked around the bustling town. More people

were arriving each minute, single riders on horseback and entire families in buckboards similar to their own. Farther down the street, in an open park with benches scattered here and there, a small brass band had set up and were playing. A crowd had formed and was taking up most of the room in the small park.

Sarah looked up and down the long boardwalk. Small tables had been set up every few feet and were heavily laden with all manner of fruits and vegetables. Interspersed with the farmers selling their crops were people peddling their goods. Freshly baked pies, homemade jewelry and trinkets, and baby clothes were just a few of the items Sarah could see.

"What's going on? Is it some type of festival?"

Cora nodded. "That's right. I had forgotten. Our harvest festival started today. It usually runs for four or five days."

Sarah smiled. "Perfect. That means there are all kinds of people in town today. I wonder how we can find some of the sheriff's men. I want to see how they're doing."

Cora shaded her eyes and slowly looked around town. While there were plenty of people milling about, they didn't recognize anyone from their performance last night. Cora tugged her arm toward a nearby store.

"Let's stop in here. They sell tack and I need to pick up a new bridle."

The store featured everything a farmer would need to take care of his animals. Saddles, harnesses, horse collars, feed, grain, and medicine were everywhere. If Cora needed a bridle, then this is definitely where she was going to find it.

Cora picked out a simple leather bridle and paid for her purchase. After inspecting the workmanship of several brand-new saddles, they moved on to the next store. They felt the heat from the forge even before they stepped inside. It was a blacksmith's storefront. They could hear the clang of metal being pounded into shape from deep within the workshop. Cora automatically stopped. "I don't think I need to go in there," she said.

It was Sarah's turn to pull her friend inside. "I'd like to look around, if that's okay. I really haven't had the opportunity to look through the shops."

"I thought you said you had been in town for six months?" Cora asked, confused. "Didn't you do any shopping then?"

Sarah shook her head. "I didn't feel like it. I was too worried about whether or not I'd ever see my husband again."

Cora nodded compassionately. "I can understand that. Speaking from my own experience, I don't think I'd ever be too distracted to shop."

Sarah laughed. "You and my mother-in-law would get along well. She literally coined the phrase 'shop til you drop'."

Cora giggled. "I like that. Yes, I think I would get along well with her. Well, what would you like to look for in here? We really must be careful. There's dirt and soot everywhere."

"I can see that. Don't worry, we won't be long. Steve has a strong interest in blacksmithing and I want to be able to tell him what this one was like."

Rows of rakes, hoes, and scythes lined one wall. Another had huge bins full of nails and spikes. And yet another had horse shoes, plows, and other bits of metal ready to be assembled into something else.

"Are you looking for anything in particular?" Cora asked as she inspected horse shoes.

"Not really. I don't see any swords or weapons in here so he probably wouldn't be too terribly interested in this."

"Swords?" a gruff voice barked from behind them.

Both women whirled around to see a huge bear of a man towering over them. Ordinarily someone that size would have frightened Sarah but he had such a harmless puppy-dog look on his face that she couldn't help but smile up at him.

Cora smiled up at the proprietor, too. "Hello, Kendall. How are you today?"

"Ms. Miller! What a surprise to find you here! How can I be of service today?"

"Kendall, this is Sarah. She's a friend of mine."

Kendall went to shake her hand when he noticed his own was covered in dark smudges. He whipped his hand behind his back and simply nodded his head.

"A pleasure, ma'am. Any friend of Ms. Miller is a friend of mine."

"How do you know Cora?" Sarah asked, curious.

"She made my beautiful Catherine her wedding dress. She still can't stop raving about it. Is there something I can help you two lovely ladies with? Did I hear something about swords? You won't find any of them in here. I'd consider it, if enough people wanted them."

"My husband has an interest in blacksmithing. I knew you wouldn't have anything like that in here but I did want to be able to honestly tell him that I went in and checked."

A huge smile appeared on Kendall's face.

"No problem. Feel free to look around. If you need anything just holler. I have to finish an order for a small plow."

Kendall retreated into the back area of his shop and the loud clanging began anew. Cora gestured toward the door. Sarah nodded and was about to take a step in that direction when she came to a stop and pulled Cora next to her.

"You know a lot of people in town. Do you know who that is?"

Cora looked to see where Sarah was pointing. On the other side of the street was the Kootenai County Telegraph Office. Leaning up against the northern side of the building, a lone man was staring straight at them. He appeared to be in his late teens or early twenties and was wearing a mish-mash outfit consisting of dark wool pants, a blue button-down long-sleeved shirt, and a red sash around his waist. He also had a revolver on each hip.

"I don't know who that is," Cora whispered to her. "I'm sure I've seen him before. He sure does seem intent on what we're doing, doesn't he?"

"Yes, he does. Let's go."

They stepped out onto the boardwalk when a group of four men walked by. Sarah was ready to pull Cora back into the blacksmith's shop when one of the four men dropped his gaze to the ground and stepped to the side, giving himself as much room from the two women as possible as they passed. The man walking beside him glanced irritably at him but didn't say anything. They kept walking, without so much as looking at the ladies as they passed by.

"Did you see that?" Sarah asked, dropping her voice. "I think that man deliberately avoided you."

Cora turned to look at the backs of the four retreating men. "Which one? The one that stepped to the side? How can you be sure?"

Sarah shrugged. "I'm not. It just looked that way. Come on, let's keep looking around. I want to put some distance between us and Mr. Creepy across the street."

The next shop they visited must have been one of Cora's competitors as she mumbled something under her breath and pulled Sarah into the store. A young girl of about twelve was behind the counter.

"Wow, she's young," Sarah observed.

"That's Hattie," Cora softly answered. "She's Miranda's daughter."

"Who's Miranda?" Sarah wanted to know. "The owner?"

"Yes. She has copied many of my designs and undercuts my prices."

Sarah went to the closest rack and pulled out a pink frock coat with ruffles for sleeves.

"Trust me, you have nothing to worry about."

"That is definitely not one of my designs," Cora told her. "I'm not a big fan of pink. Besides, the ruffles belong on the skirt or the bodice, never on the sleeves."

The young girl from the counter approached as they were perusing a rack of gowns in various shades of green.

"Can I help you with something? I... wait. I know you. Mama doesn't like you very much."

Cora smiled at the girl. "I was just looking, Hattie. I like to see what other people have done to see if I am inspired to try something new."

Satisfied with that answer, the girl returned to the counter.

Sarah pulled a lime green gown from the rack and was inspecting the skirt. None of the pleats were straight and one even had a break in the line, as though the seamstress had run out of thread. She replaced the dress and looked around. Sure, there were a few dresses that were nice but the quality of work was nothing compared to Cora's.

Cora tapped her on the shoulder to get her attention and pointed at the window. "Our friend is following us."

Sarah scowled. "What does he want with you? I have half

a mind to drop him in the middle of the lake."

"And if he drowned?" Cora prompted.

"I said I wanted to," Sarah answered, with a mischievous smile, "I never said I'd actually do it."

"Besides, he's more interested in you than me."

That got Sarah's attention. "What? Are you sure?"

"I've been watching him. I've moved around the store, in clear view of the windows. He never once turned to see what I was doing. He only has eyes for you."

Sarah frowned. "I don't know him. I've never met him. That's just creepy."

"I agree. Let's move on."

They stepped out of the clothing store and saw the same four men from before step across the street and into the closest saloon. Sarah gave her companion a quick nudge before hurrying after them. They pushed through the swinging doors and settled into chairs at a nearby table. Glancing around the room, Sarah saw that nearly two-thirds of the tables were occupied, with patrons ranging from grime-covered miners to elegantly dressed couples enjoying the day.

"Are you two lovely ladies here to take advantage of our free lunch?" a man's voice cut in, causing both women to gasp with alarm. "My apologies, ladies; I didn't mean to startle you."

Sarah recovered first. "It's okay. Did you say free lunch?"

The tall man was wearing a red vest over a white long-sleeved shirt, black pants and shoes, and had a white apron tied around his waist. A black bow tie and matching black sleeve garters completed the outfit. The bartender turned to gesture toward a long narrow table laden with plates of cold cuts, yellow cheese, bowls of black beans, and stalks of celery and carrots. There were also bowls of dill pickles, potato chips, pretzels, and salted peanuts.

"Please help yourself, ladies. Lunch is on the house as long as you each order two drinks."

"Does an iced tea count?" Sarah asked.

The bartender nodded. "Of course."

Cora smiled. "We'll have two iced teas, please."

"Coming right up."

While their drinks were being prepared Sarah and Cora wandered over to the lunch table. Sarah chose a few cold cuts and a piece of cheese while Cora selected a piece of ham, a few pretzels, and several stalks of celery. The bartender returned to their table just as they did and served them their drinks.

Sarah had kept an eye on the men sitting several tables away. Thankfully none of them had bothered looking their way, which she took as a good sign, but a little part of her pride was annoyed. Not one of the men had even bothered to check them out! She knew that she and Cora could turn heads no matter what room they were in, as evidenced by their leisurely stroll down the boardwalk. However, here in this saloon, where there were only two occupied tables, not one of the men had bothered to look up. Hopefully they had more pressing things on their mind.

Sarah took a sip of her tea and smiled. Unsweetened tea was so much better than the sweet tea most people enjoyed from their time. Then she saw Cora dump several spoonfuls of sugar from a sugar jar into her tea and mix it together. Good thing she hadn't said anything.

"That was the biggest damn mess ever."

Sarah and Cora both looked up from their tea and then together looked over at the four men sitting huddled together.

"I figure we must have angered ev'ry damn spook for a hundred miles."

"Shut yer mouth, Gene," a second man grumbled. "I don't wanna talk about it."

"Talk about what?" a third man asked.

Gene, the man who'd avoided Cora outside the blacksmith's shop, spoke up. "We were sent to burn down a house," Gene told them in whispered tones. Sarah and Cora had to practically hold their breath in order to hear them. "Didn't see why we were s'posed to burn down the house but clearly it's a good thing we didn't."

"Why not?" the third man asked. Gene's hushed, conspiratorial tones had already unsettled him. "What happened?"

"All hell broke loose, that's what happened. Spooks were

floating up off the ground and massing at that cursed house."

"Spooks? You sure you weren't drunk?"

Gene put down his bottle of beer as if he had been caught drinking after promising never to drink ever again.

"Hank, I'm telling ya I weren't drunk. Let me tell you, I started drinkin' once I made it back home, though."

"What, exactly, did you see?" Hank asked.

The fourth man, who up until this point hadn't said anything, slammed his third empty bottle of beer down and reached for another. "It ain't natural," he muttered crossly.

"What isn't?" Hank asked, growing more nervous by the second.

"The things I saw last night, that's what."

"You think you saw somethin' last night, too?" Hank asked, nervously eyeing his empty bottle.

Ever the vigilant barkeep, the bartender swooped in to remove the empty bottles and replace them with new ones. Hank grabbed another beer and swallowed noisily.

"Let's hear it. What'd you see?"

"I ain't talkin' 'bout this no more," the fourth man stated.

"Gene, what about you? What'd you see?"

"Spooks. Rising up from the ground. We watched 'em all fly into that blasted house."

"That huge manor east of town?"

"Right. Must have been a hundred of 'em. They all rose, quiet as a mouse, and flew inside."

"Weren't there people inside?" Hank wanted to know. "What'd they do?"

"They're in league with 'em. I swear it."

Hank blinked with surprise. Neither noticed the two women sitting nearby who were doubled over with silent fits of laughter.

"You're kiddin'. That's a lie."

Gene stubbornly shook his head. "It ain't. I swear it on my pappy's grave!"

"You're makin' that up," Hank insisted, growing angry. "Why would anybody live in a house with spooks in it?"

"I ain't makin' it up. I saw her earlier today."

"Who?"

"The lady of the house. She's here, in town. She was just strollin' along without a care in the world. I know her house is infested with them spooks. The only way she wouldn't be concerned was if she could control them. That's it. She's gotta be a witch. Think about it. It makes perfect sense! She summoned those spooks to her once she saw that her house was in danger. It's the only explanation!"

Cora turned to Sarah and suppressed a giggle. "I'm a witch now, am I?"

Sarah couldn't stop the smile from spreading across her face. "Oh, this is priceless!"

"She even made it rain bugs!" Gene continued. He shuddered, which caused the fourth man to suddenly stand up from the table and stride outside. "He must have been one of those unlucky fellers that was covered with them critters. Never have I heard such shrieks of terror."

Hank's eyes were open so wide that they couldn't open any wider. "She made critters fall on you? Er, just one or two or was it —"

"SHE MADE IT RAIN BUGS!" Gene interrupted, becoming more and more agitated. "Do you have any idea how terrible that must have been? I only got a few on me, but the ones that did got down into my britches, Hank. Do you hear me? They were in my *britches*!" Flecks of spit flew out of Gene's mouth as he became more and more crazed.

A soft giggle sounded from behind them. Three angry faces turned to see two women sitting at another table. Sarah, mortified that she had been unable to contain her laughter, was looking down at her hands, which she had clasped together on the table. Hank rose angrily to his feet.

"You find somethin' funny, lady?"

"You're being silly," Sarah told him, deciding to see how riled up she could make him. "The Millers live at the house you're talking about. They've lived there for a few years now. I believe that it was Luther who built the place. You're saying he built a haunted house?"

"I know how it sounds!" Gene was practically shouting at the top of his lungs. "You gotta believe me!"

Sarah made deliberate point of dropping her head to

address Cora, who sat with her back to the three men.

"Maybe Luther built the house on an Indian burial ground. I hadn't considered that possibility."

If possible, Gene's ashen face became even paler. Cora finally turned in her seat and looked up into Gene's shocked eyes.

"That's not a very nice thing to say about me, is it?"

Three grown men screamed in unison and bolted for the door.

"Hey!" the bartender shouted after them. "You forgot to pay your tab!"

Gene tossed a handful of coins up into the air behind him as he ran down the street. They darted around the bend in the road and vanished from sight. The bartender collected the coins from the ground and eyed the two women still seated at their table.

"It would appear that your gentlemen friends have left enough to pay your tab, too. Shall I take care of that for you?"

"How nice of them!" Sarah exclaimed. She looked at Cora, whose face had slowly melted into a frown. "What's the matter?"

"Don't you think this is going to have some repercussions on you when you return to your, er, home?"

Sarah slowly stood and pushed her chair back under the table. Cora did the same.

"It probably will. In my time there's no record of the manor being haunted, so this will more than likely have some effect. We can't worry about that now. I can live with rumors about my house. I can't live without my husband. If this is what it takes to keep you and Luther safe, then so be it."

Cora smiled gratefully as she and Sarah stepped back out into the bright sunshine. They hadn't made it more than a few steps before both women stopped in their tracks. A brand new aroma was in the air and it was one they couldn't ignore: freshly baked muffins.

"Whatever that is sure smells good," Sarah remarked. "That must be the new bakery which opened last week."

Cora turned and pointed in the direction they were walking. "It's that way. Fresh Baked opened next door to the barber shop. Want to go?"

Sarah hooked her arm through her friend's and together they followed their noses north. Three stores down they saw a brunette woman, wearing a white long-sleeved blouse with a black floor-length skirt covered by a white apron. She was carrying a tray of assorted muffins. The woman was greeting everyone that passed by with a smile, regardless of whether or not they chose to patronize the bakery. The bakery's door had been propped open to allow as much of the fresh cool air in as possible. On the main window was a picture of a huge orange muffin that had light colored flecks on the crown. A comical smiley face had been drawn in on the cupcake's base. Sarah stopped in front of the shop and looked through the open door. A second person, a tall balding man with his back to them, was moving trays of bread from one rack to the other. The woman with the apron appeared in front of them and held up her tray.

"Fresh baked muffins! Care to try a sample?"

Sarah looked down at the gorgeous works of art nestled on the tray and whistled in admiration. No muffins she had ever made, whether from a box or from scratch, came close to looking as good as these did.

"These look lovely," Cora observed. "What flavors are they?"

The dark-haired woman gave them a million-dollar smile. She rested a corner of the tray on her hip and started pointing at different sets of muffins.

"This is blueberry, which is quite good; right next to it is apple crumb. Mixed berry comes next, followed by my personal favorite, oatmeal pumpkin. I'm Aras. Nice to meet you!"

Sarah returned the smile. "What a pretty name! It's nice to meet you, too, Aras. I'm Sarah."

Aras smiled and handed Sarah a muffin. "You need to try the oatmeal pumpkin. Trust me, you won't find anything better."

Sarah accepted the muffin and carefully pulled it apart. She handed a piece to Cora and then surprised their new friend when she offered her a piece of the muffin, too.

"It's wonderful," Cora agreed. "I've never been able to bake like that. Your bakery is going to be a huge success, Aras."

Aras's eyes sparkled with recognition as she looked at Cora. "Wait a moment. I know who you are. You're the seamstress! Your dresses are to *die* for! I would love to own one of your dresses but, sadly, not yet. They're a bit above my budget."

The beginnings of a smile appeared on Cora's face. "Then I propose a trade."

Aras's eyes flew open. "A trade? What could we possibly trade for?"

"If you can provide a dozen muffins once a week, let's say for two months, then I will give you a gown."

"A dozen muffins? That's it? But that's nothing! Deriksen would let me have that once a day if I'd like."

"You're sure he'd let you have that many?" Cora skeptically inquired. "That's a lot of muffins."

Aras glanced back at the bakery. "It'll be fine. Trust me, Deriksen makes dozens of muffins each day. That man sure loves his muffins."

Cora turned to look inside the open door. "Is that Deriksen in there?"

Aras didn't bother turning around. "Yes. He's the owner."

"Do we have a deal?" Cora asked.

Aras excitedly jumped up and down as she emphatically nodded her head yes. She held out her tray to Sarah.

"Could you hold this for just a moment, please?" The instant Sarah took the tray Aras caught Cora's wrist and pulled her into a hug. "We have a deal! Thank you so much!"

The tray was handed back just as Aras pointed toward the bakery. "Let's go inside for a bit."

Once inside the shop they were introduced to Deriksen, a friendly man who, they were told, was famous all across the country. They learned he had operated a bakery in Philadelphia before deciding to try his luck out west. Wherever he went his baked goods drew rave reviews. In fact, in the few minutes they had spent inside the bakery, several passersby had hollered and waved, to which Deriksen had promptly smiled and waved back.

Having never been in a nineteenth century bakery, Sarah took her time looking around. The shop, while small, had everything it needed crammed into the tiny area. The far wall was comprised of bricks and encompassed several ovens. One reminded Sarah of a pizza oven and was chest high. There was a much larger oven down lower that could almost pass for a fireplace, only Sarah could see grooves along each side of the large oven where racks, or trays, could be placed.

In front of the ovens was a huge bin full of long loaves of bread. The far right of the bakery had a large work bench spanning just about the entire length of that wall. That's where Sarah could see rolling pins, canisters of flour, sugar, and other assorted ingredients.

The far-left wall had an enormous rack that had multiple shelves. She could see dough proofing and loaves of freshly baked bread cooling. Stacked on top of the racks had to be at least thirty empty trays, waiting to be used.

Sarah was about to tell Deriksen that she loved the bakery when she noticed Aras standing silently by the window, her arms crossed. Sarah glanced back at Cora, who was inspecting the fresh loaves of bread in the huge bin.

"What's wrong?" Sarah asked, in a hushed tone.

"That man is still there," Aras told her. She pointed at the figure leaning against the hitching post across the street in front of another saloon. "I saw him there a little bit ago and didn't like the way he was looking at you so I ushered you inside here. He's not going away."

As they were staring at the man he suddenly straightened and walked across the street, angling straight toward the bakery.

"Deriksen!" Aras sharply called out. "Heads up. We might have a problem."

Deriksen appeared and wiped the excess flour off his hands onto his apron. He looked at the figure walking purposely toward them.

"What's the matter? What's wrong with that guy?"

"I have a funny feeling about him."

The man stepped through the door and ignored everyone

but Sarah. He tipped his hat at her. "Good afternoon, ma'am."

Sarah, convinced there was something wrong with this person, kept her guard up. "Good afternoon. Why are you following me?"

"You noticed, did you?"

"It's rather hard to miss. One person leering at another is generally considered rude."

Deriksen inched closer to one of the many rolling pins stacked neatly on the far corner of the work bench.

"I've seen you around town," Mr. Creepy said. "I'm an admirer. I was hoping to accompany you to the festival this evening."

"No, thank you. That won't be possible."

Mr. Creepy made eye contact with everyone in the bakery. He finally grinned and again tipped his hat at Sarah. "Can't blame a man for tryin'. Good afternoon."

He left the store and immediately walked away, disappearing around the nearest building.

"I don't trust that guy," Sarah announced to the room. "There's something smarmy about him."

"You're more than welcome to wait here for a while," Deriksen offered. "I will not have one of my patrons accosted by a stranger."

"Thanks, but it's okay. I can handle myself."

Cora tapped their new friend on the shoulder to get her attention. "Remember our deal, Aras. Come by the manor, at your earliest convenience, and we'll get you fitted."

Aras's smile illuminated the room. "Thank you so much! I look forward to it!"

After they left the bakery, it was decided they should return to the manor. Something about that unsavory character had spooked Sarah. As she followed Cora back toward the wagon Sarah cursed silently to herself. If only she had been allowed to teleport Cora they could be back at the manor by now. However, since they had driven the wagon here, they'd have to drive it back.

The streets became busier and more crowded as the many activities of the harvest festival got underway. Sarah looked at the numerous people walking by. At least it was crowded. There was safety in numbers, so hopefully they'd be left alone. Nevertheless, she kept turning to look behind her, halfway expecting to see Mr. Creepy tailing them. Thankfully they didn't see any sign of him.

Their luck ran out as soon as they walked by the small park that had the band playing in it. Couples were dancing to the lively music while many others clapped approvingly nearby. Cora pulled Sarah to a stop.

"Your friend is back."

"Damn," Sarah swore softly. "Where is he? If he tries anything his sorry tail is going to end up in Timbuktu."

"Where's that?"

"Somewhere very far from here," Sarah assured her. She turned to look behind her. Sure enough, there he was about twenty feet back. "He's not even trying to disguise the fact that he's following us. That can't be good."

As she and Cora turned to hurry away from the park, they were stopped by a veritable wall of huge men deliberately blocking their way with no qualms about it. In fact, every one of the men had a nasty leer on his face until they saw Cora. Several of the men nervously eyed each other as they became unsure of what to do.

"May I have this dance, milady?"

Cora turned to see Mr. Creepy expectantly holding out his hand.

"I don't think so," Cora nervously answered.

Mr. Creepy smoothly turned to Sarah. "May I have this dance?" he repeated. He continued to hold his hand out.

Sarah shook her head. "Sorry, but I'm married."

"I don't see your husband here. I want to dance. Shall we?"

Mr. Creepy's hand never wavered. He waited, patiently, as though he was the perfect gentleman and to refuse would be a faux pas.

Sarah held her ground. "You need to leave."

Thinking that she'd be perfectly safe with hundreds of people as witnesses, she turned toward Cora and urged her to go. The instant she turned her back Mr. Creepy lunged forward to encompass her in a bear hug.

"If I ask a woman to dance, then she's expected to dance," Mr. Creepy hissed in her ear.

Sarah started to scream. "Help! Help! Get away from me!" She looked imploringly at the people hurrying by. Every single one of them had their heads down and refused to lift a finger to help her. "What's wrong with you people? Help me!"

Cora rushed forward to help but was grabbed from behind, too. She struggled helplessly against her assailant but there wasn't any way she could break out of his iron grip. She did the only thing she could: scream.

Suddenly Sarah remembered something Steve had told her. He had taken years of taekwondo lessons and had shown her some of the brutal, but effective, ways to break an attacker's grip.

She ceased her struggling and heard Mr. Creepy chortle. Sarah took a deep breath. Here we go.

She stomped down on Mr. Creepy's right foot. Hard. He bellowed and she felt his arms go slack, although he hadn't completely released her. She took a step to her left and rammed her right fist straight into his groin. He doubled over in pain. His eyes bulged as both of his hands clutched his damaged anatomy. Twisting to her right, she hooked her left hand behind his neck, planted her right hand on the small of his back, and then twisted again.

Mr. Creepy flew through the air and crashed heavily onto the ground. A hush fell over the crowd. A small child started to cry.

Smiling victoriously and running on an extreme adrenaline rush, Sarah turned to look at the thug holding Cora. She didn't want to reveal to the townsfolk that she was a teleporter, but there was no way she could let harm befall Cora. What should she do? Well, she could—

A hand holding a damp cloth slapped over her mouth. Sarah took a breath to scream, but instead she sucked in sweet, sickly fumes. Before she knew what was happening, she succumbed to the trichloromethane and passed out.

One of the heavily muscled thugs slung her over his shoulder like a sack of flour. The other tucked the cloth doused with chloroform into his back pocket. Moments later, Mr. Creepy regained his feet and gave a dismissive wave to Cora. The thug dropped her, unceremoniously, onto the grass.

Now Mr. Creepy walked over to Sarah's unconscious form, slung over one of his henchman's shoulders. He grinned maliciously at the crowd. One by one, the townsfolk dropped their gazes to the ground. Whistling a merry tune, Mr. Creepy followed his henchmen toward a non-descript wagon waiting nearby.

"So why's he want her so bad?" the thug carrying Sarah asked Mr. Creepy.

"I have no idea why the sheriff wants her. I don't care, either."

Chapter 12 — A Promise Kept

Hold tight. It'll wear off in just a moment. I'll create a couple of fireballs for you, okay? That ought to warm you up. It takes some getting used to, doesn't it? The first time it happened to me it shocked me senseless." Seeing that the young girl had started shivering, he increased his own body temp by a few degrees and waited for the dragon to break through the thick layer of clouds.

Everything was going great. Perfect, actually. Every time Pryllan beat her wings the dwarf girl giggled with delight. Now, however, the dragon decided she was going to show off a little, rising higher into the sky. The first cloud they passed through coated them with a fine chilly mist. Steve shrugged it off as his jhorun compensated by increasing his core temperature. Aislinn, on the other hand, gasped with shock and was rendered as still as a statue. Steve leaned over to see for himself that she was alright.

"I have never felt anything like that before," Aislinn whispered, after she had regained her composure.

"Really?"

The young dwarf girl craned her neck to look up and back at him. She gave him a disquieting look. "There aren't many clouds underground."

Steve chuckled. "Let me ask you something. Are all dwarves born with a healthy dose of sarcasm?"

Aislinn flashed him a smile and returned her attention to their steady ascent. The cloud bank stretched on endlessly. Higher and higher they rose as Pryllan punched her way through the clouds. Bright sunshine temporarily blinded them. Steve, directly facing the sun, saw teeny tiny little spots everywhere. His eyes cleared and he looked around. His eyes widened. Being above the clouds meant—

Steve threw an arm around Aislinn's tiny waist and held her tightly. With his other hand he gripped the large scale they were sitting on.

"What's the matter?" Aislinn inquired. "Why are you alarmed?"

"Wait for it," Steve quietly told her. "She's gonna hit it right about…"

They were slammed backward, as though they had just been released by one of R'Tal's huge catapults. Pryllan grunted with concentration as she angled her wings first left and then right. Using her tail as a rudder she kept them level as the powerful tailwinds picked them up like a child's toy and flung them eastward.

"We've been up this high a few times," Steve explained to the girl. "Once we can get high enough, and clear the clouds, Pryllan can find some really strong winds that will pretty much carry us to the other side of the kingdom, all with minimal effort. It comes in handy."

"Which way are we heading?" Aislinn asked. She looked up at the overhead sun, and then back at Steve. "Are we flying east?"

Steve nodded. "Very good, Aislinn. That's right. We're heading east."

"Why?"

"Umm, what?"

"Why are we heading east?"

"Why not?"

"That's not an answer."

Steve smiled. He was liking this dwarf underling more and more. "It's the answer I have to give."

"Have you ever seen the sea, young dwarf?" Pryllan's voice asked.

Aislinn fell silent.

Pryllan? A dwarf is generally afraid of the water. They can't swim. They sink.

Oh. I thought she might be interested in seeing a body of water larger than any she has ever seen before.

Pryllan's right wing dipped low and she started to turn.

What are you doing? Don't turn around now. Aislinn will know something's up.

Something *is* up. I don't want to frighten the poor child.

Just keep the aerobatics to a minimum and we'll be fine.

Are you insinuating I am a reckless flyer?

Not at all.

Pryllan hesitated.

Do I become so in the future?

Not really, no.

Not really? What does that mean?

Steve sighed.

From time to time, you've been known to take a few risks.

I find that difficult to believe.

I know you do.

You are a strange human.

I know that, too.

"Can you tell me how we met?" Pryllan inquired, using her normal voice so that Aislinn would feel included.

"I'm not sure …what if I change something by telling you of our first encounter and *that* influences your decisions from now on? You might end up doing something else that day besides finding me and saving my life."

"I saved your life during our very first encounter?"

"Damn. That one slipped out. Yes, you did."

"Fear not," the dragon complacently told him. "The passage of time has a way of righting itself if something goes wrong. Some things are just meant to be."

Steve looked up from the soft blanket of clouds far beneath them and saw that Pryllan bent her neck around to look him in the eye.

"I wish I had your certainty. Okay, let's see. I had been kidnapped and managed to free myself. However, I was in a strange country wandering aimlessly alone. I was lost. Anyone who knows me would attest to my lousy navigational skills. Anyway, Kahvel told you about my predicament and enlisted your aid to find me. You're the one who did."

Aislinn twisted around in her seat and gave him an appraising stare. "How could someone kidnap you? You're too big."

"Someone snuck up behind me and conked me over the head," Steve recalled as he absentmindedly rubbed the back of his head. "When I awoke, I was tied up in the back of a wagon. I freed myself and then foolishly set off on my own to try and find Sarah."

"Is she your wife?" the girl wanted to know.

Steve nodded. "Right. No one could find me, nor did I have any chance of finding my way back. Kahvel, that's Pryllan's mate, was supposed to be our guide and I know he felt bad about losing me under his watch, so he enlisted Pryllan's help to try and locate me just as quickly as possible."

"That was nice of her."

"I thought so then, too."

"I must have known who you were," Pryllan said more to herself than anyone. "I must have remembered our meeting from this time. Why else would I willingly volunteer to look for a human?"

"I don't know. Maybe you were being nice?"

Pryllan shook her massive head.

"Rinbok Intherer has said, repeatedly, that we weren't to trust humans and to keep our distance from them. I only now begin to realize just how misguided his preconception of all humans can be."

Feeling a kink develop in his left knee, Steve stretched his leg for a few moments. Aislinn also fidgeted within his grasp. She sat straighter, fidgeting with her blankets. Steve tapped her on the shoulder.

"What are you doing? Is everything okay?"

Aislinn pulled the outermost blanket from her shoulders, folded it to form a cushion, and slipped it beneath her. Twisting around, she laid a hand on Steve's chest. She stared up at him in awe.

"You are warm. Very warm."

"My wife tells me that all the time," Steve told her, with a smile.

Can you feel the child's heartbeat?

Surprised that Pryllan had switched back to communicating telepathically, Steve hesitated. The dragon turned her neck and gave them each a quick glance to make sure they were okay.

I could if I held my fingers up to her throat, Steve wryly thought to the dragon. *I might have a difficult time explaining that one. Why do you ask?*

It grows stronger. The child's health is returning.

Has the shachar been created?

It has. I felt it form the moment she was placed on my back.

I'm sorry for getting you into this mess, my friend.

And I trust you will get me out of it.

I will. I don't know how, but I will.

I believe you.

"Do you think we're far enough from the valley now? I'm sure Aislinn would love to see what's below us."

Pryllan turned her head until she was staring at the two riders on her back. "How did you know I was trying to avoid the valley?"

"Please. That's an easy one. You want to make sure we're not seen by any other dragons so Mr. Grumpypants doesn't learn what we're doing."

Aislinn let out a soft giggle. Pryllan gave them a throaty chuckle.

"We should be far enough away to avoid detection. Let us begin our descent."

"Will everyone please raise your seatbacks into the upright and most uncomfortable position and lock your tray tables into place?"

"What was that?" Aislinn asked.

"I do not understand your meaning," Pryllan added.

Steve shook his head. "Oh, forget it. It was just a joke."

Sensing her riders might like a thrill, Pryllan tucked her wings close to her body and bulleted straight down. She punched through the thin cloud layer. All Steve could do was hold on as Pryllan plummeted ever closer to the ground. Or water, in this case.

Aislinn shrieked with delight. Her eyes were alive with wonder and she clutched Steve's arm with both of hers. Steve felt a sense of shock. Aislinn was gripping with a strength she simply didn't have an hour ago. Was her health returning that quickly?

Several hundred feet above the surface of the water, Pryllan snapped her wings open and arrested their fall. A split second later she was cruising easily along. Steve cleared his throat and tapped the nearest scale to get Pryllan's attention.

"Give us a little bit of a warning before you do that again, okay?"

"Is there a problem?"

"I'm told dragons don't like anyone peeing on them."

"That is correct. It ... Have you—"

"No, I haven't," Steve assured her with a laugh. "Although I don't think it would have taken much more, let me tell you."

"My most profound apologies."

"Nuh-uh. No, you don't. No apologizing."

Aislinn sat up and flung the last blanket off of her.

"That was so much fun! Let's do that again! Everyone must love dragons!"

"I think one rapid descent will be quite enough," Pryllan told the underling.

"You're right, of course," Aislinn added, surprising them by switching gears so quickly. "Look at all the water! It's everywhere!"

"You do know that dwarves are supposed to be afraid of water, don't you?" Steve asked, giving Aislinn a friendly nudge on her shoulder.

"Because we can't swim? If we need to cross the water,

then we'll just find another way to do it. I'll bet we could build something that could carry us across."

Steve bit his lip. "Like a boat?"

Aislinn beamed her delight up at him. "Yes! You're smart, for a human. We could build boats that can carry us across the surface. That way no one would have to get wet."

"Why would a dwarf need to cross the water?" Steve hesitantly asked, afraid of what he'd hear for an answer.

"Why, to get to the other side, silly!"

Steve groaned and Pryllan chuckled.

Aislinn effortlessly rose to her feet and, holding Steve's arm, cautiously peered over the side of Pryllan's body to see what was directly beneath them. It didn't work. Pryllan was just too massive.

"A moment, if you please," the dragon told them. "I will help."

Steve held on to Aislinn's arm while Pryllan banked left. Once she was executing a flawless left turn, and with the dwarf girl stretching out as much as she was able, they could see the dark blue choppy waters of the sea.

"There's so much water," Aislinn softly murmured. "Does it have a name?"

"The Sea of Koralis, as the humans call it," Pryllan told her.

"That isn't the first time I've heard a dragon say, 'as the humans call it'," Steve remarked as he looked at Pryllan's head. It didn't matter. The dragon wasn't watching him. "What do *you* call it if you don't use the names the humans gave it?"

"Wyverians do not have the same foibles as humans," Pryllan answered as she righted herself and continued east. "We do not see the need to name every stream we discover, or each mountain peak we have nested upon."

"How do you keep track of what's what? What if you wanted to find a particular section of a river, or maybe a specific mountaintop again? How would you do it?"

"I would use the Collective. We see, we share, we know."

Steve grunted. He couldn't fault that logic. "Your way is more efficient."

"There's less chance of forgetting a name," Pryllan agreed.

Thirty minutes later, it was all Steve could do to keep the energetic youngster sitting on the scale in front of him. She wanted to stand; she wanted to count the number of scales on Pryllan's back; she asked about dragons and their babies, and of course, wanted to know what came first: the dragon or the egg. Steve grinned once the young dwarf girl posed that question to him.

"What comes first? The dragon or the egg? I'd say 'dragon' 'cause you need a dragon to lay the egg."

"But doesn't the egg hatch a dragon? Wouldn't that qualify as coming first?"

"I, er, hey Pryllan, care to help me out?"

Pryllan turned her long graceful neck to peer at the dwarf girl. She wisely avoided the question. "How are you feeling, young one?"

Aislinn smiled at Pryllan with a tenderness Steve didn't know a child could possess. "Better than I have ever felt my entire life. I am content."

She sure doesn't sound like a kid.

She seems wise for her age, Pryllan agreed.

I've heard that children with terminal illnesses have a tendency to act and behave like adults.

"You have been healed, young Aislinn," Pryllan gently told her.

"Your father told you what was going to happen, right?" Steve hesitantly asked. "He told you about the life debt?"

Aislinn turned her inquisitive eyes on Steve and gazed thoughtfully at him. "I heard him say something about it, but I am still confused as to what it is."

"A life debt, or *shachar* as it is known to wyverians, comes from ancient times," Pryllan explained. She banked to her right and began to head back toward the distant shore. "Way back before the time of our oldest elders, we dragons were given powerful jhorun. We —"

"Hold up," Steve interrupted as he raised a hand. "I seem to recall asking you before if dragons had jhorun and I do remember you clearly telling me you didn't."

"Dragons don't use jhorun," Aislinn piped up as she stared first at Steve and then over at Pryllan's head.

"Not in the conventional sense, no," Pryllan admitted. A wind had picked up and was trying to push them down toward the surface of the sea. Pryllan beat her wings a few times to gain altitude. "The humans have incorrectly defined jhorun as a mystical force within themselves that gives them the ability to do a certain task. They believe, incorrectly, that only humans have this gift."

"I already know that's wrong," Steve mumbled under his breath. The dragon heard him.

"Indeed? Good for you. As I was saying, the humans believe only they are capable of interpreting and utilizing this force within themselves. How, then, can the wyverians heal? How can the griffins see even if blinded?"

Steve blinked with surprise. "What? There's no such thing as a blind griffin?"

"Whether they've lost their eyesight in battle, or due to age, or by lack of light, a griffin can always see what transpires around them."

"I didn't know that."

"Unsurprising. Each species prefers to keep its own secrets."

"Okay, so how do you know about the griffins?" Steve wanted to know.

Pryllan's cryptic smile, the one he knew very well, appeared on her face. "We dragons have our ways."

"I'll bet you do."

I already know dwarves have jhorun, too.

I know. I felt it. I also know you refrained from telling the dwarf underling what you knew.

There's no sense in having her raise unwanted questions to her father. The dwarves of my time view jhorun as an abomination and actively avoid it.

Those same views are in place right now.

And how would you know that?

Pryllan kept smiling as she gently swayed back and forth across the waves, much to Aislinn's delight.

A few minutes later, as everyone was clearly enjoying the quiet solitude of flying above the sea, Steve looked down at Aislinn and raised an eyebrow. Something the girl had said was bothering him. Something about the shachar.

"What *did* your father tell you?"

Aislinn turned to look at him. Waves of thick brown hair caught the breeze and blew up in his face, threatening to make him sneeze. Aislinn hastily gathered her hair and started braiding it.

"He instructed me to let him know if I felt any strange urges."

Pryllan blinked a few times before turning her head around to inspect the girl. Steve also stared down at her. Aislinn finished her braid and tucked her hair under her arm to keep it from flapping in Steve's face. She looked up and noticed she was being watched.

"What?"

Steve cleared his throat. "Such as?"

"Well, whether I felt like eating raw meat, or if I started growling, or if I grew any…"

Steve's eyes widened and he held up a hand, signaling Aislinn to stop. "Did your father suggest you could grow scales??"

"Not exactly."

Pryllan's gaze shifted from Aislinn to Steve. "You told me you explained it to him."

"I *did* explain it to him."

"Obviously not."

Aislinn looked up at Steve and then over at Pryllan, and then back again. "What's the matter? Did father get it wrong?"

"Not only did he get it wrong, he wasn't even in the right ballpark," Steve grumbled.

"Ballpark?" Pryllan shook her head. "I'm not familiar with that word."

"It's … forget it. Listen, Aislinn. It's, uh, hmm. Where do I start?"

"A shachar is a bond between the dragon and their rider," Pryllan clarified. "I have now saved your life. Until you can repay the debt, and save mine, you will feel an overwhelming sense of uneasiness. Of stress. You won't be at peace until the debt is lifted from your shoulders. Do you understand?"

Aislinn was silent as she thought about what she had just

heard. "You saved my life so I have to save yours? That's fair. What can I do?"

This isn't as easy as I thought it'd be.

Tell me about it.

"It's not that simple," Steve told her as calmly as he could. "In all of the dragons' history, only a handful of these shachars have ever been created. None have ever been absolved."

"You mean I'm going to be the first to pay back a dragon for saving my life? That's fantastic!"

"Wow. You're handling this much better than I thought you would."

"I had better start thinking about what I could do to repay Pryllan for her kindness."

Both Pryllan and Steve stared at the diminutive girl with equal fascination. This child, this underling, was displaying wisdom way beyond her tender years.

We have got to break this thing.

Agreed.

We cannot let her live her life trying to figure out what to do to save yours.

Agreed.

We need to —

What happens when you return to your own time?

What?

Your goal is to get the crystal from the dwarves. Once you have it, you'll return to your own time. What about me?

I'm sorry. Perhaps I should have made that clear. I'm not returning to my own time until this is resolved. You're in this mess because of me. I got you in, I'll get you out.

I can see why we have become friends. I trust you.

Steve laid a hand on the closest scale he could reach.

And I you, my friend.

They were less than ten leagues from the rapidly approaching coast when something on the water on their left caught Steve's attention. The waters below them had started churning, as though a huge school of piranha was attacking some hapless prey.

Aislinn pointed at the disturbance. "What's that?"

"It's an oskorlisk," Pryllan answered. She wisely chose to steer clear. "A great sea serpent. It's not often one is seen near the surface when it isn't their time to rut."

"When it's their time to what?" the young girl asked.

"Think of it like a party," Steve hastily interjected, before Pryllan could answer. "They get together and, er, look for partners."

"Oh."

"As for me, I've personally seen enough of them to last a couple of lifetimes."

Steve noticed Pryllan's subtle tilt of her head. He had piqued her curiosity, he was sure, but thankfully she didn't press the issue. The last thing he wanted to do was to explain how he knew so much about the dragon's annual hunting of the great serpent.

Pryllan gently banked south as they approached the coast. Flying along at an altitude of several hundred feet, they followed the smooth cliffs for a few miles before they spotted one of the three waterfalls found on Lentari's eastern coast. This one, Steve noticed, was at least two hundred feet tall and was kicking up quite a cloud of water vapor from where it splashed into the ocean.

Aislinn pointed at the waterfall and giggled. "Look! There are faces on the cliffs. Dwarf faces!"

Steve had to give the girl credit. It did look like stern dwarf faces were silently watching them, one from each side of the falling water. As Pryllan circled around the waterfall, Steve could see the water had eroded the cliff face, creating the illusion. The dwarf faces disappeared the closer they got to the falling water. However, Steve still couldn't help but feel as though the faces had been deliberately carved into the stone.

He caught sight of a massive slab of stone, which had broken off from the cliff and fallen into the sea, remaining partially exposed.

The air chilled as Pryllan gained altitude and increased her velocity. They passed into the Selekai Mountains, home to many flights of griffins. Ordinarily griffin and dragon left each other alone, but since there was only one of her, and presumably hundreds of griffins, it was best to be safe and keep at an altitude much higher than what the hybrid eagle/lion creatures could attain.

Pryllan turned west and followed the mountain range for another thirty minutes before she turned north and headed back toward the open grassland in central Lentari. A flight of three dozen griffins appeared directly in their path. Over half the group held prey in their beaks. Evidently this was a hunting party, returning home. Several griffins squawked warnings and they gave the dragon a wide berth. Pryllan continued flying north and soon passed out of griffin territory altogether.

Steve had felt her concern as there were no other dragons near enough to fight off the griffins. He hadn't said anything but he had been ready. Both hands were ready to ignite and he was ready to throw up a wall of flames to defend his friends. Thankfully it hadn't come to that.

I agree. You would have fought the griffins for me?

Steve jumped. Aislinn turned to look at him. "Sorry. I'm fine."

"You're awful jumpy."

"Yeah, it happens when you get old."

The girl laughed and turned back around to enjoy the passing scenery.

Yes, I would. It's what friends do. I've fought a few griffins before. It wasn't fun. He left it at that.

Several hours after beginning the flight, they approached the tiny glade, which contained the hidden entrance down to Aislinn's home. The place appeared deserted.

Pryllan gently touched down and extended her wing until her wing talon had sunk deep into the grassy valley floor. Steve made a move to pick Aislinn up and carry her down when she surprised him by springing up from their seat and sprinting—leaving a trail of giggles behind her—along Pryllan's back toward the wing.

The moment her feet touched the springy leather skin on Pryllan's wings, the child let out a cry of delight and jumped into the air. The dragon's wing stretched, much like a trampoline. Bouncing along Pryllan's enormous wing, as though she was immune to the effects of gravity, Aislinn made her way toward the ground. With room for only one more bounce, she gave a mighty leap and propelled herself high into the air. She squealed with glee as she came hurtling back to the ground just in time to see her father emerge from the forest's edge with Cecil at his side. Selwyn had timed his appearance perfectly to catch his daughter before her feet came close to the ground.

"Father! We had the best time! We were soaring through clouds!"

Selwyn sank to one knee as he held his daughter. Tears fell freely down both of his cheeks. Aislinn, unaware of her effect on her father, struggled out of his embrace and walked back toward the massive dragon. Pryllan was resting her head on the grass as she watched the reunion between father and daughter. Aislinn walked right up to the dragon's snout and, ignoring the wickedly long fangs, laid a tiny hand on Pryllan's nose.

Steve rose to his feet and walked stiffly to the edge of Pryllan's wing. He slowly picked his way down Pryllan's back until both feet were on solid ground.

"You look like you're in pain," Cecil quietly observed.

"I'm getting too old for this," Steve admitted with a grimace. "My seat up there was nothing but a hard scale. Let's just say I don't feel like sitting any time soon."

Overhearing him, Aislinn turned her head to smile. "That's why I folded a blanket into a cushion. I was way more comfortable."

Steve gritted his teeth and smiled at the girl. "You're smarter than I am, kid."

Aislinn turned her attention back to Pryllan. She kept her hand in place and the two gazed silently at one another. After a few moments the dwarf girl finally spoke. "Thank you for the most wonderful experience in the world. I will never, ever, forget it."

"Don't thank me yet, young one," Pryllan softly told her. "As soon as you feel the effects of the shachar, you will feel differently."

Selwyn approached and placed his hand next to his daughter's. He tried to say something but his voice cracked. He angrily cleared his throat and waited to compose himself. Aislinn smiled at her father and took his heavily callused hand in hers. The tears started flowing again and the poor dwarf was unable to speak. Steve laid a friendly hand on Selwyn's shoulder.

"It's okay. It must be overwhelming, seeing your daughter healed."

Selwyn could only nod. He pulled a leather satchel off his chest and handed it to Steve.

"What's this?" Steve started to untie the opening when Selwyn smacked his hand. Hard. "Oh. Right. Wow, that would have been stupid. This is the athe crystal. Got it. It stays tightly wrapped."

"One cut, polished, and refined athe crystal, ready to power a portal. As we agreed."

Steve slipped the strap over his shoulder and secured the satchel against his waist.

"Are you…" Selwyn's voice cracked again. He ran a hand through his hair and scowled. He looked down at his daughter and his stern expression disappeared. "Are you well, Aislinn?"

The girl's smile was infectious.

"Never better, father."

"How are you feeling, young one?" Pryllan wanted to know. "Have you begun to feel any affects?"

Steve thumped Selwyn on his shoulder and spun him around until he was facing him. "You seriously asked your own daughter to let you know if she craved red meat? Or grow scales? Did you completely miss the explanation of what was going to happen?"

"I was just being careful," Selwyn muttered. He turned to his daughter. "Aislinn, can you feel anything?"

Aislinn took a deep breath and laughed. "I feel everything, father! I want to run and play! I want to see mother! I want to help mother cook! I want to —"

"Think about me," Pryllan gently interrupted. "What is your first impulse when you think about the two of us?"

"I want to know where we're going next."

"You are returning home with your father while I return to my nest."

"But —"

"Little princess," Selwyn began as he dropped back down on one knee, "the dragon wants to return home just as much as you do."

"But I don't want her to leave."

"She has to. She has her life, just as we have ours."

A frown appeared on Aislinn's elfin face. Her brow furrowed. "I do not think I want to be separated from Pryllan," Aislinn announced. "Yes, that's it. I want to go with her."

"I know you do," her father told her. "It's a feeling you'll have to suppress until our new friends, Steve and Cecil, can undo this life debt."

"But —"

"No *buts*, princess. It will be difficult; however, this is the way it must be. You now owe the dragon your life."

Cecil cleared his throat and waited until he had everyone's attention. "Fear not. Steve is a man of his word. If he says he'll absolve this life debt, then rest assured that's exactly what he'll do."

Steve risked a look at his friend. "Thanks, pal. No pressure there."

"How soon must we be at the waterfall?" Cecil asked as he turned to Steve. "If we miss Sarah's return then we will be stranded."

"Don't I know it. We need to high-tail it back to Verdayn so we can get the king to let us use Avin's portal. That was only about an hour west of the waterfall."

"Or I could take you."

Steve and Cecil looked up at the huge green dragon towering high over their heads. "Can you? I don't want to risk you getting into any more trouble on my behalf."

"I'd carry the two of you in my claws rather than have you ride on my back."

Cecil paled. "Be carried? By a dragon?"

"Think of the stories you'll be able to tell once you make it home," Steve whispered. He gave his companion a friendly nudge on his shoulder. "Wouldn't you want to tell AnnaBelle that not only did you make friends with a dragon, but you were also carried by that same dragon?"

Cecil took a few deep breaths. "Not really."

Steve dismissed his concerns and looked up at their large scaly friend. "Pryllan, we would be eternally thankful if you can take us to that waterfall."

Pryllan nodded. She extended one of her forelegs and opened her talons. She waited for the two of them to climb into her open palm. She carefully used the talons from her other foreleg to create a protective basket around the two humans.

Without waiting to see if they were ready, Pryllan leapt straight up and disappeared into the clouds. Cecil's panicked screams finally faded away.

Selwyn put an arm around his daughter and guided her toward their hidden doorway. The entire time, Aislinn talked non-stop about the many sights she had seen, describing the sensations of flying so effectively that Selwyn had to slap a hand over his mouth and try to keep from getting sick. Aislinn giggled with delight and launched into even more detail as they descended the dark staircase.

Standing as still as statues, concealed in the heavy foliage of a nearby tree, stood a tight group of five diminutive figures. Tools and weapons softly clinked together as they turned to look at their companions. Each of them was wearing highly decorated ornamental robes covered with emblems, insignias, and various medals.

"Did everyone see what I just did?" one dwarf finally spoke.

Four heads nodded in unison.

"Are you as dumbfounded as I am?"

The dwarves all nodded again.

"What does it mean?" the dwarf asked no one in particular.

"It means we have a lot to think about," a second dwarf softly intoned.

Chapter 13 — Rotten to the Core

The room spun, her head pounded, and Sarah swore the
floor was tilted. She took deep gulps of air and pulled
herself upright on a dusty cot with a threadbare blanket. A
simple wooden chair, a narrow window near the ceiling. Bars.
There were bars on the window and on the door.

That could mean only one thing: she was a prisoner.

It was time to get out of here.

She knew she was capable, knew without a doubt that she
had faced worse obstacles; yet the solution to this predicament
eluded her.

"Magic," Sarah mumbled, dismayed to discover her
mouth was bone dry. She could really use a drink of water. "I
can use magic to get out of here."

She sat perfectly still as she tried to collect her thoughts.
Why was it so hard to think? She had magic. This she also
knew. Why couldn't she remember what...

Teleporting. That was it. She could teleport. Easy enough.
All she had to do was bring up an image of where she wanted

to go and with a proverbial wiggle of her nose, she could... Sarah hesitated. She had never alluded to her ability as being equivalent to that of a certain nose wiggle. That would imply some part of her consciousness thought she was a witch. Wouldn't Steve get a kick out of that?

Steve!

Sarah's eyes cleared, but only for a moment. Where was Steve? Why wasn't he coming to save her?

Because he didn't have to, a little part of brain managed to squeak out before the thought became lost in the chaos her mind had become. *You can take care of yourself. Besides, he's stuck on Lentari. You dropped him off there.*

Sarah nodded, then groaned, bringing a fresh wave of nausea. Steve was in Lentari. There was no way he could rescue her from another world. In fact, the only way she would see him again was if she found a way to teleport away from this horrid place and fetch him back.

Sarah's eyes opened. The rendezvous. The meeting! How long had it been? Wasn't this the second day he'd been gone? She must get to Lentari or he'd never make it back. She *had* to escape. Her husband's life depended on it!

She pressed her temples to fight the pain. She needed to teleport, but where? Her aching brain couldn't form a picture of her safe zones. A wave of dizziness hit her when she stood, but she fought the nausea and stumbled to the door, pounding on it and shouting with no response. The headache reached meltdown status and she barely made it back to the cot before her legs gave way. A cloud of dust rose as she fell upon the horrid old blanket. Her eyes slammed shut and refused to open.

She hadn't realized she'd fallen asleep until she heard someone clear their throat. Loud. Abrasively loud. Someone was in the room with her, she realized with a start. Her eyes opened.

There, casually sitting in the chair with one leg carelessly draped over the other, was a man in his mid-fifties. He wore a freshly pressed white button-down long sleeve shirt, blue trousers, and black boots stretching up to just below his knees. His white hair was cropped short and he had an iron-gray handlebar mustache.

His expression was completely neutral, studying her. How long had he been there?

"Ah. You're awake."

"Who … who are you?"

"Sheriff Marcus Bixby. You may call me Sheriff."

Sarah tried to wet her lips but found that her mouth was too dry. "Could I have some water?"

The sheriff shrugged. "Certainly."

He raised a cane Sarah hadn't noticed and banged once on the door. A moment later the door cracked open and a tousle headed young man appeared.

"Fetch the lady some water."

The young man nodded and disappeared. The sheriff, clearly intent on watching Sarah, remained silent as he waited for the water. Once Sarah had quenched her thirst, she turned to face the sheriff.

"What have you done to me? Did you give me something?"

The sheriff gave her a smug smile.

"You could say that."

"Why?"

"All in good time, darlin'."

"I'm not your darling," Sarah angrily protested. Her headache responded with a fresh wave of nausea.

"You are now, darlin'. Words cannot begin to describe how excited I am to see you here."

"What? Why would you say that? I don't even know you."

"But I know *you*, darlin'."

Sarah automatically shook her head and winced. She seriously must not provoke the headache gods any further.

"There's no way you could know me. I can't … I don't … Why can't I think straight? What have you done to me?"

The sheriff gave her a patronizing look before he smiled at her.

"Let's just say that I gave you a little something to help you feel better."

"You drugged me?"

"You could say that."

"I *did* say that. Would *you* say that?"

"Oh, you need some clarification? Sure thing, darlin'. You've been drugged."

"Why? With what?"

"Psychoactive drugs are somewhat hard to come by in these parts, I will admit. It cost me a pretty penny, but I did find a supplier in San Francisco willing to ship me what I need, when I need it."

"What did you give me?"

"Just a little somethin' to help you relax."

"I don't want to relax. I want to get out of here."

"I'm sure you do, darlin'. However, that won't be possible."

"You can't keep me here."

"Let's agree to disagree, darlin'."

"Stop calling me 'darling'."

"I'll do whatever I want whenever I want to do it, darlin'," the sheriff snapped, his smug demeanor vanishing in an instant. "There ain't nobody in this damn town that can tell me what to do. I call *all* the shots, you hear me? If I want you to do somethin' then you damn-well better do it. You understand me, darlin'?"

Sarah thought of standing to confront him but she didn't trust her legs yet. "What is it you want of me?"

The sheriff slowly rose to his feet. His blasé attitude annoyed her but she decided against saying anything. Until she could think straight, she didn't dare provoke him.

"I am an ambitious man, darlin'," Sheriff Bixby began, hooking a thumb in his front pocket and lifting a booted foot to rest on the chair he had just vacated. "I've been in this town for over twenty-five years. Twenty-five years! Can you even begin to imagine what this town was like back then? You've seen it now. Trust me, it wasn't worth spit back then, not that it's worth that now."

Sarah stared at the sheriff with partially glazed eyes. Sleep was threatening to overtake her once more, but she was determined to learn more about her captor. There was something about him … she couldn't place her finger on it.

"War had broken out," the sheriff was saying. "Who was the enemy? Foreigners? Invaders? No. The North was fighting the South. Did the people around here care? Not one damn bit. Life moves on, darlin'. No one cared about this little backwater town and that's the way I preferred it. Then the gold rush started and people swarmed into California. This territory was essentially overlooked. So, what drove the people here, do you think?"

Sarah sensed the sheriff wouldn't continue until she answered.

"I don't know. Why don't you tell me?" Let him talk while she cleared her head.

"Silver. A silver strike is what happened. Overnight my town tripled in size. It annoyed the hell outta me." The sheriff looked at her and smiled lecherously. "The people who were willing to put in an honest day's work managed to scrape together a few dollars of profit from their mines. I ain't no miner, darlin'. I don't want to be no miner, yet there were a few people who struck it rich. That was the key. That's what I needed: a producing mine."

Sarah blinked a few times. Why was he telling her this? Had he found a mine and killed the former owner? How had this man ever become an officer of the law?

"So, there I was," the sheriff drawled, clearly enjoying the attention he thought Sarah was giving him. "I legally bought a mine when some damn fool defaulted. I had no idea if there was any silver, but if there was, then it was mine. How, then, could I get it without having to do the work? Then it came to me. Let someone else do the work. Genius, ain't it? I started a rumor that the mine had been abandoned after the owner had been killed in a freak accident. I let slip that a rich vein of silver supposedly ran in the area. The mine was simply waiting for the right person to work it.

"It worked. People started swarming the area. Everyone wanted to take a crack at my new mine. They figured if they slipped in under the cover of nightfall, they could strike it rich and be off before anyone would know. Well, I knew. I was waiting. I caught them red-handed. They were guilty of claim jumping and they knew it. I confiscated their haul and pocketed the earnings. Why not? I was the rightful owner of the mine. What they found was mine. With the proceeds from the Crusty Gulch mine I then…"

Sarah's mind wandered as the sheriff droned on. For the first time in a long while she became genuinely concerned. Her thoughts were so jumbled that they refused to stay on one topic long enough to form a coherent thought. No wonder she couldn't bring up a mental vision so she could teleport.

The drug was messing with her, still. Somehow, she had to be certain she didn't take any more. Was he tainting the food? Maybe the water? She nervously eyed the glass of clear liquid she was still holding. She *had* to clear her mind.

She tried deep cleansing breaths. No change. She tried to focus on her husband. She missed Steve, wished he was by her side. He'd deal with that pompous sheriff. Steve would be able to shut him up.

"How else could I earn a living once they dried up?" the sheriff continued to drawl. "I hired a few local boys and then we … want to know what we did next?"

Sarah tried to tune him out again. The pompous jerk wasn't even looking at her. For whatever reason, the narrow window in the room had attracted his attention. The sheriff clasped both hands behind his back as he regaled her with his story as though he was addressing an auditorium full of people. He had paused, as if expecting an answer. What was it he had just said? That's right. Something about hiring some guys and asking her what they did next. How in the world did any of this concern her?

"I suppose you're going to tell me," Sarah sighed.

"Of course, darlin'. Now, where was I? That's right. How was I supposed to make a living? The mines I had bought ran dry. I needed capital. Then I realized something. It was all around me. This city's life blood is silver. People staked claims everywhere. You couldn't walk a hundred feet in this town without stumbling across someone's discovery marker. What you gotta realize, darlin', is that in order to stake a claim you must file a mining certificate with the Kootenai County Recorder's Office, which just so happens to be located in this very town. And you know what? It's the damnedest thing. Those certificates have a tendency to be filled out incorrectly or just end up being misplaced."

"You paid off the clerk, didn't you? You've been cheating people out of their claims."

"It ain't my fault this town has so many idiots in it."

"You admit you're a claim jumper?"

"If I see a piece of land that I'd like to stake a claim to, then, to keep things legal, I investigate the land to see if anyone else has staked a claim to that chunk of land. And if they have, then I do some discreet investigations at the recorder's office to see if all the paperwork is in order. Seems I have a knack for finding unclaimed land or claims with missing certificates. Fair's fair, darlin'."

Sarah frowned. "But ... but..."

"What about the previous owners, you ask? A good question, darlin'."

Sarah glowered. Sheriff Bixby glanced over his shoulder at her.

"There are a surprising number of mines that aren't properly staked. As I said, if the recorder don't have no certificate on file for your plot o' land then someone else is free to stake a claim of their own. Many a prospector's been run outta town for filing incorrect or incomplete paperwork. This city has rules, darlin'."

Sarah glared at the back of his head; contempt written all over her face.

"With that being said, let me ask you somethin', darlin'. What's the meanin' of life? Do you know?"

Sarah was silent as she plotted what she was going to do with the sheriff once she was in full control of her jhorun again.

"Don't worry your pretty little head if you don't know it, darlin'. I'll tell you. The secret to life is happiness. So, the question becomes what does it take to attain true happiness?"

The sheriff went silent for a few seconds.

"Just feel free to blurt out the answer when you know it. Since you don't then I'll tell you. You become happy once you set and attain goals. That's how, darlin'. Goals."

"How do I fit in to this picture?" Sarah demanded, in a brief moment of lucidity.

The sheriff turned back to her and smiled. It was not a

pleasant sight. "You, darlin', are the answer to my prayers."

Sarah stared at the sheriff with confusion evident on her face.

"You are my new best friend," Sheriff Bixby continued. "You are going to be my strongest and most loyal confidant. With your help, we will be able to clean out every bank vault this side of the Mississippi."

Sarah's confusion was replaced by utter shock. "I have no idea what you're talking about. I think … I think you've made a grave mistake."

The sheriff ignored her objections. He continued to smile that lecherous smile of his. "Just think of it. My very own teleporter. The sky's the limit. Literally. You are worth your weight in gold, darlin'!"

Sarah couldn't keep the surprise off of her face. There wasn't any way the sheriff could know she was a teleporter. No one could! She had been careful. She had only teleported when no one was watching, she was sure of it. How, then, could the sheriff have known about her jhorun?

She swore softly under her breath as her jumbled mind struggled to work out the connection. Whatever he had given her had done a remarkable job of scrambling her thoughts. No matter how he had guessed her true identity, she *had* to keep the sheriff from knowing he was right. She *had* to convince him that this was just a case of mistaken identity.

"I — I don't know who you think I am," Sarah faltered, fighting to keep her voice from shaking, "but you clearly have the wrong person. I have no idea what you're talking about or what a 'teleporter' is."

The sheriff refused to be dissuaded.

"Sure you do, darlin'. After all, that's who you are, ain'tcha? You are the teleporter, which means, correct me if I'm wrong, that you are Lady Sarah."

Sarah's eyes flew open before she could stop herself. It was impossible! How did he know her true identity?

Sheriff Bixby chuckled as he turned to face her. He nodded as he saw the terrified look frozen on Sarah's face.

"That's right. Thanks to your little show last night I finally pieced it together."

"But… how…?"

"I've had men following you, darlin', from the moment I suspected that one of the famous Nohrin had arrived in my town."

"I don't … I'm not…"

"Oh, let's be honest with each other. I know who you are. Your face tells me that I'm not wrong. Lady Sarah, is it?"

"There's no possible way you could know that."

Sheriff Bixby grinned, displaying a mouth full of yellowing teeth. "Isn't there? You sure you ain't overlookin' somethin'?"

The chaos in Sarah's head tripled as she desperately fought to make sense of what she was hearing. One thought became crystal clear to her.

"That's why you drugged me. You believe that if I can't think straight then I won't be able to escape."

The sheriff casually walked back to the chair and sat. He leaned back and crossed his arms over his chest.

"You think you can escape? Go on, then. Prove me wrong. Teleport outta here. Come on, princess. I know you don't want to be here. Leave. I'd love to see how you do it."

Sarah valiantly tried to bring up one of her safe zones so she could teleport out of that dingy cell, but once more her swirling thoughts were unable to conjure a mental picture. Switching tactics, Sarah tried to visualize anything. Any place was better than being in that dusty cell with the sheriff. As before, her mind continued to betray her.

The sheriff smiled that smug smile of his. "You're still here, darlin'. Is there something wrong? I can save you the trouble. If you can't concentrate, then you can't teleport."

Sarah frowned at the sheriff. "Yet you're expecting me to teleport to the insides of a bank vault? To help you *rob* it? Are you kidding me? Why in the world would I ever cooperate with you? Who do you think you are?"

Sheriff Bixby's posture relaxed. He stretched back in the chair, clasped his hands together, and then hooked one ankle over the other. "I'm just someone who's tryin' to make the best of an otherwise lousy situation."

"I am *not* helping you rob a bank. Forget it. Rest assured;

I am teleporting out of here the moment that I can."

"That's not much motivation to play nice, is it?"

"What's that supposed to mean?"

"Aren't you even remotely curious how I'm keeping you from using your jhorun against me? Whether to teleport or otherwise?"

"I already know. You said you've been drugging me."

"That's right darlin'. But you'll never know *how* I've been doing it."

Sarah wasn't concerned. There was no way this pompous ass was going to get the best of her. "Clearly, you've been drugging my food or water. That's a problem that is easily remedied."

"Is it now, darlin'? You might think so, but it ain't."

Sarah finally smiled. "Well, there's the proof I needed. You just confirmed that you've been drugging the food or water. Now I know not to take either from you anymore."

"Starvin' to death ain't a pretty way to go," Sheriff Bixby haughtily told her. "You'll be changing your tune shortly. Besides, I don't think I'll need to drug you anymore. You're going to help me of your own free will."

"Like hell I will," Sarah vowed.

"I'm finding that I really enjoy proving you wrong, little darlin'."

Sarah folded her arms across her chest. "You have no hold over me. There's no way I'll ever cooperate with the likes of you."

"Aww, now that done hurt my feelings. That's not very nice, is it? Perhaps I can convince you otherwise."

"You can try," Sarah coldly told him as she turned to face the door, "but you'll fail."

"You love your husband, dontcha?"

Sarah's blood ran cold. No. He couldn't know.

"You'd do anything to protect him, wouldn't you?"

Sarah was silent.

"That includes keeping him alive, don't it?"

Sarah turned to look back at the sheriff. His cold green eyes were boring holes into hers.

"What … what do you mean?"

"You will help me, Lady Sarah, or so help me I'll personally shoot Luther and Cora Miller right between the eyes. With his ancestors dead, how do you think your husband will ever be born?"

Sarah stared at the cold-hearted man in horror.

"Yeah, I know who they are, darlin'. If some accident befalls either of those two, then poof! No more husband. Do you catch my drift?"

"How could you possibly know…"

The sheriff's voice dropped dangerously low. He stood up so that he could stare down at Sarah, still sitting on the cot. "Twenty-five years, darlin'. That's how long ago that damn portal dropped me here. Trust me; I've had plenty of time to put two and two together."

"You're from Lentari! No Lentarian would behave like this."

"That opium must have really messed with your mind. Interesting stuff, really. There's nothing like it back home, that's for sure. I've never touched the stuff myself, but it has proven itself useful on many occasions in convincing the judge to declare certain people, shall we say, mentally unstable. To answer your question, yes, darlin', I am Lentarian. Or should I say, *I was*."

Chapter 14 — Flaw Detected

"What do you mean you can't find it? You told me you've been here before. Many times, you said. And you! You're a dragon! How is it you can't find a simple waterfall?"

"I could drop him into the nearest nest of griffins," Pryllan casually suggested, instantly silencing Cecil's outburst.

Steve glanced irritably at the person sitting next to him safely inside the dragon's interlaced talons. "Would you? Please?"

Cecil's exasperated face quickly transformed to one of genuine concern. "Don't tell her that! She might do it!"

"And she'd be well within her right to do so," Steve grumped. "I'd help her. You've done nothing but complain for the last two hours. Do you have any idea how much walking Pryllan is saving us? Hours. Days!"

"So, I should cease my complaints, is that it?"

"Yeah, that's it alright."

"You sound like AnnaBelle."

"You're accusing me of sounding like a woman? Dude,

you realize you're talking to a fire thrower, don't you? Not only will I push you out, but then I'll use you as target practice as I watch you go down."

Cecil fell silent as he stared at his companion. Steve glanced over and saw his concerned expression. "Relax, man. That was only a joke."

Cecil visibly relaxed. "I knew you were bluffing."

"Of course. We need to be much higher so that you'll fall longer. I can get more shots off that way."

Pryllan chuckled as she flew over yet another clump of tree covered hills. They had been searching for the small waterfall for close to an hour. Of all the hiccups he had imagined befalling them, this was nowhere on the list. Steve squinted as he stared at the passing treetops. They all looked the same! It suddenly felt as though they were looking for a needle in a haystack. Perhaps they should…

"A waterfall suggests mountains or hills," Pryllan's voice cut in, interrupting his thoughts. "As you can see there are mountains and hills everywhere, yet no falling water."

Steve thought a moment. "Okay, tell you what. Go west. Let's find Avin. We'll work our way east from there."

"How far is the waterfall from the human settlement?" Pryllan wanted to know. She banked left and swung in a gentle arc until she was facing due west.

"It's about an hour's walk," Steve answered. He shrugged. "I have no idea how far that is as the dragon flies."

"We're about to find out," Pryllan observed. "Once we find the settlement then it should be a matter of minutes, since bipedal locomotion is slow and cumbersome."

"Is she suggesting that we're slow and clumsy?" Cecil asked, as the corners of his mouth crept upward in the beginning of a smile.

Steve nodded. "Yeah, she is. That's okay. She's right. Find the village and we find our rendezvous point."

Thirty minutes later, after canvassing an area nearly the size of R'Tal and the surrounding area, they were forced to come up with another plan.

"Things don't appear to be going our way," Cecil quietly observed.

Steve patted the leather satchel around his waist and shook his head. "We have the crystal Luther needs to activate the portal. That's one item checked off our To Do list. We'll be seeing our wives tonight. We're flying, not walking. I think things are finally going in our favor. In fact, the only thing that would make it better now is if Pryllan found the village."

"Your luck holds," the dragon told them as she dipped a wing and angled herself north. "I think the village is near."

Steve cast a discerning eye at the sky and noted that sunset was only an hour or two away.

"No time like the present," Steve mumbled as he stuck his head through Pryllan's talons. He looked down at the passing landscape and saw nothing but trees and an occasional glimpse of grass-covered forest floor. However, he didn't see any signs of human habitation anywhere. "Are you sure? I don't see anything."

"Nor do I," Pryllan admitted, adjusting their course so they were flying more northeast than true north. "But I can smell them."

Cecil scoffed loudly. "What's that supposed to mean?"

Steve grinned and gave Cecil a slap on the shoulder. "It means that we stink."

"We most certainly do not!" Cecil disagreed.

"Yeah, we really do," Steve argued. "You have a few years before deodorant will be invented. Trust me, it can't arrive soon enough."

"So, you're saying that I stink?"

"Dude, I'm saying that *I* stink. If I can smell myself, then I can only imagine what you must smell like. And no, don't even ask. I'm not going to tell you."

Cecil was mortified. "I had no idea. Do you think AnnaBelle finds me malodorous?"

"Let's just put it this way. Never *ever* argue with a woman when she suggests you take a shower or a bath. The two most important words in the English language are 'yes, dear.' Got it?"

Cecil nodded. Steve poked his head back through the dragon's talons and scanned the ground far below. Nothing but quiet, swaying treetops met his eye.

"We are very close," Pryllan told him. "I will accelerate so that the humans living in the settlement do not panic."

"Smart move, my friend."

Pryllan's wings began pumping her wings as she gained altitude and velocity. Within moments the world had become a passing blur.

"The village approaches," Pryllan announced, followed almost immediately by, "we have passed the village, maintaining a heading due east. By my calculation we should arrive at your waterfall in about five minutes."

"I never realized how slow humans walk," Cecil murmured.

"What you should consider instead is just how fast we're flying. I've ridden Pryllan when she's flown much faster than this."

"Indeed?"

"Yep."

Five minutes later Pryllan slowed and began methodically inspecting the ground. There were still no signs of their elusive waterfall. They finally caught a break when the trees cleared and they saw a thatched cottage on the banks of a small river.

"I'll be damned," Steve said, as he saw the approaching cottage. "I've been in that house. Or a newer version of it belonging to Kornal and his wife. Pryllan, follow this river. It should lead you straight to the waterfall."

Pryllan nodded and executed a sharp turn until they were facing the rapidly sinking sun. Now that she had a river to follow, Pryllan easily tracked it to its source and found the tiny lake formed by the waterfall's excess water.

"With all these trees, it would be best that I set you down in an open area," Pryllan said. She found a suitable location nearly a mile away and deposited them on the soft grass without touching down. She verified the two of them were safely on the ground, nodded her head, and rapidly beat her wings to give her some clearance from the ground.

I certainly hope to hear from you soon, Steve.

You will, my friend. I won't return to my time until we have dealt with this shachar thing. I need to talk to Sarah. A solution exists. We have to find it, and we will.

You have my thanks.

And you have mine. I'll be in touch.

Until then. Farewell.

Pryllan turned to the north and climbed high in the sky, disappearing from sight after a few moments. Steve turned to look at Cecil and pointed south. "That way."

Cecil wasn't convinced. "Are you certain?"

"Yes. I was watching Pryllan like a hawk. Do you think I want to get lost out here?"

Cecil turned to look at the western horizon. "Dusk will be here soon. Let's get going."

The waterfall was just as they had left it two days ago. Two days. Had it really been only two days since he had last seen Sarah? It felt like two weeks! If luck was on his side, she'd already be here somewhere, waiting for them. Keeping his fingers crossed, Steve, with Cecil following close behind, strode into the tiny clearing and looked around.

Luck was definitely not on their side.

A dozen or so small black rodent-like creatures were at the water's edge, clearly quenching their thirst. One of the fuzzy creatures must have been assigned to keep an eye on the small group because that one reared up on its hind legs and let out a shrill squeal. The rest of the black creatures rose up on their hind legs as well and silently studied them.

Steve didn't know who was studying whom. The fuzzy black rats with thick fuzzy tails remained motionless. Finally, one of the creatures dropped back down onto all four of its legs and started squeaking and trilling like crazy. It began advancing on Steve and Cecil, as though it didn't want them there.

"Blast them with fire," Cecil urged. "Clear those revolting things out of here."

Steve clenched his right hand into a fist and was ready to ignite it when he hesitated.

"What are you waiting for? Do it!"

"No, Cecil. They are just protecting themselves. What if I drive them away from the water? What if because I did that then something irrevocably changes down the line?"

"From scaring off a bunch of black rats? No, you're fine. Please. Get rid of them. I cannot begin to tell you how disquieting I find them."

The squeaking rat thing was getting closer. Steve started backing away, and the creature became bolder. Its warning chirps and whistles got louder.

"Sarah!" Steve called out in his loudest voice, silencing the fuzzy black rat. Only for a moment. The moment Steve's voice trailed off, the creature returned to its attempt to force the intruders to leave. "Sarah, are you here? If you can hear us, we're heading over to that log. Are you here yet?"

The only thing they heard was the chirps and trills coming from the tiny glen's new residents.

"At least we didn't miss her," Cecil happily informed him. "I was concerned that we might have."

"We still might have," Steve told him. "I doubt it. The sun is ready to set. This is the official end of day two. This is our meeting spot. We're right where we're supposed to be."

Cecil nodded, pleased. "This is definitely one adventure I won't be forgetting any time soon."

Steve turned to look at his friend. "I don't blame you. I've never traveled through time before. Your friend is my great-great-grandfather. How do you think that makes me feel? It's crazy."

"What's the first thing you're going to do when you make it home?" Cecil asked.

They arrived at the fallen log and sat down at the same time.

Steve grinned. "Give Sarah a big hug and a kiss. What about you?"

"Oh, the same. AnnaBelle and I have never really been apart before. I can't even imagine what she must be going through without me."

It was nearly an hour past sunset and the woods continued to darken. For the tenth time in as many minutes, Cecil gave him an anxious look. "Perhaps we should go to the castle and wait for her there?"

"Cecil, do you have any idea how far away the castle is? Even if we headed straight there and didn't stop it'd take us at least two days."

"Couldn't we have the dragon drop us off there?"

"And create a panic in R'Tal when an unknown dragon touches down? There's no way I'm asking her to do that. Besides, even if Pryllan did give us a lift to the castle, it'd be too late. Flying would take a few hours. Sarah and I agreed that either this place or R'Tal would be the meeting point. We're at one of them. She can jump between here and R'Tal literally in the blink of an eye. We cannot, so this is where we are going to wait. Don't ask me again, okay?"

"I mean no offense. I can see that you're worried. That's what worries me most. Your sense of calm and confidence has been my source of strength ever since we stepped foot here. I cannot begin to tell you how troubled I am to see you so worried."

"Sorry. You're right. I am worried. I didn't think Sarah would be this late."

"Could something have happened to her?"

"You're not helping, Cecil."

"I'm sorry, Steve, but I feel this topic must be addressed. What happens to us if something has befallen Sarah? How are we to return home?"

"She'll show up. Drop it, okay?"

"Very well. We should at least make it easier for her to find us."

Startled, Steve looked up at Cecil.

"What do you have in mind?"

"Shall we make a fire?"

Steve nodded. "That's a good idea. Come on, let's see if we can find some rocks to make a firepit."

Thirty minutes later they were sitting on their makeshift bench in front of a roaring fire.

"Alright, look…" Steve took a deep breath and let it all out with a loud sigh. "We don't have many options. If something *has* happened to Sarah then obviously we'll need to find another way back."

"But there isn't another way back," Cecil countered.

"Therein lies the problem. We're going to have to find a way back ourselves. What we need to do is some brainstorming. Do you know what that is?"

Cecil nodded. "Sure, only I don't know how much help I could be here."

"That probably means you'll be perfect," Steve told him. "Start shooting out ideas. What are our options?"

When Cecil was silent Steve figured he'd start them off. "The first logical choice would be to consider the portal. The *interdimensional* portal, as the king called it."

Cecil beamed his approval. "That's perfect! We can use the same portal Luther used to get to Idaho. All we have to do is —"

"Hold up," Steve interrupted. "That's the one option we don't want."

"We don't? Why not?"

"Think about it. When Luther went through it dropped him off three years into the past. Sarah went through and was dropped off six months ago. I don't know how I managed to make it to the present."

"What if Sarah went to the present and you went to the future?"

Steve held up both hands, palms out, and shook his head. "If I start thinking about that I'll give myself a headache. I'm not touching that one. The point is that portal is unstable. It messes with time. We could end up arriving in Coeur d'Alene ten years before Luther does. Then we'd have to wait until we caught up with present time again, like Sarah had to do while waiting for me to arrive. Do you really want to risk that?"

Cecil was speechless as he shook his head no.

"I didn't think so. We have to rule that portal out. Maybe if we…"

Steve trailed off as both of them heard twigs snapping in the distance. Someone was out there. Was it Sarah? Had she finally arrived? They heard a few more small sounds, signaling whoever it was had wandered a little closer.

"Sarah?" Steve called out. "Is that you?"

The sounds disappeared. Whoever, or whatever, it was had stopped moving.

"Sarah?"

The forest fell silent.

"I don't like the sounds of that at all," Cecil whispered to Steve.

"What sounds? I don't hear anything at the moment."

"Right. That's what concerns me. We just did. Someone is out there listening to us. I don't think its Sarah."

Steve rose to his feet. Cecil began to stand when Steve ignited both hands. Cecil hastily sat back down. "Perhaps I should wait here."

Steve nodded. "Good idea. I'll check it out."

As he left the comfort of the fire he unconsciously increased the jhorun flowing into his hands; they blazed even brighter. For thirty seconds he walked west, moving as quietly as he dared. However, he didn't hear anyone else moving about. Maybe it had been an animal and it had scurried off?

He heard a soft moan and then what sounded like a few quiet sobs. No animal, save humans, sobbed like that. It had to be a person! Was it Sarah? Was she wounded?

"Sarah! Are you there? Are you hurt?"

The sobbing fell silent. He heard the person moan again. He was close, less than a dozen feet away. Maybe hiding behind one of those trees? The question was, who was it? Sarah would have said something. Was someone spying on them?

"Who's there? Identify yourself."

Now both the moaning and the sobbing vanished. Steve increased his flames and looked around the area. Trees, trees, and more trees. The person could be hiding behind any one of them. Perhaps he should not sound so intimidating?

He cleared his throat and tried again. "Who are you? Are you hurt? I know you're here 'cause I can hear you."

He heard a soft moan, this time coming from behind him and to the left. He glanced in that direction and saw a small foot wearing a simple brown slipper. He reduced his flames back to standard torch level and ordered his jhorun to remove the heat.

"Hey there. I see you. Are you okay?"

The person didn't answer.

Steve walked around the base of the huge tree and squatted down low. It was a girl. A young girl, perhaps barely in her teens. She had shoulder length brown hair and was wearing a plain brown blouse with a matching brown skirt.

Steve leaned over to tap her on her shoulder. "Hey, are you okay?"

The girl didn't answer. From the light of his lit hands, he could see that her clothes were scratched and torn in several places. She had a scratch running along her left cheek and had numerous cuts and nicks along her arms.

The girl moaned again and fidgeted on the ground. Then the sobbing began anew. Again, Steve tried to rouse the girl. As before, he was unsuccessful. Then he noticed beads of perspiration running down her brow. From him?

Steve scooped her up into his arms and made his way back into camp. Cecil was on his feet in a flash.

"Who do you have there?"

"Haven't a clue. I need you to do something for me."

"Of course. What do you need?"

"Hold a hand to her forehead. Tell me if she's running a fever. I see beads of perspiration on her face and I'm pretty sure it's not from me."

Cecil held the back of his hand against the girl's forehead. He looked up at Steve the moment he was touching her skin. "She is. She's burning with fever. We need to cool her down."

"If she was on fire then I'd be the one to talk to," Steve told him. "I know absolutely nothing about first aid."

"I do. Somewhat. We need to cool her down. Quickly, let's get her into the water."

Steve scooped the girl back up and made it a few steps before he bumped into his companion. He leaned to the left to see what the holdup was. "What are you doing? Get going."

Cecil gestured at the near pitch-black darkness surrounding them. "I can't see where I'm going. I'm going to walk into a tree."

A large chaser flared into life and moved out in front of them. "Follow the fireball," Steve instructed. "I'll follow you."

Cecil hurried toward the sounds of falling water. He waited by the water's edge for Steve and the girl to arrive. As soon as they did, Steve waded into the water and started to kneel down while holding the girl. Cecil held up a hand.

"This isn't a question and answer session," Steve pointed out. "If you have something to say then just say it."

"I think the girl is supposed to be undressed for this to work properly."

Steve hurriedly straightened and looked down at the girl he was holding in his arms.

"Hell no."

"We need to lower her body's temperature. Fast. Her life depends on it."

"She's underage. There ain't no way in hell I'm taking her clothes off."

"She could be wearing underclothes."

Steve stared incredulously at his friend. "Do you want to check? Because I don't. I don't know what kind of laws you're used to in your time, but in my time it is highly frowned upon to undress a girl without her consent. I'm not going there."

Cecil held out his arms. "Give her to me. I'll do it. It's medically necessary."

Steve passed the girl over and instantly closed his eyes. He heard the sounds of clothes rustling about and then Cecil's sharp hiss of surprise as he lowered the girl into the water.

"This is going to cool her down in no time," Cecil called out. "This water is absolutely frigid. I'm going to need you to warm her once we get her temperature down."

Steve groaned. "Was she at least wearing something under her clothes?"

"Yes. She had on a nightshirt. I left that on."

Steve sighed. "Good. Let me know when you're ready."

"I think we're about ready now."

"Are you sure? That was awfully quick."

"You should feel this water. It's incredibly cold. Are you ready? I need you to take her now."

Steve reluctantly cracked an eye open and looked down at the two of them. Cecil was struggling to rise to his feet while holding the girl in front of him. Her thin night shirt fell down to a few inches shy of her knees.

He took the girl from Cecil and was surprised at how cold she felt. He increased his jhorun and allowed himself to gradually heat up.

"Did it work?" Steve worriedly asked, as he looked over at Cecil, who was huddled by the fire. Did her fever go down?"

"As soon as I get some feeling back into my hands, I'll check again. Why don't you feel her forehead?"

"That never works," Steve told him. "My hands are always warm."

A few minutes later Cecil laid his hand across the girl's forehead once more. This time he smiled. While her head was warm, it was nowhere near the blisteringly hot skin he had felt before.

The girl stirred in Steve's arms. Two strikingly blue eyes opened and fixed upon his. "Who are you? Why are you holding me?"

Steve smiled sheepishly. "I was trying to warm you up a bit. We had just dunked you in a cold lake to lower your body temperature. You were burning up with a fever."

"Where are my clothes?"

"Cecil draped them across that log right over there."

"Please put me down."

Steve carefully lowered the girl to the ground. The young teenager took a few steps before she started swaying dangerously. Steve caught her before she could topple over. The girl clutched his arm as she tried to regain her balance.

"My heartbeat is elevated, I'm short of breath, and I have a fever. I don't suppose either of you have any goatweed, do you?"

Steve shook his head and indicated he didn't have any pockets. "No, I don't. I don't think he does, either."

"Do you think you could find me some?"

Steve gave the girl an appraising stare.

"You know about herbs?"

The girl nodded. "Goatweed is commonly used to reduce a fever. It grows no higher than a few feet. It has narrow, oblong yellow-green leaves with translucent dots seen throughout the leaves and tissue. It grows like a weed so you should be able to find some nearby. If it's flowering, look for pontal with five yellow petals."

Cecil stared at the girl with a mixture of uncertainty and

skepticism. "How do you expect us to find it at night?"

The girl looked over at Steve and smiled. "I'm sure he can find some."

Steve sighed. He pointed at the log and indicated the girl should sit down. "Fine. I'll go. What's your name, anyway?"

"Lissa."

"I'm —"

"Sir Steve, I know."

Cecil's mouth fell open. "You know him?"

"Of course. He's the Nohrin. Everyone knows who he is."

Steve stared at Lissa for a few moments more before heading off into the dark forest. Fifteen minutes later he was back. Steve handed the girl a plant with bright yellow flowers, in the process of closing its petals for the night, complete with clumps of dirt still falling from the roots. Lissa nodded approvingly. Following the teenager's incredibly detailed instructions, Steve mashed the ingredients into a paste. Once he found a stone with a natural depression in it, he filled it with water and mixed in the ground plants, heating the liquid as he did.

Once it was ready, Steve gently poured the mixture in the girl's mouth.

"Are you going to be okay?" Steve asked.

Lissa nodded. "The goatweed should break the fever overnight. I should be fine by tomorrow morning."

"You sure do know a lot about plants. Wait. You're that kid from Capily! The constable's daughter! You're on the list of people that Sarah and I are trying to find!"

"Lady Sarah is the teleporter. Can she take me home? I don't know where I am. The only thing I do know is that I'm nowhere near the sea."

"True. We're ... well, forget about that. We're waiting for Sarah to arrive. Once she does, we'll get everything sorted out."

Cecil eyed Steve. "Do you think she knows?"

Steve shook his head. "No, I'm pretty sure she doesn't."

Lissa warily eyed the two men. "What? What don't I know?"

"You're in Lentari," Steve began, as he sank down next to Lissa on the ground, prompting Cecil to follow suit, "but not the Lentari you're familiar with."

"What does that mean?" Lissa asked, confused.

"Clearly you fell through that portal, right?"

Lissa slowly nodded.

"Well, I hate to tell you this, but that damn portal dropped us in the past."

"The past?" Lissa repeated, frowning. "How far into the past?"

"Over a hundred and twenty years."

"What? But ... but my father will be worried about me!"

"Honey, your father hasn't been born yet."

Lissa's eyes widened. "So, you're waiting here for Lady Sarah to take you back to our time? Can she take me with her? I don't want to stay here."

Steve glanced helplessly at Cecil, who returned his frank stare. Comforting a young teenage girl in distress was way above and beyond the two of them. Steve noticed that Lissa was openly crying. She turned her tear-streaked face to his and grasped his hand.

"You will take me with you, won't you?"

Steve nodded. "Yes, we will. You're in this with us. The only way you're going to make it home is to stick with us. Everyone is looking for you, including the Kri'yans."

Lissa's crying abruptly shut off. She stared at Steve in shock. "The Kri'yans came to Capily because of me? I only went searching for herbs yesterday."

"I think you'll find that you actually disappeared about four days ago."

Lissa shook her head, sending her brown tresses tumbling about. "No, it was just yesterday."

"I keep forgetting this portal messes with time. Sarah fell through and I went in immediately after she did. She arrived six months before I did."

"Why aren't you with her now?" Lissa wanted to know.

"We had to split up. I had to come here for a few days and am now waiting here for her to take us back."

Lissa looked up at the thousands of stars twinkling above

them. Then she turned to look back at their rudimentary campsite.

"She's late," Steve confirmed, answering Lissa's question before it was asked. "I don't know what's happened to her. She should have been here by now."

"What happens if —"

"No, no more 'what ifs'. Let's give her some time. She could be running late. For now, we stay here for the night. I'll stand guard. You and Cecil should get some rest. I'll make sure you two stay plenty warm through the night."

"You cannot be expected to stay awake the entire night!" Cecil protested. "The least I can do is stand guard a few hours. If anything happens, I can alert you. Fair's fair."

"Fine. I'll wake you in a couple of hours. Get some sleep."

* * *

Dawn arrived without preamble. The sun was just peeking over the eastern horizon when their campsite finally stirred. Cecil yawned, stretched, and sat up. Lissa, looking much more refreshed, sat up and smiled shyly at Cecil. Then her brow furrowed as she frowned at him.

"Weren't you supposed to be standing guard?"

Cecil, in mid-stretch, froze. "He never woke me. Where's Steve?"

They searched the campsite but could find no traces of the fire thrower anywhere.

"Steve!" Cecil called as loudly as he could. "Can you hear me? Are you alright?"

Lissa tried. "Sir Steve! Where are you?"

"Sir Steve?" Cecil repeated, puzzled. "Why did you add a 'sir' to his name?"

"Because that's what he's called in my time," Lissa informed him. "He and Lady Sarah were Kre'Mikal's bodyguards. Did you know they defeated the evil sorceress Celestia in a magnificent battle? There were trolls, therons, and malwerns, too. I wish I could have seen it."

"I'll let you tell me all about it later," Cecil promised. "In the meantime, let's find Steve."

They headed toward the lake when they saw movement in their peripheral vision. It was Steve, but he was pacing. He had paced so much, for so long, that he had created a path through the grass and had worn it down to bare dirt and rock.

Lissa looked up at Cecil. "Is he alright?"

"I don't know. Steve? Can you hear me?"

Steve lifted his bloodshot eyes and stared at Cecil. "Sarah didn't come. Something has happened to her."

"What do we do now?" Cecil asked in a quavering voice. "How do we get home?"

Steve turned to look at his two companions. He dropped his hands to his sides.

"I honestly have no idea."

To be concluded in ... *Thoughts For a Portal*

Author's Note

Okay. Don't hate me. I know that this is the first ever cliffhanger I've ever done and it certainly wasn't planned that way. I could have, as my wife pointed out after she read the story, have probably condensed the full story into something that could be released as one title. However, the story wouldn't have flowed as well as I wanted and I would have had to cut out parts that I wanted to share. So there you have it. My first cliffhanger.

I tried to keep the nineteenth-century town of Coeur d'Alene just as authentic as possible. Yes, the military fort was there. Yes, so was Wyatt Earp, and he did, in fact, open a saloon there.

Did you enjoy the story? Hate it? I always encourage my readers at the end of each book to leave a review wherever they bought the book. I'm an author. The best way for someone to help out an author is to leave a review. Tell your friends. Share the book with your family. Nothing makes us authors smile more than hearing how their books were enjoyed.

So, how will Steve and Cecil (and Lissa!) find their way back to Idaho? Better yet, how in the world will they manage to return to their own time? Yes, I have left Steve and Cecil in quite a pickle. And let's not forget Sarah. She's been kidnapped and is now being held against her will. How is she going to escape? Who will help her? Does Sheriff Bixby actually win in the end?

I hope you're intrigued enough to find out!

Are you looking for something else to read while you're waiting for the next Tales of Lentari book to be released? In the past, I have included some recommendations in the back of the books for other titles you may be interested in. Oftentimes I've been asked what are some of my favorite books? Well, wonder no more. Here are some of my favorites. If you haven't checked them out before I strongly encourage you to do so.

The Blue Moon Detectives Agency series by JH Sked
Hemlock and the Wizard's Tower by B Throwsnaill
Dragon Blade by J.D. Hallowell
Klondaeg the Monster Killer by Steve Thomas

They are all indie authors, just like I was when I first began writing, and would love to get their books into the hands of some new readers. I've read all of them and enjoyed every single one of 'em.

Finally, I wanted to take the time to thank you, the reader, for picking up a copy of this story. These books only exist because of dedicated readers like yourself. So, from the bottom of my heart, I give you my thanks. Thank you for reading.

Want to be sure you don't miss another book release? Sign up for my newsletter. The Daily Scroll is the only official source of Lentarian news. You'll never miss another contest, or giveaway, or book release ever again! Sign up for my newsletter! Fans are also encouraged to follow me online through Facebook (www.fb.com/BakkianChronicles). You'll never know when I'll ask for some name suggestions, or ask an opinion about weapons, monsters, etc.

I hope to see you online!

J.

P.S. Read on to see a list of fan submissions!

Fan Submissions

Where would I be without the help of my fans? I owe you guys a lot! I asked for help naming some characters. Here's what was used!

Erik Munson — Leanna, Bertol, Torya, Eslac
Toni Trick — Tessler
April Enos — Graylan, Ruskin, Quinn
Gunnar Kristjansson — Gunnar
Derek Pritchard - Breet
Brett Gable — Melvyn, Fensham, Zevern, Merrith
Rachel Gardner — Tyril, Ruan
Duncan Wheatley — Duncan
Kendall Davis — Hattie
Deb Shapiro — Brent
Heather Doyle — Gabriel
Tina Batson — Calin
Claire Jones — Selwyn, Aislinn, Jonquil

And I need to give a hearty thank you to my friends at Fresh Baked Disney (www.FreshBakedDisney.com) for their permission to use their likenesses in the book. Deriksen and Aras were inspired by David and Sara of Fresh Baked fame. Thanks again, guys! See you in the Happiest Place on Earth!

ABOUT THE AUTHOR

Jeffrey M. Poole is a professional writer who writes in both the fantasy and mystery genres. His series are listed below. Jeffrey lives in picturesque Southern Oregon, with his wife, Giliane, and their Welsh Corgi, Kinsey. His interests include archery, astronomy, archaeology, scuba diving, collecting movies, collecting swords, and tinkering with any electronic gadget he can get his hands on.

In March, 2015, Jeffrey became a proud member of SFWA, the Science Fiction & Fantasy Writers of America! Jeffrey encourages readers to connect with him on Facebook (facebook.com/bakkianchronicles). Fans can also follow him online at: www.AuthorJMPoole.com.

Scan the QR code to sign up for his newsletter and receive a free short story!

BOOKS BY JEFFREY POOLE

Epic Fantasy
BAKKIAN CHRONICLES
The Prophecy
Insurrection
Amulet of Aria
Disneyland Debacle (short story)
Winter Wonderland (short story)

TALES OF LENTARI
Lost City
Something Wyverian This Way Comes
A Portal for Your Thoughts
Thoughts for a Portal
Wizard in the Woods
Close Encounters of the Magical Kind
The Hunt for Red Oskorlisk (short story)
May the Fang be With You (Pirates trilogy #1)
The Hammer is Strong with This One (Pirates #2)
These are Not the Stones You're Looking For (Pirates #3)
Blast from the Past

DRAGONS OF ANDELA
Harness the Fire
Strike the Spark
Clear the Water